THE SECOND COMING

B.Z. PIERCE

Formatted with Vellum

1

"Miss Julie, I ain't lyin', the ghost of General Stovall burned the courthouse down," said the man sitting across from me in the diner booth.

"And Mr. Lyons," I replied, "why should I believe the ghost of General Stovall burned the courthouse down rather than, say, someone who is alive and perhaps against the reason I'm in this town in the first place?"

"Well, Miss Julie, you should know that Pothos is a town of honest people, and no one wants to stand in the way of your case." Mr. Lyons peered down at the table and shook his head. "I'm just afraid that you've upset the ghost of the esteemed General Stovall."

"I don't believe in ghosts, Mr. Lyons."

Mr. Lyons offered a polite smile. "Miss Julie, I'm not one for all these ghost stories either, but the General was born and laid to rest right here in Pothos and lived a life of morals that you're trying to upset. He—"

My hand signaled for pause. "Mr. Lyons, disenfranchising the rights of Black voters is not a moral high ground, and frankly, I'm offended by your continued attempts to hurt my case, most recently the burning of the courthouse. Please know there will be a criminal investigation into this matter, and we will find the *living* person who committed the crime." I stood, knocking a fork that slammed against the ceramic plate loudly enough to startle the crowd. The diner fell quiet; the jukebox, usually unnoticed, played "Eternal Flame". I gave Mr. Lyons my best steely gaze and said, "This isn't close to being finished."

After exiting the diner, I could see where the stately courthouse had once stood, now a brick skeleton of what used to be the centerpiece of this town. The water steamed off the debris in the sun as firefighters admired how the flames turned objects they once knew into abstractions. People gathered behind yellow tape; a woman I recognized as a court clerk was crying. I walked back toward my car, dialing my firm in Washington, D.C. After a secretary told me everyone was busy in a meeting, I hung up.

I was certain my colleagues didn't like me, which is why I was sent to this shit town of Pothos, Georgia. I didn't particularly care whether or not they liked me, but I had a suspicion the other junior associates had plotted against me to give me this assignment. I could imagine some of them lobbying my boss that I was the best associate to take this case.

Perhaps my unshakable professionalism was off-putting to them. I sneered when the men in the office would complain, "Oh, my mother is coming for the weekend," and they'd all groan and laugh over their lunches. I would look up from my phone and wonder how these women raised such ungrateful men. When my parents visited, though a truly rare occasion, I would have my apartment professionally cleaned and hire a chauffeur for them, the difference between these spoiled Americans and my inherited Taiwanese values. I just couldn't imagine revealing much about me to these people. The women in the office tended to bore me, but I'd still eavesdrop on their Monday morning bathroom stories about *what* a weekend they had. Plus, I dressed better than they did, if more conservatively, perhaps another reason the men didn't like me.

Yet, looking around this town, I suddenly missed my colleagues. The people in Pothos had no ambition, mixed with a lack of imagination for what life outside this small, impoverished place could be like. They were born, filling the gaps where needed (priest, mechanic, grocer), married, and multiplied. Anyone of higher education in this town either moved to New York City or spent half the year somewhere more interesting, like Orlando.

The reason I was stuck in this Confederate hamlet was because they'd violated the civil rights of the minorities in the town, mainly the Black population. In an effort to rig the elections, the Election Board, to combat "voter fraud", sent police to three-hundred Black citizens with letters summoning them to court to prove their residency or lose their right to vote. All the records needed to prove said residency were located in the courthouse—the very courthouse that had burned to an unfinished jigsaw puzzle of what used to be a grand building.

I looked down at my phone, seeing a message from a town clerk. I was copied on an email, along with others with emails like "redwhiteandblue4life@aol.com" and "southernrevolt1861@gmail.com" on an announcement that a temporary courthouse would be established in a Baptist church down the block from the City Hall, a structure of two single-level brick ranches connected together. City Hall was also two blocks away from Forbidden Palace Chinese Buffet, the restaurant I'd been consistently recommended by the townsfolk.

I took a look at the courthouse and sighed. The diner was well-positioned in the town, with a clear view of the burned courthouse. It was too bad the fire had happened at night, when no one was at the diner to witness it. I looked around at the other buildings and noticed one dilapidated Victorian house. It stood a couple of hundred feet from the courthouse, but also with a good view over its overgrown front lawn. I could only hope that someone had been in the round turret at the time and clearly witnessed the arsonist who burned down the courthouse.

I crossed the street and walked toward the house. It looked as if it might be abandoned, but I could only be certain by seeing if anyone was home. The wooden steps creaked with each ascension until I stood on the porch at the front door. Once a statement of wealth, time had reduced this house to a monument of neglect. The outdoor lights were covered in cobwebs and dried flies, which I hoped wouldn't fall on me as I stood there. Hanging pieces of paint fluttered in the light breeze. Past colors peeked through the shingles deformed by decades of repainting. For this incarnation, the house was dark blue.

I walked up to the front door, painted an accent of yellow. The whole thing screamed eccentric inheritors; the house was probably owned by a family member who'd inherited it without the means to take care of it. As the child of recent immigrants, I wouldn't inherit any such estate, just some humble property, and money my brother would try to exclude me from getting.

I knocked and waited. I swore a little dust felt off the door with each knock. I heard nothing, so I knocked again, making out a little bit of movement inside. From within the once grand house, I caught a disgruntled, "I'm fucking coming!"

A middle-aged woman opened it. She was Black, with a light complexion. Her face was round with a scarf tied across her head. She wore a tasteless mu'umu'u and stood about a head lower than me.

"Can I help you?" she asked, with a deeply unhelpful attitude.

I said, "Yes, I'm looking for the owner of this house."

"You have an appointment?" she asked.

"An appointment for what?" I couldn't imagine what anyone would walk into this dilapidated, unwelcoming house for.

She sighed heavily. "I'm a psychic. If you're not here to speak with the dead or find the love of your life, then leave."

This seemed fitting for this town. I'd never believed in psychics, or astrologers for that matter, so I'd just have to appeal to her sense of justice. I said, "Unfortunately, I'm just looking to speak with a *living* person who might have witnessed what happened on the night of the courthouse burning."

Her eyes narrowed. "Are you police?"

I scoffed. "Absolutely not. I'm actually a lawyer working to reinstate the rights of Black voters in this town."

She swept a dismissive gaze over me. "You look bougie. What are you actually doing here?"

I could already tell she disliked me. Furthermore, I hardly considered what I was wearing to be "bougie" —my blouse was well-made and fit nicely. I could see her leaning awkwardly to read the emblem on my purse.

She asked, "Is that a real Prada? Then you can afford one of my readings. Follow me."

I followed her into the foyer. The staircase was full of books and other belongings, piled along the edges to allow careful movement around them. I got the sense she was a bit of a hoarder. I tried not to look at the tables filled with unopened mail and magazines, not wanting to have a lethal anxiety attack and be stuck as a trapped spirit, haunting this shitty house forever.

"I charge $75 an hour for my readings," she told me, leading me into what must have been the old dining room.

"I'm not paying you," I told her firmly.

She ignored me and busily made her way around the room,

turning on accent lighting. I assumed this was supposed to transform it into a seductive space for spirits to enter her.

"What's your name?" I asked.

She sat down and adjusted her bulk in the chair. "I'm Ms. Honeypaw."

"I'm Julie Chen," I said, then genuinely curious, asked, "That's an interesting name, where is it from?"

"We're not here to talk about me. Let's get to the heart of the matter. Are you in love?" She started to shuffle a deck of cards.

I shifted slightly, feeling a flash of discomfort. "I'm not here to talk about my personal matters. I'm just here to gather information on the courthouse fire."

The cards snapped into a neat pile. "Five hundred dollars," she said.

"What? For what?" I asked, confused.

"You want to know what happened on the night of the courthouse fire. I can help you, but information has a price."

I gave her a stern look. "No. That's illegal, and your testimony wouldn't be valid if I paid you."

"Fuck the law. I want my money." She crossed her arms and locked eyes with me.

"Ms. Honey...paw. If you witness a crime, you are morally and legally obligated to report it. I can promise you won't be endangered; my law firm and partner organizations will protect you."

She squinted, pulling a card from her deck and studying it. "You got a man?"

I said, "That's hardly relevant to why I'm here."

She smirked a little. "It's more relevant than you think." She pulled another card and her eyes widened. "Oh, that's messy."

I refused to take the bait.

"Aren't you interested in what fate has in store for you?" she asked, looking genuinely curious.

"I think fate wants me to win this case."

She pulled another card and made a concerned noise, shaking her head. "Not gonna happen."

"What? What's not going to happen?" I asked coolly.

She pulled another card murmuring, "Oh, that makes sense," then yet another card, laughing a bit. "Wow, what's your name again?"

"Julie, Julie Chen."

"Right, you got a lotta shit coming your way. I can help you be prepared for it, if you're interested."

"Ms. Honeypaw, I'm only interested in whether you saw something on the night the courthouse burned down." My impatience was starting to heat my blood.

She only hesitated for an instant. "Okay, three-hundred."

I stood up and said, "Oh my god, I'm leaving." I fished out a business card from my purse, "Please, when you're ready to talk, call me."

I made haste to the front door and down the creaking front steps, shaking off the bizarre feeling of my nonconsensual psychic reading.

I looked out toward the courthouse, then back at Ms. Honeypaw's house. She stood behind the dirty glass at the front door, her gaze fixed on me for a moment before she turned and walked back into the dusty darkness of her house.

THAT EVENING, I collapsed on my hotel couch with a glass of wine. I usually cooked in my hotel suite's mini kitchen, and tonight I sprung for the most expensive bottle of wine in the local grocery store ($34.99) and some frozen shrimp. I was inspired to drink after my frustrating encounter with Ms. Honeypaw. It seemed that she had information that was deeply important to my case, yet was stubborn about sharing it. Was she actually facing dire economic ruin and the only way to make some money was through extorting me? Or was she just a pseudo-psychic grifter who always knew how to make a buck out of people? I would have to figure out a new way to convince her to help, but everyone in this town seemed frustratingly blasé about this fire, or voting in general. The frustration carried all the way until I lay in bed, attempting to sleep. The only joy I found here was sleeping alone because it meant I could masturbate before going to sleep.

Sometimes, when my boyfriend Matthew was asleep, I'd sneak a hand under the covers, but here I could do it with abandon. The problem was that I struggled to come up with something to think about. Sex with Matthew had never pleased me enough to reference it as pleasure material. We'd sort of fumble our way through with the expectation that this was what a couple should be doing.

Matthew worked for the State Department and traveled a lot. He was in India at the moment. We'd met on a dating app three years ago, and we both seemed agreeable enough that we settled with each other rather than continue the bizarre struggle of meeting someone in the digital age.

I did like Matthew. He was a respectable and decent guy with a pleasant, boyish face and an incredible brain, but I think the biggest impediment to our sex life was his insistence on using the "sex sheets." He kept them separate, so we would have to negotiate our carnal desires around the changing of bedding. He also insisted on a top sheet, which I thought was overkill. We could have sex without the sheets, but he preferred being covered. There was no oral sex. I'd offered a few times to give him a blowjob, but he insisted that it was degrading to see me "down there". Honestly, I understood because I was too embarrassed to ever let a man go down on me.

I thought about the last time we had sex. As usual, after we'd changed the sheets, we undressed, and I briefly admired his smooth and slightly doughy figure before hopping under the covers. The duvet cover could remain unchanged as long as the top sheet was between us and it. He was a decent kisser, but I didn't always love the way he tasted. Usually, he brushed his teeth before sex, but on this occasion, I'd gotten the faint essence of truffles when I dug my tongue into his mouth. After we kissed, he entered me and I put my hands on his shoulders. Sometimes I moved my hips to brush my clit against his groin, but this time I'd ended up sneaking a hand away from his shoulder to rub myself, which occasionally did the trick. It helped a little, but not enough. As usual, he kept kissing me until the last moment when he turned away, so I didn't see his stupid orgasm face.

There was also that post-coitus survey when he'd ask, "Did you finish?"

"Yeah." I'd lie, the same old lie. This last time I'd lied yet again, and as usual, he had no idea. He rolled off me and got up. "Hey, do you mind changing the sheets? I'm gonna go shower."

He also always showered immediately after sex. Sometimes, while he was showering, I'd quickly masturbate to completion. I'm not sure why I feel compelled to hide this, but if he walked in on me touching myself, I would feel uncomfortable, probably because I wasn't thinking about him. What's worse is that when I knew he was sleeping deeply enough, I'd try to quietly fish my vibrator from the nightstand and hope I didn't knock anything over in the process.

Tonight, alone in my hotel, I couldn't think of anything to get me off. I found myself numbly rubbing my pussy while thinking about buying a water carbonator. While I calculated my weekly intake of sparkling water, I tried desperately to come up with something sexually stimulating. It was frustrating because I had a good imagination and usually fantasizing came easily, as long as it didn't involve Matthew. That was too much reality.

In DC, usually I'd see a hot guy at the gym or running, and if they were intriguing enough for me, I could orgasm with the split-second memory of them. In my fantasy, I was charming and outgoing enough to convince them to have a quickie, perhaps in my vacant apartment while Matthew was on a work trip. In my fantasy, I was also cold enough to kick them out when done, without letting them shower, and never tell a soul.

It's sad that I was in Pothos, where I had all the time in the world to play with myself, yet nothing to stimulate me.

I continued to try, but still nothing. I picked up my phone and searched for water carbonators instead.

THE NEXT MORNING, I drove to the temporary courthouse. Apparently, there were enough churches in Pothos that a spare one could be used to conduct the legal necessities of the town. The sign outside said "Get rich quick: count your blessings."

I walked into the Baptist church. Folding tables had been placed between the pews and the front of the altar. The walls were white, and cracks with brown water stains decorated the ceiling.

"Julie Chen." I heard the voice of the attorney for the police department, Jim Smoke. He reached out for a handshake. I reluctantly put my hand against his wet palm, but my reluctance meant I didn't give a firm enough shake. He forced my hand to turn and placed his other hand on top of mine, an act of dominance. I cursed myself for being afraid of his sweaty fingers and not gripping harder. He held it as he said, "Wonderful to see you're still here. I believe this will only be a minor hiccup of a case, and it should be over quite soon."

I pulled my hand from his smothering grip. "I'm not sure how it will be over soon," I replied, trying to sound tough, but the prospect of having a drawn-out case here scared me more than losing. "All the records needed to prove residency burned with the courthouse. However, if you put everyone back on the voting rolls, then we could have this done by the end of today."

He said, "Ah, well, we will do this after a probationary period of one year for every voter affected, while we take the appropriate measures to validate their residency."

I laughed at his audacity. "Mr. Smoke, that's long enough for them to miss the next election. Doesn't that seem suspicious?"

He glanced at the two other men surrounding him, tugged on the sides of his tweed blazer as if it would close over his fat stomach, and laughed. "Ms. Chen, I think you're making us out to be criminals. We're on the side of the law, not *against* it." His pair of groupies laughed too.

"Who are these two?" I asked.

"This is my paralegal, Tim, and my hunting partner, Steve."

I didn't bother to ask why Jim Smoke's hunting partner needed to be here. I also didn't want to shake their hands. I was fast learning to choose my battles in this peculiar town.

BY THE END of the day's session, we'd made no progress. Jim Smoke's talent lay in discussing things completely unrelated to the matter at hand. My attempts to interject were met with the judge's raised palm. Now the judge, his chin resting on his palm, seemed far more interested in Mr. Smoke's story of boar hunting in Hawaii than in the facts of the case. We ended promptly at 3 pm so the judge could have his diabetes injections. I'd accomplished nothing, other than ensuring we'd have another day in court.

As I exited the courthouse, Mr. Lyons spotted me and threw

his cigarette on the ground, grinding it into the sidewalk with his heel as he walked toward me. "Miss Julie!"

There was nowhere to run, so I said, "Yes?" I was beginning to worry he was just a creepy old man who went after younger women.

"Hi, Miss Julie, I hope you're well." He tipped the brim of his baseball cap. "But listen, I have to warn you about something. Last night Ms. Lee saw something. Do you know Ms. Lee?"

I kept a healthy distance from him. "I don't."

He said, "Right, well, she lives near the ole Stovall Plantation. You know the one northeast of here?"

I simply said, "No."

"Okay, well, she was out last night, gettin' ready to coop her chickens, and she saw a man standing on the edge of her property. He was dressed in an old general's outfit, and she thought 'Ain't that odd.' Now imagine, Miss Julie, that you're her and I'm the man."

Mr. Lyons moved about fifteen feet away, shouting to me from a distance. "...So she said to that man, 'Who are you? This is private land!' And pointed her shotgun at him, which she always carries ever since coyotes ate her wiener dog one evening 'bout twelve years ago. So she points the gun at him like this," he continued, raising his pretend gun and aiming it square at me. "And ole Ms. Lee said 'You got five seconds to get off my land or I will blow you off myself!' Now the man didn't move one inch, and Ms. Lee always keeps a promise, so she counted to five and then pulled the trigger. I'm telling you the truth, Ms. Julie, the pellets went right through him. Ms. Lee ran back toward her house, but he just appeared in front of her door, and you know what he said?"

I rolled my eyes. "I don't."

He walked closer and shook his head, "The ghost of the

great General Stovall told Ms. Lee, 'Get that Oriental out of my town!' He hollered it at her, then disappeared in a blink of an eye. I'm afraid it was a warning to you, Miss Julie. It ain't safe for you here."

2

I climbed into my Volvo sedan and took a deep breath. It wasn't the first time I'd been called "oriental", and far worse slurs had been hurled my way. I expected to face racism in this backwards town. However, the surprise of hearing it always made me emotional. I decided to walk away without a word after Mr. Lyons's warning.

I pressed the ignition button and saw all the dashboard lights come on, but no engine turnover. I tried pressing the button again and again, until the eleventh time I just screamed, "Fuck!"

Someone must have sabotaged my car. It was the only one without a Georgia plate or a full-size Confederate flag creatively attached somewhere on the body. I slid down the driver's seat and squeezed my eyes shut, wishing myself anywhere but here.

I thought about life back in my law office. I thought about the white walls, aluminum window frames, and the bland abstract art that hung above fake orchids. I remembered my cubicle. The only personal item on my desk was an extra water bottle. I also remembered the fucking day I received this assignment in our junior associate meeting.

"Julie, we're assigning you a landmark civil rights case," Senior Partner James Livingston had unexpectedly announced.

All the associates turned to look at me, and all I could say was, "Okay."

James continued. "We're taking on a pro bono case about voting rights in Pothos, Georgia. Since you completed law school in Georgia and are barred there, this is a natural fit."

At least four other people in the firm were barred in Georgia. They were either White or Black, and I guess in this case, my neutral ethnicity would be an advantage.

Later in the breakroom, one of my new colleagues, too new and too much of an idiot for me to bother learning his name, asked me how I felt about the assignment.

"I haven't read the briefs yet, so as of right now I have no opinion." A diplomatic response.

Another Junior Associate, who only bought things branded with her alma mater, Yale Law School, took a sip of coffee out of her blue YLS mug and said with what was clearly a smirk, "You know, I heard James is trying to get a judgeship. He's only taking this voting case to suck up to the establishment."

I replied,"That seems possible."

"So just be careful." She leaned in toward me. "If this case goes south, then that might put his dreams in jeopardy."

"Well, this case is already going South," chimed in Useless Idiot. Yale Law let out a shriek of a laugh. *She wants to fuck him*, I concluded. Only someone who wanted sex would laugh at such a stupid joke. I imagined her beige pants pulled down while he humped her boney ass. When he got close, I'm sure she'd shriek in panic about getting cum on the back of her blazer. I smiled a little at the thought.

"You seem happy about the case, though," said Yale Law.

"I haven't read the briefs yet, so as of right now I have no opinion," I repeated and walked out of the break room.

Snapping myself out of my office reverie, I searched my phone to find a garage. There was a small one called "Steve's Toybox" and a dealership, but I didn't trust dealerships after my firm got a windfall on a class-action from a dealership conglomerate lying about repairs.

The closest one was about a ten-minute walk down the road. I called and got no answer, but didn't want to lose the possibility of an easy solution, one that didn't require me dragging myself all over town in my business heels, hauling my heavy Prada bag with me.

I walked along a crumbling sidewalk past a sad strip mall, plants growing in the cracks of the parking lot, to Steve's Toybox. When I arrived, I found a three-bay garage with an alarming number of derelict cars parked off to the right of the building.

"Hello?" I called out as I got closer, "I'm just here to ask about fixing my car." I felt the need to establish my intentions in case some redneck with a shotgun popped out from underneath a truck.

I reached the entrance to the first bay and there was still no one in sight, just some cars with their hoods popped up and one on a lift. But I could hear some country music playing and someone was singing along. The voice was rough, but it complemented the song.

"Hello?" I called out again.

A head popped out from behind the hood of the car. "Hey there. What're you looking for?"

"I need help with my car. It's broken down in front of a church farther down the road."

He stood up, wiping grease off his forearms with a dirty rag. The grease stopped at his wrists, as his hands were covered in black gloves. He pulled off the gloves, and tossed them to the side as he walked toward me. He was surprisingly handsome except for the long, dirty blonde hair under a hat embossed with some beer brand. His shirt's armholes extended almost down to his hips and I could make out a small tattoo with some kind of writing on his ribcage, which I'm sure had something to do with the Bible. If he'd had a haircut and proper attire, he might even have competed with my fantasy gym men.

"Broken down, huh? You got a tow?" he asked, chucking the rag onto a table.

I said, "Not yet. I just wanted to check if you guys had space before I have it taken to the dealership and they rip me off."

He let out a little laugh. "Yeah, you gotta be careful with those dealership boys. Especially if you don't come from around here."

"How do you know I'm not from here?" I asked.

He looked me up and down and said, "Because I grew up here and know just about everyone. I even know what kinda cars they have. What are you driving?"

"A Volvo sedan."

"Nice, what year?"

"It's a 2021."

He nodded and said, "It might be a little complicated for a small garage like us, especially with the new ones. If it's a battery issue, I might be able to jump it."

I asked, "Do I need to get it towed here?"

"Don't bother. I'm finishing up for the day here anyway. We'll just take my truck and see if we can jump it." He walked a little toward me, "I'm Josh, by the way. I'd shake your hand, but I'd prefer to wash them before I do. "

"That's alright, I'm Julie Chen, nice to meet you."

He smiled. "I'm going to run to the bathroom and wash up. Can you wait a minute?"

I nodded as he disappeared into an office. I looked around at the garage. It was certainly aged, but fairly organized, enough so that I didn't feel anxious about letting him work on my car. I saw buckets labeled for disposal of hazardous chemicals, which made me happy to know he wasn't dumping them in the river, but the thought of his strong arms pouring a barrel of chemicals into a fragile ecosystem suddenly seemed naughty, in a different kind of way.

My newfound fantasy as an environmental steward meeting a sexy polluter in the woods was short-lived as he walked back toward me. He reached out strong hand, drops of water still beaded on the hair, and took mine. Our palms met and I squeezed his hand tightly, which made his eyes widen a bit.

"Wow," he said. "You have a strong handshake." He extracted his hand and shook it a little.

"Oh, sorry." I was a little embarrassed, realizing that I took out my residual frustration from being overpowered by Jim Smoke on Josh's hand.

"It's alright. I can tell you're someone that doesn't want to be messed with," he said.

"What do you mean?"

Josh grabbed his wallet and phone and looked at me. "You just want people to know you're in charge, right?" He winked at me. God, he was patronizing me. He moved toward his truck and I followed. I hauled myself up the passenger side. It was an older Toyota, that much I knew from the logo on the steering wheel. I waited until he moved a few papers, an empty sandwich bag, and a water bottle off the passenger seat. "Sorry."

"It's okay, I know you weren't expecting company." I used my feet to gently push some trash to the side to clear a space for them.

"So where are you coming from?" he asked as he started the engine and pulled into the street.

"I'm a lawyer from Washington, D.C., prosecuting a case here."

He looked surprised. "A lawyer, that's fancy."

"Is it?" I asked, puzzled. I saw my job as practical, but certainly not aspirational.

"Yeah, you gotta go to a lot of school and pass some big exam, right?"

The way he simplified my seven-year journey to becoming a lawyer as "a lot of school" and "pass some exam" made me laugh a little, but how would he know the grit and determination it took?

"What's funny?" he asked, glancing over at me.

I said, "Nothing really, it's just that where I live, everyone is a lawyer or works for the government. I can assure you, there's nothing fancy about me."

He grinned. "Well, I'm impressed. I don't know any lawyers, so as far as I'm concerned, you could be on the Supreme Court and I'd be none the wiser."

I rolled my eyes. "I'd rather be anywhere than the Supreme Court right now. It's not a good situation there."

"Yeah, I don't really pay attention to it much, but I don't like them taking away rights from women."

"Oh, I'm surprised that's your position."

"Why? Because I'm a guy?" he asked, his grin widening.

I wrinkled my nose. "Umm...I'm trying to figure out how to say 'yes' without saying 'yes'."

He nodded. "You're not wrong, but I have known enough women who at some point got together with the wrong guy. Some got stuck, had a kid, and weren't able to leave, and some got the support and help they needed. And for some of them, if they hadn't been able to choose what was right for them, it would have ended badly."

I was taken aback by his unexpected insight and could only say, "Yes, that is the truth."

We sat in silence for a moment before he said, "Besides, doesn't 'Supreme Court' sound kinda North Korean-y?"

With that, the truck halted to a stop next to my Volvo.

He spent the next twenty minutes trying to jump the car without anything happening. He bravely got on the ground and looked underneath the car while I scanned the pavement for used needles.

I heard him call from underneath. "Okay, I'm looking at where the electrical wires enter the interior, and it looks like something damaged them."

"They were cut," I stated.

He said, "Hmmmm...maybe not. I think it's more likely a rat ate them."

He moved away from underneath the car, "Some of these newer cars have wires insulated with a soy-based plastic. The rats and squirrels love it."

"That sounds like a good class action lawsuit," I said, quietly calculating the potential numbers in my head.

"Yeah, well this car ain't moving on its own. I'm gonna call a friend for a tow," he said, pulling out his phone.

While Josh was on the phone calling his friend, I checked work emails on my phone. I saw a group email from Yale Law about a case where the Useless Idiot replied with a question, then realized it was already answered in the original email, replying again with an apology. Yale Law replied to him with a message to soothe his embarrassment, writing, "I apologize for not creating a more strategic email. We all don't have time to deeply read these."

I could tell she was still horny for him. Useless Idiot needed to just bang her so she can go back to being only a moderately pathetic woman.

"Julie," I heard Josh call. I looked up. "My buddy Ricky is

gonna pick the car up but it might be a while. He's out on a call in another town."

I said, "Okay, I don't mind waiting."

As I LEANED against my car and checked my emails, Josh watched something on his and laughed. I assumed it was a compilation of monster trucks crushing cars or skateboarding accidents.

I asked, "What are you watching?"

He said, "It's a video from a geologist, but he's doing a series on using Jane Austen books to describe rock formations. He's pretty funny. This is called 'Sense and Sedimentary.'

I raised an eyebrow. "You read Jane Austen?"

He shook his head. "Nah. I could never make it past the first page."

"Same," I said, trying to fit yet another incongruity into the picture of this Pothos garage mechanic.

I looked at my phone. I'd received a seven-word email from my mother about a cousin getting engaged. I could see her drawn-on eyebrows pursed with judgment. Just when I imagined myself walking down the aisle toward Matthew, feigning a smile while wiping anxiety sweat off his forehead, a tow truck pulled in.

A tall, dark-skinned man with a strong, muscular build hopped out. He and Josh performed some sort of bro handshake hug. They spoke with familiarity while I stood and waited for them to finish.

"Julie, this is my man, Ricky," said Josh.

I studied Ricky. He was also attractive, but in a more polished way than Josh. His hair was buzzed to his scalp, and he moved with an almost militaristic intent. Since he was Black, I wondered if he had been affected by the courthouse fire.

"Hi, Julie. I'd shake your hand but mine are a little dirty," he said, echoing Josh's earlier greeting.

"All the men in town seem to have dirty hands, but that's fine. It's nice to meet you. What is Ricky short for?"

"Ri'Chard," he said.

"I like 'Ri'Chard'," I said with a smile. "He must be your alter-ego with clean hands."

Ri'Chard returned my smile. "Then call me that if you like," and walked off toward my car. Pulling out a silver hook, he searched along the bumper for a hole covered in plastic. Then he crouched down, popped the cover off and screwed the hook in. I watched the muscles in his forearm flexing with each turn, thinking this was something I'd never witness Matthew doing, any more than I would ever witness Matthew's muscles flex in such an appealing fashion. And when Ri'Chard bent over to tie one of his boot laces and he pulled those laces taut, I felt a little jolt in my body as if static electricity had shocked me.

Ri'Chard, oblivious to my contemplation, swung into his truck and in a flash had backed up, loaded the car on, and was ready to take it to the garage.

"Ri'Chard can drive it over, and I'll give you a lift to where you're staying," Josh said.

I said, "Thank you, that's kind. Can I get a receipt for the tow, though?"

"Don't worry about it," said Ri'Chard. "It's only down the road, I got you."

I objected, but he was firm. It was oddly nice for him to do that, but I'm not sure why. He seemed very formal with me, in contrast to Josh, who was probably the hot stud everyone loved.

I asked, "How about I take you guys out to dinner as thanks? I'm hungry anyway, and I get to expense it for work."

They both agreed, and Josh said, "The Forbidden Palace is right there, you wanna go there? It's pretty good." I tried to hide my lack of enthusiasm. It was inevitable I'd have to end up there someday. When I'd checked into my hotel, I asked the receptionist if there were any restaurants in town that used cloth napkins, and she'd said, "Maybe Olive Garden?"

They walked a few paces ahead of me as I checked my phone again. More emails, and one lame message from Matthew apologizing for missing our scheduled call because of "Iran." I glanced up at Josh as his stupidly large arm holes in his shirt caused it to catch wind like a sail. Ri'Chard wore a black t-shirt and dark navy work pants. I admired the shoulders and backs of these two men. They carried themselves with an innate athleticism, and I couldn't help comparing them to Matthew again and how stupid he looked when he ran, with no control over his arms. But to be fair, what Matthew lacked in brawn he certainly made up for in brains, and he was on track to secure a higher position in the next election cycle.

I was still looking at my phone and barely noticed Ri'Chard holding the door open for me as I walked into the restaurant. The aged walls were teal and the tables red. The hostess did a double-take when she saw my face.

Josh and Ri'Chard sat next to each other on one side of a booth, studying the menu, while I sat across from them, next to my Prada bag. I dropped my phone in it and politely smiled at the older Chinese man who came to take our order. He said hello to the men first, then looked at me with obvious excitement. I'd already heard him speaking to the hostess in a Beijing accent, which grated in my sensitive ears. Being Taiwanese, we speak in a different Mandarin accent, one I find cleaner, while the Mainland Beijing accent has the long "rrrs" that my classmates in American schools used to taunt me with unfairly.

"Where are you from?" he asked.

"Washington D.C." I replied. I could tell he was unsatisfied, so I said, "But my parents are from Taiwan."

"Oh, so you are Chinese. I can tell from your face."

I said, "No, I am Taiwanese." I rejected belonging to the mainland.

He said, "But it is still China," holding his teeth together at the end.

"No, it will *never* be part of Mainland China," I said sweetly as he continued to stare for an uncomfortably long time, the fixed smile not reaching his eyes. He was probably thinking of all the creative ways the cooks could poison my food, and I hatched a plan to foil them. I'd order whatever Josh was having and ask to switch with him. His body mass would take longer for the poison to kick in, and maybe we'd get to a hospital in time. Hopefully. However, being in this town had dulled my will to live.

After we gave our orders, Josh, who'd been listening to our exchange, asked, "So where exactly is Taiwan?"

I was not surprised by his ignorance. "It's a small island nation off the coast of China. It has a long history, including being a Japanese colony, but after the KMT lost the Chinese Civil War, it became a refuge for them. My family immigrated there from mainland China around that time, but now we consider ourselves Taiwanese."

"That's interesting. Have you ever been?" Josh asked.

"Yes, a few times. The food is great," I said, knowing I was going to be disappointed by whatever came from an American-Chinese restaurant kitchen. I suddenly missed Matthew, who understood the differences, not just in food, but in the political and historical subtleties impossible to explain to the uninitiated. I was surprised to find Ri'Chard gazing at me quite intensely.

"I was stationed in Okinawa when I was in the Navy," he said. "Often I would fly through Taipei and sometimes would spend a few days there."

That made sense. I've seen a lot of military men in D.C., and

I'd already noted that he carried himself in a similar way. "Did you finish service?"

He said, "I almost finished my contract, but I had to leave early for family reasons. My father got really sick, and he needed help with his towing business, so I'm back here."

"Will you go back to the Navy at some point?" I asked, and he took a moment before he replied.

"I'm not really sure what I'd be fighting for," he said carefully, as if trying to gauge my reaction. "I don't know what America wants to be. I joined under Obama because I thought we were making progress, but then the country went back to being racist as hell, and I'm not fighting to protect that."

"Did you join up for the education?" I asked.

"Of course. I would never have enlisted otherwise," he said.

As this was the first time I'd actually had a chance to converse with a non-hostile and apparently intelligent Pothos resident, I decided to take advantage of the moment. "Were you taken off the voter rolls here?" I asked.

Ri'Chard shook his head, "No, I live just over the bridge in the next county, but some of my family members were removed."

Josh, clearly surprised, chimed in. "Oh, are you working on a case here, Julie?

I said, "Yes, your town has been actively disenfranchising the rights of Black voters."

Josh's brow drew down. He turned to Ri'Chard and said, "Dude, you didn't tell me about this?" Josh seemed genuinely concerned. I twisted my head and stared at his furrowed brow. Why did his concern about voting rights make my pussy tingle?

Ri'Chard shrugged and said, "It's nothing new for us here." He looked across at me and asked, "How's the case going?" Staring deeply into his eyes, I suddenly forgot about Josh's furrowed brow.

I said, "I can't discuss the details of an ongoing case, but it's weird." They both laughed a little bit, as if they got that Pothos was a peculiar place, and I had to admit, it felt nice not to be treated as the enemy. "The courthouse burning down has totally fucked everything up, and the consensus is that some ghost did it. Do either of you know anything about this supposed ghost of General Stovall?"

"Hell yeah, it's an old town legend," Josh said. "He was some old Confederate general. Some people say his ghost still hangs around the woods near his old house. A bunch of teens go up there to mess around, and they joke that he'll come out and shoot you if he catches you having sex."

A ghost story to encourage abstinence. This was new to me. I glanced over at Ri'Chard. "Have you ever seen anything like a ghost in there?"

He laughed. "Are you asking if I hooked up in those woods?"

"I've hooked up with a lot of girls in those woods, and I didn't see anything," said Josh, unabashed.

"I ask for a reason, because I don't think a ghost did this. Yesterday I went to the house of a Ms. Honeypaw. Do you know her? She's that psychic who lives in the blue Victorian near the courthouse."

Josh blew out an exaggerated breath. "Who doesn't know Ms. Honeypaw? She is...something else."

Ri'Chard nodded in agreement.

"What about her?" I asked curiously.

"She owes everyone in this town money, including me," Josh said. "She never pays, only promises to pay in a few days, then disappears into her house and no one sees her for the longest time. I feel bad because I've known her my whole life, but after a while, I learned to say no. Everyone started leaning on her to pay her debts, so she started leaving jewelry as collateral, saying it 'belonged to her grandmother'. Some people fell for it, and they were really pissed when they realized it was just copper and glass." He shrugged. "She's trouble; I would avoid her."

I nodded slowly. "So do you think she might have been lying when she told me she saw something on the night of the courthouse burning?"

Ri'Chard said, "I'd be careful of anything she promises. You don't want her to think she can get anything out of you, because then she will definitely bleed you dry."

All these warnings made me wary, but also curious about this woman. I was split: she could be lying to get money out of me, but still, she had such a clear view of the courthouse that it was just as possible she could have seen something. Just then our food came. I looked at my plate with no enthusiasm, hungry as I was. The cook didn't need to poison me; American Chinese food already felt toxic enough to my body.

As dinner began, Josh asked, "So, Julie, do you have any hobbies?"

I considered it. "I don't know. I think work takes up most of my time. I run, if that's a hobby. Sometimes I go to museums."

Josh said, "Oh right, you have all those museums in D.C. I've always wanted to go to the Natural History Museum there. I really want to see the Hope Diamond."

"Why?" I asked a little rudely.

"I like gems and rocks. It's my hobby, I guess," said Josh.

"Oh, are you a closeted geologist?" I asked, not sure why I was needling him.

"Who says I'm in the closet?" He pulled a chain from underneath his shirt to reveal a reddish rock. "This is a garnet I found in this state. It's the find I'm most proud of."

I couldn't help but be a little impressed. "Garnet is my birthstone. I was always sad it wasn't a diamond or sapphire, but I'm glad to know you think garnets are cool."

"They're a great stone. Lots of interesting combinations. This one is an almandine garnet." He rubbed his fingers over the stone.

I looked over at Ri'Chard. "You're quiet. I don't want you to feel left out."

Ri'Chard said, "I'm just naturally a quiet guy. I'm more of an observer, I guess. I'm happy to just listen to you guys talk about rocks."

I challenged him. "Oh, come on, you must have some hobbies."

Ri'Chard folded his hands together on the table. "All right. Josh already knows this, but I'm kind of a nerd. I really like computer games, mostly the civilization builders. I think in a past life I must have been a war strategist."

I wasn't exactly turned off. I was already dating a political strategist, but I was beginning to fetishize Ri'Chard as a rugged hunk, not a computer game junkie.

Ri'Chard said, "It's strange, but I definitely feel like I've commanded armies for vast empires; it comes so naturally to me."

I nodded, unsure of what to say. "Sometimes I wonder what my life would have been like in an ancient empire. I think I would have probably been a mouthy concubine who ended up poisoned by an evil queen."

Ri'Chard raised an eyebrow. "I don't see you as a mouthy concubine, but I could see you as a cunning queen."

"I like that," I said, imagining myself in the role and already feeling the power go to my head.

Josh asked, "What position would you give me in your empire?"

I considered, then tapped my chopsticks on the edge of my plate. "I'd give you the title of Minister of Rocks. You could make sure the pebbles of my footpaths are chosen to the highest standard."

Josh smiled and kept eating. Frankly, I thought he should be more grateful he hadn't been made food tester for the cunning queen.

AFTER DINNER, we walked outside. We were all quiet, unsure of what to say after our polite dinner.

Josh broke the silence. "I have a car you can borrow from the garage until your car is fixed."

I thanked him for the offer. I figured that might be easier than trying to find a rental. I turned to Ri'Chard and said, "Thanks for helping today. It was really nice to meet you."

"No problem, it was nice to meet you too. I guess I'll see you around?"

"Yeah, I hope so." I didn't know what else to say to Ri'Chard. He was a nice surprise in this otherwise mediocre town.

Josh gave me a ride back to my hotel in his truck and dropped me off directly in front of the hotel's main double glass doors. He told me he'd bring me the new car in the morning. I thanked him and said goodbye.

As soon as I walked into the lobby, I noticed a new woman behind the desk. She was looking in my direction and I nodded in acknowledgment.

She nodded back, but I thought I caught a slight smirk on her face. It continued to bother me as I walked down the hallway to my room. I wanted to know what had put it there, so I turned and walked back to the desk.

"Do you have any teas without caffeine in them?" I asked.

"I can check." She went into the back and came back with a few bags of some cinnamon orange mixture. "Will this do?"

"Thank you," I said, taking the teabags from her. "I haven't seen you before. Are you new here?"

She said, "No, I've been here for a while, just got back from vacation. What brings you to Pothos?"

I said, "Work, just work. But my car broke down today, which is why I was getting dropped off now."

She nodded again. It was that same damn smirk. I put the tea bags in my purse and walked back to my room. Maybe she was a Born Again Christian who'd assumed I was one of Josh's easy marks. That was the kind of mistake I could have gotten away with before the age of 25, or maybe 27, but I was past 30 and knew better than to sleep with a guy like that.

I couldn't, just couldn't, but then why did I lay in bed that night and think about Josh while touching myself? I let him lift me onto the hood of my car as his hands cupped and lightly squeezed my breasts and my palms slipped underneath his douchebag shirt and ran up his torso. I slid my tongue over the dip in his collarbone and tasted the salt that lingered on his skin after a long, hot day of work. Strangely, I imagined Ri'Chard watching us. He stood in the corner of the garage with that same intense gaze.

Suddenly the scene shifted. I was back in my D.C. apartment and Ri'Chard was there. I imagined myself on all fours on the bed, his hands holding my hips as he thrust into me from behind. His boots were tied so tightly they had to stay on. I was just about to reach orgasm when Matthew walked in and started yelling about Ri'Chard's shoes on the sheets – our regular, non-sex sheets. There went my climax.

I made Matthew disappear. As he faded away, I conjured up a new fantasy. Ri'Chard was now on top of me, and with each imagined thrust he sent me back centuries until I could practically feel my silk robes pulled up over my naked hips, collapsing the dragon embroideries into golden abstractions. My legs splayed open around his thighs, as his beautiful, broad hands pressed hard into my buttocks while we fucked by candlelight in my imperial chamber. After all, I had to reward him for such daring maneuvers that led to my empire's victory. He was the brilliant general, and I, the cunning queen. He stared into my eyes if I were a code to be deciphered, focused, obsessed, and addicted to my riddles. He ripped the silk of my dress and leaned down to kiss my breasts, his tongue lightly lingering on one erect nipple before slowly drawing across my neck, like the sword of a traitor. Our eyes locked again as he gave me an heir to the empire.

THE FANTASY suddenly ended as an orgasm ricocheted through my body and was immediately met with guilt. *What the fuck?* I said to myself, in awe of the bizarre scenario my brain just concocted and my body's enthusiastic reaction to it.

As I considered whether this was a new sexual awakening, I turned over to see a message from Matthew asking "Chat now?"

I decided to go to sleep instead of answering it.

3

The next morning Josh showed up in front of my hotel in some old shitbox car. It was a modest black sedan, the paint now matte from years of scratches across the surface. He got out and asked, seemingly without irony, what I thought of the car.

"Does it have airbags?" I asked.

"This thing has everything you need. It's a 2004 Corolla, the perfect car. I even installed a media system with Bluetooth." He seemed proud to offer this to me, so I would have to accept, even if it had a faded Phish sticker on the bumper. I hated bumper stickers.

Josh asked for a ride back to his garage, and I got a feel for the car. He thanked me for dinner last night, and I surprised myself by replying, "I'm grateful for the company. It's been pretty lonely here."

"We can hang out again if you'd like?"

I gave him a sideways glance and said, "Possibly."

"I also put a rock in the cupholder to bring luck. It's citrine, but not a high quality one. Still a nice color though."

I glanced down at the yellow stone. "Thanks, that's very considerate. I wish I had brought you a gift as well."

"Oh, the rock isn't a gift. It's just on loan so you don't crash the car."

"Is that a racist remark, since I'm Asian and you think I can't drive?" I asked accusingly.

He stuttered, "Uh, I didn't mean it like that. I'll just be quiet now."

I laughed a little. "I'm just kidding. I understand this is a very valuable car and you're just worried about it."

Josh studied me for a second. "I know you're making fun of this car, but it will grow on you, I promise."

We pulled into the driveway of Steve's Toybox. He started to open the door while the car was still moving. I almost screamed and put the car in park, but before I knew it, he was out of the vehicle and leaning on the open window frame. He said, "I'll call you when your car is fixed. In the meantime, if you have questions about this car or Pothos, you can text me." He gave me a wink, tapped the window frame rhythmically a few times, and walked into the garage. Today he was wearing a regular t-shirt and looked like a functioning adult male. *Damn, I think I would have sex with him.*

I shook my head to get those thoughts out. I had never cheated, or even had sex with a hot dumb guy. I'd chased academic accolades and stability and achieved all of it, so why did I feel empty? And why did I want Josh to help fill this emptiness?

I wondered about this as I sat in one of the back pews at the Baptist courthouse. Typing on my computer was slow as I made many mistakes. Instead of remembering punctuation, I was fantasizing about Josh. For a brief moment, I thought about us having sex in the back of the Corolla, then the darkness of my mind wondered about what would happen if I got pregnant and he were the father. Would I want to raise a child with him? He'd never leave this shit town, and I'd be stuck here running a personal injury law firm on the second floor of a former brothel turned office building. To my left was a brochure rack that had pamphlets taunting me with "Life Starts at Holy Conception." I shuddered.

I saw Jim Smoke enter the central aisle and nod at me. He sat on the pew across the aisle, then turned to me and said, "Nice to join you here again this morning. I'm starting to think you just want to spend time with me."

I looked up from typing on my computer and turned to face him. "Mr. Smoke, are you lonely without your hunting partner?"

He laughed. "Well, Steve is out since bow hunting season just started. Do you like to hunt, Miss Julie?"

He was testing me. Of course I've never hunted in my life, but he was challenging me with his fragile idea of masculinity. Mr. Smoke was an archetype; most men like him somehow end up in power. They're outgoing, with ambition influenced by insecurity and fear. Fear drives everything. Jim Smoke was scared of the unknown, and the unknown here was a Black population with the right to vote. I could see right through him, like the ghost that was haunting this town.

I replied, "Mr. Smoke, I don't hunt."

He looked satisfied, and I continued typing while he carried on. "I could tell a woman like you isn't cut out for it. You have 'city' written all over you. But it's just great, going out in the early morning, spending hours on the ground, tracking and waiting until just the right moment to make a choice between life and death. It really makes you feel like a man."

I looked at him. "Well, if you're so good at tracking, why don't you find the person that burned down the courthouse? Then I can go back to the city, and we can both be happy."

He just smiled. "Well, when this is all over, Ms. Julie, why don't I take you hunting?"

I felt a little pang in my stomach, and it wasn't Josh's imaginary baby. I said, "I don't think it's smart to give your enemy a gun, right?"

Mr. Smoke grinned creepily. "Are you threatening to shoot me?" He seemed excited by the idea of violence.

I decided to be provocative. "If I did and blamed it on the ghost of General Stovall, would people believe me?"

He laughed and shook his head. "You're quick, Ms. Chen. I think I'll have to keep an eye on you."

I suddenly wondered if he'd cut the wires to my car. Perhaps Josh was a spy luring me into the Corolla with faulty brakes. I couldn't trust anyone in this town, and with the way I'd started sexually fantasizing about him and his friend Ri'Chard, I didn't think I could trust myself either.

Thankfully, our conversation broke when Sasha, a woman from a voting rights organization I was working with, joined me and we began to strategize our court agenda. She sat next to me, and I glanced back at Jim Smoke, who continued to look at me with that unsettling grin.

THE HEARING, surprisingly, went nowhere. The injunction against the town government to immediately reinstate the voters failed, and I was left with another wasted court session watching Jim Smoke confidently dodge my legitimate claims. He wasn't exactly brilliant, but he wasn't an idiot, and certainly knew how to bend the law to his will. I exited the Baptist courthouse pissed and even more driven to destroy him.

As Sasha parted with me on the sidewalk, she asked, "What are you going to do now?"

"I don't know. There's just something bothering me about all this. It's so obvious this is a cover-up, but I need something convincing."

"Listen, more than one Pothos is happening in this state, hell, even this country. Even if you don't figure this case out, there are plenty more to fight."

"You're right, and thanks for what you're doing too."

She said, "I know. I don't get paid enough for this shit, and sometimes I feel like voting doesn't even matter. This fight never ends." She got into her car and asked, "Do you need a ride? I didn't see your car parked here."

"I have a loaner," I said, and gestured at the Corolla.

She raised an eyebrow. "Does that come with food stamps?" She left me with my mouth slightly agape at the insult. I looked at the Corolla and tried to see the potential in it, perhaps the same potential I saw in Ms. Honeypaw.

I drove toward the old courthouse, still a void in the town center. Today no one was at the scene, and the caution tape fluttered with only a few spectators pointing over it at what was left of the brick façade, now vandalized by fire. I parked close to Ms. Honeypaw's house, where I thought I could see someone smoking a cigarette on the porch. I decided to get out and walk closer.

Sure enough, Ms. Honeypaw was sitting in her big old rocker, enveloped in another equally tasteless mu'umu'u and staring down Main Street, an impressive billow of smoke wafting from the tip of her cigarette toward the sagging ceiling. She didn't see me walking up.

I smelled weed and realized she was smoking a joint. "Hello, Ms. Honeypaw."

Halfway through an inhale, she turned to look at me, coughing clouds of smoke. "Shit, I wasn't expecting to see you," she sputtered through the hacking.

"I wasn't expecting to see you either, but I guess fate brought us together again."

"What do you know about fate? You have no idea what a tricky bitch fate can be." Ms. Honeypaw did not look pleased.

"Maybe fate wanted us to meet again because you have information that can help a lot of people."

"I ain't snitching for free. The ATM is two blocks down Main Street, so go withdraw some cash, and then we can talk. Oh, and my fee has gone up to $800." Ms. Honeypaw coolly took a big draw from her joint.

I rolled my eyes. This version of Ms. Honeypaw was much more obstinate than the beckoning psychic I had met earlier. I said, "Listen, I just spent a frustrating day in court trying to protect the voting rights of townsfolk like yourself. Don't you care about your community here?"

"This ain't my community," she said. "And what would you know about 'community'? You got a gang of Prada-bag bitches that hang out and try to fix the problems of Black people?"

I rolled my eyes again. "Listen, I don't want to be here. I was sent here by my boss and I'm trying to not get fired for losing this case. Please, help me."

She leaned back. "Listen Miss Prada, I got bills to pay too. This town is trying to take my house, so look deep in your heart and pockets to help Ms. Honeypaw."

I sighed and shook my head. "I legally can't give you money. I'm sorry."

Ms. Honeypaw nodded. "Then, legally, I can't give you my information." She stubbed out her joint and stood. "Good luck in your case, Miss Prada. Though next time I find you in front of my house, I'm shooting your ass."

I scoffed. "I'm on the sidewalk. This is public property. You can't shoot me."

"Unless you're here to pluck my eyebrows, get the fuck outta my face." Ms. Honeypaw turned and walked through the front door of her house.

I stood in shock. Usually, a minute after an altercation like this ends, I think of the witty thing I should have said, but today I was dumbfounded. Ms. Honeypaw was a peculiar challenge, and I had the sense she would provide infinite frustration as I attempted to get information from her.

I resented her and yet was intrigued. Would she be the master of mind games, or could I break through that with my own mental acumen? I ran through all the scenarios in my head of how I could approach her the next time while I walked back to my car. I saw a flyer under my wiper for a monster truck rally. I crumpled it and thought about tossing it on the street, but I put it in my purse instead for legal disposal later.

I drove down the Main Street of the town. Sad two-story brick and wooden-clad buildings once filled with segregated stores that went out of business since the nearby Walmart opened. At least that's the narrative I decided on.

Strangely, the road was lined with plastic chairs and beach chairs, but no one was sitting on them. Some had little American flags tied on them, others with fake flowers. It looked ominous, and I was wondering if they'd parade me down the street tomorrow before I was stoned to death.

I pulled up to my hotel to change. I saw the same smirking woman from the front desk and asked her about the chairs.

"It's the Veteran's Day Parade tomorrow. Big deal among the folks in the town– well, some folks."

I asked her to clarify.

"They don't honor Black veterans in that parade. They never have, even men like my grandaddy weren't allowed to walk in it."

"Oh, no, that's illegal. They're breaking the law."

She feigned a laugh and said, "There's no law about it. It's just an unspoken thing, and you'll soon learn things work differently down here. You can say it's the law, but who is going to enforce it?"

I considered what she said. I'd noticed all the town officials I'd seen were White, hardly representative of the substantial Black population. "I'm sorry. My firm is working hard to change that and to reinstate the Black voters of this town."

"Well, I'm grateful for that. My name is Keli. It's nice to meet you."

I was pleased to see her armor drop a little. I introduced myself then asked, "The other night, you were smiling at me, like you knew something I didn't."

"Oh that..." She laughed. "I just...I know *that* truck."

I nodded. "You thought I was on a date with Josh?"

She gave me a knowing look and said, "Let's just say I've seen a lot of girls get out of that truck."

So Josh was a dumb whore. My intuition was spot-on. I said, "I figured. But don't worry, the only thing of mine he'll be touching is my car."

She laughed. "Listen, I wouldn't judge otherwise. He's a nice guy, I really don't have anything to warn you about, other than don't get your heart caught up in him."

I thought of Matthew. I never had to question his loyalty. He was a terrible liar, and he seemed generally satisfied with me, but there was no lust. Staring at Ri'Chard last night reminded me of the power of attraction, the power of two bodies in courtship. Josh also brought out those same feelings, but his accessibility was intimidating to me.

"I'm going to finish some work, but it was nice to meet you."

"Same," Keli replied, "And I'll try to get more caffeine-free teas." She ended with a wink.

I thanked her and went to my room.

I LOOKED up from my computer to realize it was already night. I'd have to gamble on another supermarket salad for dinner that hopefully wouldn't give me E. coli. I zipped over in the Corolla. It was like driving a road-legal go-kart. My luxury sedan felt like a tank in comparison to this economic model, and I enjoyed the thrill of it.

I perused the aisles for some wine to go with my mandarin orange and chicken salad.

"Surprised to find you here," I heard a familiar voice say.

I turned to see Ri'Chard. "Hi!" I said, holding a bottle by the neck. "Why do I feel like a teenager caught stealing wine?"

He laughed. "I have a feeling you were a very well-behaved teenager." I felt a little pang of truth since he was correct; I was a model kid.

"You're right, I never even drank before coming to this town." We both laughed a little. He had perfect teeth and dimples that formed when he smiled.

"It must be hard coming here from such a fancy place like D.C."

"Yeah, it's not that the town isn't fancy, it just feels backward."

Ri'Chard nodded. "I get it. It wasn't easy growing up around here, and certainly not coming back."

Curious, I asked, "Are you going to move?"

He nodded lightly and said, "I think so, but my girlfriend is still deployed for a while longer, so I'm gonna wait until we figure out where to settle. Then I'll sell the towing business."

Damn, *girlfriend*. It made sense; he was too attractive to be single and too kind not to have been sought out by other women. I hated her, wherever she was, even if she was out "defending our country" or whatever bullshit she was programmed to believe.

I feigned a smile. "I'm happy to hear that you have a long-term plan." I stood in silence, awkwardly, until I broke it with, "Anyway, I'm just going to pick out something and head out."

We exchanged a brief goodbye, and after a few steps, he turned. "Hey, I'm going to Josh's place tomorrow night to hang out, after my family's party. You should come. He doesn't have much family, so he could use the company."

I wondered if that would be awkward. I barely knew them, and it seemed untoward for Ri'Chard to be inviting me to Josh's house.

"Is Josh okay with that? I mean, we don't know each other that well."

Ri'Chard smiled and said, "Don't worry. You're interesting, so you'll be good company."

"What should I bring? Is a half-empty bottle of chardonnay okay?" I asked as I held up the bottle.

"Just bring yourself. You're more than enough."

I COULDN'T WAIT for the wine to cool in the hotel room fridge. I should've bought an already cold bottle of $7 Pinot Grigio, but I felt that was beneath me. I wanted a big gulp of wine because I felt stupid for thinking Ri'Chard was single, devastated that he already had a girlfriend, guilty because I already had a boyfriend, and even more stupid for feeling this way in the first place.

I blamed the town. Idle hands are the devil's playground, and my lack of mental stimulation caused this mental turmoil.

I paced around the room and kept opening the fridge to test the coolness of the bottle. I only liked white wine cold, so I'd have to get ice.

I went out to the front desk where Keli was working.

"Hey! How was the rest of your day?" she asked, sounding cheerful.

I said, "Not great. The stalled court proceedings and the

usual pointless bureaucracy of this town are really getting to me."

She was smiling, but it turned slightly to a grimace. "Yeah, you must have really pissed your boss off for them to send you here."

"I think my crime is that I'm a neutral ethnicity, neither the oppressor nor the oppressed here." I waited a moment, then asked, "Do you have any ice?"

"Yeah, I'll go get some. Sorry the machine has been broken, by the way."

"It's fine, it's not often I need it," I said, which felt like a lie.

I waited until she came back with a glass full of ice, "I might want some of whatever you're drinking with this," Keli said, with a wink.

"Yeah, can you sneak a little wine at work?" I asked.

"No, I shouldn't..." She looked around, "But I'm about to go on a smoke break and could meet you out front. You have a big purse?"

I understood and said, "Yes, I am a working woman."

She raised her eyebrows. "Okay, okay, I'll meet you out front in five."

"Bring the glass of ice," I said.

I walked back to my room and stuffed the bottle of wine in my purse, wrapped a towel around the glass to keep it from clinking, and walked outside.

Keli sat on the top edge of a concrete planter built into the side of the building with some green foliage behind her. She took a drag of her cigarette and exhaled a long cloud of smoke. "The camera in this part of the parking lot is broken, so we're good."

I sat next to her and took out my glass and bottle. I took half the ice from the glass and put it in mine, then gave a generous pour to both glasses. We held them up, prepared to toast. "What should we drink to?" I asked.

"Hmmm," Keli considered, then raised an eyebrow. "A toast to our successes, our failures, and those rare times when life feels like it is going right."

I laughed. "Okay, to all the above." We clinked our glasses and took a sip. "I needed that after today," I said.

She shook the ash off the end of her cigarette. "Yeah, I'm sure you make a lot of money, but your job sounds shitty."

"It is. Sometimes it's alright, but often I find myself asking, 'What is all this for?' The money, the career, the man, if it all feels empty..."

"Oh, you got a man?" she asked. "Tell me about him."

I told her about Matthew, ending with, "He's back in D.C., or actually India at the moment, for work. He works for the government, and he's really great. Very stable and very smart."

Keli looked unconvinced. "And...?"

"And what?" I asked.

"Does he make you...you know, squirm while thinking about him? You sound like you're telling me about your brother or something. I don't get the sense you have any passion for him."

"First, I could never talk about my brother without multiple expletives. Secondly, that's not true. Matthew is a very practical lover."

"Practical?" said Keli in a high tone, "This isn't about practicality, this is passion...what about Josh?"

The moment she said his name, I felt a burning through my body. I couldn't hide my smirk.

"There you go," said Keli. "Now I can see you squirming."

I took a big sip. "Josh is cute, but he's the worker, and I'm the client."

Keli took a drag of her cigarette while I looked at my glass.

"Actually," I said, "I bought this bottle because there was another guy I liked, but I just found out he has a girlfriend."

"Damn, you're hitting the bottle over this man? Who is he?"

"I don't want to say, it's stupid." I waited a moment. I was enjoying Keli's company. She had an energy about her that made me want to be open, like I could say whatever naughty thing crossed my mind and she wouldn't judge me for it. I said, "His name is Ri'Chard."

Keli's eyes rolled back in her head while she groaned. "Oh, oh shit. You gotta give me warning before you speak that man's name. He is so fucking fine!" She let out a lot of graphic noises, clearly retracing similar dirty thoughts she'd also had about him.

"I know, I know. He towed my car yesterday, and I can't get him out of my head."

She agreed. "Listen, that man will never leave your head. He's like a fucking sculpture that belongs in a museum. He's so polite, but I just know he's a freak too."

"How do you know?"

"It takes wild to know wild." She raised an eyebrow and said, "I think you got a little freak in you too."

I was bashful, but maybe she was right. I think there was depth of sexuality within me I never explored, and my fantasies with Josh and Ri'Chard were safe ways to do it. "Maybe, but I don't want to cheat on my boyfriend or for Ri'Chard to cheat on his girlfriend."

Keli nodded. "Yeah, that man is loyal, which makes him even more fine. Just fuck Josh."

I almost spit out my wine. "What?!"

"Just fuck Josh," she repeated. "He's easy, and no one will ever find out once you go back to D.C."

"I can't; I have a boyfriend," I said unconvincingly.

She said, "I don't know, I'm skeptical about this Matthew. Did you ever have a *ho era*?"

I looked at her, puzzled. "A 'ho era'"?

"Yeah, it's a constructive period in your life where you get the ho out of you before you settle down with a Matthew."

"No, I guess not. There was only one other guy before Matthew."

Keli took a drag and the smoke came out of her mouth while she spoke, like a wise dragon. "See, that's your problem. You haven't lived up to your *ho-tential.* You need to get that out, otherwise you'll just be miserable thinking about all the dick you missed out on."

"Do you think I'm miserable?" I asked.

She delicately said, "No, but you seem uptight. I hope that's not offensive."

I looked at her. She was right, no one ever considered me as "relaxed" or the "cool girl". I was never invited out with coworkers after work, or even slated to be a bridesmaid. Matthew and I only hung out with couples from his work, but he worked all the time in his new position, so that was extremely rare. I realized with a shock of recognition that I was not fun, or wild, or anything more than my Prada bag. All those things swirling in my head were never said out loud. Instead, I just portrayed an off-putting coolness while in D.C.

I guess people were nice to me here because there were so few outsiders that they were accepting of anything.

Keli said, "You look sad. I'm sorry if I offended you."

"No," I said quickly, "It's not you. Today was rough. Court was shit, and then I had to deal with this woman named Ms. Honeypaw, who is just a pain in the ass."

Keli scoffed. "Shit, you gotta give me a warning before you say that woman's name. That bitch is crazy. She owes both sides of my family money. How can you scam both my paternal and maternal grandparents? That's fucked up."

"Well, I have not heard anything positive about her," I echoed.

"That is a troubled woman. Comes with the family history, though," said Keli.

"What's with her family?"

Keli looked around, then took a long sip of wine. "You know that General Stovall that they have a statue of in town?"

I made a sound of disgust. "Yes, I'm familiar."

"Well, apparently she's a descendant of his."

My eyes widened. "What? I thought he was a Confederate general."

She continued, "That didn't stop these Confederate men from being nasty. They were all hypocrites pretending to be Christians. Just ask their wives when they came back home smelling of other bitches' syphilis."

"So, who in his family married a Black person?" I asked.

"Married?" she repeated, stunned. "There was no marriage. He raped his slave. She got pregnant, and the line continued all the way to Ms. Honeypaw."

"Whoa, I guess I see where her anger comes from."

Keli said, "Oh no, she's angry because she's a repressed lesbian."

I asked, "How do you know?"

"Is the sky blue? Her attraction to pussy is abundantly clear to everyone in this town, except for her apparently."

I started to wonder about the obvious things people notice that we cannot admit to ourselves, like being gay, or having an eating disorder, or being attracted to my mechanic.

I shook off the thought. "Thanks, maybe this will help me find a new way to approach her."

"What do you need from her? I'd stay far away if I were you," said Keli.

"She lives right across from the courthouse. I think she saw something the night it burned down, but she won't tell me unless I pay her."

Keli looked dumbfounded. "Aren't you supposed to be smart? Once a scammer, always a scammer. She'll tell you whatever you want to hear for money. The bitch can't see the future, but she can see dollar signs and desperation."

"Do you think she's lying?"

Keli bluntly said, "Yes."

I sighed. "Fine, I'll leave it alone. I guess it's good. She told me if I come by her house again, she'll shoot me."

Keli laughed. "I'm sure she's got her White great-great-great-grandaddy's musket somewhere in that house."

"Then she told me to leave unless I was going to pluck her eyebrows. Was that a racist remark?"

Keli, in a high tone, said, "What eyebrows? The bitch got alopecia."

By now, both our glasses were empty, so I poured a little more in each and said, "Let me make a toast. I'm not going to be uptight anymore."

Keli echoed with an encouraging, "Okay."

I continued, "I'm going to relax and have fun. I'm going to enjoy my time in this town. I'm going to win this court case and get a promotion. I'm going to show these men that I am not one to be messed with. I'm tired of these guys thinking they can push me around. That ends today. Cheers!"

We clinked our glasses together, and each of us took a big sip.

Keli got up and announced, "I have to get back to work. Thanks for keeping me company."

I got up, and Keli surprised me by giving me a hug. She

patted my back while telling me, “Please go and fuck Josh and come back and tell me about it. I’m so bored at this job.”

We laughed, and I said, “That’s not going to happen, but I am going to his place tomorrow night.”

We walked back inside as our conversation continued. I promised to tell her everything before heading back to my room to eat a disappointing salad.

4

I woke up to a disturbing lack of emails to keep me distracted. Since today was Veterans Day, everyone had a holiday. No work emails to digest or briefs to catch up on. I was supposed to be taking the day off, but what did that look like in this town?

I had a craving for something other than hotel coffee, so I decided to head toward the main street in the hopes of finding a café with a working espresso machine. I hopped in the Corolla and drove toward downtown. Cars lined the streets and, in the distance, I saw orange barricades across the intersection of Main Street. To my dismay, the entire town seemed to be lined up along the street. The chairs I saw set out yesterday were occupied by the townsfolk dressed in their best t-shirts and trucker hats. Most looked like piles of flesh straining the engineering of their foldable chairs.

A slight breeze ruffled the American flags that hung from the streetlights. The parade was just beginning to make its way down the street. Veterans dressed in their uniforms walked stoically or rode in old convertibles.

A convertible carrying the mayor passed, followed by a

contingent dressed in Confederate soldier uniforms. They carried their Confederate flags with obvious pride, and I had the urge to run. But this contingent was short-lived and meant to honor the soldiers of Pothos who died during the Civil War, at least according to the banner being carried by two soldiers sweating through their steely blue wool uniforms.

Then I noticed the uniforms had started to change. The marchers wore robes of red satin, and I walked closer to get a better look at the spectacle. Two men held a banner announcing that this was the Pothos Historical Society. I recognized Jim Smoke and Mr. Lyons, whose complexion was almost the same color as the robes from the heat. A woman walked silently behind them in a similar robe. She held a black and white portrait of a man.

A man next to me said to the woman he was with, "Mary, who is that woman walking?"

The lady replied, "That's the great-great-great-grandniece of General Stovall, Sally Wren."

"No shit," he said, seemingly impressed. "I didn't recognize her! She's gotten slim. Remember when she used to be all big after the kid?" The woman nodded in remembrance.

I watched Sally Wren stride confidently, holding the photo of her dear great-great-great papa General Stovall. Not far behind, I saw a little girl in a sparkly dress with an uncomfortable amount of makeup riding on top of a miniature pony. She wore a sash that said "Miss Pothos" and stiffly held her arm bent at the elbow. She gave everyone an artificial smile. The pony looked around nervously as it was guided forward.

I was overwhelmed enough by the bizarre pageantry and ready to give up on my simple mission of finding a latte. I turned to walk back to my car.

Suddenly, I heard a shrill shriek and turned just in time to see Miss Pothos bouncing on the pony as it reared up on its tiny legs. It bucked a few times, and she fell off. It wasn't a dramatic fall; she was able to get her right foot on the ground and tumble down. The pony took off disrupting the people marching in robes. They moved aside and exposed Sally Wren carrying General Stovall's portrait. The pony ran and dodged her at the last moment, but it was too late. She was startled and tripped over the hem of her robe, throwing his portrait into the air. It landed face-down on the street with a loud shattering of glass.

People started to scream, and men jumped in to catch the errant pony. Some women rushed in to help the downed niece and rescue the portrait of General Stovall. I felt myself smile so I quickly left. I started laughing when I was far enough away. I was happy to see the parade after all, and I was sure this moment would be the talk of the town for days to come.

I SPENT the rest of the day in my room. Keli had the day off, so I was challenged to find any reason to leave. I was curious if I'd hear from Josh or Ri'Chard later, but I didn't want to seem desperate by inquiring. I only wanted to go because the alternative was doing absolutely nothing, like I was doing at the moment, tapping my fingernails on the wooden veneer of my hotel desk.

I decided to look up General Stovall on the internet. The first result was a scant Wikipedia article. I found a more detailed account of the General on the Pothos Historical Society website.

The article was certainly written by an admirer. Apparently, General Stovall was born into "poverty" and "pulled himself up by his bootstraps" to expand his family's cotton plantation. He was regarded as a brilliant businessman and known as a powerful orator. During the Civil War, he found his following as a General. He lost a few battles and won even fewer, before being captured at a fort 30 miles north of Pothos. He was released on amnesty before becoming the mayor of Pothos. A few years after that, he was assassinated in the former courthouse due to a disagreement over a cotton tax he wanted to institute.

I scrolled through photos of old Pothos and the General. The silver nitrate portraits might have been discolored by time, but I could clearly see he was just another historical asshole.

I searched "general stovall slave" and waited for the results. There was nothing mentioned about what I was looking for: an explanation for the genealogy of Ms. Honeypaw. I decided to search again, adding "lover" at the end, but before I could press search, I stopped. I realized a definition didn't exist for what I was looking for. "Concubine" seemed too ornate, "lover" was dishonest, and "affair" seemed too consensual. How could I categorize a woman who was likely assaulted by someone who claimed ownership over her? The violence that existed in her past was beyond my scope of imagination. Yet a part of me couldn't help but wonder how I would have behaved at that time. Would I have stood up for injustice or remained complacent in a system that condoned slavery? Was I complacent now, considering my motivation to win the case was mostly for career merit?

I lay down and decided not to think about it. Instead, I thought about Ri'Chard. I drifted into a dream state as I thought about his pensive gaze, his purposeful movements, and his perfect eyelashes. I imagined him lying in bed next to me, what he looked like while he was sleeping. His arm was above his head while he slept, and I could see his armpit. I wondered if he was ticklish there. I imagined a military regiment tattoo on his inner bicep, slightly warped by his muscles. I reached out to graze his arm and underarm, which made him stir a little.

I continued to trace my fingertips along his body, down his chest, down his stomach, until I hit the dam of blankets. In my fantasy, he surprised me by saying, "Keep going," without opening his eyes. Like water, my hands slid under the covers, and I felt him. "Good girl," he told me softly. As I started to stroke him, I felt hands move along my waist. I looked down to see Josh's hand creeping beneath my waistband, the light pressure and friction of his fingertips arousing me. I continued to stroke Ri'Chard, who was moaning with pleasure. I moaned, and Josh continued to entangle his fingers with my wetness as I felt his erection straining against the scrap of underwear still covering me.

As I stroked Ri'Chard's steel-hard shaft, quickening my pace as he built toward an orgasm, I felt the same sensation washing over me. Josh's nimble fingers continued to tease my slick, sensitive folds as my stomach muscles tightened and my whole body began to shake. I watched as Ri'Chard's abs contorted, and I felt his release and the warmth of his orgasm drip on my hand. We both took a big breath and, smiling, I turned to kiss Josh, but was met with a different face. His lips were buried beneath a mustache, and his body by a steely blue uniform.

I was face-to-face with the ghost of General Stovall. Panic came over me as I stared in terror into his evil visage. Trapped by his weight, I was unable to move away. I stared directly into his eyes. They had faint blue rings around the irises and contained the cold calculation of an evil man. In a whispery voice that nevertheless seemed to resonate from all directions around me, he murmured: "You belong to me."

I woke up in a fright. I panted and shook off the sleep for a few seconds. It had been ages since I had a nightmare, and being fingered by a ghost certainly topped the list of my worst. I hoped this didn't become a recurring one. I looked at my phone and saw there was a text message from Josh, "Hi. This is where I live. Come later if you're free."

There was a link to a place about 20 minutes away. No

Street View available to scope it out. I searched online for the address to see if any of the real estate websites had a listing. I had a bad habit of doing that before I went to someone's house. It's just uncouth to ask how much they paid in taxes over dinner, but I liked to know. I didn't see much info online either. I'd go regardless and find a way to bring up real estate taxes over beers.

My only question was what he meant by "later"? I replied back, "7 okay?"

He replied, "All good."

I think that was enough. I debated asking what I should bring. I had an unopened jar of mixed nuts in my kitchen. I decided that's all I could offer. I wondered if Josh had a bowl to serve them in. Just in case, I brought one from the hotel.

I ARRIVED at the entrance to his driveway at 7:03 p.m. I couldn't see the house; it was a narrow dirt road that had a turn. I eased my Corolla up and saw a modest trailer, then Josh's truck and another truck parked next to it. I wondered if that was Ri'Chard's. Their big trucks dwarfed my tiny Corolla as I parked next to them. I looked around to see if I should lock my car since my wallet was in it, but I didn't see any neighbors around. I decided to bring it with me instead.

I heard some footsteps on the gravel behind me and turned to see Josh.

"Hey, you made it!" He opened his arms to give me a hug.

I awkwardly leaned in for it, then held up the jar and said, "Yes, I brought nuts!"

"Thanks. These look fancy."

I shrugged. "It's fine, they're not even organic. Do you have a bowl?"

"Yeah, what do you need it for?"

"The nuts. I brought one in case you didn't have one," I said, awkwardly.

"I have a bowl," he said. "Multiple, actually. But thanks for thinking about it."

"It's fine. I feel stupid for bringing it now," I said, embarrassed.

"Don't feel that way," he said, looking at me kindly, "You just like to make sure everything is taken care of. I like that about you."

I smiled a little. "Thanks, sometimes I can be pretty annoying about it, though."

"I think you're too cute to be that annoying," said Josh.

I was taken aback. I felt flattered by the line, but the flattery felt thin, like this was a line he used on a lot of girls before. I wasn't one of those easy ones who hopped in his truck. "Wow, that's a good line." My awkwardness was quickly replaced by my suspicious side.

"What?" he asked. "My compliment?"

"Yeah, it was smooth and almost worked for a moment."

He smiled, but his eyes showed confusion. "Well, I was just trying to make you feel nice."

"Don't worry, I'm not judging you for it. I'm just letting you know it doesn't work on me." I gave him what I hoped was a reassuring smile, but I wanted to be very clear I was not about to fall for his usual gimmicks.

"What doesn't work?" he asked.

"Those cheesy lines, the 'you're too cute to be annoying' stuff," I said. He still looked confused.

"Oh, I guess I'm sorry if that offended you."

"I'm not offended either, but I'm onto you."

He laughed a little. "Damn, I'm kinda intimidated right now. You lawyers are scary."

"It's fine, we're not that bad. Should we go inside?"

Josh looked amused. "Ri'Chard is around back."

I walked around to see Ri'Chard tending to some burgers. He said, "Hey, you made it."

"Yes, and I brought nuts." I held out the jar to him.

He looked at the jar and said, "Alright, that's cool."

I looked at the jar again. "I guess that's a ridiculous thing to bring to a party."

"Nonsense," said Ri'Chard, "Everyone loves nuts."

I turned around to see Josh laughing. "What is it?" I asked.

He said, "Oh no, you scared me, so I'm being quiet now."

Ri'Chard asked, "What happened?"

I said, defending myself, "I wasn't scary, I was just being honest."

Ri'Chard asked, "With what?"

"Josh was...trying to compliment me, but it came off as a cheesy pick-up line."

Ri'Chard gave Josh a look as if this was something he had witnessed before.

Josh said, "I was just trying to be nice. Excuse me for exercising my right to give a compliment."

I replied, "No, it was the way you said it. It felt like a line you've used before."

Josh scoffed. "It wasn't. On God, you're the first woman I've ever said anything like that to."

I rolled my eyes. "That also feels like a line. Women must eat this shit up."

Ri'Chard was laughing.

"Wow, why don't you trust me?" Josh asked.

"None of it feels...I don't know. Sincere? Accurate? It just feels trite," I said. Josh looked at me, a little puzzled. He probably didn't know what "trite" meant, so I continued, "That stuff might work on a lot of women, but you're forgetting my job is to see the truth and reveal it or disguise it. When you say that, it feels like you have an ulterior motive."

"Wow, I feel like I'm in court," said Josh.

I heard Ri'Chard say "Damn," and laugh a little. "Did he make you that mad?" Ri'Chard asked.

This was getting out of hand, and perhaps I was being ridiculous. I said, "I'm sorry, I guess that 'you're too pretty to be annoying' comment really pissed me off."

"Why would that piss you off?" asked Josh.

"Because I can be annoying, and mean, and it's not a performance for a man to fix. It's just life. That comment felt regressive, like women are meant to be cute objects for men."

Josh crossed his arms and leaned one broad shoulder against the aluminum siding. "So... what I'm learning is that you don't want a man to fix all your problems?" I knew he'd said that just to needle me.

I asked, "Do you think men can fix problems?"

Josh considered. "For me, I can fix problems with cars but definitely not personal problems."

"Exactly," I said. "Sometimes problems can't be fixed. For me, it's important to see how people exist with their problems. Do they drink them away? Take them out of others? So many of my cases are based on people who can't deal with their emotional problems."

"Shit, you're making this sound like a day in court when it's just a backyard party!" Ri'Chard exclaimed. Ri'Chard cued up some music while Josh started to clap his hands. I watched them both mime the words and groove to the song, and I couldn't help but smile and laugh. Josh danced over my way while he opened a can of beer. He wordlessly placed it in my hands and danced away. I took a big sip and tried to move my body a little.

Ri'Chard called out to Josh over the music. "Josh, can you

grab Julie's nuts?" I laughed a little. I could tell he was making fun of me in a kindhearted way.

Josh danced over to the table and picked them up. "These nuts?" he asked, opening the jar.

Ri'Chard nodded. "How do they taste?"

Josh took a handful. "Julie's nuts taste good. You want them in your mouth too?" I felt red from trying to keep composed while laughing,

Ri'Chard asked, "Are you willing to share her nuts?"

"There's enough for both of us, my man." Josh went over and poured some into Ri'Chard's open palm. "Her nuts look good in your hand."

Ri'Chard said, "They'll look even better in my mouth." He ate them while I sat down and put my hands to my forehead, laughing through the embarrassment. Ri'Chard said, "They're salty. Not bad."

"Tasty nuts," said Josh.

"Julie's nuts are delicious," echoed Ri'Chard.

Josh held the jar out to me and asked, "Want to taste your own nuts?"

I cheekily said, "I think I'm too cute to eat my own nuts."

Josh smirked and raised an eyebrow. "Yes, you deserve a man to eat them for you." I felt my cheeks tighten with a coy smile.

We locked eyes for a moment before Ri'Chard said, "Burgers are almost done? Is everyone ready to eat?" Josh turned to help Ri'Chard while I wondered if he would satisfy my appetite.

Ri'Chard joined us at the picnic table with burgers. Josh grabbed some condiments from inside.

The brief moment Ri'Chard and I were alone I said, "I'm surprised it's just us. I thought Josh would have more friends coming."

Ri'Chard looked at me and considered for a moment. "He

lost someone important to him around this time, so he likes to keep things lowkey at this time of year."

"I'm sorry to hear that," feeling a deepening curiosity about him within me.

"I figured you might be a good distraction, since you're from out of town and don't know his whole backstory." I looked in his eyes for a moment, then tore them away. I couldn't help but glance back at his arms, at how big his biceps were as his arms rested on the table. I took a sip of beer and tried to shake the dirty thoughts out of my head.

Josh came back with a bottle of mustard and ketchup. He looked excited as he started constructing his burger.

I waited until the boys finished and studied my options. It was quaint, this experience. I made my own burger and joined in. "I don't know why but I feel like a tourist in America," I said.

"How so?" Ri'Chard asked.

"This is...so American. Eating burgers at a picnic table with cheap beer. Even though I live at the center of American power, my life is so different there."

Josh asked, "You don't get burgers in D.C.?"

"You do, but it would be covered in brie and cost $28. This is fun, though. Thanks for having me over."

I genuinely felt grateful to meet these two, even if it was only for a fleeting moment. Perhaps it was the cheap beer, but I felt happy. The kind of happiness that comes from familiarity and comfort, even though admittedly, I barely knew these people, yet there was no reason for pretensions. They weren't transactional D.C. sharks or calculating lawyers, they were just two simple guys trying to figure their lives out in an unremarkable part of America.

We all ate in unison. After a brief silence, Josh broke it with, "So, were you always so..."

"Argumentative?" I suggested.

"I was trying to think of a nicer word, but the same idea," said Josh.

I thought about it and said, "Usually I'm pretty quiet. I've always been a nerd, I guess. I focused on school mostly."

"That's cool," said Josh. "It makes sense, ending up as a lawyer and all."

I grimaced. I thought back to high school and college. I was so uptight, and the uptightness followed me since. I never got invited to parties—not that I would go, and anyway, I never had any boyfriends. I'd missed out entirely on making out until I was in my 20s.

I decided to let them into my life. "There's a word in Mandarin, *guai*. It's hard to translate into English. It's basically being good and obedient, but not in a moral sense. *Guai* is being a perfect child, getting good grades, and listening to your parents. So I was *guai*."

Ri'Chard looked at me as one cheek raised into an asymmetrical smile. "You were a *guai* girl." Even as his face lost its symmetry, he was still so sexy.

I nodded. "I was a *guai* girl, so what was it like when you were growing up here?"

"It was a normal, small town experience. My town is a bit bigger, but part of the same school district. We were both on the football team for a season, then Josh did track. That's how we know each other," said Ri'Chard.

I said, "Oh, I thought high school football players would all be fat by now. You guys held on."

Josh laughed a little. "Yep, I still try to keep up with it."

I asked, "So you guys did all the stereotypical things: dating cheerleaders? Harassing theater gays? Having parties when your parents were gone?"

Josh said, "We did all the above, except we didn't have any gay kids at our school."

"Yeah, Josh was not *guai*," reminisced Ri'Chard.

"But you guys are cool with gay people?" I asked as a way to take their political temperatures. It was hard to tell if Pothos had any "progressive" minded people.

"I'm cool with it. I have no problem with whoever you wanna love. I just want people to be happy," said Josh, smiling. I looked at him and felt even more attracted. It wasn't only that he looked handsome as he smiled, as the hint of lines from age fit his face well, but also that he seemed to be a decent person. It was increasingly rare to find a man like that in the world, especially Pothos.

"My uncle in Atlanta is gay, so it was never a problem for me," said Ri'Chard.

I nodded. "Cool, I'm glad you guys aren't homophobes. That would have made this night rougher for me."

"Why, are you gay?" Josh asked.

I was about to say that I have a boyfriend, but stopped myself and just replied with, "No, but I'd probably make out with a girl." I squirmed a little internally, knowing I was saying what countless straight women had uttered when pressed about liking women.

"I once kissed a guy while playing Spin the Bottle," said Josh.

"Is that something you used to do in high school?" I asked.

"Yeah, Spin the Bottle, Seven Minutes in Heaven..." Josh looked into the distance with the fond gaze of someone who peaked in high school.

"What about Truth or Dare?" I asked.

"Oh, that too," said Josh.

I said, "I bet you did all the dumb shit people dared you to."

Ri'Chard laughed and shook his head. "Josh was definitely wilder back then."

I turned my gaze to Ri'Chard, asking, "And what about you? What were you like?"

He shook his head, acting coy. “I was *guai.*”

“Really?” I replied, raising an eyebrow in suspicion.

Josh interrupted our moment. “Ricky has always had his head on straight.”

Ri’Chard asked me, “And you really didn’t do anything wrong?”

“I was very quiet and boring. You both would have just ignored me.”

“Don’t say that, I’m sure we would all have been friends when we were younger,” said Ri’Chard. They definitely would not have been my friends, and I’m not even sure why they were now.

Josh asked, “Did you used to play Truth or Dare?”

“Oh, I was excellent at that,” I said. “I think that’s when I decided to be a lawyer.”

“Is Truth or Dare like being a lawyer?” Asked Josh.

“A little bit. You kind of have to get into people’s heads and figure out ways to embarrass them. Have you ever been deposed?”

Josh looked puzzled. “I don’t know what that is.”

I smiled. “Can I depose you?”

He hesitated. “I guess.”

“Good. I’m going to ask you some questions. Please answer them truthfully. If you feel the answer may incriminate you, then you may plead the fifth.”

Josh nodded his head. Ri’Chard stood up and grabbed new beers for all of us. I took a gulp of mine and focused on Josh, asking, “Please state your name and occupation.”

“Uh, Josh Turner. I’m a mechanic.”

“How old are you, Josh?”

“I’m 31.”

“Where do you live?”

“In Pothos, Georgia.”

"Are you in a relationship?"

"Uh, no. I'm single."

"When was your last relationship?"

"Last year. She broke up with me."

"Do all your girlfriends dump you?"

His face changed a little, becoming more panicked. "What? I mean, sometimes, but it goes both ways."

I paused. "Usually your lawyer would interrupt and say that question was out of line, but I'm doing it to make you self-conscious."

"Oh, okay, this is like some lawyer mind games," said Josh.

"Yes, are you ready for more?" I asked. He nodded. "Josh, do you think Ri'Chard is handsome?"

Josh laughed and looked over at him. "Of course, he's my boy. Everyone thinks he's handsome. Do you think Ri'Chard is handsome?"

"No, no, I'm not the one being deposed. Have you ever thought about Ri'Chard in a way that's more than friends?"

"What? No, it's not like that. I mean, I've complimented him on his body a few times, but he's got a sick body." Josh turned red, and I wasn't sure if it was out of anger or embarrassment. "Can this be over? This is getting weird."

"No, this is exactly the point of a deposition, to make the accused uncomfortable enough to make a mistake."

Josh protested. "But what mistake am I supposed to make?"

I sighed and looked around. "It's okay, I was just trying to have a little fun."

Ri'Chard leaned forward. "Why are you asking Josh these questions?"

I looked Ri'Chard in the eyes and said, "I plead the fifth."

"Oh shit, I forgot you can do that," said Josh, seeming disappointed.

Ri'Chard looked at me with a little glimmer in his eye, "I

don't know...for such an uptight lawyer, I think you have a bit of a fun side."

As the night progressed, we moved inside Josh's trailer, overserved on beers, and listened to sexy R&B. Josh had started to dance, and Ri'Chard was bopping his head to the music. I remained firmly planted on the couch.

"Julie, dance with me." Josh came toward me with seductive arms, but I declined.

"I don't really dance."

"Come on, I think you got some moves." Josh winked at me and beckoned me with a hand.

I laughed and said, "Why don't you dance for me?" In my drunkenness, I pulled out my wallet and took out some cash. Josh sashayed his way forward, grinding his body toward me. I laughed loudly, as did Ri'Chard. He pulled up his shirt, and I tucked a $1 in his waistband. He hollered, and started to put in more effort, seducing me with his moves, while Ri'Chard started to look a little uncomfortable. Josh came closer to me and moved his body between my legs. I giggled.

"Do you like my moves?" He asked.

I said, "I do. Were you a stripper before you became a mechanic?"

He laughed so close to my face that I could feel his breath. "No, I think I missed my calling, right?"

"I think you can do a lot more than being a stripper."

He was close to me. His eyes locked on mine. His cheeks strained with a smile. He leaned down and kissed me lightly on the lips. As he pulled away, I caught the back of his head with my hand and pulled him close. I kissed him back, and our lips joined, exploring one another, before the tip of my tongue met his. He lightly bit my lower lip before gently kissing it.

I shifted on the couch until he was lying on top of me. We continued making out as his hands rubbed up and down my chest. I heard the screen door open, probably Ri'Chard, leaving out of discomfort. I didn't care—I couldn't have him anyway. He was safe fun, but Josh was new territory. Oh well, I was drunk, and kissing wasn't really cheating.

However, Josh was not Matthew. Josh's body ground against mine as his hands ran all over me. He was so passionate in the way his tongue dipped into my mouth. I felt my body tingle with an excitement I'd never felt before.

He pulled back and said, "Do you want to go to my bedroom?"

"We're not having sex," I said.

"No, it will just be more comfortable."

I relented. He led me by the hand to the bedroom and fell onto the bed, pulling me with him. He took my hands and held them above my head. *Oh shit.* My legs locked around his waist as we started to grind on one another. He kissed my neck, my ear, before returning to my mouth. This continued until we both were panting and sweaty. The sensation of his jean-cloaked boner rubbing against me felt delicious, even as my brain felt like it was bobbing in a turbulent ocean from all the alcohol.

I was confused, intoxicated, and exhausted. We made out for minutes, or maybe longer. It was hard to know until we both peeled ourselves off of each other. While the booze daze kicked in, I drifted off into a shitty sleep.

5

I awoke with a dry mouth and the heavy regret from drinking too much beer. It had been a long time since I'd felt this hungover. I looked at my phone, which showed 5:43 a.m. and a low battery. My first instinct was to run to the bathroom and pee. After that, my instinct was to run before Josh woke up.

I grabbed my purse, quietly opened the door, and slipped out. Ri'Chard's truck was gone, and the memory of him leaving came back. Thankfully, I'd left my bottle of water in the car, and I chugged it all before starting the Corolla and leaving.

Things might have happened last night, but it felt unnecessary to think about any of it at the moment. I could only focus on driving and the joy of showering and sleeping in my own bed.

I was on the main road heading toward my hotel when I saw the lights of police cars ahead. I recognized the area, and my stomach sank. They were outside the Baptist courthouse. Somebody must have burned that down too.

Yet as I got closer, I saw the roof and white walls were intact.

Maybe it was vandalism? I slowed and saw a woman crouched on the sidewalk, sobbing. Some officers stood in a group, and a few other men were grouped under a tree in front of the building. Then I saw it, the reason they had gathered.

It took a moment for my brain to process...a deer? A calf? No, it was the miniature pony, strung upside down from the tree with its stomach cut open. Its guts spilled from the gaping hole like some kind of gruesome gray tangle of snakes as its stiff body spun slightly in the gentle breeze. I was close enough to see flies buzzing in and out of the stomach cavity and entrails. The lawn below was soaked brownish-red with blood, and the rest of its organs sat in an untidy pile on top.

"Holy shit," I said to myself in the car. I'd seen enough crime scene photos to not feel an ounce of nausea. I was tempted to stop and investigate myself, but I knew my breath and hair were not presentable. I sped back to the hotel to get myself in order and return as soon as possible.

I TOOK two mugs of shit coffee from the hotel lobby to my room and downed them while getting ready. In record time, I became a lawyer again–not the philandering drunk waking up in another man's bed that I'd been a mere hour ago.

At least the excitement of a disemboweled miniature pony distracted me from thinking about Josh and Matthew. I thought Matthew was in Egypt now. I'd have to check his message from two days ago. I felt a pang of guilt, but high-level jobs in the government always take a toll on personal relationships. At least that's what the wives of men in his circle tell me.

Excuses aside, the more important thing was that someone continued to fuck with my case.

I hopped in the car and arrived back at the Baptist courthouse. There was a bigger crowd gathered around now, to see the pathetic pony guts spewed onto the under-watered lawn. This was prime entertainment for the town.

Of course, Mr. Lyons was skulking on the edge of the crowd. I hadn't seen him since he called me a racial epithet, but it was inevitable. I was riding on the high of unprocessed alcohol and caffeine, and I felt invincible.

I parked my car and quietly walked up next to Mr. Lyons. He didn't notice me until I said, "Let me guess, the ghost of General Stovall killed that pony?"

He turned to look at me. "Oh, Miss Julie. I didn't see you; you're like a ninja."

"That's a different kind of Asian," I clarified for him.

"Well, I'm sorry, but in all honesty, I couldn't tell a lot of you apart," said Mr. Lyons, with a little laugh. "I think the ghost did indeed do this. Yesterday, that poor animal caused quite an embarrassment to the memory of the General, and I'm afraid he's had his revenge again."

"So, General Stovall tied the pony to the tree and spilled its guts because his feelings were hurt? I don't know, Mr. Lyons; the ghost of General Stovall sounds a little sensitive."

"Miss Julie, General Stovall was the greatest man this town has ever known. Soon you'll understand why respect should be given to him."

"I'm sorry, but I'm still having a hard time believing a ghost is responsible for all of this. If you guys are going to stage a cover-up, don't you think you should try a more convincing story?"

Mr. Lyons turned away. Staring at the pony, he said, "Miss Julie, it's my responsibility to help you see the truth. I can only tell you what I know, and I know the ghost of General Stovall is coming back for his revenge."

Well, he certainly wasn't budging from his narrative. I

walked to the front of the group and ducked under the tape. One of the police officers stopped me and told me to go back. I went back to the spectator side of the tape. It wasn't like the movies; I couldn't stroll up and make demands. I flagged the same officer and asked him, "Excuse me, has the building been vandalized in any way?"

The officer looked back at it. "Not that I've seen, everything seems to be okay here. It was still locked this morning when we came."

"Do you know when it will reopen?"

"No idea, ma'am." He turned and walked away.

I watched the officers put an aluminum ladder against the tree. Two held the base while one climbed up with a knife. He cut through the rope until it broke. The branch swayed up as the pony fell, almost knocking the officer on the ground.

The crowd gasped as the pony collapsed on the earth below. Flies erupted and swarmed above it, disturbed from their feeding. One man in the group slowly clapped.

I decided to head back to my hotel. The hangover was catching up with me, and after the pony fell, the theatricality of it all ended. I needed a nap first before I could begin to understand what happened.

HOURS LATER, I awoke. I downed some coconut water in my fridge and looked at my phone. I turned away when I saw a few messages from Josh.

I took a breath and glanced again. "Hey" read the first one. The next read, "You forgot your wallet at my place."

Shit. I wrote, "I'll come by later."

I collapsed back onto my bed. I wasn't ready to see Josh, and tried to figure out how long I could survive without my wallet.

He could bring it to work tomorrow, but it was one of my essential possessions. I could just go and pick it up. It was inevitable I'd have to face him, and maybe the sooner the better, considering he might have expected me to be there when he woke up.

I slept a little more, woke, showered, and decided to head to Josh's. I went by the front desk and saw Keli.

She saw me and said, "My good friend, what's up?"

"I'm so hungover. I went to Josh's last night."

She looked excited. "And...?"

I grimaced. "We made out, and I forgot my wallet there."

"So y'all didn't fuck?" she asked.

I quickly said, "No, I'm pretty sure we didn't. My clothes were all on. I think we just dry humped."

She nodded slowly. "Oh, that's some cute high school shit. I'm proud of you."

"Thanks?" I said suspiciously. "I'm going to grab my wallet, but I'll catch you later."

Keli said goodbye while I headed to my car. She was right, this was like high school shit, but it was not the high school experience I knew. I knew calculus and SAT prep, not going to parties and making out with boys after drinking cheap beer.

Yet the guilt of cheating was something I hadn't begun to negotiate yet. This wasn't just "high school shit"; I was an adult and in a serious relationship. I was ignoring the better judgement of my fully developed brain. I had no excuse other than I was more attracted to chaos than I ever knew. Maybe I would repress these feelings, but for now, I was actually having fun. I felt so free, driving down this rural road in my shitty Corolla, to the house of a boy that I may or may not like. That part made me feel the fleeting excitement of youth, when everything felt bizarrely fresh and important. I didn't have to get my wallet today, but something was pulling me there. There was an excuse in my head that I needed it, and perhaps in the process, I'd figure out how I felt about Josh after last night.

I pulled in and parked next to Josh's truck. I took a deep breath and headed to the front door. The door was ajar, with the screen door closed. I peered in, trying to see Josh. I saw movement from the bedroom, and then a shirtless Josh walked toward me, wearing jeans like the ones he dry-humped me in last night. I wouldn't be surprised if they were the same pair.

"Come in," he said in a friendly tone.

I tentatively opened the door and entered. He looked at me and grinned a little, understanding the awkwardness of the situation.

He said, "Hold on, I'll grab a shirt."

"It's fine, I'm only getting my wallet." I saw it on the counter. I knew I'd have to resist my urge to count my cash later; I should trust Josh. "So," I said, "Last night was a little weird. I didn't mean for that to happen, and I hope we can still be friends."

He nodded. "It's totally cool with me, you don't have to worry about it. We were drunk, and it happens."

Not to me, I thought to myself. "Yeah, it's fine. Thanks for my wallet, and I guess I'll see you around?"

I started to back out when Josh said, "Julie, wait."

I looked at him, and he pulled a $1 bill from his waistband. "You forgot this."

He held it out to me, and that same damn tingle erupted all over my body.

Before my brain had a chance to kick in with better judgement, my body had already grabbed Josh. He was on top of me again, on the same couch, and I struggled to unbutton my shirt while his hands were busy pulling off my pants. Once they came off, he started kissing all over my thighs before looking up at me and smiling.

He started kissing up closer to my vagina, which made my

eyes widen. No man had ever gone down on me before; I'd always felt embarrassed and insecure about what he might discover face to face with my pussy. It was technically no man's land because I would never know it as well as the person who tries to go down on me. Thoughts were racing through my head, *how do I smell? How do I taste? What do I look like?* With determination, I could potentially answer these questions for myself, but I wasn't prepared for this to happen. As he moved closer to the hem of my underwear I said, "Kiss me," while I pulled his head up and kissed him for what felt like the first time.

Now that I was sober, I was able to notice the details. For instance, I'd never been with a man who had his generically hot body. It was firmer than I thought, and for a moment, I almost missed the softness of Matthew. Then Josh picked me up and carried me to the bedroom, and I didn't think about Matthew anymore.

He lay me down on the bed, but I pushed him over to get on top.

"Do you have a condom?" I asked.

"Yeah." He reached over and procured from an all too convenient position next to his bed. I helped pull off his pants while he expertly slid the condom on.

I put him inside me and began to run my hands all over his chest, arms, and abs.

"You're so sexy," Josh said to me.

I didn't say anything except moan as we both disappeared into each other's bodies.

We hit a rhythm, but more importantly, his hand traced from my chest, down my stomach, to my clitoris. He lightly put pressure to it, with just enough presence to create a delightful jolt of friction. I gasped, then smiled.

He paused and asked, "Are you okay?"

Through heavy breaths, I answered, "Yes, why?"

"You just started giggling."

I paused and thought about how I should answer. I wanted to tell him I was giggling because my boyfriend had done the simple expedition of finding my clitoris, except for the one time I guided his hand there as if I were a school for the blind and trying to teach him braille. He soon forgot his first lesson. However, I still wasn't ready to bring up Matthew to Josh. I said, "No, it's just, sometimes I think sex is funny."

Josh nodded. "Yeah, I guess it's funny too."

To change the mood, I leaned down to kiss him. He tasted slightly minty, which meant he must have brushed his teeth before I came. He was either calculating or it was a coincidence. Beneath the mint I could taste him, though. The slightest hint of tea, but also pleasant nothingness. I tried not to mind it, but as I traced my tongue across Josh's, I found myself realizing I didn't have to quietly suffer through discomfort. In fact, Josh felt oddly comfortable until he began to rub my clitoris a little too intensely.

I grabbed onto his hand and held it instead. He intuitively asked, "Okay?"

I said, "Yes, it's just you rubbed me too hard. I like it very, very gentle."

He apologized, saying, "I'm sorry, I do want to know."

"Okay, flip me open and get on top." We rolled over and I found myself looking up at him, leaning up to lick a drop of sweat that lay on his collarbone like a pendant.

I said, "I think I tasted last night's beer in your sweat."

"No way. I worked out and went for a run this morning, I'm sure I sweat it all out."

I felt his biceps and reached around to feel his back. "Where do you work out?"

"I have a small gym set up in the shed out back, though sometimes I go to Ri'Chard's gym and we work out together."

The thought of them both working out together made me strangely horny, though I'd never been turned on by the thought of two men working out. "Maybe next time I can come to the gym with you guys."

Josh smiled. "But then I'll have a boner while working out."

"For which one of us?" I cheekily asked.

"I think you know which one." He leaned down to kiss me again, and our bodies melted together. There I was, underneath him, but I also felt like I was on top of him. It was strange feeling so sexually connected that we became a singular being; my pleasure was his pleasure and vice versa. My body vibrated with something beyond simple lust: connection. Like opposing magnets, the power of it terrified me and made me want to push away, but his lips on mine flipped the magnets and we snapped back together, where only a force greater than us could pull us apart.

"I'm close," he panted into my mouth.

"Me too," I moaned.

The pace quickened, urgent with release. I felt heat, like sun pouring over my naked body, then a cool wave rocked me, its power pulling me deeper into Josh, who shivered in his own ecstasy.

We lay in each other's arms, exhausted. I felt accomplished; it had been a long time since I'd had an orgasm without my vibrator. Josh lovingly rubbed his hands along my body, intertwining his fingers in mine. He held me close, which didn't give me a lot of space to process my guilt in the aftermath of our tryst. *Maybe I should tell him I have a boyfriend,* I wondered, *but he doesn't care. All he wants is sex.* I figured I'd just figure out how to process my feelings toward Matthew another time, probably when I was back to my real life in D.C., which was feeling more and more constricted than my life here.

I looked at Josh and felt his breath on my chest. He looked

cute, but not enough for me to stay in this moment. I had to leave, so I shifted my body a bit and he got the idea, moving off of me. I sat up and said, "Hey, I had a lot of fun. We probably shouldn't do this again, though, since I'm supposed to be here working, and I'm borrowing your car. Things could get complicated."

"Yeah, I get it," he said. He pushed himself up to a sitting position. "By the way, your car part will be here tomorrow."

"Oh, awesome. I'm pretty used to the Corolla now. It's like my undercover car."

"You can keep it for as long as you need," he offered.

I stood and gathered my clothes, finding mine entangled with Josh's jeans and underwear. I looked back at him, still sitting on the bed.

I dressed. "Let's get dinner soon, okay?" I told him. Instead of saying "goodbye," I strangely said, "Ciao."

I grabbed my wallet on the way out and paused to look at the dollar bill still on the floor, leaving it there as I stepped into the dusk.

Walking into the hotel lobby, I hoped that I didn't run into Keli, since I was sure I looked disheveled. I walked in and felt a wash of relief when I didn't see her at the desk, but that only lasted a second. As I turned my head, Keli walked toward me from the breakfast area. She gave me a quick once-over before saying, "Oh my god, you guys fucked this time."

"What? No." I lied, totally thrown off balance.

She leaned closer, talk-whispering. "Girl, I see the fuck still on you, and it looks good on you too."

I said nothing, feeling my cheeks flush red with embarrassment.

She said, "Yeah, turns out sex can change someone. You

should have seen the confidence you strutted into this hotel with."

I pursed my lips and broke my confession. "I don't know. I don't feel different, but it was dumb. I shouldn't have sex with Josh, it just complicates my work here...and my life." I shook my head in disappointment with my lack of discipline.

She asked, "How? He doesn't have anything to do with your case, right?"

"No, but it was unprofessional."

She raised an eyebrow. "None of your bosses are here, though, so chill. Just have some fun. I know Josh will supply plenty of it."

I was impressed by her callousness toward sex. My head spinning with the *what-ifs* was interrupted by Keli saying, "Hey, tomorrow is my day off and I'm performing stand-up at a club a few towns away."

She handed me a flyer for Amateur Hour at a club called Bubba's. "Oh, I didn't know you did this. I'd love to come support you."

"Yeah, it has been a dream of mine for a long time to make it as a stand-up. But you gotta start somewhere, and that's Bubba's." She smiled, and with a wink added, "You can bring a date."

I suddenly thought of Ri'Chard, then felt a pang of guilt. That would be cruel to Josh, but it would be so much more relaxing to be with the platonic friendship of Ri'Chard after what happened today. I'd ask them both, or go alone.

"Okay, I need to go shower and get some work done; however, I'm going to come to your show tomorrow."

Keli said, "When it's that good, I like to leave the fuck still on me."

I asked, "Should I do that? Won't I get a UTI?"

"Just drink a lot of water and you'll be all right."

I walked to my room wondering if I should shower or not. In the hallway I decided I should. It would be weird not to.

Yet, when I was back in my room, I didn't feel like showering. I changed into casual clothes and decided I liked the feeling of Josh still on my body, so I'd just have to wait until the morning to wash off a memory I wasn't ready to let go of.

6

The town was still abuzz with the mystery slaying of the miniature pony. The Baptist courthouse was set to reopen today, with an unlucky police officer stationed outside it in case someone else returned to decorate the trees with dead farm animals.

I texted Matthew about the pony, and he responded with, "So weird!" I asked him how his trip was going, and he just replied, "Busy!"

I sighed. I texted Josh about going to Keli's show tonight, and he said, "Sure." I messaged him that I'd also ask Ri'Chard, and Josh replied, "Cool." Ri'Chard messaged, "Not sure if I can make it. I'll let you know later." Finally, a real communicator.

I decided to get breakfast at the diner. It would be the epicenter of all unhinged theories about the pony murder, and I'd happily eavesdrop on the discussions.

The diner was packed this morning. There were a few seats left at the counter, but I still didn't trust having my back turned to these people. I found a booth toward the back and settled in. Luckily, Mr. Lyons didn't see me, as he was focused on a discussion with some other men.

I decided to place my order at the counter, so I could get closer to their booth. I'd just torture the waitress with my yuppie food questions while I tried to gain some information.

I walked up to the counter and asked, "Excuse me, what are your milk options?"

She looked at me, dumbfounded, and said, "Uh, cow?" She had an attitude, but I could work with it.

I asked her to check if the cherry danish had dairy in it and after she'd rolled her eyes and disappeared into the kitchen, I stood at the counter and listened.

I overheard, "...You know, it could've been some immigrants. They might have wanted to eat that poor pony."

"Or some thug doing a gang initiation," another man chimed in.

I heard the familiar drawl of Mr. Lyons. "Gentleman, I don't think it's either of those cases, plausible as they may be. I truly believe the ghost of General Stovall is enraged and disgraced by what's happening in this town."

"What could a ghost be mad about to cause this ruckus?" asked a gentleman I hadn't seen before.

Mr. Lyons dropped his voice. "The Blacks are trying to take over, and the General doesn't like it."

Ah, he was still peddling his racist ghost theories. The waitress returned and said, "So he doesn't know, but like, if you're gonna die if it has milk in it, then maybe don't eat it?"

I thanked her and ordered an omelet with no milk. She poured me a cup of weak black coffee and I turned to walk back to my table. Mr. Lyons must have noticed me, because he said, "Miss Julie, I'm surprised you're here this morning."

"Mr. Lyons, it's my right to enjoy the finest cuisine this town has to offer."

He smirked. "I just thought you would have gone back to

where you came from, unless you have more of a stomach for blood than I thought."

I laughed. "Oh, the pony? I'm not as fragile as you think."

"Well, I'm happy to hear it, because I'm afraid there might be more to come."

He looked at me blandly, and I narrowed my eyes. I'd extract myself before this got even weirder. "I'm leaving, Mr. Lyons." I walked toward my booth and settled in, keeping my eyes on the back of his balding head.

I watched the townsfolk in their diner routine, people getting up from booths, then stopping at others on the way to share a few anecdotes about their lives. It was seemingly quaint if one didn't know what lay beneath the intentions of these people. I nibbled on my somewhat edible omelet and thought of Ms. Honeypaw. Perhaps my wanting to speak with her again was self-punishment for the aftermath of my tryst with Josh; however, part of me wondered if she had an interpretation of what happened to the pony.

Before I could question my intentions further, I left cash on the booth table and found myself in front of the stoop of Ms. Honeypaw's aged house. I exhaled a deep sigh and tried to remember the date of my last tetanus shot before I took a brave step up onto the aged porch. I stared at the same door I was in front of just a few days prior, wishing I were ignorant about who was inside.

I knocked and listened for the same graceless gait. I knocked again and heard no response. I waited a few uncomfortable minutes and decided she must not be home. I slowly descended to the sidewalk and stared across at the ashes of the courthouse. It seemed that everyone had forgotten the devastation of the fire as their attention turned to the sacrificial pony. I hoped I could turn the same blind eye to my indiscretions, but that hopeful thought was interrupted by a familiar hostile shout, "Are you stalking me?"

I looked back at the porch, expecting to see Ms. Honeypaw leaning out her front door, but it was still closed.

The voice continued to taunt me. "Now I got you confused, looking embarrassed in front of my house."

I looked way up and squinted through the sunlight to see Ms. Honeypaw leaning out the window of the turret. She had a sleep mask pushed up to her forehead.

"Are you still sleeping?" I asked. "It's almost 10 a.m."

"Why do you care about my sleep schedule?" she demanded.

I considered the question. "So if you're sleeping in, that means you're up late, and if your bedroom is in the turret, then you have a direct line of sight to the courthouse."

"Stop being a logical bitch. I told you, I didn't see shit."

"Maybe because you were the one who set the fire?" I said, deliberately provoking her.

"Now why the fuck would I do that?"

I raised my arms and exclaimed, "I don't know, I'm just trying to solve this case."

She shouted, "Now, you must have paid for that Prada bag from sucking dick because you sure are a dumb bitch for a lawyer. Have you heard of 'motive'? Do you not watch crime shows? I'm just a woman minding her business, so why would I burn down a whole goddamn courthouse?"

"Maybe to get rid of all the lawsuits for all the money you owe?"

She screamed down at me, "Hold on, stay right there until I put on some shoes so I can come outside and beat your ass."

I decided to face fear with confidence, like punching a shark in the face when attacked. I waited with my arms crossed until Ms. Honeypaw came to the front door, shouting, "You don't seem like a bitch that's ever been in a fight, so I'll go easy on you."

I said, "You're not wrong, but I'm not here to fight. I'm here for your expertise. I need to communicate with the dead."

She studied me. "You're weird. You come and interrupt my morning, harassing me for information, accusing me of crimes I didn't commit, and now you're begging me to help you with my abilities."

I scoffed. "Our interaction was hardly that traumatic."

She ignored me. "And now you want to stand here and tell me how I should feel. You're a fucked-up bitch. I don't want to see you in front of my Victorian mansion again."

I grimaced and rolled my eyes. "Victorian mansion? More like *shitorian*."

Ms. Honeypaw looked at me, stunned. I was also stunned, as my internal dialogue accidentally externalized itself. I quickly estimated in my head how long it would take to run to the next block if she produced a gun.

To my surprise, her chest started to shake a little. I thought she might be in the early stages of an asthma attack, or perhaps a fatal heart attack, but instead, a deep laugh came from her chest. Her bosom heaved as she hollered, making my lips curl into a cautious smile.

She said, "I thought geisha bitches like you were supposed to be all quiet. You certainly have a mouth on you."

I decided to not take offense and to treat it as a temporary truce. Ms. Honeypaw set her hands on her broad hips. "Now, Miss Prada, do you really want to talk with the dead?"

I nodded, and Ms. Honeypaw raised her eyebrows. She said, "Well, we can't do this shit outside. We need to go to my temple."

I found myself following her to the room she took me into the last time. I wondered if Keli was lying about Ms. Honeypaw's sexuality because she clearly lacked any gay genes when it came to decorating. I brushed the seat before I sat down, anchoring myself against the shitstorm I was about to start.

She grabbed a silk robe from behind a door, putting it on before she made her way lighting candles throughout the room. "Is this your first time talking with the dead?"

I thought about it. "Does a Ouija board in high school count?"

"Don't fuck with that shit. No wonder you're weird; you probably caught a demon from that." She settled into her chair in front of me and said, "Today I'll give you a special: only $65 for thirty minutes."

I decided to needle her. "Sure, do you take credit cards?"

Her eyes narrowed. "Just remember that I haven't forgotten my inclination to beat your ass."

I acquiesced. "Fine, I'll pay cash. Actually, I'll pay you $100 because this is important."

Ms. Honeypaw perked up, giving me a slight smile. "And who would you like to communicate with today?"

"I want to talk with the ghost of General Stovall."

Her smile quickly faded. She leaned back and crossed her arms, suddenly becoming hostile in tone. She slowly asked, "And why the fuck do you want to talk with him?"

Choosing my words carefully, I said, "Well, I have questions. I want to know if he is, in fact, haunting this town as people here are saying."

She looked visibly angry. "I can tell you for a fact that motherfucker is very, very dead. He's not coming back."

I decided to play my last good cards, gambling it all. I took a breath and said, "I know you're related to him. Is that why you're afraid to talk to me? Does it have something to do with the stigma of being his descendant?"

I saw her grinding her teeth through closed lips. I wondered if, indeed, I was about to experience my first ass beating. I just hoped that there would be no dental damage. Ms. Honeypaw's nostrils flared as she continued to stare at me.

Finally, she said, "What did they say about me?"

"Nothing bad," I told her. "But they said you may be a descendant of General Stovall. I just found that surprising, given he was a racist asshole."

"He was more than a 'racist asshole.' He was an evil, evil man."

"Can you tell me more?"

Her nostrils flared again. I realized I was playing with fire, but my determination kept me focused.

Ms. Honeypaw raised an eyebrow. "Why the fuck do you want to know this?"

"To be honest, I don't know. I'm trying to figure this all out, why this is happening in this town. Why the courthouse, the pony... Is this part of a cover-up or all random? I guess I'm just trying to understand Pothos." She didn't say anything, so I continued, "Listen, I'm sorry. That was inappropriate of me to say. I'll leave now."

I turned to grab my purse from the floor when Ms. Honeypaw spoke, "GeishaBitch, wait." She took a deep breath and looked at me with a softened, vulnerable look. "You really want to know? You want to actually know about me?"

"Of course. I'm genuinely intrigued by you." I offered her a small smile.

She returned a weak smile and shook her head. I saw her quickly wipe a tear from her eye. She said, "You know, I've lived in this town for most of my life, and every person had their mind made up about me before I even had the chance to change it. The White kids hated me for being Black, and the Black kids hated me for being White. They used to call me a 'cracker' and a 'White woman'. Do you know how confusing that was?"

I wanted to tell her it was like being called a "geisha", but I held my tongue. This was her moment.

She continued, "I mean, I'm Black, and the White people definitely treated me as such."

I asked, "Do you know how you are related to the General?"

She said, "My great-great-grandfather was his son. His momma was a slave on his plantation, Betsey. The General had a thing for Betsey. He forced himself on her. The General's wife was a Confederate cunt. Betsey was worried she might do something to the baby, so one night, during a big party at the plantation, she just walked out during dinner service. She fled to the house of Dr. Samson. I guess she seemed pathetic enough that he hid her until the baby was born. He was one of those acceptable White men that they make movies about. I don't know why, but he helped her scared Black ass. She had her baby, then one night, she left without a trace. She abandoned her son, my great-great-grandaddy, with the doctor." I saw tears well up in Ms. Honeypaw's eyes. "I heard she went up North, but they never found out about her. She didn't want to be found. She made her choice to leave her family, and we're still fucking here." She used both her hands to roughly wipe tears from her eyes. "So is that what you wanted to know? How we were born to be hated by everyone. I'm sure Betsey couldn't stand to see the face of that White man in her son, and I know the General made sure my great-great-granddaddy was hated too.

"The doctor was alright though. We folded into his family, and that's how I ended up with this house. It used to be his, the home where Betsey abandoned her son."

I stared at Ms. Honeypaw. I'd been so quick to judge her, like everyone in this town. Her unpleasantness was just defensiveness, as she obviously always had to protect herself. "I'm grateful you shared that with me. It actually helps me see things more clearly."

"I'm sure a lot of people have been running their mouths about me, but they don't understand anything about my life."

"Why are you still in this town? Why don't you leave it?"

"I came back to take care of my momma when she was dying. She left me this house, and it's all I have. I don't have any money, and they're getting ready to take this house from me. When I go, I'm starting over from nothing, and that scares me."

"You come from strong people. If Betsey could do it, so can you," I told her.

Ms. Honeypaw, with red eyes, smiled wryly. "That's true, though if I see that bitch in the afterlife, I don't know how I'll react. How could she leave her son?"

"It was just a different time and complex circumstances these women were forced to exist in. Maybe she thought it would be safer for her son to leave him in the care of a doctor. I'm sure she went on a treacherous journey to leave the South. My family went through similar things when fleeing to Taiwan."

Ms. Honeypaw tilted her head. "What's Taiwan?"

I said, "It's a small island nation off the coast of China. After the Chinese Civil War...you know what? It doesn't matter. It's just a country in Asia."

"I thought you were Japanese?"

"No, I'm Taiwanese."

"Oh, is that where Thai food comes from?"

"No, that's Thailand."

Ms. Honeypaw asked, "So what's the difference between The Wan and The Land?"

I tried to break it down in a way an American might understand. I said, "The Land has ladyboys, and The Wan has really good dumplings."

"Ooh, got it." She smiled at me and said, "I got a bitch from The Wan. Well, Miss Prada, welcome to Pothos. What do you want to know?"

Finally, my invitation, but I'd need to give her a little foreplay before I could ask what I really wanted to know. I said, "Let me start with Mr. Lyons. What do you know about him?"

"Oh, he's weird, and not in a *you* kind of weird. He used to be a history teacher at the high school. Now, I'm not a scholar by any means, but I'm going to venture that his story of history wasn't always right. He tried to teach us that slavery was actually the first public education system. I honestly stopped going to class after that." She shook her head. "He's racist as hell, but like a sneaky racist. He might be all polite in your face, but he's definitely weird when he's home, if you know what I mean."

"What do you mean?" I asked.

"I mean, he sits at home every night and jerks off to porn. *That* kind of weird."

I grimaced. "Ew, gross. I don't even want to think about him masturbating. How do you know this?"

She said, "His cleaning lady comes for readings. She has to spend half an hour picking up tissues next to his recliner."

"Ugh. So nasty. What a pervert."

"Miss Prada, all men are perverts. Don't you know this? All. Men. Are. Perverts. Some women are freaks, not all, but a good number are. But there's a difference between a 'freak' and a 'pervert'."

I wasn't convinced. The flaw in her thesis was Matthew; I had a lot of empirical evidence that he was no pervert. The shower foreplay he often proposed felt more like a supervision while I cleaned myself, with him inspecting my soap-to-skin coverage. I asked, "What about Josh? The mechanic. You know about him?"

Ms. Honeypaw smiled a little. "Damn, Miss Prada, I knew you had some freak in you."

I tried not to flush and acted surprised. "What, what do you mean?"

"Many a girl has sat in that seat asking about Josh." She started to mimic, "*Does he love me? Is he the one? Why did he break my heart?* That man is a magnet for dumb bitches, and it looks like you got stuck."

I was insulted. "Uh, no. I'm not one of his 'dumb bitch magnets'. I do not get my heart broken, much less by a guy like Josh. He's just been nice to me, and I want to know what his motives are."

"Your pussy," Ms. Honeypaw said, matter-of-factly. "His motive is your pussy, and I feel like you have that nice, rich-bitch pussy. You must get it waxed, and have silk underwear for it."

I suddenly realized Ms. Honeypaw had given some thought to my pussy. I guess Keli was right about Ms. Honeypaw's sexuality, whether she accepted it or not. To be honest, I was a bit embarrassed because I often neglected my pussy. I occasionally trimmed the pubic hair, but otherwise I felt a little disconnected from it. It wasn't until sex with Josh that I felt connected to my decidedly middle-class pussy again.

I said, trying to defend myself, "Josh seems different. Not like all the other guys in this town."

She said, "Well, we're actually kinda-cousins. He was related to the doctor that owned this house, but all the brains got bred out by the time Josh came."

I gasped. "You guys are cousins? He didn't say anything."

"We're not close anymore, or actually related, but I've known him his whole life." She pursed her lips together, then said, "He's just mad because I owe him a lot of money. He's one of the few good ones, though, not absorbed in White supremacy like these other motherfuckers."

"Like Jim Smoke?" I asked.

"Like him. He certainly qualifies as a racist piece of shit," she said, nodding her head.

"What about Judge Bishop?"

"He's funny. We don't see him around much on account of his lack of toes, but he's part of *that* gang."

"What gang?" I asked.

"Weird old White men doing *funny shit*."

I cocked my head. "Like burning down a courthouse kind of 'funny shit'?"

Ms. Honeypaw looked around, and shifted in her seat. "Listen, I'm only telling you this because I'm temporarily fond of your ass, but on the night of the courthouse burning..." She took a deep breath, "I saw some *funny shit*, like these men dressed in robes and going into the courthouse. There was a whole group of them. The lights cut out, and after a while, they all ran out. Then a few minutes later, the whole thing was on fire."

"You saw Jim Smoke?" I asked.

Ms. Honeypaw nodded.

"Mr. Lyons?"

She nodded again.

"Judge Bishop?"

She shrugged with uncertainty, but it was enough.

"Holy shit. This could change everything. This could flip the entire case. This is amazing!"

Ms. Honeypaw shook her head. "No, no, no. If you for one second think I'm testifying, then you are wrong. My ass is staying out of this."

"Ms. Honeypaw, please. Don't you want to take down these evil men?" I pleaded.

"No, that's your agenda. My agenda is to sit here and count my money, so pay up GeishaBitch, put on your kimono, and get the fuck out of my house."

She looked at me with her arms crossed. She was closed off again, back to her usual obstinate self.

I sighed and picked up my purse from the ground. I put it in my lap, admiring the supple leather and nickel hardware. I bought it after winning my first big case, as an embodiment of success. I saw a bit of my reflection in the buckle; a glimpse of the woman I trained myself to believe I was. A smart lawyer, devoted partner, and happy with the narrow and safe path I lived.

I hated it. I hated everything this bag represented. I took a deep breath and said to Ms. Honeypaw, "I can't pay you. But if you testify, I could accidentally leave my Prada bag for you to find."

Ms. Honeypaw raised her eyebrows. "The Prada? The authentic Prada?"

I nodded. "Yep. What you do with it is your business, but it's definitely worth more than you are asking. However, you only get it on the condition you testify."

I heard her mumbling some choice curse words before letting out a hearty sigh. "Fine, fine. I'll do it, but this better work. You're fucking with a lot of the wrong people in this town."

"You will? You'll testify!" I almost started to cry. "Don't worry, I'll make it work. This is all going to work, and it's because of you. You are going to save this town, Ms. Honeypaw."

"Shut up. I'm tired of you already." She turned away in disgust.

"I'm going to schedule a witness prep session soon. I'll give you the bag *after* you testify," I said, grinning.

We both stood and walked toward the door.

"You don't trust me?" she asked, accusingly.

"No, but I need the chance to buy another bag."

"Well, I look forward to seeing what you get." She stopped at the door while I faced her from the porch. Her eyes narrowed as she said, “Miss Michael Kors doesn’t have the same ring to it.”

I gasped. “Damn, that stung.”

“Now get your bougie pussy off my porch.” She slammed the door in my face, and I smiled. I turned to seize the day, hopeful that justice was on the horizon.

7

I told Josh I'd drive tonight, since I didn't want him to feel like it was a date. He parked his truck next to my Corolla in the hotel parking lot and hopped out. He had on a decent enough button-down shirt and his best dress jeans.

Smiling when he saw me, he said, "Hey. Your car is almost fixed. I'll finish it tomorrow, if you want to pick it up."

"So this is my last night with the Corolla?" I asked him.

"As I said, you can use it for as long as you want."

"I mean, I paid a lot for that Volvo, so I guess I should use it," I said, rationalizing. However, the utility of the Corolla very much appealed to me—especially the fact that it was not a reminder of my past life in D.C., like the Volvo.

"You look cute," said Josh.

I was wearing a silk-ish polka-dot blouse and jeans. I thought I looked pretty orthodox. "Too cute to be annoying?" He groaned as we got into the car.

"Ri'Chard texted," I said. "Something came up with his family, so it's just us." I was already feeling the awkwardness of the situation as I plugged the location into my phone.

"Nice. I'm happy to spend a little more alone time with you."

Josh leaned forward and kissed me. I was a little surprised and slightly warm.

"Was it okay for me to kiss you?" he asked.

I stuttered, "Uh, I think so? I just wasn't expecting that right now."

He shrugged. "It's alright, just let me know when you're ready."

"And do I have to be ready? What if I don't get there?"

He looked over at me. "That's fine. I'd hate for you to feel pressured by me in any way."

Good. I just didn't want to feel like he was expecting sex, because I was still conflicted as to whether it should happen again. But as the drive went on, I eased into his presence. "I went to talk to Ms. Honeypaw," I offered.

"Why?" Josh asked, shooting me a quick glance. "What do you want from her?"

"I just had a feeling it was the moment to make progress with her. I learned a lot about her, her history, and that you guys are cousins."

Josh sighed lightly. "Oh, I guess you could say that. She was around more when I was growing up, but we're not really speaking because she owes me so much money."

"I think you shouldn't let money get between your relationship," I told him.

"Hard not to when she's obsessed with it. Also, it's better for me not to talk to her. She's just someone who causes trouble when you let her into your life."

I suddenly felt that Ms. Honeypaw and I might have that in common.

He continued, "Besides, it's just embarrassing to watch her fuck up. I don't know how to say it, but I guess my heart would hurt too much if I let her stay in it."

I nodded. "That's hard, but I understand what you're saying.

What does your family think of her?"

"There aren't many left anymore. My mom moved to Florida with her boyfriend. My dad died a while back, and my sister passed away too." I heard Josh's voice crack, which he tried to conceal with a cough.

"I'm really sorry." I tried my best to provide comfort, but these situations were never my forte, hence why I chose being a lawyer over anything that required displays of emotion.

I saw Josh looking out the passenger window, quickly wiping his eyes with one thumb. His voice sounded a little unsteady as he said, "She was a pain in the ass, but also beautiful. She loved to fight, and loved you with all her heart. But it was the painkillers that really changed her. After that, it was only a few years before she overdosed, and the paramedics were too late to help."

I sighed. "I truly hope those doctors and pharmaceutical companies are held accountable. That's why I went into law, with the hope it could do good."

Josh looked over at me. "Is it doing good?"

"I don't know," I said, quietly wondering the same thing to myself.

We remained in silence for a bit. Josh broke it by saying, "I got a tattoo dedicated to her on my ribcage. They're Jewel lyrics since she was such a big fan."

I could see Josh's eyes watering. I decided to reach out and hold his hand, which was an instinct I didn't know I had. We held hands for a bit until Josh interrupted the silence. "Let's talk about something else."

He asked me if I had siblings. "Yes, an older brother. The favorite, of course."

"What makes him the favorite?" Josh asked.

I turned to him. "Being the firstborn son. That's it. He sucks otherwise. His wife is nice. My family isn't interesting, though. Let's talk about something different."

"Okay..." Josh considered for a moment, then asked, "Who was your first crush?"

I let out a small laugh and said, "Oh, his name was Nathan. He was a few grades ahead, but I loved him through high school, and college, to be honest. He was really good at soccer, but he also played guitar and had a sensitive side."

"Did you ever tell him?" Josh asked.

"Absolutely not. Well, one time in middle school, I left an anonymous Valentine. But I wasn't built for him; he was for the hot blonde girls."

"You don't think you're hot?" Josh asked me.

I considered and said, "I think I'm attractive enough, but at that time, I was definitely not hot."

Josh squeezed my hand. "I don't know, I think I would've tried to get with you back then."

I groaned and took my hand away. "Here we go again..."

"What?" he asked, defensively.

"It's those lines. They're so tired."

"Julie, I'm being honest when I say I find you attractive," he said, defensively.

"And I'm being honest when I say that you don't have to do this shit with me. Don't treat me like one of your *girls.*"

"What girls?" he asked.

I gave him a little side-eye. "Your cousin, Ms. Honeypaw, mentioned she's had many women seek guidance from the after-life because you broke their hearts."

Josh groaned. "Oh, come on, you're going to believe *her?*"

"What's not to believe? I don't mind that you're a player, but just don't try to play *me.*"

Josh shook his head. "This isn't the night I had in mind."

I turned to him and smiled. "Well, I'm having fun."

"What's fun about this?"

"Without your cheesy lines, you have no powers," I said, my smile widening. "It's like figuring out how to defeat the monster at the end of the movie."

"Are you calling me a monster?" Josh asked.

I said, "No. You're cute, but your flirting is terrifying."

Josh grinned. "So you don't like it when men try to flirt with you? How do they ask you out?"

I thought of Matthew. We bonded over political dialogue, or his dialogues that I bear witness to. With him, I was more comfortable listening and occasionally adding a witty jab at the opposing political party, but there wasn't much flirting.

I said to Josh, "You're right, maybe I'm broken. I don't like when men flirt with me. It feels...suspicious."

"Maybe just the wrong men have been flirting with you?" Josh put his hand back on mine. "And don't you dare tell me that's one of my lines."

I smiled wryly. "I guess I'm just a suspicious lawyer."

He smiled back. "I like that about you. I like the way you ask a lot of questions."

Before I could respond, the GPS announced our arrival at Bubba's, located in a strip mall of brick and aged brown roofing.

"Quaint," I said, pulling into a parking space.

As soon as I walked in, I realized I should have brought bleach wipes with me to wipe down seats. I hoped I wouldn't get Legionnaire's disease from the cracked vinyl chairs. I was doing this for Keli anyway.

Josh ordered two beers for us as we sat at the table. I wiped the rim of my cup with a napkin before taking a sip. The program was modestly attended, but more people joined after one or two mediocre acts.

I studied these men on stage, the way they fumbled through their sets. They were pathetic in their attempts, which made me wonder what motivated them to get on stage. Was it making people laugh, or the idea of fame? I didn't let their embarrassment make me uncomfortable. In fact, I found it gave me power. I just slowly sipped and narrowed my eyes as they tried to win back the audience with another lame joke about masturbation. All of the performers so far were men, and I would not reward their mediocrity with a feigned laugh or a clap. Just because they could stand on a stage didn't mean they deserved my adoration. I hoped Keli was the exception.

I clapped while she ascended the stage. She looked confident and bubbly and started her set by saying, "Please, everyone, don't be afraid. I'm here to speak on behalf of Black women. A lot of people find Black women scary, but you *only* have to be scared of Black women if you're afraid of the truth."

Keli then launched into a series of genuinely funny tales of times when her honesty became the punchline. It wasn't perfect, but she was doing an excellent job. As I watched her, I was reminded of the unfairness of America. She was effortlessly outgoing and hilarious. If she were a White man and played lacrosse, she'd be working for Goldman Sachs and constantly promoted because people liked her sense of humor. I wish she knew that.

Toward the end of her set, she tried something else. "I'm telling you: Mars is the next great White flight. The only reason these people want to colonize an inhospitable planet is because they know no Black people are going to move there." She looked around the audience. "You're Black, are you going to Mars?"

"Hell no!" a voice shouted from the audience.

"You hear that, she said 'Hell no!' Thank God they got rid of DEI before they tried to get one of us to go to Mars, you know, for the brochure. Could you imagine waking up in a new land after a treacherous journey only to discover you were trapped on this plantation–oops, I mean planet." A few of us laughed, "I'm just saying, I'm starting to see some parallels here. I can't help but be honest. Thank you all and have a good night!" Keli took a bow, and I stood and cheered for my new friend.

We found Keli after the show and congratulated her. I gave her a hug, and again, was surprised by my outgoing intimacy.

"You were awesome," I told her. "I think you have a talent. I can see you doing this."

"Thank you!" she replied, looking pleased. "I think I can do this too."

Josh was nodding along, and Keli gestured to him. "This is your date tonight?"

I shook my head. "No, he's a pro bono case."

She said, "Oh, I'm glad you're donating your time to a man in need. What was your crime, sir?"

Josh looked a little flustered. "Uh, I think it was trying to flirt with her."

Keli smirked. "She's a woman of authority. Sometimes you have to show your power."

I scoffed. "That's not true. Just be yourself."

Keli made a noise that was a wordless way of dismantling my statement. She said, "I guess I'll see you at work tomorrow? I'm getting a drink with my cousin. You guys have fun tonight." She winked as she walked away.

As we left, Josh put an arm around my shoulder.

"What are you doing?" I asked.

"Just be quiet. Enjoy it."

"What if I don't enjoy it?" I said sarcastically.

He sighed and took his arm away. "Why are you so difficult?"

"I'm not difficult. I'm just...." He was right, I was being difficult. Why was I doing this? A gesture like an arm around my shoulder was a totally acceptable thing to do.

He said, "I feel like you're one of those girls who has to be mean and push guys away because they are scared of being liked or something."

We both got into the car, and I asked, "Why are you trying with me though? I thought we were just friends that accidentally hooked up."

He said, "I mean, I like you and want to get to know you."

I looked over at Josh, starting to feel immense guilt. I knew I needed to tell him about Matthew, much as I wanted to avoid the conversation. "Josh, I need to talk to you about something—"

"Was Keli right?" He asked.

"What do you mean?"

"That I need to show you how much I want you?"

He leaned over the armrest and kissed me. It was like before, tender, deep, passionate. He grabbed my hand and put it on his groin, and I could feel his erection through his jeans.

"Fuck," I said, and meant it in all regards of the word. His boner was turning me on; I realized we were about to have sex; I didn't have the chance to tell him about Matthew yet.

"There's a Walmart down the road. Let's drive to the parking lot," he ordered.

"Are you sure?" I asked.

"I need you right now." His authority turned me on even more, but I couldn't do this, I told myself firmly. I wasn't an impulsive person, or someone who had an insatiable sexual desire that made her fuck in Walmart parking. Yet my foot was on the gas. I zipped the Corolla about half a mile down the road to the Walmart. We found a secluded edge of the parking lot. In less than thirty seconds, we were in the back seat, bodies wrapped around each other, our tongues intertwining.

It was wrong, but part of my body told me it was right. Despite Ms. Honeypaw accusing me of having a "rich-bitch pussy", I was about to have parking lot sex in the back of an old

Corolla. I started giggling, thinking about the irony as I tried to find a more comfortable angle for my knee. Josh asked me what was funny.

"It's just that I've never had sex in the back of a car," I said, pulling his shirt out from his trousers and running my hands up the muscles of his back.

"You haven't? Never in high school?" he asked.

"Nope, I didn't date in high school."

"Let's pretend we're in high school then." He kissed me again, and in between kisses interjected, "Maybe you're the cute smart girl that tutors me because I'm failing algebra..." He kissed my neck and lightly cupped one partially exposed breast... "And I started to fall for you..." He bit my lip, "...And we just had our first date at a movie..."

"What did we watch?" I moaned.

"Hmmm, maybe *Scream*? You were scared the whole time, and I had to hold you..." His hands were in my pants, "...And after the movie I kissed you..."

Josh looked into my eyes and kissed my nose. "You're so beautiful," he said. It was convincing, and felt like he was just saying it to me. I was sold.

"I want you to take my virginity," I said. We both laughed, and he kissed me again.

"Are you sure you're ready?" he asked as his other hand slipped between my legs.

"Yes, I want you to be my first." I said as I shifted to lie flat on my back, my knees lifted and thighs spread to receive him. The backseat was cramped, but he was right; it did feel like high school again.

Somehow, he'd managed to get a condom out from his wallet and slipped it on, slowly, gently teasing me open with his tip before entering me. "I don't want your first time to hurt for you."

I fake-whimpered, desperate for him to bury himself in me. "Don't worry, it'll be alright."

He slowly and methodically moved his hips, but even with the care he took, my head began to bump uncomfortably into the car door. I put my hand between my skull and the plastic, but it didn't help. I said, "Uh, Josh, I'm hitting my head."

He apologized as he tried to slide us down. He struggled to free his leg from his pants to give him more flexibility. I lay there with a great desire to be back in a bed, any bed. I was quickly discovering I was not a girl for car sex.

By the time his leg was finally free, I'd lost my enthusiasm. "Maybe this isn't working," I suggested.

He looked at me. "Are you okay? Are you hurt?"

"Well, only my pride." I gingerly shifted from underneath him and sat up. "I think I'm a mattress kind of girl."

He collapsed into the seat. "That's no problem. This was a lot easier when I was younger, too."

We both stared at each other for a moment. He looked defeated. The failure of this sexual encounter ruined his veneer of cockiness. It was at that moment I found him most attractive.

"Wait." I put my hand on his penis and carefully removed the condom, slowly stroking as I kissed him, then faster as he grew harder.

"Julie." His voice was high-pitched. "You're holding it too hard. It hurts a little."

I released my hand. "I'm sorry!"

"It's alright. When I'm really hard, I'm also sensitive, so you have to be really gentle or use lubricant. It's fine, keep going."

I carefully put my hand back on his penis as if it were a Fabergé egg, my palm barely touching it as I stroked up and down. "Is this better?"

He said, "Try spit, that might help."

I spit in my hand and tried again, carefully and lightly

moving along his shaft. I hadn't given a blowjob since my boyfriend before Matthew, and even then, it was never a lengthy experience. I studied Josh's penis as I lowered my head down toward it. I never gave much thought to the aesthetics of penises, but if my standard was based on whether or not it looked weird, I'd say that Josh had a nice penis. It was not particularly curved and seemed to be a healthy size. It felt as good as a penis in my vagina could make me feel, but Josh seemed to be aware that the magic really happened at my clit.

I opened my mouth and felt the tip of his head hit my tongue. Flesh met flesh again, but this time it felt disconnected. He didn't ask me to do this, and I sincerely wanted to try to please him. As I bobbed my head up and down, I tried to focus on the truly bizarre act of giving a blowjob. Was it degrading? Was it empowering? After all, he trusted his precious manhood in my mouth.

With each head bob, I felt his body tense. *Maybe he's close to cumming?* I wondered. I went faster, then I heard his high-pitched whimper again. "Julie!"

I pulled my head up and asked, "What's wrong?"

His face was contorted in pain. "You're using a lot of teeth. I'm sorry, but it hurts too much."

I immediately flushed red with embarrassment. I put my hands up to frame my forehead and said, "I'm so sorry. Are you hurt?"

I saw Josh inspecting his penis. "I think it's fine. You didn't break the skin, but it was a little intense for me."

"Of course, I'm so sorry. I haven't given a blowjob in so many years, and I don't think I know what I'm doing." I started to offer unnecessary excuses, while Josh kept trying to appease me.

He said, "It's fine, but I think that's enough for tonight. Do you want me to drive back?"

. . .

I SAT LOOKING out the passenger window. I was so deeply embarrassed and ashamed that I could feel tears well up in my eyes. What a strange reverse; earlier Josh sat in this seat and cried about his dead sister. I sat there and cried about giving a toothy blowjob.

"Josh, are you okay?" I asked.

"Me? Yeah, I'm fine," he said casually enough.

"I mean your penis? Is it going to be okay?"

"My penis is perfectly fine. It's just sore, but nothing he hasn't been through before."

"This has happened before?"

"Yes, plenty of times, but it's alright. I don't need oral sex to enjoy myself."

I nodded and ran my tongue along my teeth, wishing this one part of me could become softer for him to enjoy.

8

My shame hangover lasted until the afternoon. I felt so awful for hurting Josh that I texted him to ask if he was okay. He confirmed he was totally fine and told me not to worry about it.

Yet, I couldn't help but worry. Having failed one of the basic mechanics of sex, the blowjob, I was beginning to wonder if I should just take a vow to never give one again. It didn't do much for me anyway, but I did not like the idea of limiting my sex life, even though it would be that way anyway if I went back to being with Matthew.

I mindlessly tapped away at computer keys until Keli's shift started at 2 p.m. Ten minutes after 2 p.m., I walked to the lobby.

She smiled when she saw me. I stood opposite her at the front desk and asked, "How are you feeling after last night?"

"Why would I feel anything?" She asked.

I said, "Because you were awesome. Doesn't it feel good to kill it on stage?"

"That was just another normal night for me, but for you, I feel like your night may have been more interesting..." Her sparkling eyes were an invitation for me to reveal everything.

I sighed. "Well, that's what I wanted to talk to you about. Afterwards, Josh and I went to the Walmart parking lot and tried to do it."

Keli's eyes widened. "Wow, that's...nasty. You tried to do it in a car?"

"Yeah." I grimaced. "In the back of the Corolla."

She grimaced too. "Listen, after twenty-five, the only vehicles you can have sex in are private jets and yachts. That's not a good look on you."

"I know. It was so uncomfortable. I hit my head, and we couldn't fit, so then I just tried to give him a blowjob."

Keli leaned closer. "I'm listening..."

I squirmed, then said, "But after a bit, he stopped me because he said I was hurting him."

Her eyebrows furrowed. "What was it? Too much grip? Too fast? Not enough spit?"

I took a breath and said, "It was all of the above, and teeth."

Keli moved backwards in shock. "Julie, you don't know how to suck dick?"

I bowed my head in shame.

She asked, "What are they teaching you in law school? Do I have to tell you everything? Listen, first things first: you need to get your mentality right. Don't go in scared or second-guessing yourself. You need to be confident. It's like doing standup; you have to exert power over the audience or they'll get in your head. It's the same thing: you have to control the D. You can't let the D control you."

A guest walked through the sliding doors and stood in line behind me. Keli said, "Excuse me, sir, I'm still checking her in. It's a complicated reservation, so I suggest you take a seat and I'll be with you in a moment." The person left and sat in some sad armchair in the lobby.

She looked back at me and continued. "Don't be scared of

the D. You have to make the D your own. It's your D Julie. Don't come on the stage unless you're about to fuck up the mic. You need to conquer your fears and show yourself that you can do this, and, for God's sake, curl your lips over your teeth."

I nodded, internalizing her words of encouragement.

"Next time you see Josh, it's going to be a mental game. You're going to feel embarrassed because of what happened, but you need to be strong. You're going to make me proud, right?"

My eyes began to burn. I genuinely wanted to make Keli proud. The absurdity was not lost on me, but as an adult, it felt nice to find a mentor again. Though past thirty, I still had so much to learn about life, embarrassing as that might feel.

Keli came around the desk and gave me a hug. "You're going to be alright. I believe in you."

"Thank you. I'm not going to be scared of the D anymore."

"Exactly, it's not like it's a ghost. There's nothing scary about it."

I laughed a little. "That's true." I went back to my room, repeating Keli's words of encouragement.

I ROLLED my eyes during a useless work call, listening to Yale Law discuss the intricacies of an old case we worked on together. She was remarkably unlikeable, but I didn't find her grating this time. Instead, I found a well of patience to deal with her desperate need to please the male figures at work. Perhaps the critical side was turned on myself, sparing her my internal wrath.

I looked at my phone to see a missed call from Ri'Chard, followed by a message, "Hey, I really need to talk with you if you have the time."

I called him right back, and he picked up after a few rings.

"Hey, can you hear me?" he asked.

"Yes, I can."

"Okay, cool. I'm outside the police station. Listen, I'm sorry to ask you this, but I'm wondering if you can help me? It's my nephew, he got in trouble with the police, and I think he could really use a lawyer."

I stood up. "Oh, okay, of course. Send me your location, and I'll come down right now."

I zoomed off in the Corolla. I know I was supposed to see Josh today and return it, but our awkward reunion would have to wait.

THE STATION LOOKED like it was built in the '60s and neglected since then. I met Ri'Chard standing outside the police station, where he stood with his hands in his pockets.

"Hey, thanks for coming." He looked worried, and in turn, I felt worried for his well-being.

"What's going on?" I asked.

"Yeah, last night my nephew Dante got picked up. There was a carjacking, and he was in the area. They found a knife on him and an ounce of marijuana, but the carjacking was done at knife-point, so they think it was him. He might be a stupid kid, but I know he wouldn't do that."

"What are the police saying?"

"They're saying he matches the description, and he doesn't have an alibi, so they want to arrest him for it."

"Any prior arrests?" I asked.

Ri'Chard shook his head. "No, he's good."

I nodded. "Okay, let me go and represent him."

I walked inside and went up to the officers' window. I told her I needed to speak to my client and said his name. She looked me up and down, and said, "Alright."

She took me back and had me wait in one of the interrogation rooms until Dante was escorted in. His hands were cuffed, and he looked scared. He was young, probably early to mid-twenties, and unlike Ri'Chard's perfect skin, Dante's was affected by acne.

I introduced myself and explained Ri'Chard sent me. "I need you to explain everything that happened last night, in the most detail you remember."

He told me that he was at home playing video games, then went for a walk, and got picked up by the police.

"Did you have a particular reason for going on the walk?" I asked.

He shrugged. "Not really, I just wanted some fresh air."

He was a bad liar. Something wasn't sitting right with me, but I'd return to that feeling. I questioned him more about what he already told the police and what they told him.

"And the reason you had the knife?"

"It's just a small one. I always keep one with me at night because of the dogs."

"And you've never gotten in trouble with the law before?"

"No ma'am."

The formality felt weird. "Just call me Julie. It's fine, I'm friends with your uncle."

Dante raised an eyebrow and said, "Oh, he doesn't have many friends, but I haven't heard of you."

I said, "Well, I'm new in town, and I'm sure he has more friends than you know."

Dante shrugged again. "Nah, he mostly keeps to himself."

"And Dante, you don't have any friends you were with last night?"

"Nope." He settled down deeper into his chair.

I narrowed my eyes on him. "Are you sure? You aren't dating anyone and are afraid to say?"

He shifted in his chair. "No, I got a girl, but she was in Atlanta last night."

I sat back and crossed my arms. "You do realize this makes you look like a suspect, right, the lack of an alibi?"

"I do, but I swear I didn't do anything. What would I do with a stolen car? I don't know anything about hot cars."

"I don't know much about video games, but do they have a log where we can see the time you were playing them last night?"

He looked down. "I don't know, we could try…"

"You don't seem very enthusiastic about proving your innocence."

He just stared at me and tapped his foot. He was holding something back.

"You know, your uncle is really worried about you. I promised I would help you, but you have to help me too." He rolled his eyes. He was getting frustrated. I was making progress. I continued, "I don't know much about your family, but I'm sure it would rip them apart to see you convicted for a crime you didn't commit." He shifted lower. "And you don't want your girlfriend to get up at 5 a.m. on the weekends to come see you in prison."

I could see the frustration in his face. I was just on the edge of truth. Finally, he quietly said, "I was…with someone last night."

I smirked, knowing I was right. I hid it and said, "Tell me more."

He looked away. "I was cheating on my girl last night, so that's why I didn't want to say."

My eyes widened. I knew that guilty feeling. "It's alright. This happens a lot, trust me, but we're going to need a statement from the other woman so this can go away."

He shook his head. "It's not gonna go away. My girl is gonna kill me."

I leaned in. "Everyone's relationships are tested in some way. I'm sure you can find a way through this."

He shook his head again. "No, I can't let anyone know about this."

I tried to be more sympathetic. "Okay, Dante, I understand you're young and feel like these things matter, but they don't. What's more important than your relationship with your girlfriend? Not going to prison. Give me the information of the woman you were with last night so we can get this over with."

He was still quiet. His jaw was clenched, and he shook his head a third time. "It wasn't a woman. I was with...a guy last night."

"Oh, I see..." I tried to figure out the best way to disguise my surprise. "That's fine, there's nothing to be ashamed of in being attracted to men."

He shot back, "I'm not into dudes like that."

He was denying it within himself, which was so common. This case would not be about convincing the police, but convincing Dante to accept himself. I said, "Listen, I know it's hard admitting these truths to ourselves and others, but it literally will set you free. There's no shame in being attracted to men—perhaps you're bisexual. I've seen time and time again the damage it causes when men do not accept themselves."

He shrugged. "Bruh, it's not that deep."

"Then tell me, Dante, what is holding you back from accepting yourself?"

He rolled his eyes again. "I'm not gay."

I nodded slowly; this wouldn't be easy. "Listen, you don't have to be scared to be yourself—"

"Stop!" he interjected. "Stop, just stop, alright. Last night I got head from a guy and I'm embarrassed, but they also recorded it too."

I was quiet for a moment. We both stared at each other, but I felt the muscles in my cheek tensing into a smile. It was at that moment I started to laugh. I don't know what compelled me, but I couldn't help it. All this frustration and fear, Ri'Chard pacing outside the police station, my panic driving over here, because he was too scared to tell anyone he got a blowjob from a guy.

"Why are you laughing? This shit ain't funny," said Dante.

"I'm so sorry, I don't know why I find this so funny. It's so stupid; it's just a blowjob, and you were about to go to prison?" I started laughing harder.

He said, "This seems very unprofessional."

"Shut up," I told him. "I'm doing this for free. Now show me the video."

He pulled up his phone and slid it over to me. It was a post on Twitter from an account called "@throatttgoattt", posted nine hours earlier. I played the video and watched carefully.

I could hear the bass of rap music thumping in the background. The room was lit by purple light, and Dante was holding the phone, pointing down at someone between his legs. They wore a bright red wig under a sequined balaclava, obscuring their face. They rubbed Dante's groin over his black pants.

I looked at Dante and asked, "Um, how does this person identify? What are their pronouns?"

He shrugged his shoulders. "When they're wearing the wig, they like me to call them a woman. You know, 'nasty bitch', 'slutty ho', 'wet pussy'. That type of stuff."

I nodded slowly and said, "Thank you, I just wanted to clarify." I paused for a moment and said, "Out of respect for the person who just sucked your dick, let's address them by their preferred pronouns, alright?"

I went back to watching the video. Dante's pants were pulled off, and she was rubbing her hands over his underwear. I squinted and saw he had a tattoo of a skull on his thigh.

"Perfect, that shitty tattoo is going to save your ass," I said.

"Damn, you're, like, judgmental," said Dante, offended.

I ignored him and went back to watching the video. By now, his dick was out, and she was stroking it. Dante reached for the phone, and I leaned back in my chair to get out of his reach.

He said, "I think you've seen enough."

I shook my head. "Nope, I really should watch the whole thing."

I held the phone closer and studied. The self-proclaimed "Throat Goat" began to suck on Dante, slowly and confidently, her hand leading and following her mouth with a circular twist.

"So, does that feel good? The hand thing?" I mimed the hand motion to Dante.

"Yep," said Dante, uncomfortably.

I watched more as Dante's dick effortlessly glided out of the Throat Goat's mouth. In the video, he said, "Do you like it? You like my dick, bitch?"

The Throat Goat said, "This is *my* dick, baby."

I was caught in a trance of intrigue. The Throat Goat didn't seem to be scared of the D at all. She seemed like the exact example Keli set for me, which made me wonder, how do people learn this?

"Uh, Julie, are you alright?" asked Dante.

I looked at him. "So, you don't ever feel her teeth?"

His eyes widened. "Do you think I'd be getting head from them if they used teeth? This is a goddamn pro."

I went back to watching the Throat Goat devour Dante's penis with the singular focus of an Olympic athlete. I asked, "When does she breathe? It's like she's scuba diving, and your dick is the only source of oxygen."

Dante just gave me a look of ignorance. I studied the background of the video and noticed out-of-focus shelves, but I recognized the color blocks of canned goods. "Is this happening in the backroom of a store? Why is there so much canned food?"

"They're a prepper, you know, for like the Doomsday shit," said Dante.

I looked puzzled. "Doomsday?"

"You know, like when the government decides to take over and start killing more mothafuckers than they already do."

"Right, makes sense." I watched for a few moments longer. The Throat Goat's dedication was impressive, but I wasn't sure I possessed the desire for penis that she did. I wondered why they felt the need to do it in a wig. They arguably had superior technique, but why did they need to present as a woman in order to please a man?

I paused the video and said, "My last question: does the wig make it not gay?"

Dante sighed. "Bruh, just leave me alone."

I put my hands up. "I'm not judging, I'm just trying to understand. Would you have gotten the blowjob if that person were not wearing a wig?"

Dante looked puzzled. "Honestly, probably not. That would be too weird."

"I'm fascinated. Did you request the wig color?"

Dante shook his head. "This was a mistake. I shouldn't have ever shown you this."

I stood up. "Well, I'm sorry, because I'm about to go show this to the police."

THE OFFICERS FELT the video was enough to establish Dante's alibi, but one officer wanted the Throat Goat's address to get a statement confirming this. However, they would release Dante in the interim.

We walked out and met Ri'Chard outside the waiting room. We could hear the officers laughing loudly in the back, so I said, "Let's leave."

I EXPLAINED to Ri'Chard that I worked my lawyer magic, and Dante and he could talk about it some other time. Ri'Chard wanted to take me out to dinner and offered to drive. We dropped a quiet Dante off at home; he gave me a meager "Thanks" before getting out of the car. Ri'Chard called out to him to thank me properly, but I said it was alright.

"He had a long day," I said.

"What did you do to get him out?" Ri'Chard asked.

"He provided the evidence for his alibi himself." I laughed to myself a little.

He said, "Well, thank you. I really appreciate your help with this. Seriously."

"It was no problem," I said. We were quiet for a bit as Ri'Chard drove. "Can I ask you something that might make you think I'm crazy?"

"That's an interesting way to start a question. I have to say 'yes,' of course."

"If a man gives a blowjob in a wig, does that make it not gay?"

Ri'Chard looked confused. "Why are you asking me this?"

"Oh, nothing, just a case I'm working on," I said casually.

"Okay..." He thought for a minute. "Yeah, I don't think that's the case. I don't think men who aren't into men want a blowjob from a guy."

I said, "Yeah, that's my feeling too. It's interesting that they justify it by wearing a wig, as if a pile of synthetic hair creates a boundary of what they find acceptable, for both parties. Sorry, I'm just so fascinated with this."

"Does this have something to do with Dante?" Ri'Chard asked.

I let out a high-pitched, "Nope!"

Ri'Chard shook his head, "That boy...You know what? I don't want to know more about this."

I said, "Okay, we can talk about something else."

WE FOUND a mediocre chain restaurant we both could agree upon. We sat in a booth and stared at the menus. I couldn't help focusing on his eyes, and the defined jawline that led to his lips. I noticed that so many men had dry lips, but his were wet, and he often rubbed them together and licked them a little.

"Do you have a lot of family around here?" I asked.

"A good amount," he said, undoing the paper napkin tie. He placed the cutlery on the plate and unfolded the paper napkin, and put it on his lap. "This is out of habit. My momma always got mad if we had food stains on our pants." Ri'Chard laughed. "You should have seen the food stains on me when I was trying to learn how to eat with chopsticks in Japan."

"At least you tried. I'm sure the people there were entertained by it too."

This was my first time alone with Ri'Chard. He was remarkably contained. He wasn't shy, but he seemed to hold much of himself back. He reminded me of how I acted in D.C.

I wanted him to open up, so I decided to ask a question about something I knew he'd be interested in. "You like those civilization games? If you had to build an empire, what would it look like?"

His eyes changed; I could see the excitement in them. "I've

thought about it a lot. Location is so important, especially because of climate change, so that limits things."

I interrupted, "But it's not realistic to acquire enough land to make a new country, at least I don't think."

"You can't buy it, but you can take it." He continued, "Look at Israel. They're just a modern-day version of what America did. America did it to plenty of places. It's not impossible, but it's dependent on your military capabilities and lack of accountability for destroying the lives of harmless people."

"I thought you'd be more brainwashed by the military?" I asked.

"I was, but then I started to question why I was stuck on all the military bases in foreign countries. Did you know we used to colonize the Philippines?"

I said, a little embarrassed, "No, I didn't know that." I paused and asked, "So you learned how to build your imperialist empire from watching America?"

He laughed. "No. If it had my way, we'd be like Wakanda, perhaps what Haiti should have been. Haiti was the most profitable colony in the history of European colonialism, and it was the only successful slave rebellion. They should have been prosperous, but that would be too dangerous. For the world to see the disenfranchised succeed would have upended the world order. Haiti was always meant to fail. Even today, it would be a threat to see thriving Haiti."

I tried to quell my discomfort with my own ignorance. I had a feeling I'd have to conduct some internet searches after dinner tonight. Ri'Chard continued. "I like the idea of a quiet kingdom that minds its own business, similar to Bhutan. That's somewhere I've always wanted to visit."

"What happens in your quiet kingdom?"

"Everyone is happy. Black people are free and celebrated.

Schools, healthcare, and elder care are all free. Housing is also affordable and sustainable."

"It sounds lovely," I said admiringly.

He continued, "For me, I just want a life without worry. Worrying about making ends meet, discrimination, my future kids being safe. I think that's what most people want. There'd also be block parties every month, and the national anthem would be written by Sade."

I seconded. "I'd move there just to never hear the American National Anthem ever again."

"I agree. Now that I'm older, Sade really hits differently after thirty." He looked off into the distance for a moment, probably imagining the soothing vibes of Sade's national anthem.

"Do you think about running for politics?" I asked.

"In this country?" He raised an eyebrow. He looked so sexy with his skeptical look. I wanted to keep asking stupid questions that he could dismantle with just a glance.

"Good point."

"I think power corrupts people," he said. "I saw it a lot in the military, and hell, even back here. I had hope for change, but everyone just ends up the same."

"That's true, and I live in the epicenter of terrible people in power."

"Is that what you wanted, to be in D.C.?"

I considered it. "I thought so. Before, I had this whole plan. I'd get married to someone in the D.C. circuit, a person in a high-level government position. I would be a partner at an influential firm and live in a nice house near a metro line. But now I don't know if that matters. Being here has opened my eyes a bit."

"How so?"

"Like you said before, I don't know what this country wants to be."

Ri'Chard shook his head, sharing my frustration. "I haven't

spent much time in Taiwan, but I'm starting to see myself wanting to live somewhere like there. It seems like systemic racism will always be an observed tradition in this country, and I don't want to be a part of that."

I added, "Sorry to break it to you, but my people are just as racist."

"Impossible. Although it would be easier to ignore if it's in a language I don't understand."

Just then, our food order arrived. Ri'Chard said, "I think we should toast."

"To what? Racism?" I asked.

"No, to you." He looked at me and said, "You're one of the good ones, and I'm grateful you helped my family tonight. You can be the Minister of Justice in my new country."

"I thought I was the cunning queen? Or is that position filled?" I inquired.

"In my country, the queen will be Black, I'm sorry."

"Well then, let's make a toast to the future Black queen." We both held up our glasses and clinked.

As we ate, I wondered if I should ask about his girlfriend. I felt us growing closer in a friendly way, so I was worried that discussing her might put up a boundary. I decided to go for it.

"How did you meet your girlfriend?"

He wiped his mouth with his napkin and took a sip of water. He said, "We both were stationed in Virginia. We didn't know each other on the base, though. I happened to go out with some buddies at a bar, and she walked in. I think it was love at first sight, or at least infatuation. Her name is Aisha. She had on a red dress and looked fine as hell." Ri'Chard shook his head and smiled in recollection. He continued, "I'm really shy, but I knew I wanted to try and talk to her, so I wrote my number on a note that said 'I think you're beautiful'. I got up and walked over to the table, holding the note. She made eye contact with me, and I got scared, so I walked by and went to the bathroom. Then I came back and put the note down on the table in front of her. She looked confused, and I was still scared, so I went back to my friends."

"You just put it in front of her and didn't say anything?" I asked.

Ri'Chard looked embarrassed. "Yes."

"Well, I guess it worked."

"Nope. She ignored me until I finally found the courage to go and talk to her. She was intimidating at first, but eventually she realized that I'm just shy."

"Why are you shy, though? You're really handsome and a nice person."

Ri'Chard looked taken aback. "Oh, thanks. I guess sometimes I don't really think about how I look on the outside. On the inside, I'm more insecure, you could say."

My voice softened. "Why are you insecure?"

He shifted a bit and paused, looking down. "Well, I think it comes from growing up. I had a really strict father. He pushed me into playing football, but I did not want to play. I wanted to do Dungeons and Dragons. He made me, though, and it was a rough team. I was the weakest link for a while, until I learned to run really, really fast. I never loved football, but I got good at it. I'm working on it, but somehow, I just can't shake that feeling of being a bit scared and out of place everywhere I go." He looked at me with that same intense gaze. "You don't seem like you're scared of anything."

"Me? I have plenty of fears," I said.

"I'm not talking about spiders. You don't seem to be afraid of being in different spaces, or with different people. I don't know... we're so dissimilar, but I find myself really comfortable around you."

I don't think anyone in my life had ever told me I was

comfortable. I always felt I gave off a cold aloofness to my colleagues or people in D.C., but Ri'Chard seemed to have a different interpretation. I said, "I also feel a bit out of place in my regular life. I don't connect with my colleagues, and don't have many friends in D.C. It's weird, but in a way, I do feel more comfortable here."

"Why is that?"

"I think it's because I grew up in the real world. I was part of an immigrant community; most of my friends' families owned restaurants. I didn't live in a fancy place, and I went to public school. I forgot I used to be more down to earth. I think living in the bubble I've been in has made me more judgmental." I looked to my side and remarked, "I used to be so proud of this stupid bag. It's just leather they charge more for putting a fancy name on it. Growing up, I never cared about that, but now I'm ready to give it away."

"You're getting rid of your Prada bag?" he said with real surprise, one eyebrow shooting upward.

"Why does everyone care about this stupid purse?" I asked, feeling ridiculously defensive.

"Because none of us can afford something like that."

I looked at the purse and nodded in agreement. "It is frivolous."

"Are you selling it?"

I looked at him. "No, I'm giving it to a friend."

His other eyebrow joined the first. "Damn, must be a good friend."

"Mmm. I hope so. Speaking of good friends, why are you friends with Josh?"

He looked at me suspiciously, "You're asking me that like it's a bad thing."

"No, I'm just curious about how you two fell in love. Did you slip a note into his locker and run away too?" I said, adding a wink with my jab.

Ri'Chard smiled wryly. "Josh was my first friend on the football team; actually, my only friend on it. He only played for one year, though; he joined track after that. We used to run together, and it felt like if we could run fast enough, we'd be able to get away from our lives. I know it sounds weird, but maybe you get it as well...he's one of the few White guys I feel safe around. Sometimes I think it's because he's too oblivious to be racist. but I think he has a big heart. He's smart about the things he likes, then ignores everything he doesn't. I never saw him be mean to people, and that's a rarity amongst men, especially boys. It takes someone who is really comfortable with themselves to not belittle others. I mean, I don't think my dad was comfortable with himself, so maybe that's why he was so difficult." Ri'Chard looked at me. "I'm sorry, I'm talking a lot. I'm treating this like a therapy session."

"Lawyers are more expensive than therapists, so you might be surprised when I send you the bill," I told him. "But it's fine, I'm enjoying learning more about you. Can I ask, are you comfortable with yourself now?"

Ri'Chard looked beyond me into the distance, then back at me. "For a while I wasn't, but I think that changed when I met Aisha. It's weird thinking that you know what love is, then discovering it's so much bigger and more complex than you ever imagined, yet also simple. So, the short answer is: now I'm comfortable with myself, because of her."

I asked, "Because she completes you, or tells you that you're pretty?"

He smiled at my obviously stupid remark. He asked, "Have you ever been in love?"

I said, "Sure, I've had significant relationships."

"No, have you been in *love*? Have you felt that kind of

connection that feels like it's coming from a higher place?" Ri'Chard's eyes glowed with wonder. Who knew this man was such a romantic?

My face must have shown my amusement as I thought of past dates and relationships, including Matthew. I hadn't had the grand connection he was talking about. But then my mind fell back to Josh, to being in Josh's bed the first time we had sex. That was the first time I felt connected in a way I couldn't define. I said, "In love? Maybe. I'm still figuring it out."

"We can talk after you've fallen in *love-love*."

I felt a bit unbalanced with his line of questioning and decided to needle him. "So Josh was your first love, but Aisha completes you?"

Ri'Chard tilted his head. "Why do you keep asking about Josh and me being in love?"

I said with an awkward defensiveness, "I just think it's funny because football players are supposed to be homophobic, right?"

"Yeah, I'd say sports isn't a great place to find acceptance. I don't know why gay men are so threatening to men, though. I think it comes back to the insecurity thing. If you're comfortable with who you are, then there's no need to bully others for being themselves. Maybe you're right, I do love Josh."

"I knew it!" I decided to be a bit honest, "Maybe I'm just jealous because I don't have the kind of friendship you guys have."

Ri'Chard asked, "Do you have a best friend?"

"Not really. Not anymore. It wasn't for any dramatic reason either; our lives changed, and so did the friendships. It's just part of growing up, I guess." It was true. There was no dramatic reason for my lack of close friendships, other than my apathy towards maintaining them.

He said, "Well, I consider you a friend, and I know Josh does too."

I felt a lump in my throat. How could I be their friend when I was hiding so much of myself? I knew this was the moment I should choose honesty instead of fear, but it wasn't the same fear I felt facing Ms. Honeypaw. That fear was electric; this fear was sour.

I looked at him and smiled. "I consider you guys to be my friends too. Should we get the check?"

THAT NIGHT, I sat in bed, thinking about the day's events. After dinner, Ri'Chard took me back to my car, and we said farewell. I wanted to hug him, but I was afraid that might cross the boundary I needed to draw. I like fantasizing about Ri'Chard, his steely gaze and the hard muscle under his shirt. It was basic stuff, but also fun. At dinner, we'd connected on a different level, one that made me more curious about him and also cautious. I understood why he was so quiet; it was not rooted in simmering sexuality but a necessity to study others around him. He was a watcher, probably from having to watch others in an effort to keep himself safe, as his father pushed him into uncomfortable situations growing up.

I promised myself I'd put a pause on fantasizing about Ri'Chard. I wanted us to be friends, so I'd even friend-zone the imaginary Ri'Chard who would ravish me after towing my useless European car. I regretted not being honest with him and cursed myself for pulling out more fistfuls of dirt from the grave I was slowly digging.

That brought me to thinking about Josh. I was still incredibly embarrassed after our last tryst. I didn't know how I'd face him tomorrow when I would go to pick up my car. I wondered to myself why I had never learned to give a blowjob. Was it the failure of my institutional education to prepare me for such a basic act? How did other girls learn? I reflected on the Throat

Goat's dedication to sucking dick. She was an acrobat with her tongue, and I just felt like a spectator in her circus.

Maybe people who have penises already knew how to do it, I decided. Therefore I couldn't possibly be in league with someone like Throat Goat, who already had a natural advantage. It felt unfair to be competing with someone like her. I pulled out my phone and searched her username, locating her page. I scrolled her feed and watched video after video of Throat Goat doing her best work. My mind was a mix of jealousy and admiration. I had no interest in the dicks she was sucking, but she was effortless in her approach. I wish I could approach having a penis in my mouth with the same rigor. The way she gave blowjobs was like watching the strongest dancer in the group absolutely nail the choreography, with my place in the back as I struggled to remember the moves.

I wondered about the men she was working on, and whether this was a subculture I knew nothing about. I mean, look at Dante. There was nothing about his appearance or behavior that indicated he'd be interested in seeking out a Throat Goat. Perhaps secretly adventurous men were more common than I thought. That made me wonder if General Stovall were secretly gay. I imagined him, sipping a glass of whisky at the end of the night, opening his walnut cabinet to find a horse-hair wig. He'd put it on and admire himself in the silver mirror, before summoning some poor Confederate intern to molest. Or maybe it was not actually gay, though, because he was wearing a wig.

I bet many of the politicians in D.C. had blowjob wigs. Maybe that was what bound them all, a shared society of men, bonded by their secret. I decided there would be an invitation, an initiation, and, of course, at monthly meetings, they would all arrive and put on their wigs in a dimly lit, ornate chamber. Yes, this chamber was where all the decisions that changed the world were made: this was the deep-throat state. With the backdrop of Gregorian chanting, somebody would perform ceremonial fellatio, then offer the semen to some altar featuring the blowjob wigs of our forefathers before us.

I laughed to myself, but it was true that Washington was filled with strange men horny for authority any way they could get it. Everyone was obsessed with power and penises and symbols of power and penises. I suddenly thought of Matthew and his uninspiring penis and wondered if he would fit into the secret society I'd just dreamed up? But then, if he wouldn't go down on me, I couldn't imagine him blowing a guy. Maybe he was simply scared of vaginas. Hard to tell

I yawned heavily. It had been another long day and night, and other than springing Dante, I hadn't actually accomplished anything legally, no thanks to the townspeople who were passionately throat-goating the memory of a dead Confederate general. This crew would fit in nicely to my secret society, only they didn't have the brains, the power, or the swank to pull off world domination, let alone bewigged fellatio. What they did have was a lot of secrets and potentially the power to sabotage my case, and I wasn't going to let them get away with it.

I slid down in bed and pulled the covers up around me, the smile lingering as sleep descended. My thoughts jumbled and images swam together – Mr. Lyons and Judge Bishop in blonde blowjob wigs, chanting incantations in a dead language. After all, "cum" was a Latin word.

9

I woke and checked my phone, seeing a late-night text from Josh: "Hey, you forgot your car." I was supposed to pick it up yesterday, and I stood Josh up. I felt a pang of guilt as I realized I'd found yet another way to hurt him—or maybe I was overreacting and he didn't care. I messaged him that I'd come by soon, and I apologized.

Steve's Toybox opened at 8:30 a.m., so I casually showed up fifteen minutes after to collect my car. I still wasn't sure how to approach him after the awkwardness of our last encounter, which made my mouth feel sandy as I walked toward the open garage doors. I called inside, and he appeared holding some extracted part of a car.

I said, "Hi, sorry I didn't show up yesterday. I had to help Ri'Chard with a problem."

"Oh, is everything all right?" he asked.

I nodded. "Yeah, his nephew had a run-in with the law, but it was all sorted when he admitted his alibi."

"What was he doing?" Josh asked.

I thought to myself. I cautiously said, "He was...visiting a friend." I thought about asking him my wig question, but didn't want to make things weird. I think Josh caught on that there was more to the story, but he wasn't pushy about hearing it.

"Well, your car is ready for you," he told me.

"Thanks, I need to pay."

"Don't worry about it."

I stubbornly said, "Absolutely not, I'm paying."

"No, I got you on this one," he said, winking.

I put up a hand. "I stood and said, "I appreciate the gesture, but work will reimburse me, so we'll both be taken care of." I lied about this, but I wanted to pay him. It was only fair. I also didn't want to feel like I owed him anything.

He stood and said, "I'm not taking a dime from you, no matter what."

I hated him for his generosity. I reiterated my desire to pay and said, "Josh, you don't have to sacrifice your financial security as a gesture. I know you're trying to be nice, but it costs a lot to exist, and you took the time to help me, so I need to pay you."

He stood and gave me a wry smile. "We'll compromise. You can pay for the parts, but labor is free."

I groaned. "Fine, but I will find a way to repay you, and you must accept it." He agreed, and I took a last look at my Corolla. "I'll miss you," I murmured. I'd grown quite fond of the practical shitbox.

He handed me the keys, and I got in my Volvo. I had missed the seats and was immediately reminded of the luxury of my old life as the supple leather gently supported my body.

However, I instantly caught a faint, unpleasant smell, like a mouse had died somewhere in the interior. I started sniffing around the car, pressing my nose to the air vents. I saw movement out of the corner of my eye as Josh opened the driver side door. "Is everything okay?"

I didn't want to be fussy since he'd fixed my car for free, but I also didn't think this was something that would go away with the windows down. I said, "Yeah, there's just a weird smell, like something died."

He leaned in and started to sniff. "Weird," he said. "This wasn't here before. It definitely smells like a dead mouse." He opened the rear door and started to sniff, then asked, "Do you keep food in the trunk?"

"I don't think so. There's no reason food would be in there, but let's check." I stood up and walked around the trunk with him. He felt for the button under the hood but couldn't find it. I said, "You have to use your foot." I waved my foot under the bumper to an astonished Josh, who said, "No shit."

We were hit with a wave of acrid decay. I bravely pushed open the trunk and screamed. Josh put one hand on my chest and the other behind my back. I took a breath and moved forward as I registered a dead fox in the trunk. Its neck was red with blood, cloudy eyes, and its tongue hung out of its mouth. I exclaimed, "What the fuck!"

Josh exclaimed, "Whoa. That definitely wasn't in there yesterday. Someone must have put it there last night."

I asked, "Why would someone break into my car and put a dead fucking fox in it?"

Josh winced. "Uh, I'm sorry, but I think I left it open."

I looked at him, astonished. "You didn't lock my car?"

He shrugged. "I never lock cars, honestly. It's Pothos, and there's a security camera on the front of the garage."

"Josh, this is a luxury sedan." I stood with my mouth agape.

"Listen, I'm really sorry. I'll take care of the fox, don't worry about it." Josh put his hands on his hips and frowned, the lines between his eyebrows cutting deep furrows. "Listen, keep the Corolla for now. This has never happened before. Someone is trying to fuck with you."

"No shit. Does the security camera actually work?"

"Yeah, it does. It goes to Steve's phone. I'll text him to check the footage."

"Good. If we have evidence, then maybe I can get a restraining order against whoever did this..." Although as I said it, it seemed unlikely that any justice would be served in this town.

Maybe my paranoia was actually intuition. Someone in this town definitely had it out for me, and they were only going to be more pissed after I won this case. I was also so upset with Josh that I thought I'd purposely bite his dick the next time I had it in my mouth.

I PARKED down the block from Ms. Honeypaw's house. I took a baseball cap from Josh's truck, hurried up the sidewalk onto her porch and hoped no one noticed me. I knocked and heard voices coming from the inside. Through the dusty window, I could see two people coming toward the door.

I stepped to the side as it opened. A middle-aged woman with curly brown hair and a Spanish accent stepped out and said, "....I'm so grateful. Thank you for helping me. You truly work miracles." She took Ms. Honeypaw's hands and continued to thank her. Ms. Honeypaw's face was soft as she accepted the woman's gratitude. The woman let go, wiping tears from her eyes, and walked down to the sidewalk. Ms. Honeypaw turned to me, her face now hardened and judgmental. She said, "Miss Prada, you can come back in an hour. I need to smoke a blunt and take a nap."

She tried to close the front door, but I grabbed it with my hand and pushed it back open. I said, "No, you can nap after I do witness prep."

Ms. Honeypaw rolled her eyes and walked inside. I followed her and said, "You will not believe what happened this morning.

I went to pick up my car from Josh's garage, and something smelled weird, so we opened the trunk and found a dead fox in it."

Ms. Honeypaw turned to look at me, grimacing. "A fox?"

I nodded and said, "Yes, someone is trying to intimidate me into dropping this case."

Ms. Honeypaw said, "Why do you always have weird shit happening? It's always about the courthouse burning, or a dead pony. Can't you just be normal and say 'Hey, how was your day?'" She mumbled to herself, "Fucking dead fox, stinky-trunk ass-bitch."

We settled in her reading room, and I said, "Excuse me, this is not my fault. I had nothing to do with any of this."

She looked at me with a grimace. "But you are the common denominator for all this weird shit. Maybe *you* are the problem?"

I scoffed. "That's ridiculous. How can any of this be my fault? Someone put a dead animal in my car."

Ms. Honeypaw shrugged. "I don't know. You used to play with Ouija boards. Weird shit happens to weird bitches."

I relented. "Fine, that's not the point." I took a breath. "I'm here to work with you on your testimony for tomorrow."

Ms. Honeypaw let out a noise of disagreement. "Right, I thought about it, and I'm not going to testify."

I focused on her. "No, you promised to testify. I'm not letting you out of this."

"GeishaBitch, you may have the delusional mindset that you have some authority over me, but I answer to only God and the ghost of my momma, and she is not fond of your bony ass."

I took a breath and said, "Firstly, I don't think I have any authority over you; I see you as an equal. Secondly...is my ass really bony? I think it's pretty good, right?"

Ms. Honeypaw called out in the direction beyond me. "Momma, do you think she has a fat ass?"

I waited quietly, sitting up straighter and arching my back a bit in case a ghost was checking me out. Ms. Honeypaw waited, then laughed. I asked, "What is it?"

"My momma said your ass is 'fat enough for that White boy you've been seeing.'"

I asked, "What 'White boy'?"

Ms. Honeypaw looked at me. "Don't play me. I know you've been seeing Josh."

"Is that what the ghosts are gossiping about?"

"Nope, it's because Ms. Honeypaw is a scientist. See, you're a *dumb bitch*, and Josh is a *dumb bitch magnet,* so the Laws of Dumb Bitchdom mean you were gonna wind up under him at some point."

"I disagree with your hypothesis. One, I'm not a 'dumb bitch'. Dumb bitches don't pass the bar, get jobs at esteemed law firms, then buy Prada bags to give away to fake psychics. Two, we're not discussing my personal life today."

Ms. Honeypaw stared at me and blinked. "You think I'm a fake psychic?" She called out again, "Momma, do you think I'm a fraud?" She waited a minute, then turned to me and said, "She said, 'The only fake thing here is your first name.' Shouldn't you have some weird-ass, foreign-sounding name? I mean, your parents dropped anchor all the way from The Wan just to call you 'Julie'? What kind of basic shit is that?"

I said, annoyed, "It's called 'assimilation'. They didn't want me to get made fun of in school. I think 'Julie' is elegant and professional." I narrowed my eyes. "Where did your name come from?"

Ms. Honeypaw called, "Momma, where did my name come from?" She waited, then smirked a little. "Right. She said she called me 'Honeypaw' because I always reached for the sweetest thing. I'm a dessert-first kind of bitch."

"Great, however, I really need to prepare you for your testimony tomorrow."

Ms. Honeypaw crossed her arms. "As I said, I ain't doing it."

"Why?" I asked, exasperated. "Why are you doing this to me now?"

She scoffed and said, "*You*? This isn't about *you*. Julie, you don't have any idea about the people in this town. I just try to mind my business. If they know I'm colluding with the opps, then I have a target on my back."

I tried to soften my voice. "Listen, I'm sure you're getting cold feet. It happens all the time. You don't have to worry, as I have a plan. I've reached out to various news outlets to come and observe the court tomorrow. Your testimony is going to blow this case up, and I promise it will be state-wide news, maybe even nationwide. All eyes will be on Pothos, and no one will dare mess with you. Plus, if someone does burn your house down, you can start an online fundraiser and probably have a lot of success."

"You got the press coming tomorrow?" She asked, raising an eyebrow.

"Yes, so dress up because you might be on TV," I said confidently.

Ms. Honeypaw looked around. "Well, I've always thought I'd make a good guest, you know, like a celebrity psychic or something." She looked at me and smiled, then called out, "Momma, you hear that? I'm gonna be on TV!"

I smiled in return and said, "Okay, so let's prep your testimony."

I worked with Ms. Honeypaw to refine and speak her testimony clearly and concisely. She was going to be a surprise witness and needed to nail her part for my plan to work.

When we were done, she grabbed a deck of cards. She said, "Let me do a quick reading. What question do you have?"

"Will I win tomorrow?"

She grimaced. "Don't ask that. It might get in your head what the cards say. Sometimes it's best to be ignorant to fate. Ask something else."

I thought for a few moments before Ms. Honeypaw interrupted with, "You're taking too damn long. Just let me pull some cards."

She laid playing cards on the table, then considered them. Her brows furrowed as she studied what I thought were meaningless colors and numbers. She pulled out another card, then started to speak, "I don't know...I'm getting mixed messages. Obviously it's telling me Josh has blown your back out already... but there's something else, like someone else? Do you have a man or something?"

My eyes widened as fear entered my body. Ms. Honeypaw looked at me, and I saw the face of the same shark I already punched. I took a breath, and instead of coming clean, I diverted. I said, "I don't know. I did have dinner with Ri'Chard last night."

"Who?" Ms. Honeypaw asked.

I clarified and said, "He's Josh's friend, they used to be on the football team together, or something, but he lives one town over from Pothos."

She started to recall. "Oh, yes, yes, Lil'Ricky. He used to be skinny before he got so fine."

"Yes," I said, "He is fine."

Her face turned. "No. No. Leave our Black Kings out of your messy pussy. Josh might have already gotten trapped in it, but Ri'Chard is a sweet boy."

"My pussy doesn't trap men in it."

She reiterated, "There's a lot of messy shit in these cards. I always liked Ri'Chard; he's a good, gentle boy, but I do get the feeling he can lay pipe better than a plumber."

"Gross, I don't think of Ri'Chard that way. He's just a friend, and besides, he has a girlfriend that he's very much in love with."

She gave me a look of suspicion and pulled another card. "See, I'm just seeing a lot of confusion and chaos around you. I feel like you're keeping some relevant shit from me."

I looked in her eyes and said, "Nope, I have nothing to say."

She leaned closer. "So you're definitely fucking Josh, but you have no desires for that fine-ass Ri'Chard, is that right?"

"We're just friends, if that even," I said.

"Do you like Josh?" she asked.

"Josh? I enjoy spending some time with him, but we still don't know each other that well."

"You know, my momma was always fond of Josh. She actually used to help babysit him. His mom wasn't bad, but she wasn't always right, if you know what I mean."

"What do you mean?"

"I mean, she was bipolar. The switch would flip, and that bitch would hit zero to sixty like *that*." She clapped her hands together to add an effect. "Almost as fast as Josh had you bent over the back of his truck."

"Oh my god, it was not like that," I protested.

"So, I feel like while Josh dates these stupid crazy bitches, he's also protecting himself and is closed off, you know, like emotionally or some shit." Ms. Honeypaw grimaced. "So I'm just trying to let you know now so later you don't come and sit in this chair and start crying your *dumb bitch* shit about him, okay? Because I will not have any patience for it then."

"Well, if you testify tomorrow and we win the case, I'll be out of town long before he can break my heart."

"By the way, my momma said if *you* break Josh's heart, she's going to give you the ass-beating I promised. She doesn't care what Kung-Fu, Tai-Chi shit you know. Momma is a black belt in putting hands on bitches who had it coming."

"Jesus," I said, "Like mother, like daughter." I stood up and grabbed my bag, which I noticed Ms. Honeypaw eyeing.

She looked at me and said, "And don't you dare try anything with Ri'Chard. My ears are to the streets and I *will* hear about it."

I rolled my eyes and started to walk in the entryway. "I'm leaving, I'll see you at the courthouse tomorrow. Do you need a ride?"

She turned back in her chair to look at me, "Hell no. You got roadkill in your trunk. I always knew your kind of people ate weird shit, but damn." She looked at me in disgust. I left and walked to the door while she continued, "Just stick to dogs and shit. Why do you gotta stir-fry a fox?"

I was through the front door and closed it behind me. I took a breath and hoped the *right* things would come out of Ms. Honeypaw's mouth tomorrow.

10

For the second time that day, I pulled into Steve's Toybox. Josh messaged that I should come by and take a look at the security footage. I thought I had forgiven him, but the rage boiled in me as I saw him milling about the popped trunk of my Volvo.

I got out of my car, and he was leaning in the trunk, tugging at some of my expensive lining. I asked, "What did you do with the fox?"

He righted himself and looked at me. "I buried it out back. I'll burn some sage in here too to get rid of any negative energy."

"Then we can bathe in the moonlight and read our astrology charts?"

He stared at me, a little lost.

"Oh, are you serious about burning the sage?"

He said, "Yeah, and I'll also put together some crystals that will help purify the energy. It's only a car, but we should do it to be safe."

"Right, thank you." I looked at him, a little puzzled. When did I go from fucking the town slut to a hippie? Also, which one was I more ashamed about?

"Oh, Steve sent me the footage," he said, interrupting my thoughts. "You should watch this."

Josh pulled out his phone and handed it to me. I watched the black and white footage, which contained a good overview of the front of the garage. My car was in sight. There was no movement until I saw a figure walk toward my car. The figure wasn't very large and seemed to be dragging the dead fox by the tail. I held the phone closer and saw the figure stand at the back of my car. Like Josh, the figure struggled to find the trunk button. I saw it kick the car in frustration. The person, mostly obscured by my car because of the angle of the camera, walked around the car, and the light from the garage hit them. My eyes widened in shock. I recognized the tiny frame, over-produced hair, even without the metallic sash that read "Miss Pothos." She opened the driver's door and searched for the trunk button. She slammed the door shut and moved to the back. I could just make out her climbing into the trunk and hauling the dead fox up. She at least found the button to close the trunk and hopped down. She walked to the end of the camera frame, giving a little skip and a curtsy on her way out.

I looked at Josh and then back at the phone. I was entirely speechless.

Josh broke the silence. "Weird, right?"

I glared at him. "You're acting like this shit is normal? Does this happen all the time in Pothos?"

He shrugged. "Not really. It's freaky, but at least we know it's just a little girl messing with you and not some creepy dude." I wanted to tell him that when there was a damaged little girl, there was usually a creepy man close by her, but my mind was racing in anger.

I said, "Why are you acting so casually?"

"I mean, this is definitely concerning, but you're also ruffling feathers in this town, and I don't see this as out of character for some of these people. If you want, we can report this to the police, though."

"This police?" I asked incredulously. "Do you think the police will care about this?"

"I know a few guys that are cops in the area. I've fixed cars for them. I can call them, if you like," offered Josh.

"No, just wait. I'll talk to my boss first." I rolled my eyes. "Should we call Child Protective Services though? It's not normal for a child to be dragging around dead animals at night."

Josh's brow furrowed. "Honestly, I know that family deals with animals a lot since they got a farm. I bet her dad shot it, and she was just playing with it."

"Playing with dead animals?" I turned away, then turned back to look at him. "I'm really upset at the moment, so I'm going to leave, alright? I just need some time alone."

Josh said, "Julie, wait, I'm sorry." He caught my arm, "I'm sorry; don't go. Why don't you come over to my place tonight? You shouldn't be alone."

"Josh, it's okay. I need some time to myself."

He let go of my arm and instead gave me a hug. He repeated, "I'm sorry, please don't get angry."

I let him hold me for a bit, absorbing the comfort of his body. It was a sincere hug, and it was nice being held for a moment. I pushed back and said, "I was already angry, but it's passed."

"That was you angry?"

"Yes, but I get over things quickly."

"You were so calm, though," he said, with a slightly puzzled look on his face.

I explained, "I come from a long line of emotional repression. The women in my family train their whole lives for it. I'm fine, really."

He hugged me again. "I still want you to come over."

I said into his chest. "I can't. I have to go buy a new purse."

"Where are you going?" He asked.

"To some discount store a few towns over. I just need something temporarily."

"I'll go with you," Josh offered. "I hate shopping but it will be fun to keep you company."

I released myself. "Fine, let's make a date of it. I wish you were gay, though, because then you might add value to this trip."

"Sometimes I wish I were gay too. I could steal my boyfriend's underwear when I run out of clean ones."

My eyes narrowed. "Are you wearing clean underwear now?"

"Yes," said Josh, defending himself, "I do laundry, but once in a while I get down to those last pairs, and I start to panic."

I asked, "Why does doing laundry make you panic?"

"A cousin locked me in a washing machine when I was a kid."

"Jesus!" I exclaimed, "Did he happen to grow up and produce Miss Pothos?"

"No, he's in Wisconsin now. Divorced, twice," he said, with a hint of a smile.

"I guess you won?"

He changed the subject before he had time to think about it. He asked, "Do you want me to drive?"

Josh wanted to stop at his house on the way home to shower before heading out. He invited me to wait inside, so I'd be forced to revisit the scene of my first infidelity. Since I was sober this time, I was able to take in his trailer. I noticed the rows of rocks lining the window.

"Nice pebbles. Are they special?"

"All rocks are special, Julie, but go ahead and look at them. I have some interesting ones."

I leaned in to inspect the rocks while he went into the

bathroom. They all looked the same to me, but perhaps I couldn't see what he could. I decided to think about my case instead.

I made a mental note to look into Miss Pothos, as well as Sally Wren. Since she was related to General Stovall, she was technically related to Ms. Honeypaw. I couldn't imagine Ms. Honeypaw taking that query well, but it was worth seeing what she knew. As I recounted my witness prep from earlier, Josh emerged from the shower. He had just a towel around his waist, and his back was dripping with water. He walked into his room, then leaned out the door frame and asked, "What should I wear?"

I answered, "Something normal. We're just going shopping."

"Do you want to help me pick something out?"

I couldn't imagine he had much other than a few dressier tank tops, but I relented. I walked over toward his bedroom, and he followed behind me. I stood looking at his closet. "Do you want to present your options?"

He pulled out a button-down shirt and held it to his chest. "How does this look?"

"Good," I said. "With or without it, both look good."

He lowered the shirt and asked, "Do you like me better without it?"

I stared at his torso, defined by muscles and a light sprinkling of body hair. I followed it down toward his penis and asked myself, *Can I own his D?*

"Julie?" He raised his eyebrows.

"Oh sorry, I was just thinking about something," I answered, blushing a little.

"No problem." He pulled out a black shirt and asked, "What about this one?"

I took a breath. "Josh, can we talk for a second?" I sat on the bed while he stood in front of me. "I think we should address what happened last time, because I'm still embarrassed about it."

"Julie, you don't have to apologize, it's fine." He kneeled down so he was eye level with me. "Don't beat yourself up about it."

"It's just...I feel really bad. Is your penis alright? I've been worrying about it."

He laughed a little and said, "It's totally fine. Honestly, it's not something I always enjoy anyway. I'm more into my partner's pleasure."

"Well, I got some advice from my friend about how to give blow jobs, so we can try again if you're up for it?"

"You don't have to worry about just trying to please me. That's not what I like. I want you to enjoy yourself, too." He said, looking at me with a sweetness in his face.

"I think I will enjoy it. I'm just nervous because of the last time."

He reached out and placed his arms on my legs, moving them up my calves. "Why don't we just focus on you this time?" He leaned down and kissed my knees, then slowly began moving upward as his lips traced my thighs. His hand moved above him to push up my dress. I had to tell him to stop.

"Josh, wait," I said, biting my lip in nervousness.

He looked up at me, "What is it?"

I didn't want to tell him that this had never happened before; no man had ever gone down on me. I didn't want to tell him I was insecure and worried he'd be turned off by the way I tasted, but what excuse could I say other than I was on my period?

He spoke first, "Are you nervous? Have you done this before?"

"No," I said quietly.

"Can I show you?" He pulled himself up and kissed me on the lips. He tasted minty, and I hoped my mouth didn't taste sour from nervousness. He gently laid me back then kissed down my neck, my chest, and I felt his hands hike up my dress. He slowly slid down my panties, and I looked down at him. "Relax, just enjoy yourself."

He disappeared between my legs as his kisses got closer and closer to the center of my insecurity. When his kisses landed, I let out various tones of "Oh." There was "Oh?" and "Oh!" and "OH" and "ooooh" before they melted into generic moans of pleasure. The soft, wetness of his tongue caressed my clit, creating the most bizarrely pleasurable sensation. Josh was not afraid of the C. In fact, he owned my C. He controlled my C. Though it was so small, I found men were often intimidated by it, but not Josh. He was not scared of the C at all.

I relaxed. My breaths became slower and deeper. My body writhed, and his hands gripped my thighs. The sensation heightened as my moans became louder, leading me up the roller coaster of orgasm. Each flick of his tongue brought me one rung higher, until I was at the top of the track. And knowing he was next to me, I put up my hands and screamed.

AFTERWARDS, I lay on his chest while he played with my hair. My hands glided along his stomach, and the same guilt I'd been negotiating before came back. It was so easy with him. Why complicate it now? I'd be gone soon, hopefully, and then could wrestle with these emotions from a faraway location. Tomorrow I would win this case, setting in motion my departure. These might be the last moments I had with Josh, so I'd choose to enjoy them. As the gold of a waning sun danced across his skin, I wondered to myself if I should just stay? Even if I won this case, what was I going back to? This confused little voice started to agitate my post-orgasm meditation, but I took care of that by saying, "We should head out soon."

"We still didn't pick out my outfit."

I rolled off of him and said, "Jeans and black t-shirt. Go."

He got up, quickly grabbed them, and put them on. He looked perfectly handsome, and I was pleased with my creation. "You look nice," I told him, and he returned the compliment with a kiss on my cheek.

As we drove, I looked out the window as the woods blurred by. I remembered looking out the window at my suburbia when I was young, so confident that when I was an adult, everything would be perfect. I just assumed people made money, bought houses, and stumbled upon a husband between the ages of twenty-seven to thirty-two. I thought that adult me would know everything, but as I looked out the window, then at Josh, I realized that I knew nothing.

I was still renting and paying back student loans. I didn't know how to admit to myself that I hated my job, or that my perfect match of a partner had never given me a proper orgasm. I didn't know how to accept that I was an adulteress, or that I probably wasn't going to tell the men it affected.

When I was young, I didn't know how much I'd still be lying to myself. I promised I'd never be with a man like my father, or wind up in the position of my mother, the stoic wife who accepted her husband's infidelities. I'd catch her crying sometimes, which she excused as thinking about her younger sister who passed away when she was thirteen. Yet I knew it was another one of my father's wanderings that was hurting her.

I didn't know I'd end up just like him, too.

I think the younger me was a much more admirable version of myself. I was so dedicated and focused, so *guai*, but perhaps because I hadn't acted out then, I was doing it now. Perhaps my undoing was inevitable, just as my success was built on an empty promise I'd made to myself when I was young that, by now, everything in my life would be perfect.

Josh reached over and grabbed my hand. He held it as we drove, which I found both comforting and unsettling.

"What are you looking to buy again?" asked Josh.

"I'm just looking to get a purse."

"Why? You have one, right?" I wanted to tell him about my deal with Ms. Honeypaw, but I knew it was best to keep it between Ms. Honeypaw, the ghost of her dead mother, and myself. "I want a more casual bag. My work purse is getting too heavy to always take with me."

Josh nodded. "My ex loved shopping. She had, like, seventeen purses. I don't know what someone does with all those. She'd get mad when I questioned her about it."

"I wish I had space for seventeen purses. My apartment is small so I try to keep things minimal." It was true that my apartment was small, but my closet space was also compacted from sharing it with Matthew. "Your ex sounds awful. Why would she get mad when you asked her about her purses?"

Josh sighed. "Yeah, she just wasn't good for me. We shouldn't talk about her. But I do know she used to shop a lot at the store we're going to."

Once at the store, we perused the aisles until I stopped and studied a rack of cocktail dresses. The store was sadly understaffed, so thankfully we were left alone while I scrutinized the tacky selection, desperate for something designed with taste.

I turned to Josh. "This is the first time I've been shopping with a guy before. You're proving your worth." He looked bored, with a few dresses draped over his forearm. In the middle of the rack I found a black dress. It seemed tight, high hemmed, with a horizontal neckline and cute enough sleeves. I actually liked this one, but wanted to try them all on.

"I thought you were just getting a purse?" said Josh, with a tone of desperation.

"Right, we'll get there. Are you not having fun?"

"Uh, I'm just not that great at shopping."

"Me neither, so help me out. What do you think would look good on me?"

He looked at the racks, and with his free arm he pointed toward a translucent gray short-sleeved blouse with koi fish printed on it. "What about this?"

I looked at the blouse and laughed. "Wow, that is essential A-B-G attire."

He looked confused, "An A-B-what?"

I doubled down, "Asian Baby Girl. You want me to dress like an A-B-G."

"I don't even know what that is."

I patiently explained. "It's the hot, trashy Asian girl aesthetic. A lot of makeup, eyelashes, tattoos, drinking boba, and wearing *that* shirt." I grabbed the shirt and held it up to my chest. "Could you see me in this? Maybe with a sexy bra underneath?"

Josh squinted and shook his head. "No, I was wrong. I shouldn't be giving fashion advice."

I looked back at him and said, "I'm just a B-A-G: a Boring Asian Girl. I appreciate you trying to look for me." My eye caught a black purse stuffed between some garish ones. I snatched it out like a lizard eating a fly. I looked at both sides of it and said, "This is it! I found my purse!" I handed it to Josh and proceeded to the dressing rooms to try on my finds.

Josh dutifully waited outside the dressing room while I changed. Most were an immediate "no", and the only one left was the black one I'd had a feeling about. While I was changing, I heard Josh's voice. He was talking to someone; I stopped to listen and caught him saying, "Yeah, I'm hanging out with a friend."

A woman's voice responded, "Oh, I thought you were here to pick up girls outside the dressing room." She had a thick Southern accent and sounded trashy.

I heard Josh's voice say, "Nope, I'm not that desperate, Cassie."

The other woman's voice said, "I'm just kidding. When did you get so serious?"

Josh sounded a bit exasperated. "Listen, I don't want to have this conversation now."

I zipped up my dress and carefully opened the dressing room door. I peered out and could see Josh talking to a girl with bleach-blonde hair and daisy dukes on. The voice matched the aesthetic. She was like the White girl version of an ABG, an acronym I'd have to come up with later. I had to focus on eavesdropping. She continued, "Fine, you always like to run away from stuff anyway, even if it's just a friendly 'hello' from an ex."

Josh rolled his eyes and looked pained. I had to do something, but I was not a do something kind of girl. I thought of Ms. Honeypaw and all of her shit talking, and pretended she was in the dressing room behind me, shoving me out. Suddenly, by the force of myself or Ms. Honeypaw, I was standing outside.

"Josh, how does this look?" I said.

He turned to me, and the look on his face was already confirmation. "It's good," he said.

I glanced at her, then back to Josh, "I guess I'll buy it then."

Cassie raked her gaze over me as if I were one of the dresses hanging on a rack. "Is this your new girlfriend?"

I prayed to Ms. Honeypaw, then looked at her and said, "I'm sorry, how do you two know each other?"

Josh looked uncomfortable. Cassie said, "We used to date before I broke up with him."

I looked her up and down and said, "Hmm, I'll be confirming that with another witness later."

She let out a sound of disgust and asked Josh, "So, you've run out of girls in the town, and now you have to import them?"

"Cassie..." Josh said, "You need to stop. That's not cool."

"What?" She defended herself, "You'll never be happy with one woman anyway."

The voice of Ms. Honeypaw entered my head, *GeishaBitch, are you going to let that bleach-blonde Dixie bitch talk to your man like that?* Ms. Honeypaw's taunts echoed in my head while I watched them until I simply said, "Bitch," which caused both Cassie and Josh to turn and look at me.

"Excuse me, did you just call me a 'bitch'?" exclaimed Cassie.

My eyes widened. I needed Ms. Honeypaw's slippery tongue to finish that sentence. I panicked for a split second and looked her over for something I could use against her. Her legs were athletic and perfectly tanned. She seemed to have a great ass and a fit body. Her breasts were small but perky, and the worst part was that she had a really pretty face.

I turned to Josh, "I'm trying to find something to make fun of her for, but she's hot. I see why you liked her. Sorry, I can't help. 'Bitch' is all I got."

She looked offended. "Ew, what are you, a dyke or something?"

I replied, "No, I actually don't like cunts." As I walked back to the dressing room, I heard Ms. Honeypaw congratulating me in my head, *Good one, Miss Prada*.

I could hear Josh say, "Julie, I'm going to wait in the car. I'll leave the purse up front."

"Okay!" I said, hoping Cassie wasn't getting ready to shank me with a broken perfume bottle when I exited.

I opened the door, peering around to see if she was going to jump me. I grabbed my black dress and stepped out. As I turned out of the dressing room area, I heard someone call out, "Hey!" I froze and turned to look around, seeing Cassie peer out from behind a rack of discount swimsuits.

I exclaimed, "Jesus!" I hoped she wasn't going to strangle me with last season's bikini.

She said, "I'm not going to hurt you. I just wanted to apologize about earlier. I'm working with my therapist to not get triggered so easily."

"Fine, that's fine. Thank you," I told her, hoping to end this encounter.

It didn't. She proceeded to ask, "Are you seeing Josh?"

"No. Why are you asking?"

She looked around and said, "I'm not trying to ruin anything you guys might have, but I just wanted to warn you that he cheated on me when I was in a relationship with him. It broke my heart. I'm only saying this because sisters need to help sisters."

I glared at her. What was she trying to gain from this? Sabotage our presumed relationship or embarrass Josh? Or was she lying and still trying to fuck with him? The lawyer in me knew a wolf in daisy dukes when I saw one. I said, "I think it's pretty obvious we're not sisters. This is something you need to deal with inside, and not make it my problem, okay? Good luck."

I walked away from her, waiting for a jab in the ribs from a discount bottle of Paris Hilton's perfume.

I walked to the car with my shopping bag, puzzled by the weird interaction. I got in the passenger seat and was greeted by Josh, but I could tell he was in a different place. He wasn't the charming and confident Josh I knew, but a little smaller and strange. I think this encounter triggered something within him.

Josh asked, "Got everything you needed?"

"Yeah, I did...Cassie found me again, though."

Josh sighed. "Jesus, I'm sorry. She's really a pain in the ass."

"Seems like it." I waited, then said, "She warned me about you, that I might get my heart broken because you cheated on her."

Josh's expression turned. It was a mixture of anger and embarrassment as he nodded his head and stared straight ahead. I continued, "I just wanted to let you know that what she said doesn't make me think of you differently. Being in law, I've seen so many cases of people on their worst behavior that cheating is so benign. From what I've seen, you're a perfectly nice guy, so don't let her get in your head."

The pained look on his face gradually subsided. He took a few deep breaths and said, "Thank you." He grabbed my hand and squeezed. He let go and said, "We were at a bad place in our relationship when I cheated, but it was actually never in a good place when I was with her. However, I was wrong to do that to her."

I asked, "Is cheating really that bad?"

Josh turned and said, "Yes, it's the worst thing you could do to a partner, especially if you lie about it."

I tried to hide the look of guilt on my face. In my head, I thought murdering your partner might be worse than cheating, or stealing all their money, abusing them, et cetera. When I really thought about it, there were a lot of flaws in Josh's summation.

I decided to change the subject. I said, "If it weren't for that footage, I would've thought Cassie might have left the dead fox in my car."

"Yeah," said Josh, distantly. "Do you want to listen to music?" Thankfully, he put on something to alleviate the tension.

AFTER AN AWKWARD CAR RIDE BACK, I was happy to be back in the familiar quietness of my hotel. I held up my shopping bag to Keli as I walked in.

"Oooh, what did you get?" she asked.

"Just some unnecessary things. I bought a cute dress I might wear to court," I said.

"Nice, nice. So, have you seen Josh since we last talked?" Keli asked, desperate for information.

I teased her a little by looking around, then said, "Wine on the terrace in five?"

She nodded as I walked back to my room.

THIS SECTION of the parking lot was the closest thing to a terrace this hotel had to offer. We had our procedure down, and I realized this would be the last time I'd be sneaking a bottle of wine out in my Prada bag.

After our generous pours, Keli asked, "So, how did it go?"

I took a big sip and said, "I offered today, but it didn't happen."

"Julie, you can't 'offer'. That's your D. You gotta take that D!" she said heatedly.

"I know, I know. But I was nervous. Instead, Josh owned my C."

She sat back a little. "Oh, he gave you head. I'm liking this dynamic."

I said, "I liked the dynamic too. It was incredible; I didn't know it felt like that."

Keli choked on her wine. "Wait, you've never had your coochie licked?"

I meekly confessed, "No, that was the first time."

She said my name as she hugged me. "I had no idea. I didn't know you were so sheltered. I wish I could have been there to see it."

"You wanted to watch Josh go down on me?"

"I wanted to be there for moral support. You know, cheer him on, tell him some plays, give him some Gatorade when he got thirsty. You gotta stay hydrated if you're going to give good head."

I laughed and said, "You're like the Coochie Coach."

Keli made a noise of delight. "Wait! I like that: the Coochie Coach. I feel like I can brand that."

I think you can. I see a big future ahead of you."

"Awww, thanks, but you'll always be my MVP." Keli held up her glass as we toasted.

Keli said, "Julie, I fuck with you in a way that I don't with most people who aren't Black. Why are you cool?"

I stuttered for a second and asked, "I'm cool?"

"Yeah," said Keli, "You're dope as fuck. You're, like, sneaky cool. You don't really show it, but when it hits, *it hits*."

I hesitantly said, "Thanks, I don't think *anyone* has called me 'cool' before."

"Did you have a lot of Black friends growing up?" Keli asked.

I thought for a moment. "Not really. Most of my friends were Asian, or nerdy White kids. Although I was sort of friends with this group of really cool Black kids in high school."

"Tell me more," said Keli, leaning in.

I explained, "I paired with them for a group project, and I ended up doing most of it, as I always did with any group project. Then after that, we became friendly, and they always asked me to help write their papers."

Keli looked at me with her mouth agape. "Julie, I'm sorry, but that's fucked up."

I protested, "No, no, it wasn't like that. I see why you're concerned, but I actually enjoyed the challenge of it. School was pretty boring, so I loved coming up with different themes and writing styles. Sometimes one of them would wait until the last minute to ask me, and I'd write a whole paper during lunch. I loved the thrill of it."

Keli still looked concerned. "Julie, they were using you."

"Right, you could say that, but I wanted my intellectual powers to be used. It made me a great lawyer; I'm incredibly fast at writing briefs now. It actually cuts into my billable hours, and I should learn to slow down. Anyway, the point is that I enjoyed being around that group. Even though I was mostly writing while they were talking, I could just listen and have a good time. They even tried to teach me to dance, but I never picked that up."

Keli took a sip of wine. "Well, I'm glad you made it out a better person. Next time, though, tell me if anyone is using you, and I will fuck them up for you."

My mind flashed to Ms. Honeypaw. Tomorrow was our big day, and I hoped that she wasn't using me, too.

I thanked Keli for her offer. I said, "I met one of Josh's exes tonight, at the store. She was being mean to him, so I called her a bitch."

Keli said, "Good for you. Stand up for your man. After the adrenaline of all that, that's when you should've owned his D. You need the delusional confidence to get you going."

I continued, "I actually watched a video of a blowjob for work and thought of you."

She asked, "How can I get a job at your firm?"

"No, no, this wasn't work for my firm. I was helping out a friend. He was really embarrassed because his alibi was a video of him getting a blowjob from a guy in a wig. It made me wonder, do you think if a guy gets a blowjob from a man in a wig it's still gay?"

Keli pondered and fired off a series of questions: "How good was the wig? How many inches? Was it natural or synthetic hair? Was it glued down? Could you see the lace?"

"This is out of my expertise. The wig was bright red and probably synthetic."

"Then it's gay," said Keli, confidently.

"I just don't know why he can't let it be gay then. Why is he so scared of it?"

Keli took a sip, "You know, actually, it's complicated. Some men like feminine men, some are in denial, and some like a girl with a dick, but they don't see it as gay. I actually had an ex who dated a trans woman, and he identified as straight, so naturally, I challenged him until he put me in my place. He told me he enjoyed being with a trans woman because he could see her pleasure, like having an erection or literally seeing her cum. It was visual validation for him that he could hit it that good."

I said, "Huh, I never thought of it that way..."

She continued, "The pussy is like Pandora's Box. It's mysterious and complicated. Like, you have one, and you barely know it. Does your pussy have a name?"

I gave a confused look. "Should my pussy have a name?"

She said, "Mine is named Whitney, because I loved Whitney Houston growing up. I did it to honor her."

"Oh, okay, then maybe I'll name mine Ruth Bader-Ginsburg?"

Keli shook her head. "Julie, no. It has to be *sexy*."

I nodded in agreement. "I'll think about it."

"So my girl Whitney is complex. She needs her man to take his time. She doesn't often orgasm from penetration, and she loves to be kissed. Penises are so easy by comparison. You just make it slippery and go up and down."

I said, "The person in a wig identifies as a woman while wearing it though."

Keli let out a noise of agreement. "I think people equate femininity with giving pleasure, or possibly this person likes to play with gender. Maybe this person grew up wanting to be a girl, and the only time they feel they can express it is by putting on the wig. When they take it off, they're a regular dude in the real world."

I thought about what she said. As a woman, I used to have the notion that I had to give men pleasure. In a strange turn of events, it was Josh and his gentle, simmering masculinity that taught me pleasure. Maybe that softness in him was actually his feminine side? I wished it could also be masculine, but I'd experienced too many years of watching men take, including the right to vote, that my definition of men was marred by this rapacious need to appropriate. Yet, I didn't want to draw lines between "feminine" and "masculine" as what made a person do good things. Instead, I think it has to do more with a fascination with power and the courtship of evil that comes with its pursuit.

I said, "It's weird because I don't feel that connected to being a woman myself. I guess I'm just wondering about all this because sometimes I feel like I'm performing as one as well. I don't really know what I'm supposed to be doing. Am I supposed to be married? Having kids? Having a great career to provide? I feel sort of...blank right now. Maybe I should try putting on a wig and see if that makes me feel different."

"Maybe you're one of those non-binary people," suggested Keli. "But what makes you feel 'blank'?

"I'm from D.C. where it feels like everyone is sucking dick, literally or figuratively, trying to get power, and I don't think I want to suck dick."

"This is a big realization. It's just not your energy," said Keli, adding, "And if you want to go to a city where everyone is sucking dick, then go to Atlanta."

I laughed and said, "I don't think I'd last long in Atlanta with my toothy blowjobs."

Keli agreed. "Definitely not, but don't worry about it. You got yourself a man who loves eating your coochie. God has blessed you, my child." She clinked my glass and took a sip of wine.

I looked away. "Yeah, I don't know. When I finish this case tomorrow, I might not be around for much longer."

"Are you going to take Josh with you?" Keli asked.

I took two large sips from my glass and swallowed hard

before answering. "Uh, I have that whole Matthew situation to deal with."

Keli said, "Oh shit, I forgot about him. You need to dump his ass."

"Honestly, sometimes I forget about him too. I know that's horrible."

"You can replace him with Josh, though. Matthew might be sad, but he should've learned to eat your coochie. We'll put his ass on the bench and drop him from the team."

I laughed. "Yes, Coach, but I think Josh is meant to stay in this town. I don't think he's made to be in my city."

Keli agreed. "True, and you definitely aren't meant to be here. Love finds a way, though."

I wondered about love. Was love lying to someone about being in a relationship? But after tonight, I saw that Josh has been in the same position as me. Would he understand, or had that ship sailed? Was I even falling for him? There were so many questions, so many unknowns, the biggest being whether I would win in court tomorrow. I hugged Keli goodbye and walked to my room with a head made heavy by Chardonnay. I undressed, turned on the shower, stepped in, and as the warm water drummed against my skin, tears poured down my face and mixed with the pleasure washing off of me.

11

Waking from an inadequate sleep, I saw a text from Ri'Chard that read: "No problem. I'm happy to help you out."

My brain had yet to ignite, and I scrolled up to see a text message I'd written at 2 a.m. asking him to chaperone Ms. Honeypaw to court tomorrow, and ending with, "Please make sure she's there!!!" Despite my exhaustion, anxiety about the hearing had kept waking me throughout the night. I'd kept imagining a scenario in which Ms. Honeypaw refused to leave her house and thought Ri'Chard could leverage her fondness toward him to get her to court.

After washing, I saw the dress I bought yesterday hanging out of the shopping bag. Thankfully it was some synthetic material that required no ironing. I ripped off the tag and slithered into it, a black number that was a bit sexier than anything else I brought or even owned. I put a blazer over it to convey some professionalism.

Before I walked into the Baptist courthouse, I felt my phone vibrate and fished it out of my purse, seeing a text from James that said, "Good luck, this is a big day." I hadn't even told him about the dead fox yet, but I couldn't lose focus on the hearing today. I slipped my phone into my bag and hoped that giving up the Prada for adoption was worth it.

Jim Smoke was behind the folding table designated for defense with his hunting partner, Steve. They were looking at something on a cell phone, and I overheard them say, "The idiot shot the buck with his AR-15. It left a hole big enough to see through."

I sat down and took out my briefs. I looked around to see some of the sparse attendees, with Mr. Lyons among them. I tried not to think about his nocturnal hobbies and instead focused on my opening statement. My focus was limited as my brain was agitated by the absence of Ms. Honeypaw. With only five minutes until the proposed start time—and as the only case on the docket—her punctuality was essential. I uncomfortably shifted in my folding chair and nervously tapped my foot. I spotted Sasha from the voting rights organization, who was supposed to help bring the press into the court. I stood and walked over to her.

"Sasha, hi." I looked to see if more people were following her. "Where are the journalists? The TV crews should have been set up by now."

She looked perturbed and explained, "Julie, there are no TV crews. No one cares about this shit. I called everyone, but this was the best I could do. He's from the Ethel College newspaper."

I looked at the nerdy kid holding a recording device and asked, "Have you graduated from high school?"

He said, "I'm a freshman, but I look young."

Sasha shrugged. "I tried. Listen, they've been doing this voter disenfranchisement for years, each method more creative than the last, but people don't care anymore. If that damn courthouse was filled with dogs, *then* White people would've turned the fuck up for this."

I cursed the gods that they didn't let an illegal puppy mill operate from the basement of the old courthouse. Sasha was right. If only they had gutted a Golden Retriever in front of the courthouse instead of a miniature pony, then it would have been nationwide news.

Just then, a welcome sight: Ri'Chard holding the door open for Ms. Honeypaw. I smiled at them both, hopeful that this day might go as planned.

Ms. Honeypaw looked at me and said, "Miss Prada, I'm about to be the Kato Kaelin to your Marcia Clarke, though we all know O.J. was innocent." I raised my eyebrows; she looked at me and held up a finger to exert authority and said, "It was his son." I must have looked confused, because she changed the subject and asked, "Where are the cameras facing? I need them to get my good side."

I grimaced, knowing what was about to happen. "This is the press," I said, gesturing to the adolescent reporter.

Ms. Honeypaw looked at him and said, "*This* is the 'press'? You've got more hairs on your chin than he has on his balls."

I touched my chin, then snapped back to reality. "Firstly, I'm Asian, and we have virtually no body hair. Secondly, I know. I was expecting a better turnout, but let's give this kid his big break, okay?"

Ms. Honeypaw seethed, "I'm going to drag your hairless ass back to your lagoon, you slippery, eel-ass bitch," before she stomped off to take a seat in the stands.

I caught Ri'Chard's eye, and he asked, "How's it going?"

I sighed. "Not great, and it hasn't even started. Thank you for helping me out. It means a lot."

"You don't have to thank me," said Ri'Chard. "You're doing something to help people, so I want to support you."

I took a breath. He was right: ultimately, I was trying to help people *and* not get fired.

He gave me a little smile. "Remember, you are the cunning queen of your empire." He ended with a wink that made my stomach flutter.

I walked back and sat behind the folding table. I looked toward Sasha, who gave me a thumbs-up. The reporter started taking notes, while next to him, Ms. Honeypaw sat with her arms crossed, looking angry. Ri'Chard sat next to her with great posture and nodded at me.

The Judge sighed. "Okay, Ms. Chen, we know why you're here, so I'll just let you start talking so we can get this over with faster."

I wasn't prepared to start so quickly, but I stood up. "Your Honor, we're here today to argue our motion seeking the immediate reinstatement of all the challenged voters to the active voter rolls pending the outcome of the investigation of alleged voter fraud."

Jim Smoke interjected, "I object, Your Honor. It is well within the laws of our town to investigate voter fraud."

I retorted, "Not when the voters you are investigating are the entire Black population of your town."

The Judge declared, "Sustained. He is right, Ms. Chen, we have laws in this town, and we respect them."

It was not off to a good start. I continued, "Due to the suspicious circumstances surrounding the burning of the courthouse, it seems like it was an intentional act to sway the next elections. Therefore, if these voters are barred from casting ballots, then the criminal who burned down the courthouse would be getting exactly what they want."

"Objection—there has been no progress on the case of the courthouse burning. It could have been an Act of God, or a rat, so it's perverted to suggest that we're endorsing the act of a criminal when we are abiding by the laws of this town," said an expressionless Jim Smoke.

"Sustained." The gavel smacked down.

Fuck. This wasn't going well, and if I didn't win this case, I knew I wouldn't be up for any sort of promotion, and I'd be assigned to shit cases until I decided to get a job at a different firm. My future rested on my ability to sway these simple men, but they weren't the sinister idiots I thought. They had a cooperative agenda, and I was just annoying them with my incessant protests.

I pressed on. "Your Honor, I checked the voting records for the last county and town elections. The voter turnout rate was about 17% of the registered voters in the town. It's highly unlikely that if the Court reinstates these voters that all of them will even vote in the next election. If you wait to reinstate them until after the election, and there is no proof that they committed voter fraud, they will be disenfranchised and will be denied their fundamental right to vote. I will also be forced to keep pursuing this case. I think it's in all our interests to reinstate the voters. The town can review their statuses at its leisure if they cannot produce sufficient evidence that they committed voter fraud. I truly think this is the most practical bureaucratic solution."

Jim Smoke said, "Objection—Ms. Chen isn't here to speak on the bureaucratic efficiency of the government."

The Judge said, "Sustained," and banged his gavel once again.

I heard the door to the Baptist courthouse open and saw an unexpected figure slip in. It was Josh, wearing a button-down shirt and ill-fitting khaki pants. He quietly took a seat next to Ri'Chard and gave me a smile of encouragement.

I watched him. In all the years Matthew and I had dated, he'd never come to see me in court. Yet, two men who barely knew me had come to support me. I looked at them sitting next to each other as my eyes started to burn and my upper lip quivered. I felt a tear run down my face and couldn't help overhearing Ms. Honeypaw hissing to Ri'Chard, "Is this bitch on her period? Why is she crying right now?"

Judge Bishop asked, "Ms. Chen, are you finished with your opening remarks?"

I grabbed my briefs and held them in front of me, reading the rest of my opening statement through the cracks in my voice. "In conclusion, all the voters affected should be reinstated for the next election cycle."

Judge Bishop's saggy eyelids did little to hide the boredom on his face.

I gave him a verbal cue only because he looked as if he needed one. "Your Honor, I'm finished with my opening remarks."

He shook his head. "Oh, right." He sighed and said, "Defense, I give you the floor."

Jim Smoke stood up. "Your Honor, this is frankly a waste of time and government resources. My office should be prosecuting criminals, but our time is spent on frivolous lawsuits like this, leaving murderers and rapists to prowl the streets. It seems Ms. Chen's agenda is to help these evil people roam free."

"I object. My agenda is to ensure the rights of this town's citizens are respected."

"Overruled," said the Judge, "Mr. Smoke isn't actually accusing you of aiding and abetting criminals, he's just making an argument, isn't that right, Mr. Smoke?"

"You're surely correct, Judge Bishop," said Mr. Smoke. He looked at me and winked.

I said, "Your Honor, respectfully, I'd like to say that the law is meant to create structures for all aspects of society, and it's misleading to say that by prosecuting a voting rights case, we're taking away resources from criminal cases. The United States Supreme Court has said that the right to vote is considered a fundamental right, preservative of all other rights. This has been established in the cases of Yick Wo v. Hopkins in 1886, or Reynolds v. Sims in 1964, or Harper v Vir—"

"Stop." The Judge held up his hand and looked at me. He said, "You know what your problem is? You're one of those elites who comes from a city and thinks you understand everything about the world. I'm frankly ready to dismiss this case for wasting my time."

I looked at the audience sitting in the pews and caught a glimpse of Ms. Honeypaw seething with suppressed fury. Instead, I looked at Ri'Chard, and then at Josh, who was rapidly tapping his foot in apparent angst. He looked at me and held a thumb up. Josh was paying attention to what I was doing. I thought back to all those moments I'd talked about cases with Matthew, who pretended to pay attention while typing work emails on his phone. He'd chime in with the appropriate, "Oh, really?" or "Wow, that's incredible," but he wasn't actually listening to me, and the worst part was that I had accepted this as normal.

I felt my eyes burn again. I bit my lower lip and said, "Your Honor, I'd like to introduce a witness."

The Judge looked at me. "Ms. Chen, are you crying?"

I shook my head. "No, Your Honor, I'm having allergies."

The Judge asked, "Ms. Chen, why was this witness not disclosed earlier?"

I wiped a few tears from my face. "Because of witness intimidation by counsel."

Mr. Smoke scoffed. "That's ridiculous. We don't intimidate witnesses in my office. We hold truth and justice to the highest standard."

The Judge looked back at me. "Ms. Chen, this is highly unusual and frankly unfair. Can you provide any evidence of this intimidation?"

I shook my head. "It's just a feeling I have."

"A feeling?" asked the Judge, "The law is not based on feelings. I'm afraid you haven't given enough cause to call for a surprise witness. Motion denied."

I looked down in shame. *What the fuck was happening to me*? My effortless predator instincts in court had been replaced by a pathetic, sad kitten. I wished somebody would put me in a sack and throw me in the river.

"Does the Defense have any remarks?" asked the Judge.

Jim Smoke said, "No, Your Honor, but I have a tissue to offer Ms. Chen."

The gavel smacked like a guillotine, beheading my dreams as the Judge declared, "Case dismissed."

I was in shock. Had I fucked it up that badly? I was going to be fired, blackballed, and would have to start grading LSATs to make the monthly payment on my stupid Volvo. Yet I didn't want to cry. This was work, this was what I knew, even though losing wasn't something I was accustomed to. What had made me cry earlier...well, that remained a mystery to me.

Jim Smoke stood and patted his hunting partner on the back. He looked at me and pointed a finger gun, firing it with a wink.

I numbly packed my bag and walked toward the pews. Ms. Honeypaw stood in my way. "That was a fucking embarrassment," she said, looking as if she'd wanted nothing more than to punch me in the nose. "You started crying up there! You just set working women back a goddamn century. Now I'm even thinking bitches just need to stay at home and raise kids." She held a finger to me and cautioned, "You better find someone who'll hook your eel-ass up because I don't think this lawyer shit is for you."

I couldn't say anything. I heard Jim Smoke's familiar drawl

say, “Ms. Honeypaw, what brings you to this courthouse today? Are you getting familiar with all the laws you like to break?”

Her face changed. She became saccharine sweet and said, “Why hello, Mr. Smoke. I thought today was my hearing for a traffic violation, but I got the days mixed up.”

I saw him look at her. “Is that right? Interesting that you seem to know Ms. Chen. Is she representing you for your traffic violation?”

“Oh, Miss Pr—Chen. I don’t know her. She was just asking me if I had a tampon.”

Mr. Smoke let out a sound of disgust. “Well, that’s good. You’ll stay out of trouble now, won’t you?”

Ms. Honeypaw gave a fake laugh. “Of course, Mr. Smoke.” As he moved past us to walk out with Steve trailing behind, Ms. Honeypaw’s expression changed, and she became the usual hard person I had grown fond of. She lowered her voice. “I told you that I didn’t want to fuck with these people.”

She turned and walked out. Ri’Chard looked at me and said, “Sorry, it happens, though. I’m going to check on Ms. Honeypaw and make sure she’s alright.” He left, leaving Josh, who’d been standing behind him.

He walked forward and put a hand on my shoulder. "I don’t exactly remember what you said to me last night, but it was something like, ‘This doesn’t make me think of you differently.’ I haven’t seen a lot of court cases, but you’re still the smartest lawyer I know.”

I laughed a little and wiped a tear from my eye. I also cried the first time I lost in court, though in the courthouse bathroom. I locked myself in a stall and was overcome with the guilt and shame of failure, and the fear of consequences at work. However, this time it wasn’t just about work; it was about everything happening to me in Pothos. I said, “Josh, thank you. Do you want to hang out later? I think it’s going to be a rough day for me." I was anticipating being fired in the afternoon meeting.

"Of course, we can do whatever you want," said Josh.

"Thanks. I have to deal with some work stuff, but I'll talk to you later."

He gave me one more small hug and left, tugging at the waist of his ill-fitting khakis.

The freshman reporter approached me. "Can I get a statement from you?"

I looked at him. I wanted to tell him to fuck off, but I'd once been in his position, in school, and optimistic about the bullshit called "adulthood". I said, "Can I email you one?"

He agreed and left with Sasha, who gave me a lukewarm goodbye, probably cursing me for having to drive all the way from Atlanta for this.

I WALKED out of the Baptist courthouse and stared at the ground as I made the way to my car. I heard "GeishaBitch, are you running from me?" I looked up in confusion, surprised to see Ms. Honeypaw walking toward me. "You forgot about our deal?"

I looked at my bag, then back at her. "But you didn't testify."

"A deal's a fucking deal. I earned that bag the moment I stepped into that courthouse." She held out her arm.

"But what if I want to appeal and need your testimony?"

Ms. Honeypaw moved forward and snatched the bag from my hand. "Hey!" I shouted. She turned and grabbed a plastic shopping bag from the tote bag she wore over her shoulder. She started taking my Prada purse contents and putting them in the plastic bag. "You can't do that!" I protested, moving forward.

She moved to keep her back to me, shouting, "You're going to try and scam me? This is my bag, bitch!" I tried to wrestle the bag away, but she was faster and stronger than me. We went a few revolutions before she held the Prada upside down to see if anything fell out. She thrust the plastic shopping bag into my chest and said, "A few things you should know about me: I always get what's owed to me, and just because this paw is made of honey doesn't mean it don't have claws, bitch."

Ms. Honeypaw turned and marched back toward her house with the Prada bag under her arm. I watched her go, taking a part of my old self with her.

12

I logged on to the dreaded meeting with my firm, and unhappily found a packed room of my colleagues.

"Welcome, Julie, we're all just settling down now," said James.

He stood at the head of the room and read some notable updates for the firm from his papers. He asked some of the other associates about the progress of their cases, but sadly, none had fucked up as badly as me.

He turned to the camera and said, "Julie, can you give us an update on your case? We're expecting you back in the office next week."

Everyone stared at me through the monitor. I was tempted to slam my computer shut and run, but I knew perfectly well I didn't have that option. I needed to rip this bandage off. "Yes, I just finished court this morning." I spoke as neutrally as I could, praying no one could see my internal agony. "...And the case was dismissed by the Judge."

The room remained silent, so I awkwardly pushed on. "I can appeal, but it seems like the burning of the courthouse was a coordinated effort on the part of the town. I actually tried to introduce a witness who could testify to the collusion of the prosecutor and potentially the Judge in the burning of the courthouse. Many people believe a ghost burned the courthouse down, but this witness can prove them wrong."

"Ghost?" James said, signaling for me to elaborate.

I obliged. "Yes, there was a Confederate General from this town, and I've been told his ghost is responsible for these strange events. However, as I mentioned, the story seems to be a coordinated effort by the White authorities in this town to subvert the voting rights of the Black citizens."

Again, the room remained unnervingly quiet for a few moments. James finally spoke. "Well, I don't have to explain what a disappointment this is. You've already been there for almost two weeks, and it's a considerable drain on our firm's resources, even if we're doing this as a pro bono case. I really thought the outcome would be different."

I replied, "Yes, I was hoping the outcome would be different too, but I also think filing in a higher court would help. I don't believe my witness will make a report to authorities. They've been intimidated by the defense."

He sighed. "As of now, I'm not sure how we'll proceed."

I nodded and said, "Yes, I'll await your instructions for my return."

The meeting ended, and I took a deep breath. I sat in miserable silence for five minutes until an email from James came in. I was sure it was my termination letter, but to my surprise, it only contained some questions about the case. I answered them quickly, with excessive detail. James then sent a curt email thanking me and I began to gather my belongings and pack them up for my return to D.C.

My phone vibrated and I glanced down to see a text had

come in from Josh asking how I was doing. I replied, "I just had a meeting with my boss. He didn't fire me, or not yet. Maybe he likes to watch anxiety eat me from the inside. Are you still down to hang tonight?"

He immediately replied, "What do you wanna do?"

I cheekily replied, "Just talk about rocks."

Josh replied with a smiley face and told me to come over after he finished work. Until then, I'd just have to survive being alone with my stomach-churning anxiety and spinning thoughts.

On the way to Josh's, I took a detour driving through downtown Pothos. I hadn't been down Main Street since the parade, and by today, it had returned to a regular downtown drag, and the modest storefronts were getting ready to close. The wide street ended at a roundabout, where a statue of General Stovall claimed center stage on the central island. I circled around it once, staring at the bronze figure that loomed so heavily over this town, then exited the roundabout and headed straight toward Ms. Honeypaw's house, having had enough reminders of General Stovall's apparently eternal presence for one day. Slowing as I approached, I craned my neck to see if she were on her porch, but there was no sign of her, and I didn't see any movement through her dirty windows. Her house seemed quiet from the outside. I wondered if, like an animal, she was hiding in her den out of fear. Perhaps the court appearance had truly spooked her. Maybe I'd never see her again, and maybe that wasn't a bad thing. In fact, if I were ordered to return to D.C. tomorrow, then I wouldn't stop at her house on my way out; I didn't need more verbal abuse before my long drive back to my old life.

There were so many questions that would be left when I departed Pothos...and one of the biggest was the one I'd least expected: What were my feelings for Josh?

TEN MINUTES LATER, I knocked on the side of Josh's screen door.

From somewhere inside came, "Dude, you know me. Just come in."

I opened the screen door. "Am I the dude you were expecting?"

Josh smiled when he saw me. "You are, but also Ri'Chard is stopping by to pick up something."

"Oh, Lil'Ricky is coming," I said.

Josh's head tilted. "How do you know to call him that?"

I said, "Ms. Honeypaw mentioned that's what he used to be called, before he got big."

Josh smiled fondly. "He'll always be Lil'Ricky in my heart."

I asked, genuinely puzzled, "Why does Ms. Honeypaw like him? She seems to like him a lot more than you, which is weird given that you're 'kinda cousins'."

Josh grinned, probably at my jab, but when he spoke, his voice was gentle. "I think she likes him because he never treated her as if she were different from anyone else. I know growing up in this town was hard on her. People have a lot to say about where she comes from, but he was always nice to her, even as a kid."

I paused for a moment, considering the depth of their relationship. I'd only known these people for a short time and couldn't begin to understand the complexities of their lives, just as they didn't know mine.

I decided it was time to begin talking with Josh about some of those complexities. I was still in semi-denial about what happened in court, but was also aware there was something shifting within me, and I was pretty sure Josh was responsible for it.

"Josh," I said, "I wanted to talk about what happened today."

"In court? Does it have something to do with your emotions?" he asked.

"Was it obvious?" I asked.

"I didn't notice." It was nice of him to lie.

I continued, "Yeah, I—"

Just then, I heard Ri'Chard's truck coming up the driveway. I said, "We'll talk about it later."

Ri'Chard opened the door. He looked surprised when he saw me. "Julie, hey. I didn't know you'd be here. How did things go with the boss?"

I clenched my teeth as if I could lock the subject away, and had to forcibly unclench them. "I don't know," I said tightly. "We had a meeting this afternoon, but he didn't fire me on the spot. I think he's waiting for me to return before firing me, because it would be cruel to leave me stranded here with no future."

Ri'Chard said, "Oh, come on, I think you'll easily find another job."

Josh chimed in, "Yeah, you're definitely smart. You'll get a job fast."

Confused by this show of support when I'd so obviously blown it. "Did you not see me in court today? I think you have too much confidence in my abilities."

Josh said, "Listen, we all have bad days, but you must have good ones, right? Remember when you were interrogating me? You seemed like a good lawyer then."

I smiled, remembering how I made him squirm. I said, "Yes, I do have my good days." I turned to Ri'Chard and asked, "What are you doing here?"

His eyes darted around the room while he said, elongating, "Well...." Suddenly, he caught a small bag that Josh tossed him. His eyes widened, quickly tucking it in his back pocket.

"What was that?" I asked.

Josh answered for him, "Weed. Lil'Ricky is picking some up."

"Oh," I said. "You're a stoner."

Ri'Chard looked mortified.

Josh answered again, "He's not a stoner. He only smokes occasionally, right?"

Ri'Chard stuttered, finally saying, "Sometimes I smoke, but it's not a habit."

"That's alright," I said, "I'm not judging."

Ri'Chard still looked cautious. He added, "Sometimes I like to get high and play my civilization building games. It makes it feel more real."

"Nice," I said, trying to sound like I knew his experience. "Sounds really cool."

Josh interrupted. "Dude, I forgot to tell you, we ran into Cassie the other night."

"Where?" Ri'Chard asked, frowning.

Josh said, "Remember that clothing store in the old shopping plaza? I was there with Julie. Cassie totally flipped when she saw us, and said some pretty nasty shit."

Ri'Chard shook his head. "I never liked her."

The devil in me couldn't help adding, "She was hot, though."

Josh shrugged. "Maybe. But now that I know the ugliness within her, she's no longer attractive to me."

I said to Josh, "It was the first of your exes I met. I can't wait to meet more." He turned a bit red, so I said to Ri'Chard, "Do you have a lot of exes running around?"

"No, not here. I didn't date much growing up around here," he said.

I asked, "Why?"

He looked at me and said, "These are not my people."

I tilted my head toward Josh. "Even him?"

Ri'Chard said, "He's family, so that's different."

I sat on the couch and asked, "So, you're just here for family?"

He nodded. "Basically..."

I asked Josh, "Why are you still here?"

He considered. "I don't know...I guess I never had a plan to leave. I mean, I dreamed about living in all these different places, like California, but time just went by fast, and I'm still here."

I said, "There's still time, you know. You could go back to school and study geology if that's what you're really passionate about. It would be difficult being the old guy on campus, but I know you could do it."

Josh smiled, but he didn't seem happy. "I don't think that's going to happen for me. I'm pretty terrible at chemistry and, well, geology is just a hobby, something that makes me happy."

I thought back to our first conversation at the Forbidden Palace, where I struggled to come up with any hobby I enjoyed. What would that look like for me? At this rate, I was going to be a disgraced lawyer, and I'd have to transition into a stay-at-home wife. I sighed. I still had yet to figure out what would make me "happy."

I wondered why Ri'Chard felt he needed to be here for "family". His loyalty was perplexing, since he didn't like his father. I never felt the same pull to be there for my family, even though there was the assumption I would take care of them in old age. It was always the burden of the daughter.

"Julie?" I heard Josh's voice and snapped out of my thoughts. He said, "Do you know when you're going back?"

"I don't, but I expect it will be soon." I looked at Josh and felt a deep breath escape.

Josh said nothing, but Ri'Chard said, "We'll miss you. Think you'll visit here again?"

I laughed a bit and said, "Depends on what parting gift I'm given. Little Miss Pothos put a dead fox in my car, but perhaps I'll get something else before I go."

"What?" Ri'Chard exclaimed. "What's going on with this dead fox?"

"Oh shit, I forgot to tell you," said Josh.

"I came to pick my car up, and there was a dead fox in it. Josh got the camera footage, and it showed Miss Pothos putting it in there."

"Who is Miss Pothos?" Ri'Chard asked.

Josh said, "She's Sally Wren's daughter."

"Oh, those people," said Ri'Chard.

"What do you mean by 'those people'?" I asked.

Ri'Chard said, "I mean, those are some strange people. They're very, very religious and not friendly. They don't like to mix with folks like me."

"Ah." I understood what he was saying, but it was obvious given the bloodline. "Sounds like a family that would raise a little psychopath. One of her parents must have chaperoned her to drop the fox off in my car?"

"She can probably drive," said Josh. "All the farm kids I grew up with were driving by 10 years old."

I didn't like the idea of her behind the wheel of a truck. I asked, "Where do they live anyway?"

Josh said, "They live on a farm that's next to the Stovall Plantation. I think it used to be a part of the plantation back in the day."

"And who owns the plantation now?" I inquired.

Ri'Chard said, "I heard someone from out of town bought it. They must have a lot of money because apparently, they're always flying in and out with helicopters. They're very secretive."

"Strange," I said. "So, the sex woods are off-limits now?"

Josh looked curious, "They're still there. Why do you ask?"

I said, "Because I want to go."

Ri'Chard grimaced. "I don't know. It's kind of creepy with all these ghost sightings."

"What ghost sightings?" I demanded to know.

Ri'Chard said, "The stuff people around town have been talking about. I don't know...ghosts are already scary enough, but a racist ghost is just another level for me."

"Come on, you don't actually believe that? Ms. Honeypaw was supposed to testify that she saw a group of men, including Jim Smoke, entering and exiting the courthouse on the evening of the fire. There's no fucking ghost."

"Holy shit," they both said in unison.

"Yeah, she was supposed to change my case, but everything went wrong."

Josh asked, "Do you actually believe Ms. Honeypaw saw this?"

"Why would she lie?" I asked. "Testifying would put her in danger, so I think she was actually telling the truth."

"Wow," said Ri'Chard. "That makes a lot of sense now. I'm really surprised she was willing to do this."

"Well, I did wager my Prada bag, which she took in the end."

Ri'Chard said, "That sounds more accurate."

Josh gave me a look. "You gave her your fancy bag? Is that why we had to go purse shopping?"

I looked guilty. "Yes. I know it was wrong, but I really thought I would win this case."

Ri'Chard said, "If all these people were in on the courthouse burning, then you were never meant to win that case."

"Yeah, you're right," I said. "I just thought if we could expose the truth, in front of the press and the people, it would become bigger than Pothos, however, that didn't happen. But, more importantly, it means that there is no ghost."

"Why do you want to go to those woods?" Ri'Chard asked. "You already know there's no ghost."

"Because I have a feeling something might be going on there," I said. "If everyone is afraid of this ghost, then I want to see if he's real. It will be fun, I promise."

Josh looked at Ri'Chard and asked, "Should we have fun?"

I said to Ri'Chard, "You can get high and play games tomorrow night."

He stared at me and smiled. "But what's your plan? You just want to go walk in the woods?"

I nodded toward Josh. "Ask him since he's the most familiar."

Josh said, "There is an old road that runs along it. We could go that way and check it out."

"What exactly are we checking out?" Ri'Chard asked.

"I'm just curious if we'll find something there. Are you thinking we'll actually run into a ghost?" I asked with a smile.

Ri'Chard said, "I just don't know what the goal of all this is."

"The goal," I said confidently, "is to satisfy my curiosity as a distraction since I'm entirely certain I'm going to be fired when I get back to D.C., if not before."

Josh looked at Ri'Chard and shrugged. "I think we should go. I haven't been out there in years."

Ri'Chard said, "Listen, if we get arrested, it will be a different experience for me than you two."

Josh and I looked at each other. I sighed and said, "He's right."

Josh nodded. Ri'Chard got up and said, "But you two have fun. Let me know if you see a ghost."

I GAVE my keys to Josh, saying, "Will you drive?"

I waited a few minutes before attempting my potentially disastrous personal conversation with him again. "So, I was talking earlier about court today."

Josh quickly glanced at me, then back to the road.

I thought about how much I should say. If I ruined it all now, we'd be trapped in a car together, and I'd never get to find out what was going on in these woods. However, I did want to tell him how I felt, but it never seemed like the right moment. I settled on a half-truth.

"I got emotional today seeing you guys there in court, supporting me. My parents didn't come to a lot of things when I was growing up, and I guess I got overwhelmed by you being there."

Josh reached out and grabbed my hand. "It's alright. I wouldn't have come if I'd known."

I protested, "No, no. It's fine. I didn't know it was something I'd get emotional about."

Josh said, "Sometimes I cry too. I'll be reminded by a memory about my sister, or who knows—it could be something else that's sensitive in me. It's just part of the human experience, I guess."

"Yeah," I said, a bit unsettled.

Josh pulled off a dirt road onto what seemed like the beginning of an old driveway. The headlights shone on a gate ahead that said "Private Property." We got out, and I noticed the air was heavy with humidity, so much that I almost felt as if I could chew it. Crickets chirped from the long grass at our feet, but they became quiet within the radius of each step. Josh had brought a headlamp, and I used my phone light to navigate by. We descended down the road into the old woods.

"Try to keep your lights on the ground, okay? We don't want to be obvious," Josh advised.

I wanted to shine my light everywhere because the woods

were filled with mysterious noises at night, some I assumed were owls calling across the trees. I heard things falling on the leaves, or perhaps running on them. I imagined eyes following us. I felt tense as we walked, wondering if this had been a bad idea after all. I quietly said, "This is terrifying. How could you have sex in these woods?"

"That's part of the fun. It gets your adrenaline going," said Josh.

"Did you do it in the trees?" I asked, wondering about the logistics.

"You'd bring a blanket, or just do it in the car. Are you asking for a reason?" He shot me a grin.

I said, "I'm just trying to distract myself from thinking about what creature is going to come out and eat us."

"There ain't anything much bigger than a fox out here," Josh said.

I finished his sentence, "...And if Miss Pothos can kill one, we should be able to hold our own."

"Exactly," he said in agreement.

I asked, "Do you think Miss Pothos is going to jump out and kill us? That might actually be the scariest creature in these woods."

"I didn't think of that. Now *that* would be fucking scary."

I imagined my flashlight reflecting off her sash and the kitchen knife she held in her hand, then shuddered at the thought.

After a few more minutes, Josh paused. We were close to a grouping of dilapidated buildings, and I peered through the dark, trying to make out what their purpose was. "What are these?" I asked him.

"I think they were the slave quarters," he answered.

"Whoa," I said, "I've never seen these before."

I looked at the modest wooden houses, no more than shacks,

really, and shone my light on their weathered boards. They'd been left to rot and slowly return to the woods. I felt a mixture of sadness and discomfort.

Josh said, "We're getting close to the main house now. We should keep our lights off."

A hint of light glimmered faintly through the thick cover of leaves, and we slowly crept forward toward the perimeter of the trees, ducking here and there to avoid getting swatted in the face by low-hanging limbs and Spanish moss. It seemed to take forever, but it was really only a few minutes before the woods opened and the white plantation house appeared in all its glory, the acreage around it only sparsely populated with trees.

It was majestic; a massive four-storied house with four Dorian columns rising two stories, supporting an upper veranda running the length of the main building. Below, a set of double wrought-iron staircases led up to the main veranda. The dark green, double-sided front door in the center looked big enough to drive a truck through with room to spare. Beneath the veranda was the foundational story, built of faded red brick. I suspected this was probably the old kitchen quarters, given the size of the chimney that stretched up from it. A pair of huge magnolia trees stood in front of two generous wings, and a perfectly manicured lawn punctuated with perfectly manicured bushes and flower beds spread from the tree perimeter, stretching all the way around the house and down to what might be a lake on the other side. It was too dark to tell if the shimmer I saw was water or an optical illusion.

I'd expected the same signs of neglect that we'd passed on our way in, but even from this distance, I could see that a vast amount of money had gone into its restoration. This was why there had been helicopters flying in and out—bringing in the architects and owners to inspect such a project. Money obviously wasn't a concern, and I wondered if the place now belonged to some big corporation or if the owners were just ludicrously wealthy. I knew the elites had been buying up the ranches and private land out West. Maybe that applied to these old Southern plantations as well.

Josh stopped and gestured toward the house, "So this is it. They probably have cameras around the house, so we shouldn't go any further. What exactly are you looking for?"

I swept my gaze around the fields that had blended into the night, and out of the corner of my eye, I caught the flickering of fire. I cautiously poked my head around a tree, holding onto its bark, and saw what looked like torches.

"Josh, do you see this?"

He stood right behind me, his body pressed against mine as he looked over my head.

He said, "It looks like some people are over there."

"We need to get closer," I said.

"We gotta be careful," said Josh. "Follow behind me, and watch where you step."

I trailed behind him, carefully pushing aside branches and stepping around entangling vines until we were close enough to make out a group of people illuminated by the flickering light of tiki torches. Josh crouched down and gestured for me to join him.

"What is going on?" I whispered, my mouth so close to Josh's ear I could feel the heat coming off his skin, carrying his unique and subtle scent, the faint aroma of palo santo which he often burned in his house.

"They're in the cemetery," Josh whispered back. "Every plantation had its own." He turned his head slightly and nodded toward a separate section to our right, where broken pieces of stone lay, stones that must have once been simple grave markers. "That must be where the slaves are buried, over there. I'm guessing that they're in the Stovall family plot."

I could make out Jim Smoke, Mr. Lyons, and Sally Wren, accompanied by a few other people I had never seen before. They were all dressed in the same red robes from the parade, as if they were in some kind of strange nighttime choir. The other Julie was reading from a book, but it didn't look like any hymnal I'd ever seen, and instead of singing, she was chanting. I couldn't understand a word, and I wasn't that religiously ignorant.

She turned to Mr. Lyons, and pointing at him with one long, bony forefinger, she commanded: "Get the chicken."

He immediately stepped backwards and straight into a tiki torch, jumping in surprise and receiving a chorus of yelps from his alarmed companions.

"Pay attention!" Jim Smoke barked sharply. "Don't forget what happened at the courthouse!"

The courthouse? My eyes narrowed as a new, intriguing possibility dawned. "Josh!" I hissed. "Do you think they might have burned down the courthouse *by mistake?*"

Josh didn't respond. He was laser-focused on the scene unfolding before us. Mr. Lyons grabbed a squawking chicken out of the box and held it up in front of his chest. The chicken struggled mightily in Mr. Lyons's hands, but he had a good grip over its midsection and wings.

"Be careful with it," Jim Smoke warned. "If it escapes, you'll have to go find it."

Sally Wren resumed reading more jumbled words aloud from her book again. She stopped speaking after another two minutes and a deep silence, broken only by the squawking chicken, fell and held there, as if the choir was holding its breath in anticipation of the choirmaster's signal. And sure enough, once more the hand with the long, bony forefinger stretched out and pointed at someone toward the back; then the palm rotated upward and beckoned that same someone to come forward. Cloaked bodies shuffled and moved aside, and out of the dark emerged Little Miss Pothos in her own red choir robe, cut down to size, and a bright shade of cherry rather than a burgundy red. She headed straight toward the tomb, looking like a cherub with her halo of pale blonde hair backlit by the tiki torches. The other Julie said, "You ready, sweetie?"

Little Miss Pothos nodded at her mom, reached down and picked up a small bowl that had been resting on the top of the tomb. She held it out in front of her, walked over to Mr. Lyons, and put the bowl down at his feet. Then they both dropped to their knees, Mr. Lyons struggling with the chicken. Miss Pothos reached out with her left hand to grab the chicken's head and pulled straight. The chicken went quiet.

With her right hand, Miss Pothos began to pluck feathers from its neck, her glittery red nail polish sparkling in the torch-light. After a few plucks, she pulled a small knife out from her robe. She looked over at her mother who nodded, then returned her focus to the chicken and placed the tip of the knife against the featherless flesh. She sliced once, a shallow cut. The chicken began to buck again in Mr. Lyons' hand as its blood spilled into the bowl.

Sally Wren said, "Cut it a bit more deeply; we need all the blood."

Miss Pothos jiggled the knife into the neck of the trembling chicken. This time blood gushed from the wound, and when the chicken had bled out and became still, Mr. Lyons dropped it on the ground.

I grimaced. "Jesus Christ, that child must be homeschooled."

Josh whispered, "I think we should go; this is creepy."

"No, we need to see what happens," I protested. Frankly, nothing could have dragged me away at this point.

Miss Pothos handed her mother the bowl of blood, which her mother escorted back to the top of the tomb with the same pomp as her daughter had delivered it. Sally Wren gathered the book off of the tomb and handed it to her daughter to hold open for her. She dipped a broad paintbrush into the blood, and began to draw something on the top of the tomb. She glanced at the book and continued painting.

I murmured, "What do you think she's looking at?"

Josh soundlessly shook his head, his brow heavily furrowed. He was clearly not cut out for this.

Sally Wren dipped her brush again and made some more strokes, then peered at the book. This continued until she set her brush in the bowl and said, "It's done."

Carefully taking the book from Miss Pothos, she closed it. Then she nodded and said, "We've completed the ceremony for tonight."

Everyone held their arms out with balled fists and put their right hand on top of their left. They tapped them together twice before alternating, saying, "Our country, our culture, never surrendered, and forever alive."

They bowed their heads, then looked up at each other.

Jim Smoke said, "Good job, everyone. I'm glad tonight went off without a hitch."

"We're outside," said Mr. Lyons, "So it's not like anything would have caught on fire."

"Well, I'm not the one who didn't tie up the torch correctly," said Jim Smoke.

Mr. Lyons grumbled to himself, and everyone began packing up. Jim Smoke grabbed the chicken and tossed it into the woods in our direction. It landed a few feet in front of us, its bloodied neck dangling limply. We both froze.

"Hey! I was going to eat that," Sally Wren grumbled.

"Oh shit, my bad," said Mr. Smoke. "Do you want me to go get it?"

"Forget it," said Sally Wren. "It's too much work to clean it tonight."

I felt Josh breathe a sigh of relief. After the group extinguished the torches, they walked back toward the main house. Josh said, “We need to go.”

I put my hand on his shoulder. “Hold on, I want to go look at the cemetery.”

“Julie, no. It’s too risky.”

I ignored him and lifted into a low crouch. I crept along the woods for about thirty feet before I was close enough to the cemetery to get a good idea of its layout. It was small, holding about nine or so tombstones.

Looking to my right, I could see the departing headlights of cars across the drive lined with immense live oaks. Josh appeared behind me. “I think everyone has gone now,” he said.

I darted out from my cover and opened the creaking iron gate, stepping inside. I glanced around at the headstones, but I could barely make out “Stovall”, let alone the given names of various family members. I walked over to the large standing tomb, the one that the ‘ceremony’ had been conducted on, and turned on the phone light.

Josh quickly said, “Don’t use that. Just use your screen light.” I switched the light off and held up my phone screen. I looked at the top of the tomb. Parts of the fresh chicken blood hadn’t yet dried, and they glimmered as I shone my light on it. The other Julie had drawn some sort of symbol on the tomb, a complicated intersection of lines and circles, crosses, and bizarre shapes.

“What is this?” I asked, baffled. I’d never seen anything like it.

“I don’t know…” he replied softly, adding cautiously, “As crazy as it seems, it looks like it could be some sort of spell.”

“What is not crazy about any of this?” I said, taking a picture for reference later.

“Hey! Your flash!” Josh shook his head.

I mumbled “Sorry,” and carefully moved my phone screen

light toward the tombstone, but it was so worn away with age I could only read bits of the inscription:

...A MAN with the ultimate courage, a rare breed of instinct and brilliance...He fought valiantly for our Confederacy...Trust in God and the wisdom of the scripture...

...HERE LIES General Edward Wilbur Stovall.

13

I was too wound up to sleep. The theater we'd witnessed continued to replay in my mind. Josh and I had walked back to the car in near silence. Once the woods had vanished from the rearview mirror, he asked, "You wanna spend the night?"

I said, "Um, I didn't bring anything. I don't have a toothbrush or clothing."

"I have an extra toothbrush, and you can borrow some of my clothes… I'm just creeped out and don't want to sleep alone."

There I was, in his bed. I had on a t-shirt with a Harley-Davidson logo on it, and borrowed some of his boxers to sleep in. He didn't put the moves on me tonight. Instead, in bed, he grabbed my hand and held it as he fell asleep. Eventually, his hand fell out of mine as he shifted, and I turned to look at him. This poor man trusted me enough to let me sleep in his bed, yet he really didn't know who I was. Was he this comfortable with most women, or was I special? Either answer would hurt me in some way.

I turned to the ceiling and recounted the ceremony we witnessed tonight. If the courthouse was burned down accidentally, then what were they doing there in the first place? I'd been convinced it was intentional as it fit perfectly with their plan to throw the Black voters off the rolls, but perhaps it was a convenient accident. I thought about this until sleep turned all my worries black.

"JULIE, JULIE, HEY, WAKE UP." I awoke to Josh rubbing my arm. He said, "It's 7 a.m."

I was groggy and sat up, rubbing my eyes. He said, "I didn't know if you had to work today."

I gave him a polite smile. "Probably not, but I should be up anyway. Thank you. Do you have coffee?"

Josh said, "Sorry, no. I don't drink anything with caffeine, only herbal tea. An ex made me quit coffee, and it's been good for me."

"I'm glad, but I have to go get coffee." I got up and got dressed, giving my teeth a quick brush.

"Are you leaving now?"

"Yep, I really need to go get coffee."

I hugged him goodbye and left quickly, choosing to head to the diner for a nostalgic breakfast. My brain felt empty without the caffeine kick. I needed the constant whirring of thoughts, but my sole focus was getting to the diner and finding a spot where I wouldn't have to parallel park in.

I found a booth and ordered the healthiest item on the menu, so seldom selected that the waitress had to squint at the menu before she believed me that it was actually available.

I took a sip of weak coffee from the weathered diner mug and looked at my phone to see an email from James. My stomach dropped. The subject said, "Please Review," and I opened it expecting to be reviewing my termination letter. Instead, there was a link to the opinion page of a national newspaper. The title read "Busting Oppression and Ghosts." I started to read the first sentence when I sensed someone's presence next to me. I looked up to see Jim Smoke standing next to my table. "Ms. Chen," he said cheerfully, "I'm dreadfully sorry you lost your case. Is this your farewell party?"

"Yes, did you RSVP?"

He laughed. "I would love to join, but I'm afraid my wife would find it remiss of me to dine alone with another woman. Do let me know when the others come, and I'll be sure to drop by."

"Wonderful, and do let your wife know there's not a chance in hell I would ever sleep with you." I added a wink as a flourish.

He scowled as he skulked away. I noticed the diner door open, seeing Mr. Lyons walk in and look around. *The gang of witches must be gathering for breakfast,* I thought as I waved to him, catching his attention. As he started to walk over to me, I realized I had no plan for what to say to him.

"Miss Julie, nice to see you here," he said.

I asked him, "Do you care to join me? It's quite upsetting for a woman to dine alone."

He stuttered and looked around the diner for any excuse to not sit with me. I said, "Just sit for a minute and share a coffee with me." He sighed and slid into my booth.

I said, "Mr. Lyons, sadly, I'll be departing this town by the upcoming weekend."

He nodded. "Yes, I heard your case was dismissed through the great clarity of our town's judicial process."

"Right, that is true, but I'm more concerned with the unsolved crimes seemingly related to this case."

He looked at me sternly. "You mean the reprisals of General Stovall?"

"Sure, those 'reprisals.' Do you really and truly think it's the ghost, or are you just trying to fuck with me?" I asked him.

"Miss Julie, I ain't lyin'. The ghost is real." The waitress came over and gave him a cup of coffee, which he tipped a few packets of sugar and creamer into.

I asked, "How can I meet him then? I want to check if he's the reason I'm probably going to get fired for losing this case."

"The ghost of General Stovall is benevolent. You'll see him when he wants you to," said Mr. Lyons cryptically.

"So, in your opinion, there's no way a living person could have committed these crimes?"

"I think this is only the beginning until the balance of this town, and nation, is restored, then his spirit can rest comfortably."

I felt like this conversation was filled with White nationalist dog whistles that were going over my head. Was there actually a ghost? Was this a movement? Was my theory about everything being controlled by a cabal of men blowing each other in bad wigs correct? I didn't think Mr. Lyons would take too kindly to such a suggestion. I didn't know what strings I was tugging at, other than trying to make sense of why a chicken was bled out over a pile of bones.

Mr. Lyons looked mightily pleased with himself. "Do you have any more questions about General Stovall?"

I had many questions. I almost wanted to confess that I saw them last night and blow my cover because I'd be leaving soon, but I decided to feign ignorance.

I could only manage, "What does the ghost look like? Is the ghost a white, see-through figure? Does he look like Casper?"

Mr. Lyons stood and took his coffee. He looked at me and said, "Miss Julie, all ghosts are white." I swore he smiled a bit before he turned and headed to a different booth in the diner.

I took a deep breath and went back to looking at my phone. I scanned James' opinion piece until I came to a spot that made me choke on my coffee. James had written, "Another incident of intimidation was the slaying of a Golden Retriever, which was hung outside the temporary courthouse for all in the town to see, a savage act of barbarity by those seeking to keep lawful citizens from voting."

I reread the sentence multiple times in confusion, wondering what the fuck James was thinking writing this, then panic set in. I hurriedly went to my emails, adrenaline coursing as I found the email I sent yesterday. I read through all the details I sent him about the case, stopping at one point: *A Golden Retriever was hung and gutted outside the temporary courthouse in an act of intimidation.*

I put my hands to my forehead and said countless *fucks* inside my head. In the haze of confusion and embarrassment yesterday, my wires must have been crossed. I had joked with Sasha before the hearing about people caring more if a dog was killed, and I accidentally typed it in my haste to perform for James. My forehead went lower in my hands. I was definitely going to be fired now.

The waitress put down my egg white omelette, which I stared at in disgust. I had to tell James, and I began to write an email, but something in me made me second-guess myself. *Does it really matter? No one cares about this town or case anyway...* This side of me that I had become so familiar with began to brush over my worries, and perhaps that side was right. Like with Josh, these men were living under an illusion I temporarily created, but it wasn't an intentionally evil one. I had the best intentions, but they got fucked up along the way. I decided to hold off on telling James for now.

I turned over my phone and stared out at the people in the diner. Mr. Lyons was huddled with Jim Smoke and a few others I recognized from the cemetery last night. They seemed to be ensconced in a conversation, probably plotting their next fowl offering. *They are the evil ones hiding things*, I told myself, *not me.*

. . .

By midday James's op-ed had gone viral. He was invited onto some liberal cable news show to talk about it later in the evening. James was ecstatic; he was a fame whore, but who in D.C. wasn't? *Too late now*, I thought, and I felt that a miniature pony and a Golden Retriever were close enough that the same segment of outraged people probably had both running around their farmsteads.

I spent the afternoon on and off the phone with James, preparing him for his interview, editing and re-editing points of the case so they'd be TV-ready, bite-sized segments.

I said, "Maybe don't mention that animal killing though, because it really distracts from the political elements of the case."

"Are you kidding me?" he said, incredulously. "When my wife read about what happened to that poor dog, she started weeping. This is going to win us this case." Not only was I going to get fired, but I was also going to betray weeping White women everywhere.

Caught up in the flurry, I forgot to text Josh back from his earlier inquiry as to whether I got coffee.

I texted, "Sorry for leaving so suddenly. I just have a thing for coffee in the morning."

He told me it was fine and asked if we could hang out again tonight. I wondered if he was still spooked. I asked if he had cable, which he didn't, so I invited him to come to my hotel because I needed to witness the shitshow I created in real time.

Later, I paced around my hotel room until I was interrupted by a knock on the door. I opened it to see Josh holding a bag of takeout. I welcomed him, and he looked around my suite.

"Nice. You got a sitting area and a kitchen." He angled his head to take in the two rooms.

"This is home. It feels like I've been here for so long that I should start to decorate."

"I could lend you a few decorative rocks if you like. I have a cool celestite if you want."

"I think I'll decline for now. I'm still not sure when my boss is going to order me to come back."

Josh looked disappointed for just a moment, then said, "Well, hey, if your boss is on TV talking about the case, maybe you'll get to stay for a while."

I grimaced. "Yeah... About that. I might have fucked up again." I paused, took a breath, and said, "I accidentally told my boss that a Golden Retriever was killed instead of a pony."

Josh looked confused. "How did that happen?"

"Someone from a voting rights organization was at the courthouse, and we were talking about dogs being slayed instead." Josh looked more confused. "It was a joke. Really, as in 'people would care more if a dog had been gutted outside the courthouse' sort of thing. It was funny at the moment... you had to have been there. Anyway, after I lost, I emailed my boss and accidentally gave him the wrong information."

"Whoa, damn... and you didn't want to tell him the truth?" Josh asked.

I said, "I was worried that if I wasn't already fired, I definitely would be after this."

Josh shook his head and laughed a little. "Julie, it's funny but also kinda fucked up. You shouldn't lie to him like that because it's just going to snowball."

I dismissed his concern. "I think it will be fine. Are you horrified by my behavior?"

Josh said, "No, as I said, it's funny."

I felt myself getting defensive, but Josh was right; my lie

could snowball, and I was already watching it become bigger than any of us could stop.

"It was a mistake," he added, seeing my dubious expression. "And I could see why you got scared to say anything."

Relaxing again, I said something I never thought I would, "I wish you'd been here to talk me through this earlier. Maybe I would have come clean."

"I don't know. The truth, even though it's hard at first, is the easier way. But I think you'll find the right time. If your boss is on the news, maybe that's a good thing?"

I sighed. "I guess. Should we eat?"

I grabbed some plates from the cupboard and unpacked the food, carefully checking the time on my phone. "All this TV stuff really distracted me from what happened last night."

Surprised, Josh said, "Oh, I almost forgot." He pulled out a bundle of dried herbs, and held it up. "I got in touch with an old girlfriend today who is a witch, but a good one. I don't know what we saw last night, but in case it was Satanic, we should sage ourselves."

I reluctantly agreed. "Are there smoke alarms?" We looked up at the popcorn ceiling and didn't see any we could recognize. We opened the windows, and Josh lit the bundle. As I held my arms out and Josh swirled the acrid-smelling sage around me, I said, "Aren't you a little nervous about having a witch for an ex?"

Josh's eyebrows furrowed, "No, she's not that kind of person."

"Why did you break up?"

He shrugged one shoulder. "She had to move, and I wasn't ready to go. I was still dealing with my sister and stuff."

I nodded. "It's never too late, unless she's found a hotter mechanic."

He laughed a little. "Sometimes I think about it, but I wouldn't know what to say. She's really smart, like you, and maybe she wants a guy she can talk to stuff about."

"What stuff?"

"You know, like politics or history. I just stick to the stuff I like."

Josh was selling himself short. Though he didn't possess the intellectual prowess that Matthew had, his care and quiet approach spoke more to me than any endless monologue on post Cold War hegemony.

"Josh, you have a lot to offer. If she liked you in the first place, then why wouldn't she now?" I could feel part of me becoming jealous for suggesting he pursue another woman, but it would be delightful for Josh to end up with her quickly so I could avoid having to confess my complications.

He said, "People change. She might not like me now."

"Yes, people do change," I echoed.

Josh said, "I never talk about this with anyone, though. I guess I'm just really comfortable with you."

As he focused on enveloping my body in smoke, I felt my eyes water again and my lips tense. I put up a hand to wipe my eye.

"Are you alright?" Josh asked.

"Yes," I said, "I think it's just the smoke. It's making my eyes tear up."

He apologized and quickly stepped away, swirling the smoke around himself.

I wiped my eyes again and looked at my phone. The news segment would begin soon.

AFTER DINNER, Josh and I settled on the couch. My foot shook in anticipation, while Josh looked at something on his phone. Finally, after a commercial break, the graphic introducing the show came on. The host was a blazered brunette with a fast cadence and pretty good rejoinders. She introduced James and asked him to explain the case, which he presented just as we'd rehearsed. Winding up, he said, "I think the most shocking of the attempts to intimidate the people of this town was the tragic murder of a Golden Retriever named 'Sunny'."

A generic picture of a Golden Retriever came on the screen with its name underneath.

I said in shock, "He gave it a name."

James continued, "...And the strangest thing is that all this is being blamed on the ghost of a Confederate General."

I slunk into the couch and exclaimed, "Oh fuck."

The host raised her eyebrows. "People are blaming a *ghost* for this depraved behavior?"

"It's not an excuse we take seriously, trust me," James said quickly, "But this town loves their dear leaders. They still have a statue of the General prominently displayed."

The host said, "I'm going home tonight and holding my dog. I can't believe these sick individuals are roaming free. It's so sad that this is still a problem in backwards American towns like this. Stay safe, and I hope the ghost doesn't get your puppy!" In about eight minutes the segment was done and cut to commercial. As much of a prick James could be, he certainly knew how to work the television angle. And I really had fucked up.

I sat silently on the couch, trying to control the anxiety washing coldly through my entire body. "I didn't expect this to become a national tragedy," I finally managed to say in a small voice. I numbly felt Josh put his arm around me.

He pulled me close against his side. "Listen, your secret will remain safe with me," he murmured against my hair. "I won't tell anyone."

I leaned into his shoulder as my breathing gradually slowed. "Thank you. I'm going to be haunted in my dreams by the face of 'Sunny' tonight."

"Are you scared of having nightmares?" he asked. "Do you want me to spend the night?"

I tilted my head to look up at him, and said, "You'll have to borrow my clothes, though."

He grinned. "I think I'll look pretty good in your underwear."

I sat up and raised an eyebrow. "Challenge accepted."

Grateful for a distraction, I went to my room and grabbed a clean pair of the sexiest underwear I could find, red lace with a modest cut, and tossed them to Josh.

"Here you go. I hope they fit."

Josh picked them up and inspected them. He looked at me and said, "You really want me to put these on?"

I decided to needle him. "I knew you weren't enough of a man to do it."

That got him. He laughed a little at the insult, "Not enough of a man? Oh, I'll show you how much of a man I am."

"Then go change in the bathroom. I want to be surprised."

Various lewd remarks about how sexy he was going to look floated out from the bathroom while he changed. After a couple of minutes his head poked around the side of the door. "Are you ready?" he asked with delicious confidence.

"I'm waiting," I said while trying to maintain a straight face, amused, but at the same time a little titillated by the idea of Josh wearing my lingerie.

He confidently walked out, and my breath caught in my throat. I started at his feet, then his knees, then my gaze wandered up past the thigh muscles that flexed with every step and settled on the red scrap of lace that covered his groin. The fabric of the underwear hugged his form tightly, and as he stood in front of me, he turned in a circle to give me the full display. My panties cut halfway down his plump ass cheeks, and I stared in a combination of jealousy and arousal, saying, "Your ass looks better in my underwear than mine does."

"You think?" He tried to glance over his shoulder to see his ass, then turned back to face me, his flaccid penis straining at the red lace. Tonight, it didn't look intimidating. Perhaps it was the effect of the underwear, but his penis actually looked friendly, familiar. *Is that my D?*

I rose from the sofa and walked over to Josh. I stood in front of him and kissed him. He kissed me back, and my hands traced his back and down to his butt, which I squeezed. I put my hand on his penis, which I felt slowly grow in anticipation.

This is my D. I lightly brushed it, then said to Josh, "I'm going to try something, but tell me immediately if you're uncomfortable, okay?" Josh nodded.

I slowly got down on my knees and brushed my hand along his stomach, down his thighs, and over his D. *I have to own his D.* I brushed it through the synthetic lace. *I have to control the D.* I slowly pulled down my underwear, watching as his D sprang free. I put it to my lips and kissed it lightly. *I can't let the D control me.* I took him into my mouth, using all the advice Keli gave me. As I brought him in and out, I kept repeating my mantras, and at no point did I feel afraid of the D.

I heard Josh moan. I stopped and looked up, asking, "Are you okay?"

"Yeah, it's good," said Josh.

"It's not uncomfortable? It feels nice?" I asked.

"Yeah, actually, it feels great. How did you learn this?" He asked.

"The Coochie Coach," I said with a wink.

I went back to owning Josh's D while my fingers were intertwined with the sides of my underwear. After a bit, Josh suggested we move to the couch. He laid me down and kissed me. He asked, "What do you want me to do?"

"Hmmm." I considered this tantalizing question.

"Do you want me to go down on you?"

I replied, "Do you want to go down on me?"

He kissed my neck, then helped me out of my shirt, feathering light kisses down my chest before stopping at the waist of my pants.

"Of course. What's the secret code?" he asked.

"Sunny," I said.

Josh laughed and, as he slid them down, made me forget all the lies that had brought me to this moment.

14

"Hey, I'm back home. I saw your boss's segment last night. Things are going well?"

I read Matthew's perfectly sterile text and thought about how I should respond. I couldn't believe I'd spent so many years developing a relationship with someone that felt more professional than romantic. Seeing his message made my mind slip into the context of responding to a colleague, rather than a lover. Maybe this was how relationships age, but we never had that hot and heavy phase. It was always beige, at least compared to last night.

Josh was so open with his lust. He was an effortless lover, with just enough of a naughty side to intrigue my own that seemed so buried inside. I thought of the way he took off my underwear and held it to his face. I think if I shoved my used underwear in Matthew's face, he'd start sputtering as if he were being waterboarded.

Yet, reading this text felt like an out-of-body experience. It was the sensation of looking at my life on a screen, thinking it was just a character, then having this sinking realization that it was, indeed, *my* life. I felt like two separate beings: D.C. Julie and the present Julie. I just hoped the reunification would be peaceful.

I looked up the town and saw a flurry of articles on the case, inspired by James's article and appearance on TV. Pothos was going viral, and there was even a protest scheduled for tomorrow. I replied to Matthew, then logged on for a hastily called morning work meeting.

Again, I was in the awkward position of being on the screen in front of a room of colleagues. I saw Yale Law and was reminded of my sexless, uptight past life, and immediately felt pity for her. Why did she feel the need to try so hard to impress men? I suddenly wanted to invite her for a drink and try to understand her inferiority complex.

James arrived and began. "Good morning, everyone. I decided to write an op-ed piece regarding Ms. Chen's case, and to my great astonishment, it went viral, generating a lot of interest regarding the case." I heard someone clapping and realized Yale Law started applauding James. She was disinvited from drinks.

He continued, "That's not necessary, but thank you. I'm planning on extending Ms. Chen's stay there for another week to see if we can capitalize on the momentum generated by this. I'd also like to send two associates to assist her."

I was deeply comfortable being alone here, and the last thing I wanted was people from work to be around. I wish James had discussed this with me before announcing it in the meeting. While this was running through my head, I almost missed his announcement of the two associates: Yale Law and Useless Idiot. I remained stone-faced while I screamed on the inside.

He continued, "They'll be arriving tomorrow afternoon, so please make sure to get them up to speed. This case is evolving, so we'll see what legal actions we can pursue in a higher court."

The meeting went on for a while longer, but I was mentally

checked out. That feeling of two distinct Julies was comfortable. It felt organized. That partition was still intact, and with my colleagues arriving, that safety would disappear.

I looked down at my phone to see a text from Ri'Chard saying, "Hey, just checking in..." I scrolled up to see he had texted yesterday and late the evening before, asking about our time in the woods. He obviously was a worrier.

I apologized and explained that I'd been busy with work. He texted back, "It's fine. Josh already told me about the chicken in the woods. What is the Sunny thing by the way? I missed that."

I didn't want to ask how he knew about that. In fact, I needed to distract myself from all this and focus on what happened the night before last. I asked Ri'Chard if he was free later, and when he confirmed, I texted him, "Meet me at Ms. Honeypaw's house."

I HADN'T SEEN Ms. Honeypaw since our day in court. I wasn't sure how to approach her: as a thief, a friend, or a psychic. She was all those things in one way or another. I waited on the sidewalk, and at almost the same time, Josh and Ri'Chard's trucks pulled in and parked behind my Corolla.

They walked over to me, and all three of us gathered on the sidewalk in front of the house.

I said, "Game plan: Ri'Chard goes up, Josh and I hide off to the side, he gets her to open the door, then we all go in, agreed?"

Josh looked confused. "Why don't we just ask her if we can all come in?"

Ri'Chard said, "I'm not going to trick Ms. Honeypaw. If she has to shoot through me to get to you, I wouldn't put it past her."

I said, "Fine, but you're still standing in front, okay?"

Ri'Chard knocked while we all simultaneously took deep breaths and waited. After half a minute, Ri'Chard knocked again. Still no answer.

Suddenly, we heard the steps creaking behind us. I turned and was surprised to see Ms. Honeypaw walking up the steps, carrying my Prada bag on her shoulder. She looked right through me and instead glanced down to fish her keys out of her purse.

I said, "Hi, I'd really like to talk with you about something Josh and I saw...."

She didn't acknowledge me, or the other guys. She just put her keys in the door and started to turn the lock.

I glared at her back. "Excuse me, what's going on? Why aren't you talking to me?"

She opened the door, stepped inside, and slammed it shut, locking it behind her.

I turned to stare at Josh and Ri'Chard. They both looked uncomfortable and confused. "Is she giving me the silent treatment?" I asked in disbelief.

"Seems like it," said Josh. "You must have really pissed her off."

"Pissed *her* off? She was the one who robbed me!"

I looked at Ri'Chard. "She likes you. Can you talk to her?"

Ri'Chard looked exasperated. "I don't know...she seems to be in one of her moods. I think you have to wait for her to calm down."

I was mad, and this couldn't wait. I noticed a window cracked open a few inches and went over to it. I bent down, put my face to the crack, and screamed, "Hello! Hello! I've got some Chinese medicinal cream to help with your balding ass! You hear that? I called you a bald bitch!"

I stood up and looked at the boys. They both looked back at me with widened eyes as if questioning my sanity. I said, "Sometimes you can't get through to people if you try to be nice, you know what I mean?"

We stood in front of the door, and relatively soon, I could

make out the outline of Ms. Honeypaw as she stormed toward us. All we had to do was talk to her, so I had moderate confidence my plan would work—until Ms. Honeypaw flung the door open and aimed a shotgun at me.

Before I could react, Ri'Chard grabbed the business end and pushed it down, maneuvering the gun from her hands. It had only been pointed at me for less than a second, but it was enough to shut me up.

Ms. Honeypaw's eyes blazed with fury. "Give it back," she said with a seething tone. "I got a barking bitch I need to put down."

Ri'Chard said, in a voice so soft and calm he might have been settling a tantruming child, "We're not doing this today. No ma'am."

"Listen, we're not here to cause problems," Josh added, echoing Ri'Chard's placating tone. "We're here because Julie and I saw something strange at the Stovall Plantation the other night, and we want to talk to you about it."

Ms. Honeypaw crossed her arms over her bosom. "I'll talk to you, but this teriyaki-stick-bitch is staying outside." She turned to Josh and, with an exasperated tone, said, "I can't believe you're fucking someone with no ass. I thought I taught you better."

Ri'Chard cleared his throat. "Listen, Josh told me what happened earlier, and I think you need to hear about it. Please, it's important."

She looked at Ri'Chard. "Fine, but if this is a waste of my time, then I get my gun back, and I get to clap her bony ass." She shot me a look of disgust before turning on her heel and marching back into the house.

Ri'Chard followed her in. Josh rubbed the back of his neck hard, then dropped his hand and said only, "Yup. She's in a mood today."

I trailed after him in silence. Ms. Honeypaw led us to a

sitting room that contained an old couch and some chairs. This room was characteristically cluttered, with multiple clashing blankets on the couch and piles of old newspapers and magazines crowding the edges of the room and spilling into every corner. Ri'Chard leaned the shotgun safely against the wall next to the door and sat in one of the chairs. I pushed some blankets to the side and took a seat on the badly-sprung couch with Josh, while Ms. Honeypaw lowered herself into a faded blue velvet armchair and glared at me.

I glared steadily back and finally said, because no one else was jumping in, "What's your problem with me?"

"Problem?" Ms. Honeypaw planted her clenched fists on her ample thighs and leaned over them as if she was keeping them from stretching across the room and wrapping around my neck. "My problem is that your lying ass told me that this was going to be the case of the century, that the media was going to be all over it, so I risked my safety for you. Now these people know I've been communicating with you, and I'm trying to un-communicate with you and banish your basic-name-demon-ass from my life. That's my problem."

I shrugged and said, "To be fair, now the media is all over the case."

Ms. Honeypaw looked unimpressed. She turned to Josh and said impatiently, "Since you're here to tell me something, let's hear it."

"Right," said Josh. "I suppose the best place to begin is a couple of nights ago when Julie and I decided to go into the woods at the Stovall Plantation. She was curious about what was happening near the old house."

Ms. Honeypaw interrupted, shooting a foul look at me. "See, now you got Josh risking his safety."

I said in self-defense, "The only threat was a ghost that

supposedly lives in the woods, and since ghosts aren't real, I didn't think it was risky."

Ms. Honeypaw snorted. "Ghosts are real, you ignorant bitch."

I rolled my eyes.

Josh ignored us both. "And when we snuck closer to the house and saw a group of people—"

I interjected, "The same ones you saw coming out of the courthouse." Ms. Honeypaw glared at me again, then went back to looking at Josh.

He said, "Yes, they were performing some kind of bizarre ceremony in the cemetery at the grave of General Stovall. Sally Wren was reading something from a book, then her creepy daughter sacrificed a chicken, and Sally Wren used the blood to draw some kind of symbols or something on the tombstone. Julie took a photo. She can show you on her phone."

Ms. Honeypaw remained quiet, gazing down at her hands, now spread flat and lying still on her lap. After a long moment, she spoke. "What was Sally Wren reading?"

I said, "We couldn't hear very well, but the little we did catch was incoherent. There must have been about eleven of them, and they were all dressed in red robes."

"And you're sure it was the grave of the General?" Ms. Honeypaw asked sharply.

Josh nodded. "Yes. We went and checked after they left to make sure."

"Ms. Honeypaw, do you have any idea what they might have been doing?" I asked. "I mean, could it have been some kind of archaic memorial service for the General?"

Ms. Honeypaw scoffed. "How the fuck am I supposed to know? You can't even tell me what they were saying, or what book they were reading from. Show me the picture."

I held out my phone and Ri'Chard took it from me and gave it to Ms. Honeypaw.

She studied the photo, squinting at it, then handed it back to Ri'Chard with a wave of dismissal. "I don't know what this shit is. I only like to use cards and spirits. This is beyond my expertise."

I exhaled in exasperation, but then the absurdity of the situation suddenly struck me, and the sigh turned into a chuckle and then an outright laugh.

"What's so funny?" Ms. Honeypaw demanded, suddenly looking more curious than annoyed.

I smiled wryly. "Last night I heard Jim Smoke giving Mr. Lyons shit for knocking down a tiki torch and lighting the whole courthouse on fire."

Ms. Honeypaw's face broke into a broad smile that matched my own. "That makes sense," she said, slapping her knees with her broad palms. "You should have seen the way they were running out of that building like the husband came home and caught them cheating." Her face settled into more familiar lines as her smile slowly faded and she fixed me with a hard gaze. "Just because you made me laugh doesn't mean I'm not gonna make you cry."

Josh pressed his mouth into a tight line as if he was trying not to laugh, but Ri'Chard looked anything but amused. "I think we're done here," he said, running both hands over the back of his head. "This isn't going anywhere."

Ms. Honeypaw released a deep breath and nodded to herself, as if she'd come to a difficult decision. "Wait," she said tightly, her expression grim. "Just hold your goddamn horses and give me a moment. This is troubling; I can feel it. Those idiots are definitely disturbing the spirits somehow. I've been feeling it for a while now, that darkness is on the horizon."

Ri'Chard asked, "What do you mean? What's being disturbed?"

Ms. Honeypaw looked at him sideways. "It's just what I've been hearing from the other side. That something has been stirring up shit in this town. At first I thought it was Miss Prada's uppity ass, but I realized that she hasn't got a fucking clue about what's really going on."

"What's really going on then?" I asked, intrigued by this new slant, not that I thought for a minute Ms. Honeypaw's 'other side' had anything to do with it. "I understand there's a conspiracy amongst the government in this town; that's been proven. It seems they've formed an organized group, and this was one of their...their meetings. That's probably it."

Ms. Honeypaw looked at me and said, "Sounds like you solved the case then. So go on, bring this to court and work your lawyer magic. Show us all what a smart bitch you are. But try not to cry and embarrass yourself in front of everyone. Can you do that?"

I was exhausted from her endless shit. I understood she was upset, but her dedication to obstinacy was wearing my patience thin. "Fine, I'm leaving," I said. "I might not have a clue as to what's really going on, but it sounds like you don't have the faintest idea either."

I didn't even look at Josh and Ri'Chard. I stood up and began to walk out, then paused in the doorway and turned back for a final shot. "Have fun gossiping about me with the spirits."

Ms. Honeypaw pretended to ignore me and looked at her nails. She said to the guys, "This is your moment to choose sides. Are you Team Yellow or are you Team Black?"

Ri'Chard shook his head. "I'm not choosing sides. You both need to work out your differences like adults." He and Josh stood in tandem and headed toward the door.

Ms. Honeypaw called to Josh, "I know Jackie Chen has been

swinging your nunchucks, but you too?" She gestured toward Ri'Chard. "I thought at least you would be on my team." She crossed her arms and haughtily said, "Fine. Go, but mark my words, that bitch *will* get you in trouble."

The guys walked out, but Josh paused for a moment and said, "You know, if we worked together, we could be a force."

Ms. Honeypaw and I both let out distinct snorts, immediately dismissing the idea. It was kindhearted of Josh, but he was an optimist rather than a realist. There was no way Ms. Honeypaw and I would be working together.

When we got out to the sidewalk, I said, "Sorry for wasting your time. She's obviously not going to be cooperating anytime soon."

Ri'Chard agreed. "Yeah, something is up with her. Maybe she really is worried about retribution. Do you think she's in danger?"

I said, "I don't think so, but she's doing the right thing, laying low. I do know that there are no whispers from the 'other side'. She's just still mad at me. But maybe you guys can go back and talk to her some other time. I still want to get some information on Sally Wren."

Josh said, "We can try, but she seemed pretty pissed off. Something is getting to her."

I said, "She's just worried Jim Smoke is going to harass her. Listen, if I can produce the facts I need, this case is going to blow up, so he'll be busy and forget about her. But if I can at least get her to testify in a higher court, then everything could really change around here."

Ri'Chard looked skeptical, an expression I was coming to know a little too well. "I don't know, Julie, she seems genuinely scared. I think you might have to leave her be."

"Ms. Honeypaw doesn't get scared. She's an opportunist.

When she sees what testifying in such a big case could do for her, she'll be begging me to get her back in that courtroom."

Josh and Ri'Chard exchanged a glance that told me I wasn't going to convince them, and I was too tired and depressed to fight anymore. I said, "I'm heading back to my hotel, though. I have a protest tomorrow, and my colleagues are arriving in the afternoon. Are you guys coming?"

"To the protest?" Ri'Chard asked.

"Yes, it's tomorrow morning," I said.

Ri'Chard shook his head, "I can't. My family worries too much about stuff like that."

I turned to Josh. "Uh, crowds aren't really my thing," he said, putting his hands into his pockets.

I wasn't really surprised to be met with apathy. To be honest, I didn't even want to go. A protest might stir up enough interest to pursue this case in a higher court. I shrugged. "Okay. That's fine. I'll let you guys know how it goes tomorrow."

Ri'Chard walked to his truck, while Josh accompanied me to my car. "Are you sure you want to work tonight?" he asked as I dug out my keys from my jacket pocket.

I didn't, but I didn't really have a good choice, and anyway, I was too spent to go into my confused feelings about him. "Yeah, I need to finish some stuff before my colleagues get here tomorrow. Best if I'm alone anyway."

"Why is that?" Josh asked, parking a lean hip against the driver's side door and folding his arms across his chest, gazing at me steadily.

I wasn't sure if he was asking because he was hurt or if he was honestly interested, but he clearly didn't plan on leaving till he got an answer. I felt an unusual but powerful urge to unburden myself and give him the truth, which in itself unnerved me. Vulnerability was not my strongest muscle. It was absolutely not one that was accustomed to being taken out and exercised.

"I have to admit..." I was about to confess the emotional mess I'd made of my life, but my throat felt as if a stone had lodged in it, and I had to clear it before starting again. This time I decided to give the easier answer. "To be honest, I'm a bit on edge with having the team from D.C. coming here. My boss expects me to supervise them, which is so weird. I was sure he was going to fire me, and this is almost like a promotion. So I just can't fuck it up again. It's my entire career on the line, and I've worked too hard for too long to completely blow it."

Josh was quiet for a moment, his penetrating gaze seeming to bore a hole straight through me. I could see the frustration in his eyes and met it with my own. He broke the silence by saying, "It's okay. I get it. You're back-to-work Julie. I'll head out then. Let me know how tomorrow goes."

He walked over to his truck, and I wanted so badly to call him back, but I needed to focus. I wondered what he meant by 'back-to-work Julie.' Was I really that different when I was in working mode? Maybe he also felt a need to talk about what happened last night, and all the nights before that. I drew in a shaky breath as I turned the key in the ignition, wondering what had happened to the Julie who had first arrived in Pothos, the Julie who had complete confidence in herself and her ability to control all aspects of her life...

As I slid the car into gear and edged it out onto the street, I thought that Ms. Honeypaw was right: I really had no idea what was going on with these people, let alone with myself.

I ENTERED the lobby to see Keli sitting behind the check-in desk, writing something in her notebook.

"Hey," I said, "What are you working on?"

Keli looked up. "I'm working on my Mars joke, something about how hard it will be to get a man in space when you can't shake your ass in zero gravity."

"Oh, that's an interesting thought," I replied absently.

Keli agreed, giving me a closer look. "I think so too. How are you doing, my friend?"

I said, "Good. Actually, I took your D advice, and it worked."

Keli let out a screech of delight. "Yes! I need to hear everything! I can go on break in twenty. Meet me at our usual spot and don't forget the wine."

All thoughts of work flew straight out the window. This was what I needed more than anything.

EXACTLY EIGHTEEN MINUTES LATER, I grabbed the half-empty bottle of white from our last meeting. It didn't fit in my new purse, giving me a momentary stab of sorrow for my Prada. Instead, I stuffed the bottle in a shopping bag I'd found under the sink and headed out the door. Keli arrived with an ice bucket under her arm and two glasses she'd commandeered from the dining room. We made a good team, I thought, as she separated the ice into the glasses and I poured the wine.

"Thanks," she said, grabbing her glass and clinking it against mine. She lit a cigarette, took a long puff, exhaled her comforting plume of smoke, and said, "Now tell me everything. I already know it's going to be good."

I happily launched into the story, so proud of myself for having conquered the D demon. "Well, Josh came over last night to watch my boss on TV talking about the case," I said, smiling softly at the memory. "Anyway, I dared him to try on my underwear for fun, which he did."

"Damn, girl," said Keli, sitting up straighter. "That's freaky. This is scintillating."

I grinned. "Yeah, I don't exactly know where the impulse came from, but I found it kind of hot, seeing his bits in my underwear. For some reason, they felt less threatening, and I wasn't intimidated. I felt like I was looking at *my* dick. I followed what you'd said, and it worked."

"So you weren't afraid of the D?"

I shook my head. "Nope, not at all."

"You took control of the D?"

I nodded. "I did."

"And you made that D your own?"

"Is that even a question?"

We both burst out laughing and clinked glasses again.

"So where is that D tonight?" Keli asked. "Why are you sitting outside with my sad ass?"

I considered telling her the truth, but didn't want my throat to seize up again. "I'm busy with work stuff," I said, hoping I sounded more convincing than I had to Josh.

"You don't seem busy..."

"I'm taking my work break now, too."

She gave me another, even more curious look. "Wait. Are you getting *ho heart*?"

"What? I don't know what that is," I said, feeling both confused and exposed.

"It's what you get when you're fucking someone but realize you might have feelings for them and block them out because that's easier than actually addressing them. I feel like that might be the case, given your whole situation."

I briefly considered this insight, mainly because I liked to think of myself as an objective and fair person, even if I had recently discovered I was also an idiot. "Maybe," I said, "but I don't think I'm blocking Josh out. We're still friends, and you don't have to hang out with friends every night."

"Yeah, but you're not really experienced at being a ho,"

Keli pointed out. "You're not cutthroat either. I feel like it's inevitable you might catch feelings for Josh, but you feel guilty because of your other man and all. Does Josh know?"

A small, icy stab of something deeply uncomfortable threaded through my chest and landed in my stomach. "No, not yet. I haven't found the right time."

Keli was quiet for a moment while she took a drag of her cigarette. "I feel like you're going to start shutting him out, and that's not going to help your dick drought."

I watched the smoke from her exhale curl and spiral like little white pinwheels, thinning into nothingness against the night sky. It was kind of how I felt, vaguely insubstantial, passing through the Pothos night and soon to be disappearing. I knew she was right.

"I don't think that's going to happen," I said, trying very hard to ignore the sadness the thought of leaving Pothos brought. "We're not actually dating and…and I know it's complicated, and I know I should tell him about Matthew, but there truly hasn't been a right time because everything's been so crazy and stupid and…I don't know. I think I'll do it after tomorrow though, when the protest is over."

"But do you actually have feelings for Josh?" Keli asked.

I didn't even try to be fair. "I like him as a friend," I said in my best clinical voice.

"But will you miss him when you go?"

The sharp pang in my stomach silently answered along with that same burning behind my eyes. My body had become the ultimate traitor. It didn't care what my brain wanted; it was going to do exactly as it pleased, as it had amply demonstrated since arriving in Pothos. All that had done was distract me and get me into trouble. I thought about work and the second chance James was giving me. I had to prove myself this time and couldn't afford more mistakes. And distracting myself with Josh was a mistake.

"I could see missing talking to him from time to time," I said in my best objective voice. "But beyond that, we don't really have that much in common."

Keli flashed me a broad smile. "I was wrong. I think you've got the icy-ho mentality down."

I remained silent for a moment, then gave a light laugh of acknowledgment. "Well, you helped create this monster." I reached over and poured the last of the wine with a practiced twist of the bottle at the end. At least this was something I could do without making a mess.

Keli raised her glass. "To the monsters within us."

"And to the ones we slay that stand in our way." I took a sip and felt the wine wash over my tongue, puckering as it turned my saliva acidic.

15

"WE DEMAND THE TRUTH! WE DEMAND JUSTICE!" a woman screamed into a microphone. I stood on the outskirts of the protest, sipping coffee as I looked at the crowd of people gathered underneath the statue of General Stovall.

It was a good crowd—more than a hundred people. I looked at signs with Sunny's face on them, with questions like "What happened to this good boy?" and "Ghosts shouldn't decide elections." It seemed to be an even split between the two, though the Sunny crowd seemed to be the most enraged.

To my horror, the local police department had put out a statement on social media saying that the animal in question outside the courthouse was a miniature pony. However, to my delight, the public didn't believe them. They accused the department of covering up the truth and burying Sunny, at least according to the thousands of comments on the post about the matter. It only enraged people more, and I was watching the result in front of my eyes. More people filed in from the streets. They looked like out-of-towners, many seemingly young and probably from a nearby university. The woman got back on the microphone and screamed, "THIS IS A CONSPIRACY! THEY WANT TO KEEP THE TRUTH FROM US!" I couldn't tell if she was talking about voter disenfranchisement or the dog.

The crowd cheered. They shook their protest signs, and I could see some had phone numbers written on their arms, probably for lawyers in case they were arrested. I laughed a little at one sign that read, "We want votes, not ghosts!"

I took a few videos and sent them to James. I received a text from Ri'Chard saying, "Be safe today." I replied with a thumbs up. I saw the town police circling the protest, seemingly waiting for a moment to shut it down. Among them was Jim Smoke, my nemesis. I decided to walk over and greet him.

"Mr. Smoke, are you here to support the rights of your townspeople?" I asked.

"Ms. Chen, I'm missing a good day of hunting for this."

"Is it always hunting season here?" I inquired. He definitely looked irritated, and that pleased me.

"There's a private club, stocked with birds. Not as thrilling as the wild, but available all year round."

I really, really wanted to make a joke about the chicken, but decided against it. Instead, I said, "Well, I'm empathetic about having to work on the weekend. I'm sure we'd both rather be elsewhere."

"You're not excited by this chaos?" he asked, gesturing around him with obvious distaste.

"This is a very well-behaved protest," I replied easily, "but I fear it will be in vain. A lot of people would have to lose power in this town for things to change."

His eyes narrowed. "That sounds a bit like a threat."

"Are you afraid of losing power?" I asked. "Isn't that what this whole thing is about, maintaining a power imbalance in favor of the White residents of this town?"

He scoffed. "No, Ms. Chen. This is about protecting our voting institutions and rooting out fraud."

"No, Mr. Smoke," I said, shaking my head with a little smile. "I think this is about your fear. Your fear of no longer automatically being on top as a White man. I think you're scared of the alternative, because, I can tell you, it's not fun being anything other than a White man in this country."

He smirked at me. "You have the wrong idea about me if you think I'm doing this out of fear."

"I think if men admitted they were actually scared of things they don't know about, things would be better in this country."

"Well, Ms. Chen, maybe you should run for office since you have some big ideas about this country," he suggested.

I laughed. "Oh no, Mr. Smoke. Running for office is for the millionaires. I'm just here to watch it all go to shit."

Jim Smoke scowled. "Don't you worry your pretty little head about these things. Soon enough, order will be restored in this country, and you'll find your new place within it."

I said, "Hmmm, is that a threat?"

He said nothing, turning to whisper something to an officer by his side.

The woman got back on the microphone, screaming, "WE WILL NOT BE INTIMIDATED! WE ARE HERE TO FIGHT FOR JUSTICE FOR ALL!" I admired her determination; I took a sip of my coffee and remained on the periphery. Someone yelled, "General Stovall was a racist dog-killer!" and I smiled, pleased with his rebranding.

The crowd had formed a circle surrounding the statue of General Stovall and was shouting at anyone who would listen. I inched away from Jim Smoke to get a better idea of the overall picture. The only threat I could see was the police, who were taking the brunt of the shouting, but most stood with their fingers locked around the armholes of their bulletproof vests, and a few were busy making sure the protest didn't interfere with the sparse flow of traffic. Personally, I thought the protesters should all be shouting at the General, since he was really the one who deserved their ire.

The faint sound of drumming in the distance caught my attention, and as the taps grew progressively louder, I stood on tiptoes, trying to see where it was coming from, and unfortunately had to move back close to Jim Smoke to get a clear view of Main Street. A solitary man marched up the street toward the crowd, banging on the drum hanging at waist level and held up by thick straps over his shoulders. He was dressed in a Confederate uniform, and his walk was purposeful and exaggerated. He stopped in the middle of the street but continued drumming, marching in place until two more drummers caught up and flanked him, banging out some military march anthem. Soon after, the first soldiers appeared, all cosplaying Confederates. The marching band moved forward as the soldiers fell in behind them, waving their flags and holding what I hoped were replica rifles.

Many of the protesters, rightly infuriated, shouted profanities at the marchers. As they started to circle around the protesters, I coolly said, "What do you think, Mr. Smoke? Are they disturbing a peaceful protest? Do you think the police will do anything?"

Jim Smoke looked at the officers around and said loudly, "I don't think there's anything wrong here. Everyone is just exercising their right to free speech."

A protester hollered from across the street, "The war ended a century and a half ago. Go put on a t-shirt, buddy." Another taunted, "Y'all came out of your mother's basement for this?"

I felt my phone buzz and pulled it out of my pocket. It was a text from Josh saying that he'd try to talk to Ms. Honeypaw again today. I thanked him and said that I was at the protest now. I texted, "The Confederate soldiers just showed up on the battlefield. It's getting exciting!"

He texted back, "Be careful. Everyone has guns around here."

While I was looking at my phone, I missed the spark that ignited the flame. Out of the blue, a shoving match broke out between the protesters and the Confederates. Reflexively, I held up my phone and started recording. Some of the protesters took their signs and started beating the Confederates. Luckily, they only used the guns as blunt objects, responding with shoving and punching. I saw the face of "Sunny" moving up and down as a protester used his placard to fend off an attacker.

The officers started cursing and ran into the protest with batons. A handful of sly protesters had managed to climb the statue and tie some ropes around it. I had the sinking feeling of where this was going, but my feet were glued to the asphalt as a spectator. They hopped down as others pulled on the ropes. The police were shouting, tearing protesters away from the soldiers, and beating them. Someone unleashed a smoke bomb, creating a thick, choking plume in the center of the chaos. The woman on the megaphone yelled, "PULL IT DOWN!"

At this point, all sides lost any semblance of control, and in the melee, the protesters managed to loosen the statue enough that it started to list forward. Shouts turned into screams of panic, and the crowd splintered apart as people began to run, pushing and shoving as they tried to get out of the way of the statue slowly leaning toward the street below.

I watched in a kind of horrified fascination as it gained speed and toppled off the stone base. It hit the ground with a crash, rebounding off the pavement. In one last, surreal bounce, the General's head detached from its bronzed shoulders, popping off like an ejected cork and rolling away.

Sound and movement seemed to stop for a split second as we all took in the shocking spectacle. The General was toppled.

And then the moment broke.

As sound rushed back in, I felt a strong urge to run, but the Julie-at-work part of me somehow kept my feet from moving. I held my phone in front of me, recording everything.

As the main body of the crowd hurriedly began to disperse, people, mainly protesters, continued to knock into each other, but mostly in an effort to escape, since the police had multiplied in numbers and were actively making arrests. The only ones who didn't seem to be concerned about the police were a handful of the marchers, who had gathered around the fallen, headless statue of General Stovall in apparent mourning.

There was nothing impressive or glorious about the General now: he looked small and pathetic lying on the ground, the perfect metaphor for a once mighty man toppled by some young kids trying to bring justice to the wrong side of history. I also realized that although I might be on the right side of history, I was very much on the wrong side of town politics, given that the white supremacists remained gathered near the statue, and the protesters were fleeing. I decided I had enough video for my legal needs, and quietly walked in the opposite direction from the chaos and the retribution that was brewing. I figured hiding in my hotel would be my next act of resistance.

James found the whole thing to be quite entertaining as I recounted the protest to him. Videos were already starting to go viral on social media. I paced around my room, removing various items of clothing from my half-packed suitcase and hanging them back up in the closet while he strategized about how the firm could assist with arrested protesters next week.

I explained that Yale Law and Useless Idiot aren't barred in

Georgia. "If they can't defend in court, you might as well keep them in D.C. with you."

"They can still assist you. I appreciate your confidence, but I also think the extra minds will be useful during this time. It could be a pivotal week for the case," James replied.

I suppressed my irritation. We both knew there were other, more practiced lawyers in the firm who would be far more useful, but James seemed intent on punishing me. I could only hope my acquiescing would lead to a promotion at the end of all this. But as I was imagining the new corner office and personal paralegal that were surely to come, a voice asked *Is it the perks and the status you care about, or are you just programmed to believe it's what you're supposed to want?* I shook off the thoughts.

I'd only just gotten off with James and was contemplating the notes I needed to finish and the energy I needed to summon from somewhere, when my phone buzzed. Josh was calling.

"Hey, are you okay? I heard there was fighting! I just got home and was about to watch the news, but I wanted to check in with you before anything else."

"Yes, shit did hit the fan," I said, a little tension seeping out of my body at the familiar, reassuring sound of his voice. "I don't exactly know what happened, but the protest turned violent. I'm fine, though; I wasn't actually in the crowd."

"Are you safe now?" he asked, the question heavy with concern.

"Yeah, I'm in my hotel," I said. He really was worried about me.

"Okay, do you want me to come over?" he asked.

I sat down on the bed and thought about it for a moment. Part of me wanted him to come, but the Julie-at-work part questioned why. I ignored both of them, deciding my conflict had nothing to do with either lust or responsibility and everything to do with having promised myself last night that I'd have an honest talk with Josh after the protest. I split the difference and decided to procrastinate a bit longer. "Maybe later, I still have work to do. Did you talk to Ms. Honeypaw?"

"I just finished," he said. "It took a while. She wasn't feeling very friendly to start with, but she warmed up after we talked about her mother a bit."

"Did she say anything helpful?" I asked eagerly.

"Uh..." He paused for a moment. "She said I should stay away from you, that you have bad energy or something. It was weird, but with her, what isn't? She said something about your ignorance getting all of us in trouble."

"Wow," I said, feeling oddly hurt. "I'm not surprised, but I also don't know what I did to make her hate me so much."

"It happens to everyone, at one point or another. She's hot-headed, just like her mother was."

"Oh, did her mother's ghost say anything about me?" I asked sarcastically.

"Say what?"

"Never mind, forget it. "I'll get in touch later about hanging out, alright?"

"Yeah, no problem. Talk to you later." He hung up.

I looked around at the piles of paperwork, and my own stack of folders related to this lawsuit. Plopping backward onto the bed, I fell straight into a deep sleep.

A KNOCK on my door brought me out of a hazy dream. Reaching for my phone, I was horrified to see I'd slept for hours and it was now deep in the afternoon. I righted myself, wiggled my feet into my indoor slippers, and had to steady myself as I stood, as the blood rushed to my head. I wondered if this were maid service, and I'd have to vacate my room.

I opened the door and saw that there was no one there. I

looked around, confused. Someone had definitely knocked, but there wasn't a soul in the hallway and no sign of the maid's cart. Just as I was about to close the door again, I glanced down. A black duffel bag sat on the floor directly in front of my door, so close that I would have tripped over it while walking out. I crouched down and felt the bag, prodding the exterior with my fingers. There was something roundish and hard inside, but that was all I could tell. Nerves battling with deep curiosity, I carefully pulled the zipper down.

General Stovall's head stared up at me, his bronze visage framed by the folds of the unzipped bag, like a head peeking from behind a black curtain before a performance.

I gasped, zipping the bag up as fast as I could manage with my fumbling fingers. Dragging the ludicrously heavy bag into my room, I closed and bolted the door. I stared at the bag. I needed facts before I could draw any conclusions. Obviously, this was a message meant to scare me, but the question was: *cui bono*? Who benefited?

Kneeling, I unzipped the bag fully, gingerly poking my hands around the bottom and sides, searching for a note or clue of some kind. I couldn't find anything.

I sank onto the couch and stuck my chin on my fist. I ran over all the facts I had, but I came up empty-handed when I tried to link how leaving a head from an accidentally decapitated statue at my door. Was it a joke? Did someone think it was funny to give me this because this was indirectly my doing?

I turned on the TV, hoping to pick up a random clue from the local news. To my surprise, a live press conference was in progress featuring none other than Jim Smoke, once again flanked by police officers. I'd come in at the end of his speech, which he concluded dramatically with: "Anyone involved in planning, participating, or profiting from the violence and vandalism of our historical monument will be pursued, arrested, and prosecuted to the full extent of the law. Period. That is a promise." He glared into the camera as if he were directly addressing me.

Suddenly, it clicked: I was being framed. Even though I'd had nothing to do with the destruction of the monument, I was now in possession of evidence. Circumstantial or not, I was an attorney for the other side, and this looked bad. Very bad.

I wouldn't be surprised at all if they tried to arrest me.

The press conference ended, and my self-protective instincts kicked in. The first thing was to get rid of the evidence; I called Josh and told him I was coming over, and to call Ri'Chard if he were free, but I hung up before he could ask more questions. I suddenly regretted asking Ri'Chard to get involved in case I implicated him in this mess, so I quickly texted Josh, "Forget Ri'Chard."

I changed, put on a hat, and grabbed the duffel bag. It was ridiculously heavy, and I struggled to get it onto my shoulder. I headed out into the lobby, but before I rounded the corner toward the desk, I overheard Keli.

She said, "I'm sorry, Officer, but according to my system, Ms. Chen checked out a few hours ago. I don't know where she might have gone, but she is no longer staying at our hotel. Did you try the motel off the highway?" She enhanced her lie with needless typing as she pretended to check the system.

Blessing Keli's quick thinking, I quietly slipped back to my room and slowly shut and bolted the door again, feeling sweat gather on my body. Ms. Honeypaw was correct: I was fucking with the wrong people. I waited a few minutes before texting Keli, asking if the police had left. I then grabbed the duffel and made it to the front desk before I dropped the duffel, which landed with a thud on the ground.

"Shit, this is heavy!" I said, panting.

Keli stared at me. "What the fuck is going on? You got the police after you? What did you do?"

"Listen, I'm being framed. I think it's the prosecutor and the police. Someone left this duffel bag with the head from General Stovall's statue in front of my door about half an hour ago. Did you see anyone?"

"Shit, I don't know..." I could see Keli trying to remember. Her face looked a little guilty. "I might have been fighting with a fuckboy on Facetime in the back. I can try to check the cameras?"

"I don't have time!" I exclaimed. "I have to go now! They're after me, and if they catch me with this head, I'm going to jail!"

Keli nodded in agreement. "Probably. And you're not made for jail, honey."

"I know! Prison scares the shit out of me. I've seen too much from the other side of the bars," I confessed.

"But if you go, I'll answer your jail mail," Keli said, not looking terribly concerned about my potential future."So what's your plan to get rid of this?"

"I'm heading to Josh's. I feel like he'll know what to do."

"Good idea. I have a feeling he knows what to do with illegal shit, and he fixes cars so maybe you can melt this down, no one will ever know. Let me help you carry this thing, though." Keli grabbed one strap while I grabbed the other. "Fuck!" she exclaimed. "This motherfucker is heavy. You're so lucky I like you."

After making sure the coast was clear of any cops or potential witnesses, we shuffled out to the parking lot and toward the Corolla. I popped the trunk, and on the count of three, we heaved the duffel bag into the trunk, sinking the car a bit from the weight. I slammed the trunk shut and hugged Keli.

I said, "I think it's going to be okay. If the cops come back, keep lying. I'll defend you if they arrest you for obstruction of justice."

She said, "Oh, no. As soon as they threaten jail, I'm snitching. I'm sorry, but I'm just being honest with you."

"Okay, I understand," I said, and I did. "Thanks for your help. Try checking the cameras!"

I waved goodbye as I sped out of the parking lot, down the road toward Josh's house, a bronze head rolling around in my trunk.

I SCREECHED to a halt on the gravel drive that ended close to Josh's front door. He must have been concerned because he was waiting right there, his face peering through the screen. He immediately came out to meet me. I managed to throw open the car door myself and emerge before he asked if I was okay.

I didn't even know how to begin to answer. "No, I mean, yes, I'm okay. Someone's trying to frame me, though, and I need your help."

"Frame you? For what?" Josh asked, his eyes sharpening with alarm.

"I'm not sure," I said honestly. "Could be any number of things. Theft, desecration of a historic monument; I'm sure there are other felonies they could cook up." I popped the trunk. "The evidence is in this duffel bag. I need your help getting rid of it."

He laughed. "Right, are you pranking me right now? Is this some lawyer role-play shit again?"

"No, just grab this bag for me. And be careful, it's heavy."

He leaned over and picked up the bag. "Holy shit, this *is* heavy. What's in here?"

"Just take it inside, and I'll show you."

Once inside, he set the bag down on the living room floor with a thud.

"Go ahead, open it," I said, anxiously waiting to see his reaction.

He crouched down and unzipped the bag. His mouth dropped open, and his head snapped up, his eyes reflecting shock and, behind that, a flash of anger. "Holy fuck. Damn, it was just all over the news that the statue's head had gone missing and the police were looking for the thief. Where did you find it?"

"That's the problem. Someone left it in front of my hotel room door." I sank onto his couch and planted my hands on both sides of the beaten-up seat cushion.

Still crouched in front of the duffel, he looked over at me and grinned. "This is wild. I had no idea your life was actually exciting. I thought law was boring and shit, but this is like a movie. Let's figure out what to do with this." He rolled the head over and lifted it onto the coffee table. He carefully placed it down so we could see it clearly.

We both stared at it in silence. "How do we get rid of it?" I quietly asked.

"I think I know a spot, but we have to wait until the middle of the night."

"Is it safe? No one will see us?"

He looked at me and tried to seem optimistic. "It will be alright."

"Do you think Ms. Honeypaw did this? She hates me, and I wouldn't put it past her."

He looked skeptical and said, "Ms. Honeypaw? I highly doubt that. Besides, she was going to smoke some weed and take a nap when I left her."

I shook off the thought. "You're right. It was obviously Jim Smoke." I shook my head. "They're dirtier than I thought, so we have to get dirtier than them."

I looked at Josh, who was probably regretting the moment he offered to fix my car.

AFTER SOME PACING, I heard a car pull in. My stomach dropped. I ran to the window, and saw Ri'Chard's truck pulling in. I thought I told Josh to lay off telling him. I asked, "Josh, why is Ri'Chard coming?"

"You told me to call him?"

"Yeah, but then I sent a text about not telling him."

"Oh, I was confused and just ignored it."

It was already too late. Ri'Chard knocked, and Josh told him to come in. He immediately sensed I was agitated and asked, "Are you alright?"

I said, "Not really. I have a tricky situation."

Ri'Chard frowned. "I'm glad you're safe. I messaged when I heard what happened, but I didn't hear from you."

I sighed, "I'm sorry. I fell asleep after and woke up to this in front of my door." I pointed at the table, and Ri'Chard turned to look.

"What? Is that actually the head?" He walked over to get a closer look at it.

"Yep, it was left outside my hotel room. Then the police came to the hotel to try and find me with it and arrest me, but my friend who works there lied and saved me. I came here because I need help to get rid of it."

Ri'Chard studied it. "Is it solid?"

Josh said, "Nah, it's heavy but definitely not solid."

Ri'Chard tipped the head on the table enough so he could look inside the head. He squinted, reached in his hand, and pulled out a piece of paper. He unfolded it and revealed an illustration. I got closer and peered at it.

"It looks medieval," said Ri'Chard.

It was filled with symbols, but no words. It did look medieval with crosses and intersecting lines forming unknown meanings. Ri'Chard handed me the piece of paper.

Josh took a closer look and said, "Oh, I think it's that same sigil."

I echoed, "A 'sigil'?"

"The same one from the graveyard," he replied. "It's a spell. Those symbols form some powerful, mystical spell. Weird that it's in the head. Maybe a witch is trying to frame you?"

I stared at the paper and realized he was right. "How do you know this?" I asked, puzzled.

Josh chuckled. "I forgot to tell you I sent the grave site picture to my ex, Alana, and she said it was a sigil."

"Oh," I remarked, "A sigil? What is this for?"

Josh said, "Only the person who made this knows what it's for, if you believe in that stuff."

"Do they work?" I asked.

"I don't know," said Josh. "I've never used one. I can call Alana if you want me to ask her?"

"I don't think it's important." I set the sigil down next to the head of General Stovall. I sat back on the couch and wondered. Perhaps I was trying to tie strings between things that were unrelated. My thoughts were interrupted by Josh asking, "Anyone want a drink?" Both Ri'Chard and I nodded our heads and he handed us beers.

I took a sip. "Thanks. It's been a long day."

Josh joined me on the couch while Ri'Chard sat on the chair in front of the head. Ri'Chard asked, "What are you doing with this thing?"

I looked at Josh, who looked at me. He raised his eyebrows in uncertainty, saying, "I was thinking we could throw it in the quarry."

Ri'Chard nodded. "That's what I was thinking too. It's deep and secluded."

"What's the quarry?" I asked.

Josh said, "It's an old rock quarry that's been filled with water. It's really deep, so no one will ever find this at the bottom."

I agreed. "That sounds perfect."

Josh said, "Let's wait until dark, though."

I looked down at my hand and noticed a small cut on my finger. I examined it as the slightest bit of blood began to color it crimson. Josh noticed and asked, "Are you alright?"

I said, "Yeah. I think I got a papercut on the sigil."

He leaned over and looked at it before getting up and going to the bathroom. I looked at Ri'Chard and declared, "Josh went to talk with Ms. Honeypaw earlier. She still hates me but doesn't have much to say."

"What are you trying to find out from her?" Ri'Chard asked.

Josh returned and sat close to me. He grabbed my hand and carefully affixed a band-aid to my finger. I looked at him, focused, then back to Ri'Chard. I saw his eyes flicker between Josh tending to my hand and meeting my gaze. I said, "I'm still trying to figure some things out. I'm really interested in Sally Wren and her bizarre daughter. I think I'm more scared of that child than anyone in this town."

"I don't know much about them," said Ri'Chard.

Josh asked me, "How does that feel?"

I moved my hand and felt the tightness of the bandage stuck to my skin. I said, "It feels perfect, thank you."

"You're welcome," said Josh. "You have nice hands, by the way."

I looked at my hands, which seemed unremarkable to me. I said, "Really?"

"Yeah, I think they're pretty." He smiled at me, but this time I didn't question his sincerity. I looked at Ri'Chard, who was smirking a little. I decided to needle him, asking, "Do you agree? Do you think my hands are pretty?"

He said, "I haven't taken a close enough look at them to judge." He got up from his chair and knelt in front of me, lightly putting his right hand under mine and gently lifting it toward him. It was the first time our hands touched, and I felt a tingling radiating down my arms. He inspected my right hand, carefully lifted my left hand, then looked up at me. My mouth was slightly agape as my body vibrated with a warmth that I'm sure turned me red.

Ri'Chard said, "I agree, I think they're pretty." He moved back to his chair and settled in it.

I asked slyly, "Are you allowed to say that?"

He smirked. His eyes lowered, then locked on mine as he said, "It's only looking, right?"

16

I leaned a little closer to Josh so our shoulders touched. I felt his left hand grab my right hand that was resting on the couch between us. He began to trace his finger along my palm. I looked at Ri'Chard sitting back in his chair. I said, "I remember that you like to watch people and figure them out."

Ri'Chard's eyes flicked back to my hand, intertwined with Josh's, and nodded. "It's true."

I asked him, "Have you been watching what's been happening in this town? Do you have any ideas?"

"Honestly, since I live in the next town, I haven't been paying much attention. I only know about stuff because you're involved in it."

I raised an eyebrow. "So you're just watching me?"

He said, "You could say that. I just get all my updates through you or Josh."

I looked at Josh, who was smirking a little. His hand was now entwined with mine. I looked back at Ri'Chard and said, "That's not helpful to my case, though. There's a lot of stuff to figure out."

Ri'Chard said, "I think it's simple: the courthouse burning

was an accident. Ms. Honeypaw confirmed who was involved. You heard them admit it at a secret initiation ceremony for mystical white supremacists. Now they're trying to arrest you before you can get them. That's what I think."

"Okay, so I get the chicken sacrifice as part of an initiation, and even putting the dead fox in my car to chase me off, but why slaughter the pony and leave it for everyone to see?"

He said, "It's just another distraction to scare people and try to keep them from seeing the truth."

"It's a pretty intense distraction," I said. I felt Josh's arm slide along my back and his hand rest on my waist. I leaned a little closer into his side.

Ri'Chard asked, "What will you do tomorrow? Try and leave town?"

"I don't know. I just want to get rid of this head first." I glanced at the decapitated head of General Stovall on the table next to Ri'Chard. I said to him, "You look like a king sitting with the head of your enemy."

Ri'Chard smiled. "It was a long battle, but the war has yet to be won."

"What war are you fighting?" I asked him.

He laughed a little and said, "I think we're fighting different fights. I'm just fighting to feel free."

He was right. I was just fighting this war to keep my job, though now it felt more personal. I was tired of being fucked with and didn't want to surrender. I said, "You're right, but I think I'm ready to join your fight."

He looked at me skeptically. "Are you fit for battle?"

"I think I'm fit to film it? That's all I managed to do at the protest today."

Josh said to me, "I was really worried about you. You shouldn't go alone to stuff like that. It can be dangerous."

Ri'Chard agreed. "I was worried too. You need to be careful, especially now that they're targeting you."

I looked at Ri'Chard and jokingly said, "Yes, my king."

He smiled and said, "I'm not king material; I don't like being the center of attention. I'm much more comfortable behind the scenes."

"You're an observer," I reiterated to him.

"Exactly," said Ri'Chard, giving me a slight smile.

I looked down at my pretty hands, then said out loud to no one in particular, "I'd like to find out more about the Stovall Plantation and who owns it now. I wonder how they're cooperating with the group we saw there."

Ri'Chard said, "I thought you were going to stay out of trouble?"

"Sometimes I can't help it."

"True. I can tell you're stubborn and don't like to listen to people," said Ri'Chard.

I raised my eyebrows skeptically. "Really? Then test me. Tell me to do something."

Ri'Chard smiled slightly. "I think you were more of a 'truth' person when it came to Truth or Dare."

Our eyes focused on each other. I said, "Well, tonight I choose *dare*."

I felt Josh adjust his arm tighter around my waist. Ri'Chard looked at me and asked, "I thought you were a *guai* girl?"

I raised an eyebrow. "Well, even *guai* girls can be naughty sometimes."

Ri'Chard smirked. "If we were back in high school, I'd dare you to kiss Josh."

I heard Josh laugh a little to himself. He said, "Yep, I remember those dares."

I didn't. Ri'Chard was spot on: I'd always chosen "truth", until recently. I never knew what it was like to kiss someone out of a dare, so I turned to Josh and looked at him. We didn't need to say anything to each other. We leaned in and let our lips touch before our tongues danced in union. I ran my hands up and down his back, up into his hair. Our kiss lasted about ten seconds before we pulled apart and smiled at each other.

I turned to Ri'Chard, who looked pleasantly surprised, and asked, "Was that a successful dare?"

He nodded, "I think you lost your *guai* card now."

"Oh, I should lose it for something a lot naughtier than that." I bit my lip. I could tell Ri'Chard wanted to say something, but instead he kept whatever was on his mind inside. "My turn," I said. I looked at Ri'Chard with his intense gaze and said, "I dare you to kiss Josh."

Ri'Chard's cheeks tightened in a knowing smile. "You didn't give me the option of 'truth'?"

"That's boring. I think a dare is much more fun." I turned to Josh. "Josh, are you comfortable with Ri'Chard kissing you?"

Josh opened his mouth. "Uh, I guess. I don't want to say 'no' because he's a friend, but I don't think either of us swings that way."

I said to Josh, "I dare you to swing that way, for one kiss."

"Fine," Josh agreed easily. "Dare accepted. It's not the first time."

I looked to Ri'Chard. He smirked at me. "Since you're stubborn, you'll make me do this, right?"

I said, "I don't think I can make you do anything. Is your girlfriend okay with you kissing another guy?"

"It hasn't come up in conversation," said Ri'Chard.

"But other women are off limits?" I asked him.

"Definitely," he said, sounding certain.

I explained the logic, "So then, the only other two people allowed to kiss here are you and Josh."

Ri'Chard looked at me with a knowing smile. He shook his head a bit and said, "I can't do it."

I leaned back into Josh, disappointed. "Alright, then it's game over."

Ri'Chard suggested, "Doesn't that mean I have to tell the 'truth' instead?"

"Yes," I nodded. I lightly walked my fingers down Josh's thigh. I felt like a cat toying with a mouse, yet I was ready to go for the kill. I looked at Ri'Chard and asked, "Instead of kissing Josh, would you rather kiss me?"

I felt the air escape the room. Ri'Chard's look changed. He looked concerned, consumed with the guilt of my admission of what we both were feeling. He took a heavy breath and said, "Maybe I should have chosen 'dare'."

"There's still time," I told him.

"Maybe we can come up with a different 'dare' then?" Ri'Chard suggested.

"Are you scared, bro?" Josh asked. "I don't want to make you uncomfortable."

"I'm not scared...but...it's just..." Ri'Chard was at a loss for words. "Yeah, maybe I'm a bit scared."

"Why?" I asked him. "It's just Josh. Is it because you're not attracted to guys?"

"Do you often kiss your friends?" Ri'Chard asked, quizzically.

He was right. I'd never kissed any of my friends before, and the thought of it was bizarre, but I was suddenly comfortable enough to tease these boundaries that once felt so immovable to me.

I said, "You're in a tough position. You don't want to tell the 'truth', and you're too afraid to follow through on the 'dare'. I feel like you're letting our team down."

Ri'Chard huffed. "You sound like my father."

"Oh, I'm sorry." I apologized genuinely. I knew the feeling of being reminded of one's shortcomings as a child. "I was just trying to have some fun. I thought it was funny. I'm really sorry."

Ri'Chard looked like he was sitting on the sidelines. His hands were clasped, elbows resting on his knees, thinking. He stared at the ground and said, "I don't want to let the team down. I'm not afraid." He looked at me, and I could see the anger behind his eyes.

He said, "Fine, I'll kiss Josh." He stood up, and I tapped Josh to stand. They met in the middle, in front of the head of General Stovall, who was witnessing my agenda, and awkwardly looked at each other. Josh said, "Dude, I don't know where to put my hands."

Ri'Chard said, "I don't know where to put mine either. Just close your eyes."

Josh closed his eyes, and Ri'Chard got a little closer and put an arm around Josh's shoulder. He leaned in and let his lips touch Josh's. For the first few seconds, Josh didn't move much, but he gradually eased into the kiss and put his hands on Ri'Chard's waist. Josh's eyes remained closed, but Ri'Chard's face was slightly turned, looking at me. He stared at me with that same heat behind his eyes. He was not backing down from this challenge. I watched him kiss Josh, holding him close with his powerful arm. Ri'Chard's other hand slowly rose up Josh's chest, up his neck, holding his jawline.

Ri'Chard pulled back, and I saw a strand of spit stretched between their lips before snapping. They took a step back, allowing an opening large enough for me to fit between them.

"Stand up." Ri'Chard ordered me to come closer. "You like giving orders? Well, now it's my turn." His voice conveyed an authority that both intimidated me and made me wet.

"Kiss him." I did as I was told. I looked at Ri'Chard in the eyes before turning and kissing Josh, hoping to taste Ri'Chard on his lips. Josh kissed me passionately, and I felt his hands climb my side and wrap around my back. I searched his mouth with my tongue, hoping to find traces of the man I couldn't have.

I disconnected from Josh and pulled back a bit, while Josh kept his hands around my waist. I locked eyes with Ri'Chard. We stared at each other in anticipation of what to do next, uncertain, yet fully willing. It was the same anticipation I once knew, the memory suddenly entering my mind. There was a vine that grew in my grandmother's house in Taiwan. The plant grew austere, its long, thick fleshy tendrils held tiny thorns, forbidding us from touching it. Occasionally, from the tips burst forth with buds that grew until the moment it was announced it would bloom, only for that nocturne, The Queen of the Night.

We sat on her veranda, waiting. I moved out from under the eave to see the sky turn to night. As it grew dark, the flowers opened, and a subtle fragrance filled the courtyard with its sensuous release. The flowers could not be kept; they faded by morning. My cousin dared me to take a flower and drink it as tea. After we poured boiling water into the cup, it turned a faint gold. The liquid became thick and slippery from the flower, the same feeling between my legs.

Tonight my blossoms swelled. Touching was forbidden, and this moment would quickly pass, but with an audience assembled, I would put on a show and let my blooming be witnessed.

I thrust my tongue into Josh's mouth. I felt his hands unbuckle my jeans as he moved them down to touch me.

I opened my mouth and moaned as Josh's fingers were enmeshed in me. Josh continued kissing my neck. Ri'Chard gazed at me with a naughty intensity. I looked at Ri'Chard. He lightly shook his head, like he was mad at me for putting him in this position, like he was furious that I finally said what we were too afraid to say.

Josh pulled down my bra as his tongue moved along my

nipples. He continued to touch me as my legs became weak. I unbuttoned Josh's pants and took out his hardened shaft, lightly stroking it. I looked at Ri'Chard, pretending that I had his own cock in my hand. I smiled and pulled Josh toward the couch.

He slowly lowered me down until I was seated, kissing me the whole time. I moved my legs around his waist, and I leaned back on the couch as he held himself above me.

I felt him gyrate into me. He started kissing along my jaw and down to my neck. I looked over his back and caught sight of Ri'Chard, who was now sitting in his chair. I could see he was aroused, focusing on us as we were swept in the raging flood of lust. Though this time, he didn't leave through the screen door.

Instead, he remained on the chair, with the head of the General on the table as a trophy of war. I felt Josh on top of me. I wanted him there, but I wanted Ri'Chard with the same devotion. A rare moment where fantasy came true, nights of longing, when my lust already conjured countless scenarios of how this would happen.

I got on top and pushed Josh so he was against the couch, straddling him while he helped me lift off my shirt. Josh, our naughty, mischievous vessel, would dance the line between friend, lover, and provocateur. My back was to Ri'Chard, and as I undid my bra, I looked back at him as it rolled off my shoulders. His hand was in his pants, slowly massaging his cock. I turned and leaned down to kiss Josh as his hands palmed my ass and squeezed. He worked his kisses down my neck to my breasts. I let out a loud groan and pushed him back against the couch.

I stood and took off my pants, and with my panties remaining, I bent over and slowly lowered them, putting on a little show for Ri'Chard. I turned and sat on Josh's lap as his hands slowly ran up my body to my breasts. He lightly squeezed them and kissed my back; his right hand retraced my torso and teased me again, making me moan even louder as he started to touch me. I started to gyrate against Josh's hand as I felt his erection through his jeans. I loved the feeling of his clothes against my naked body, just a layer of cotton between our heated flesh. As Josh's fingers explored me, I stared at Ri'Chard, and he gave me the same intense gaze, while his fingers gripped his own flesh.

I wanted his skin on mine and to grip him, but I didn't want to betray his values, and the thought of his devotion to Aisha only made me more aroused.

Josh asked me through heavy panting, "Do you want me to fuck you?"

I answered "Yes," with a breathy, desperate longing to feel his hardened shaft inside of me. I undid his jeans and pulled them from his waist, down his legs, and over his feet. I got on my knees and began to kiss his knees, up his thighs. He raised his hips slightly, and I peeled off the last remaining layer of cotton between his hard trunk and my slick flower.

I slowly moved up and straddled Josh, kissing him as I sank my hips onto him with the desperate need to feel him filling me. I knew the feeling of Josh inside me, but this time the experience was heightened by my desire to please Ri'Chard. I wanted Ri'Chard to want me, to witness the sexual energy within me, even if it was too dangerous for him to play with.

As Josh let out moans of pleasure, I turned to look at Ri'Chard, whose own cock was out of his pants. He was moving his hand up and down, and I moved my hips up and down Josh's cock to the same tempo.

I got up and turned around, lowering myself back onto Josh. I put my legs on the sofa as my back leaned against Josh. I wanted Ri'Chard to witness everything as Josh pulled himself in and out of me, his hand placed on the top of my vagina like a grape leaf for modesty, though his hand delicately rubbed my clitoris as I moved up and down. His left hand moved up and down my torso until he put a finger in my mouth to suck on.

I looked at Ri'Chard while Josh drew his finger in and out of my mouth. His eyes moved around my body before his filthy focus met mine. I danced my tongue around Josh's finger.

I bobbed my head to take this finger deeper, until my lips kissed his knuckle. I kept eye contact with him while I did this, knowing he was imagining my mouth taking his own member deeply.

He licked his lips as he took in my body with pleasure. We both focused on one another, fulfilling our lust through our eyes. I stared at his hand moving up and down, lips slightly parted, and eyes wandering along my body, glistening with a slight sweat.

Josh removed his finger, allowing my moans to escape. I moaned louder as I ground down deeper onto Josh. I could see Ri'Chard mirroring our tempo, feeling exactly what we were. Ri'Chard and I stared at each other; beads of sweat had formed on his forehead.

I could feel my legs start to tire, so I slid off and commanded Josh to get on top of me. I gasped as he slid into me, and like the first time he dry-humped me, my legs locked around his waist. Though, this time, our flesh pressed against each other, glossed with sweat. I grabbed his ass and squeezed his plump cheeks as his hips swirled and dove into mine. I turned my head to look at Ri'Chard as Josh's tongue entered and aroused my ear. I moaned as both men pleased me, one physically and the other watching me. Knowing he was turned on by watching my sexual release drove me towards climax as time was counted with kisses and moans.

The breath-softened words, "Cum for me," came from Ri'Chard's mouth. I nodded while panting, moaning, and whimpering. It was happening. We both were climaxing. I moaned, and as I shut my eyes, it was like fire sweeping my body, carried by a strong wind. I ignited and screamed from the sensation. I came thinking of both Ri'Chard and Josh, and the moments we all shared—from my first ambivalence to this moment of complete openness. My clenched eyes released to see Ri'Chard orgasming, his face contorted from the finale of pleasure. My wave continued as I panted, gradually subsiding until I felt Josh pull himself out of me and felt the release of his cum on my stomach, his warmth on me.

The lust was exhausting and overwhelming; we were weak from this tension almost being broken, or just teased in the most beautiful way. It was then, both of us barely holding ourselves together after our orgasms, that I realized that I loved Ri'Chard. I loved the way he spoke, cautiously and concisely, and occasionally with seductive authority. I loved the way he studied people and worried about them. I loved the way he envisioned building a world, while also working on building a safe one for his partner.

Truth be told, I also loved Josh. I felt safe with him within me and around me. I loved his aloofness, or the fact that he had other, quiet dimensions. I loved that I felt comfortable making mistakes around him, and they wouldn't bring shame, but an opportunity to learn. I turned and kissed Josh's forehead, tasting the salty sweat that accumulated below his hairline. I felt my eyes water, overwhelmed with emotion. This was the first time I ever truly loved a man, or in this case, two. I looked at Ri'Chard as he looked at me with passion and regret, the kind felt for a fork in the road that could never be taken.

The tide of my orgasm finally receded. I was released from the riptide of desire.

We all remained quiet, breathing heavily. I felt Josh gently encourage me to lie on my side on the couch while he spooned me. I looked at Ri'Chard, who was collapsed into the chair, his breath visible as his chest moved up and down. He looked at me and smiled, shaking his head a little. He said, "Maybe I should have chosen 'truth'."

I smiled wryly. I saw Ri'Chard weakly point to the head of General Stovall on the table. He laughed a bit and said, "Guys, I got cum on the General."

I sat up and looked at the head, and sure enough, there was a streak of cum on the cheek, dripping from his eye. It looked like a white tear. I started to laugh, and so did Josh. We all broke out in laughter, a deep uproarious laughter that diffused the awkwardness of what just happened.

Ri'Chard gathered himself. He zipped his pants and asked Josh for a paper towel.

Josh told him, "There's some in the kitchen." I felt Josh kiss my back as I watched Ri'Chard search for a paper towel. I looked at the head of General Stovall, the solitary white tear from witnessing us. Ri'Chard came back and crouched down in front of the statue, carefully wiping his cum off of it. He bunched up the paper towel in his hand and looked beside the head. He reached out and picked up the sigil and held it up. Ri'Chard said, "Shit, I also got some on this."

As he held up the sigil, I could see where the streak of his semen made the paper transparent. I said, "I feel like you should win a prize for your aim."

He put the sigil on the edge of the table and gave me a guilty smile.

I decided to needle him and asked, "What if there's DNA evidence left behind?"

Ri'Chard looked at me with wide eyes. "Oh shit."

I laughed a little. "Then we'll have to do a really good job of hiding it." Ri'Chard didn't look convinced. "Besides, water will destroy any evidence, but now you have some incentive to not fuck this up."

Josh said, "Yeah, let's get ready then. I don't really want this head in my house for much longer. It has a weird energy; I'll have to sage the shit out of this place when I get back."

I grabbed our clothes from the floor and began to separate them. Ri'Chard wiped the head with some cleaning spray and grabbed a towel. He put it around the head and lowered it into the bag. He said, "We should be careful of fingerprints, in case. I think I wiped off the ones that were there, though."

I pulled my shirt down my torso and said, "I'm ready." Josh nodded at me, and so did Ri'Chard.

WE DROVE MOSTLY in comfortable silence. I wasn't certain if it was because of the crime we were committing, or the sex act we all just took part in, but it felt like we didn't need to fill the space with talking at the moment. I had never thought about the dynamics of friendship in the aftermath of a threesome.

I pondered if this would change the friendship of Josh and Ri'Chard until we reached a dirt road. Josh's truck bounced along until we came to a stop. Beyond us was a body of water, illuminated by the truck lights. He turned off the truck, and everything went dark. We let our eyes adjust, then opened the car doors in unison. I felt the tall grass brush against my pant legs. I looked behind to see Ri'Chard muscling out the duffel bag. Josh was waiting on the other side of the truck and told us to follow him. We walked along a dirt path illuminated by my cell phone light. The water was on our left, making appearances through the shrubs and gaps in the trees. The moon was bright tonight, close to full, its reflection scattered against the choppy waters.

We walked up a bit of an incline and came to a cleared area.

"I think this is our best spot. The water is really deep right here," said Josh.

I nodded. Josh offered to take a strap while Ri'Chard held

the other. They swung it back and forth, but I panicked and screamed, "Wait!"

They both turned to look at me. I asked, "Should I say something?"

"Say something about what?" Ri'Chard asked.

I said, "I don't know. It feels like we're getting rid of a body. Like a prayer or something, out of respect. I don't actually want his ghost to come back and haunt me."

"I just cleaned my cum off his face. I don't think he has much integrity left," said Ri'Chard, haughtily.

Josh joined in, "Besides, you hate him, right?"

I agreed. "Yeah, you're right. I just want to say that this secret doesn't leave this group, alright? No matter what happens, I hope we can remain loyal to each other."

They both looked at me and nodded. Josh said, "I'll keep quiet until the day I die."

Ri'Chard said, "Soon this will feel like a bizarre dream."

They turned and began to swing the bag until they hit "Three!" and released the duffel bag. It made an attempt at flying before its weight brought it down. It splashed and disappeared under the water.

The whole event was over quickly. I breathed a sigh of relief, and we all walked back to the truck.

JOSH DECIDED to play some music on the way back. Ri'Chard requested some hits from their school days, some of which I even knew. I found myself relaxed again. The General's head was in his watery grave, and I was off the hook of being arrested, for now.

When we arrived back at Josh's house, we got out. Josh said he had to pee and walked off towards the treeline, leaving Ri'Chard and I alone.

I said, "So, tonight..."

He cut me off. "Yep...it was...different."

I bit my lip, but not in a flirtatious way. "I also don't know what to say about it.."

He took a breath, like there was a lot more on his mind. My intuition told me it was guilt for doing something that could impact his relationship with Aisha. I couldn't tell if this constituted cheating because we didn't touch each other, but I could tell his heart was heavy.

I said, "I'm so sorry if this complicates things for you. I didn't plan for this to happen, and—"

Ri'Chard put his hand on my shoulder. "Julie, stop overthinking this. It's not your problem; this is something I will have to deal with." He looked at me and smiled. "I think you finally lost your *guai* card tonight."

I let out a small yelp of laughter. "Yes, I can never be *guai* again after tonight. I just hope my ancestors aren't mad. I'm going to have to burn a shit ton of 'ghost money' for them to forgive me next time I'm in Taiwan."

"You have to give ghosts money in Taiwan?"

"Yeah, gods too." I looked at Ri'Chard and tried to hold in some laughter.

"What?" He asked.

"You gave a 'ghost money-shot' tonight."

"Oh my god," he exclaimed as he broke out into laughter. "How do you know what that is?"

"Come on, I'm not that out-of-touch!" I exclaimed with a joking defensiveness.

"What's funny?" I heard Josh ask as he joined us.

"Oh, Julie's just being...Julie." Ri'Chard looked at me with a sparkle in his eyes.

I explained the joke to Josh, which made him laugh too. It was nice to diffuse the tension of tonight with some laughter.

"Okay guys, I need to head home." Ri'Chard and Josh did a bro-hug, then he leaned in and gave me a warm embrace. I felt the hardness of his body around me, and tried to remember this moment. Maybe this was the closest we'd ever get. I felt my eyes burn for the brief time he held me. He let go, turned and got into his truck, while I quickly wiped a tear. I felt like I wasn't only ruining my life anymore, but had started causing chaos in others. Who was this version of me? My disappointment in myself was tempered by my feeling of liberation. Maybe I was a psychopath because, as the tears of guilt built around my eyes, all I wanted to do was smile, especially since I felt Josh's arm drape across my shoulders. Ri'Chard rolled down the window and waved goodbye before leaving down the driveway. I stared as the red lights disappeared into the darkness.

"Do you want to spend the night?" Josh quietly said into my ear.

I smiled and nodded. As we walked into his house he asked, "Do you need anything? I'm going to go shower now."

I shook my head, then said, "Only a shirt to sleep in."

He came forward and hugged me. "I have it waiting for when you'd stay over again."

I breathed into him, looked up, kissed him, and dismissed him to take a shower. I collapsed on the couch and took a big breath. When I thought back to earlier, I just felt a gentle ease. It certainly was weird, but it was also right.

Out of the corner of my eye, I caught sight of something white on the floor. I angled down to see the sigil underneath the coffee table.

"Shit," I said. It must have been knocked down while Ri'Chard was panicking over cleaning his fingerprints. Now, I'd have to get rid of it here. I walked to Josh's kitchen and found a lighter in a catch-all dish. I tested it and saw an adequate flame. I took the sigil and went outside.

I looked up at the sky. It was clear tonight, and the stars were beautiful. If I stared long enough, I could make out the faint ignitions of distant galaxies, vast and incomprehensible. I turned my attention back to the sigil. I held the flame to the corner of the paper and watched it ignite. When the flame got halfway up, I dropped it on the ground. The orange edges turned black and collapsed into ash. Soon, it was gone.

17

I woke up bleary-eyed to Josh lying beside me. A little bit of dried drool was on the edge of his mouth. I was sure I looked similar.

He started to open his eyes and said, "Hey."

"Hey, I'm just watching you sleep," I told him in my raspy morning voice.

"It's alright," he said, stirring. "I forgot to buy coffee, though. I'm sorry."

I tried to hide my sadness. "I think I can do without it for one day."

I rolled over and looked at my phone, seeing multiple missed calls from Keli around midnight. I immediately felt worried, so I dialed back.

She picked up and started screaming into the phone, "JULIE! I DON'T KNOW WHAT THE FUCK YOU DID, BUT I'M GOING TO KILL YOU!" She continued breathing heavily and loudly crying.

"Keli, calm down. What's going on?" I asked. I put her on speaker for Josh to listen in as well.

I heard her take some deep breaths before starting. "Oh my

god, I don't know where to start. I was at work yesterday, and everything was normal except for lying to the police to save your ass. I was getting off at midnight, so I was just roaming around, cleaning up the lobby, getting everything ready for the end of my shift. I go outside for one last cigarette, and I see this man on a horse in the parking lot. All the lights are off out there, so it's hard to see, and it's late, so I assume maybe he's a drunk cowboy. He's just sitting there, though, so I ask him if he's alright. He turns to look at me, and I see he's wearing one of those Confederate outfits. I said, 'Not this shit again,' but I also noticed he had your Prada bag hooked on his saddle. I'm squinting at him, trying to make out who this purse-carrying Confederate is, then he hops down from the horse, grabs the purse, and starts walking toward me.

"At first, I thought he's on meth, then I realized this motherfucker looked like General Stovall. I was in a state of disbelief, but I just dropped molly like two nights before, and honestly, I wasn't sure if some of it was still working through my system.

"Anyway, he was coming toward me, and I was uncomfortable, so I decided to throw my lighter at him. The lighter bounced off him and landed on the ground. I thought shit was supposed to go through ghosts, so now I'm thinking he's just a regular old white guy with cataracts. He stopped, looked at the lighter, then picked it up. He looked at it like he ain't ever seen a lighter before, then tried to spark the flint. It took him a bit to get the point, then he finally got the fire to light. I'm like, 'Damn, maybe he is from the 1800s.'

"I'm watching this whole spectacle while still smoking my cigarette, but by now it's gone out. I say, 'Excuse me, I'm sorry I threw my lighter at you. I was scared. Can I have it back?'

"He walked toward me, still holding your goddamn purse. It's dark in the parking lot, so I can't see him too well. He holds up the lighter, and I lean in with my cigarette, so again, I can't see well. He sparks up, and I light my cigarette. I lean back and see his face lit up by the fire...and, Lord, Julie..." Keli's voice was beginning to crack, "His face wasn't right."

"So I screamed, Julie, and that motherfucker grabbed me by the neck and started choking me. I couldn't scream, and he lifted me up so I'm looking in his fucked-up eyes. He threw me onto the ground, but I'm a scrappy bitch so I'm up quick and ran inside the hotel. I grabbed some salt shakers off the table and emptied them in front of the doors, because I saw something about ghosts not being able to cross lines of salt. The lights in the lobby started flickering, and then everything went dark. When the power goes out, the sliding doors automatically open, so I'm standing in front of the door while he's like ten feet away from me.

"He started walking toward me while I moved back. He gets to the line of salt, looks at it, and steps right over it. I almost pissed myself right there.

"The lobby went completely dark, and he walked inside, honestly looking like a bad bitch cuz he was still holding the Prada. I'm still moving backwards and then fell over a chair and was on the ground. He looked at me and said, 'Where is she?' I said, 'Who do you want?' And he said, 'Julie Chen,' so I told him, 'Room 104. Her room is down there.'

"He turned to walk down the hall, and I grabbed my purse and ran. I'm sorry, but I'm not lying to a ghost. My boss has been blowing up my phone asking what happened, because I quit this morning. He said there was nothing on the cameras last night since everything went out. He's accusing me of being drunk and making this shit up, but on God, I saw his ghost last night."

I asked Keli, "Where are you now? I'll come find you so we can talk about this in person."

"You won't find me. I'm on my way to Atlanta. I do not do

ghosts. I'm taking the rest of my molly and processing this trauma elsewhere."

I looked at Josh with a skeptical look on my face. "I honestly don't know how to respond to this. Are you certain of what you saw last night?" I asked.

"Julie, I'm not even going to debate this with you because I know what I saw, and what I saw is the ghost of a Confederate General that is after your ass. If I were you, I'd be getting out of town, but I have to take a step back from this for my mental health. Call me when the ghost is vanquished, or whatever. I'm staying with my cousin until then. Good luck."

She hung up the phone, and I looked at Josh. I asked, "Am I dreaming? Are we awake?"

Josh also looked confused. "I think I'm awake. How can we tell?"

I gave him a light slap across the cheek. He said, "Okay, I'm definitely awake."

"Let's go back to my hotel and see what's going on."

WE BOTH GOT ready and headed out. We took Josh's truck. The weather was faintly stormy today. Gray clouds, the humidity of coming rain, and a moderate breeze. It felt like a storm was teasing us.

I asked Josh, "Do you believe in ghosts?"

"Not really. I've never seen one, but I guess they could be out there."

"I don't believe in ghosts. Now that I think about it, it was probably one of those Confederate cult members coming to attack me. I'm sure Keli was just startled, and her mind was playing tricks on her."

"That sounds about right, and I'm glad you were at my place

last night. If people are coming to your room, you really should stay with me until you leave," Josh advised.

"You're right. I'll stay with you." I looked at him and smiled.

"Are you moving in with me?" he asked, jokingly.

"Is that too fast?" I replied.

"No, it feels right for now." Josh reached out and grabbed my hand.

"What if the ghost is real and follows me back?" I asked.

"I'll be there to protect you." He squeezed my hand, and my eyes widened as I realized I hadn't replied to Matthew's last text message in two days. At this point, in my mind, things were over with Matthew. I just had to do the dignity of ending things in person.

WE PULLED INTO THE HOTEL, expecting to see police or local news, but everything was quiet. The automatic doors were working again, and when they opened into the lobby, it was the same as when I left it yesterday.

I didn't see anyone behind the desk, so I called out, "Hello?"

A man I had never seen before walked out from the back, wearing a white button-down.

"Yes, can I help you?" he asked.

"I'm looking for someone who works here named Keli? Do you know when she'll be in next?"

The man rolled his eyes. "She quit this morning. I would have fired her, though. This place was a mess when I got in this morning, and her excuses made no sense." He leaned a bit closer "Between you and me, it was either a mental episode or drugs."

I hesitated to contradict him, so I said, "Right. That's unfortunate, but what was a mess this morning?"

He scoffed. "There was salt everywhere, chairs turned upside down. It looked like she got into an altercation. Maybe a drug dealer or a fellow addict?"

"Interesting. Keli struck me as a remarkably good and dedicated employee. I never saw her act in such a strange way. Perhaps there was an incident not related to stereotypes about someone like her?"

"Oh. I see you're one of those people. Are you a guest here?"

"Yes, I am."

He feigned a smile. "Well, let me know if I can help you with anything related to your stay."

We walked through the lobby, veering toward my hall, when I heard a shrill voice call my name, "Julie?!"

My stomach dropped as I turned to see Yale Law, clutching a Yale travel mug with both bony hands. "I've been wondering when I'd see you. How are you? We just got in last night. Charming town!" She did a once-over of Josh and said, "Oh, hello."

"Hi, I'm Josh." He reached out and shook her hand.

She turned to me. "Who is this friend?"

"He's actually my mechanic..." I spoke very slowly, "My car broke, and he lent me one. He's here to check my loaner car, and I forgot the keys in my room."

I think she caught on. "Right." She turned to Josh, "It's a small town, so people must help each other out, right?"

He agreed. "Everyone becomes a friend once you get to Pothos."

"Well, that depends on your skin color," I said.

"I know, I'm excited to dig into this hotbed of bureaucratic racism!" said Yale Law enthusiastically.

I said, "Wonderful, but we'll catch up later in the afternoon?"

She squealed, "Great, we'll text. Bye!"

Once down the hall, I turned to Josh. "I totally forgot my

colleagues were arriving today. Shit. I'm not prepared to be dealing with people who are clueless about what's going on."

"It's alright," he said. "Maybe you need to tell them? Aren't they here to work with you?"

I sighed. "What can I tell them? About sigils? About the head? They'll think I've gone crazy here and gossip about me to everyone in the office. Let me just go and change my clothes, then we'll figure this all out." I felt problems beginning to pile up before I had a chance to solve any.

We turned and walked to my room. The door was a bit ajar, and I saw it had been broken. We cautiously pushed it open. I started looking around the living area to see if anything had been stolen while Josh walked into my bedroom.

"Uh, Julie," I heard him say, "Come look at this." On the bed was my Prada purse, executed with an old knife through the middle of it.

"Motherfuckers," I whispered.

Josh said, "Keli was right. Someone was definitely in here last night."

I reached out to grab my purse and held it up. "Ms. Honeypaw did this. I know it."

"What?" asked Josh in surprise. "Why would she do that?"

I said, "Did you not see how she treated me the last time we were at her house? She hates me."

Josh said, "Well, you did call her a 'bald-headed bitch'."

"Josh, that was only to get her attention so she could help us, which she refused to do."

Josh still looked confused. "But Keli was attacked by a guy last night."

"Yeah, I'm sure Ms. Honeypaw has muscle. She's probably running more than just card readings through that house."

"What does that mean?" Josh asked.

"I don't know. She's shady, and I wouldn't put it past her to fuck with me like this."

Josh said, "I think we should go talk to her. It's weird that your purse is here now. This doesn't make sense."

I looked at the bag with a knife through it. I thought it made perfect sense.

ON THE WAY DOWNTOWN, I realized I still hadn't had coffee or anything to eat. I asked Josh if he wouldn't mind stopping at the diner for a quick bite and some intelligence gathering, if possible.

Walking through the door into the diner, I expected to see it abuzz with the usual townsfolk, gossiping about the protests or other happenings. Strangely, as I looked around the diner, I saw it was almost empty.

Josh and I took a booth. "Something is going on," I said, "Everyone should be here right now."

Josh agreed. "Also, I thought there would be more newspeople after the riot. It's pretty quiet today."

I nodded and looked up at a TV hung below the ceiling in a corner of the diner. The news was reporting on a story about a pastor from a megachurch indicted for money laundering. I pointed at it and said, "I guess everyone is outside his mansion. Things move quickly in the news."

I looked around while Josh seemed to focus on the menu. The same waitress who helped me before looked bored behind the counter and eventually made it over to our booth.

"What can I get ya?" she asked.

"It's very quiet this morning. Where is everyone?" I asked her.

She looked around. "I don't know."

"Is there an event happening in town?"

She looked annoyed. “Listen, I’m just here to get you breakfast. Are you ready to order?”

I couldn’t tell if she was actually dense or just challenging me for her own entertainment. I relented and ordered breakfast.

Josh looked at his phone. “Oh, Alana responded. I forgot I sent her a picture of the sigil from last night.” He focused on her message, speaking slowly as if he struggled with reading text out loud. “‘I don’t recognize the sigil, but usually they are harmless unless you go through the process of activating them. That involves giving some energy to them then destroying them. Hope that helps.’”

“Can you ask her to clarify what ‘giving energy to a sigil’ is?”

He texted her back, and we waited for her response. “‘Chanting incantations, dancing, or sometimes a physical offering.’”

I recounted the previous night. “Does that include semen?”

Josh’s eyes widened. “Uh, I feel like she might think I’m coming onto her.”

“Just ask her,” I demanded.

We waited for a response, which Josh read with a sigh. “‘Actually, orgasmic energy is incredibly potent. Sex can be used to activate the sigil. I’m sad we never had the chance to try that.’ Oh, sorry, I should have left that part out.”

“Ask her more about activating it.”

He read, “‘A lot of times activation is done by destruction, like fire, but water also works. Are you trying to create a sigil?’”

I looked at Josh. “So, what if the sigil we found last night was accidentally activated with Ri’Chard’s cum, then destroyed by fire?”

“That’s possible. But what was the spell for? Are you suggesting we brought back the ghost for real?” Josh asked.

“I don’t know.” I looked around the empty diner and said, “But maybe everyone is hiding from the ghost.”

The waitress served us, but I had already lost my appetite. After a few minutes, Josh leaned back in his seat, satisfied with the mediocre diner food. "I don't really believe in all this ghost stuff. I think the person who left the head yesterday came back last night and tried to get you."

"That's a good point. Then how did he get Ms. Honeypaw's purse?" I asked.

Josh said, "They could have gone there first to try and find you."

My stomach dropped. Maybe Ms. Honeypaw was right; perhaps she was under threat because she was associated with me. I thought of Keli and the fear she had this morning. People shouldn't be getting hurt because of me.

I took out my phone and texted Ri'Chard, asking if he was alright.

He responded, "Yes, I'm doing fine. How are you?"

I said I'd call him after we went to check on Ms. Honeypaw. He replied, "Did something happen?"

I took a deep breath and texted: "We'll find out."

I ASKED Ri'Chard to meet us at her house if he had the time. When we arrived, I saw his tow truck already parked out front. He was leaning against it, looking at his phone. We pulled in behind it. I took a breath since this was the first time seeing him since last night.

I got out, and he smiled at me and said, "Hey."

I blushed a bit and greeted him. I decided to start by filling him in on what Keli told me earlier, then what we saw at the hotel. He asked, "Do you think something happened to Ms. Honeypaw?"

"Let's go check," I said confidently. We walked up to the front porch, and I followed behind the boys. Josh looked down at something on the top step. It looked like snow. He picked one up and tasted it. "It's salt."

Our eyes followed the line of salt left, all the way around the porch. We heard someone moving and cursing and leaned right to see Ms. Honeypaw struggling as she poured a very large bag of salt along the foundation of her house.

We watched her shuffle along as the line grew until she made it to the edge of the porch.

"Nice of you to fucking offer to help me," she said. "I got two strong men and an ovulating bitch watching me, and no one offers to give me a hand?"

They both apologized and quickly made their way down the porch.

I asked, "How do you know I'm ovulating?"

"I can smell that pussy from over here. You need to double up your underwear or something. That shit is stanky." She gave me her classic look of disgust. When the men reached her, she scolded them. "I'm already fucking done. You should have been here an hour ago."

Josh said, "I'm sorry, we didn't know you needed help."

She brushed him off. "Yeah, well, it ain't every day a fucking ghost visits you in the middle of the night." She wiped her hands on her dress and looked at me. "What?"

"Did someone attack you last night?" I asked cautiously.

Ms. Honeypaw looked around, then down. She said quietly, "I got away before he could get me."

I asked, "What happened?"

I could see her face contort and her body become shifty. She walked toward the porch, and when she made it up the porch, her eyes were watery. She said in a shaky voice, "If I talk about it, I'm gonna get all emotional." She sat in a chair on the porch and leaned back. The boys also walked up onto the porch.

Ri'Chard knelt and took Ms. Honeypaw's hand. "Tell us what

happened if you can, so we can understand." She squeezed his hand, then brought both hands up to wipe her eyes.

"Fine," she said, "I'll tell you. I was walking back from the gas station last night. I had to buy wrappers because I had the urge to smoke a fat blunt. The street was empty, and I'm not really paying much attention, but when I got close to my house, I noticed the lights down the street. One by one, they're slowly going out down the block. My eyes aren't the best, but I saw someone on a horse, and every time they went under a light, it went out. When the person on the horse got in front of my house, they stopped.

"I'll admit it, I was fucking scared. Horses freak me out, and the weird people that ride them freak me out even more. I realized I forgot to put my gun in the bag and was trying to figure out what to do. Meanwhile, the person on the horse got down. I realized it's a guy in a uniform, and he looks like one of these reenactor people. I decided I gotta show him that I'm not a bitch to be messed with.

"I said, 'What the fuck do you want?' He said nothing. I walked closer and started talking my shit, saying I got a man inside who's about to step out and solve this problem for me. I tell him I'm carrying, and if he doesn't want trouble, he should pick up his reins and ride off.

"He still just stood there and still said nothing. I got closer, and I took out my phone light and shined it on him." Ms. Honeypaw paused for a moment, and I could see the hopelessness in her face. Her tears remerged, and her voice was weakened as she continued, "I saw it was *him*. I recognized him, his statue, his stupid fucking face, but it also looked like he'd been hitting the crack pipe for a few centuries. I screamed and threw my bag at him, then ran up to my house. I was struggling with the keys, and he was coming toward me, but I finally got the lock undone and slammed the door shut. He was almost up the steps, but I keep a bag of salt by the front door just in-fucking-case, and I threw that shit down as fast as I could. He was at the door, but couldn't cross it. He just stood there, an inch in front of the glass, but there was no fog on the glass from his breath. I don't know what that was, but it wasn't a living person."

She shook her head. "He just looked at me for a minute, then walked off the porch. I saw him pick up my purse from the ground and put it on his saddle. He got on the horse and rode down the street. The weird thing is that the lights went back on as he moved past them."

Ms. Honeypaw's eyes were wide as she recollected the memory. I looked at Josh in confusion and said, "So he might have gone and attacked Keli afterward, and that's how my purse got there."

Josh nodded. "That's right. It has to be the same person."

Ms. Honeypaw asked, "What do you mean someone else was attacked?"

I retold Keli's story, and at the end, I said, "But Keli said she put down salt, and he crossed it, so I don't get why that would work here? Perhaps it really was just someone dressed up and trying to intimidate them."

Josh considered. "Sometimes they use potassium chloride as table salt instead of sodium chloride; it's supposed to be healthier. It's just a weird fact I remember."

"That sounds plausible," I reasoned. "But how did he know it was *my* purse?"

"Because everyone in this town knows you're the bougie bitch with a Prada bag," stated Ms. Honeypaw. I frowned at the truth.

Ri'Chard said to Josh, "So you think this was an actual ghost?"

Josh shrugged. "I don't know. I can't figure out how the electricity would go out all of a sudden."

I said, "Do you really think the sigil worked? That the ghost came back?"

Ms. Honeypaw gave me a look that made me shiver and slowly enunciated, "What fucking sigil?"

I looked at an uncomfortable Ri'Chard and Josh, trying to decide how to spin this. I said, "Ahhh, yesterday someone dropped the head from the statue of General Stovall at my door. I believe they were trying to frame me for theft. I took it to Josh's, and we discovered a sigil inside of it. We got rid of the head but forgot the sigil..." I winced and quickly said, "And I burned it."

Ms. Honeypaw's eyes widened in anger. "You burned it? You just go around burning sigils like you know what the fuck they're about? How are you the most educated person among us, yet you keep doing the dumbest shit? Is everyone who has a fancy degree a fucking idiot?"

"I mean, they don't teach us witchcraft in law school. How are regular people supposed to know about the occult? This is a very niche subject."

Ms. Honeypaw rolled her eyes. "How about you use common sense. Why don't you *ask* someone who might know instead of being a little know-it-all bitch."

I said, "Well, Josh did ask his ex, but she only got back to him this morning, and it was too late."

Ms. Honeypaw turned to him. "Which ex?"

Josh said, "The one that moved to Asheville."

Ms. Honeypaw nodded. "Oh, CrystalBitch. I liked her." She looked me up and down. "Her pussy didn't stink like old Chinese food." She continued, "So that motherfucker stole my purse. Where is it?"

I said, "First, it was *my* purse. You stole it from me. Secondly, he left a knife through it."

She winced, "The Prada? He gave the Prada a buck fifty?"

"What's 'a buck fifty'?" I asked.

"It's when you trash a lying bitch's face with a knife." She looked at me like it was obvious.

I felt a tingling in my cheek and slowly nodded. "Yes, the Prada is trashed." We all took a moment of silence for the bag.

Ms. Honeypaw asked Josh, "What did CrystalBitch say about the sigil?"

He replied, "She didn't know what it was for, but it was the same pattern that was drawn in chicken blood on the grave when we snuck to the plantation house."

I thought for a moment. "Sally Wren was reading from some when they drew the sigil on the grave. I wonder if that book has answers?"

Ri'Chard said, "It would be impossible to get that book, though. They must keep it guarded if it's important."

I said, "You're right, and the only bargaining chip we had was thrown into the quarry..."

Ms. Honeypaw asked, "That book, could you see a title on it?"

I said, "No, we were pretty far away."

She said haughtily, "How are you going to spy on a place and not bring binoculars? Do you see what I mean about you being a dumbass?"

I was too exhausted to disagree. "You know what, you're right. We weren't prepared to witness an occult ceremony and gather intel."

Ri'Chard chimed in. "Okay, so we still don't know exactly why they left the head for you. We assume it's because they were trying to arrest you, but we can't be certain. We don't know what the book is or what it's used for. We don't know if the ghost is... real."

Ms. Honeypaw interrupted, "That fucker is real."

Ri'Chard continued, "Right, there's that issue."

I added, "We also don't know who owns the plantation

house and whether that group trespassed onto the property to do their ceremony."

Josh said, "We need to figure out a way to get the answers. Who would know?"

I said, "Anyone in that group...but we can't kidnap them."

Ms. Honeypaw said, "Says who? Bring one of those bitches here, and I've got some pliers to rip out their fingernails."

Ri'Chard tried to defuse her. "Hey, we're not doing that."

Ms. Honeypaw was heated. "Why the fuck not? If you send a ghost to my motherfucking house, then there will be consequences."

Josh said, "That doesn't mean ripping someone's fingernails off. Stop making yourself seem tough."

Ms. Honeypaw looked at him. "Little boy, you have no idea the shit I would do to someone that hurts me or my family, and that includes you. If a bitch breaks your heart, then I'm using her fingernails for a windchime."

I felt the nerves in my fingers light up. I glanced down at my nails and tried not to think about them being pried off by her. It didn't help that the porch already had three wind chimes that quietly played in the subtle breeze.

I said, "I think we need to figure out a realistic way to get information. Perhaps there's another meeting we can eavesdrop on? Maybe if we can figure out where they meet and leave a recording device there?"

Ri'Chard nodded. "That's an idea. I have to think about it some more."

Josh agreed. "Same, I don't have any ideas at the moment."

I added, "I think we have to reevaluate and decide later."

Ms. Honeypaw said, "I have a whole house to protect by sunset, and you're just sitting here shooting the shit like we ain't got a supernatural entity trying to pull up on a horse and clap me. Y'all are fucking useless. Get off my porch."

Ri'Chard stood, and we all walked down as she went back to inspecting her salt line. Ri'Chard said, "Well, I gotta go back to work. I'll keep thinking and get back to you guys later."

I said, "Same, we'll let you know if we come up with anything." I awkwardly went in for a hug. He returned it, and I said, "Please be safe. We don't know who this person is and what they're capable of."

Ri'Chard smiled. "If it is the General, I might be high on his list..."

I smirked and turned to Josh, who was also smiling. He said, "Yes, he certainly has a boner to pick with you."

We laughed. I said, "You guys, the General was probably a repressed homosexual. All the angry ones are. Maybe he enjoyed it?"

Josh said, "I mean, Ri'Chard is a catch."

I seconded, "Maybe you helped him come out of the closet?"

Ri'Chard grimaced. "I just hope to God I didn't help him come out of the grave first."

We all took a deep breath for a moment and said goodbye. Josh and I went back to his place to think.

Inevitably, we were in Josh's bed. I was lying on my side. Josh was on his; his hand brushed some hair behind my ear, and he lightly pinched my earlobe. He smiled at me and asked, "Should I get my ears pierced?" I reached out and felt his tender lobe with my fingers. In the light, I could see the light hairs that secretly grew across our skin.

"I don't know," I said. "I like you plain, but you might look nice with some sparkle."

"I don't think I'll be wearing diamonds," he said.

"Diamonds would suit you, though," I said. He pinched my earlobe and leaned in to kiss me. Our clothes were still on. We weren't intending to have sex, but pulling at straws got boring. We were much happier in our own world, with each other.

Our moment was interrupted by my phone. I untwisted myself and found it buried in the sheets. It was an unknown number, but I decided to pick it up.

"Hello?" I asked.

"Ms. Chen, it is a pleasure to be speaking with you," the voice said. My spine tingled with recognizing the voice of Jim Smoke.

"Mr. Smoke, what brings you to call me?"

"Well, I'm just trying to help out a friend. That's all."

"Oh, did Steve have a hunting accident?"

"No, not Steve. I consider you a friend, Ms. Chen. It's part of the Pothos promise: come as a stranger, leave as a friend."

"I don't think that's true. Why are you calling me, Mr. Smoke?"

"That's a shame, because we have a situation here. I found your little friends trespassing earlier around the statue of General Stovall. You see, it's still a crime scene and an active investigation, yet they ignored our barriers, and well, we had to arrest them."

I was confused. I asked, "What friends?" Ri'Chard and Ms. Honeypaw were accounted for, it could only be—

"Those two lawyers from D.C., aren't they your friends?" He asked.

I sighed. Imbeciles. "Right, those are colleagues of mine. On their behalf, I sincerely apologize for their negligence and disrespect for the laws of the town."

He continued, "See, I thought we'd be on the same page. I can make this whole thing go away if you help me."

"Ah, the good old *I'll help you if you help me*."

"Yes," said Mr. Smoke. "That's called *friendship*. Now, I think you have something that's very important to the town. I'd like you to bring it to the temporary courthouse at 6 pm tonight, then we can settle this misunderstanding."

"And how do I know you won't arrest me upon arriving with what you need?"

"Ms. Chen, do you consider me a man who doesn't keep his word?"

I wanted to say yes, but instead I said, "I hope you prove me wrong, Mr. Smoke. See you at six." I hung up and said, "Fuck, fuck, fuck."

Josh looked concerned and asked, "What's going on?"

WE SPENT the next hour on the phone with Ri'Chard, solidifying a plan. We decided they might take our phones, so I couldn't record this meeting for evidence, or be in touch with anyone outside the church. Luckily, I had a smartwatch I was supposed to use while working out, but the hotel gym TVs only played a home shopping network, so I never went. I could hide the watch in my bra, connected to a call with Ri'Chard so he could monitor the situation. He said he'd look for backup, in case, which I thought was ridiculous. Judging from what we'd seen in the cemetery, this was not a militant group. It also wouldn't take much to apprehend my colleagues; all one had to do was lure in Yale Law with the promise of an alumni networking party.

However, we really didn't know what was going to happen on the inside. We couldn't bring the head, so perhaps admitting we got rid of it would cause them to spill their intentions. Nothing was certain, but it was the only shot we had.

Our plan was going smoothly until we were ready to leave Josh's house. "I think we should take the Corolla," I told Josh. "It's small and fast, in case we need to make a getaway."

He suggested, "But my truck is big and strong in case we need to ram the cars that are chasing us."

"That's a male fantasy. We're not ramming cars, but we might want to be able to drive away quickly. Plus, it's easier for passengers to get into the Corolla."

"The passengers could always hop into the bed of my truck, and what if there are more than two hostages? Maybe they have many, and we can fit them in the back of my truck."

"That's ridiculous. It's not like they're being trafficked and we're busting an operation. A sedan makes way more sense."

He shook his head. "I think the truck does."

"Fine! Let's take our separate cars, and then we have both available depending on the situation."

He squinted at me. "Are you serious?"

"Yes, I'm done arguing about cars and trucks."

I got into the Corolla, and he hurriedly hopped in the passenger side. He said, "Damn, were you about to leave me?"

I looked at him and smiled, "I don't think so, but sometimes I can be stubborn. I think I'm right about this."

He grabbed my hand and squeezed it. "I think you're right too."

18

We parked a few spaces down from the Church. There were some cars in the parking lot, including a large black SUV. Perhaps it was an undercover police car, so I made note of it.

I dialed Ri'Chard on my watch and stuffed it in my bra. "Can you hear me?" I asked.

"Yes, I can hear you. I'm going to record everything, but I don't know how well I'll be able to hear what they say. However, if you get in any trouble, say the word 'lemon'."

I smiled. "Okay, we have a safe word. Thank you."

Ri'Chard said, "I'll be listening in a nearby location." I thanked him again before he muted himself. I looked at Josh and said, "I'll be back soon."

"No, I'm going with you," he said defiantly.

"Jim Smoke is just being a sleazy lawyer. I can handle that. Besides, I don't want him to create trouble for you after this. I don't want you to be involved."

He looked at me and said, "I got involved the moment you came to ask me for help with your car. We're in this together." He leaned in and kissed me deeply, his palm gently resting against my cheek. I took his hand and held it as our kiss tempered our anxieties.

I pulled back and said, "Let's go fix this."

Josh smiled. "That's my job."

We got out, and I narrated to Ri'Chard, "We're walking toward the courthouse now. We are about twenty feet from the front entrance. Remember, our goal is to get information, so only come if I tell you."

I hoped he heard me and agreed. We walked up to the front door and stood outside of it. I looked at Josh and asked, "Should we knock? They are expecting us."

Josh shrugged. "I don't know. Is it locked?"

I grabbed the handle and twisted it, opening the door. "I guess not," I said as I slowly pushed the door.

As the view widened, I saw Jim Smoke standing in the middle of the aisle. "Julie, welcome. Come on in."

We cautiously stepped in. I said "I see we're on a first-name basis now." I looked sideways and I saw two men on either side of the door in bulletproof vests. They had buzz cuts and were strongly built, perhaps cops, but none that I recognized from this town.

I looked them up and down and asked, "Who are they?"

Jim Smoke smiled. "Personal security, on loan from another friend. Don't mind them; we've had to take on volunteers to help restore law and order in this town."

I saw they were armed at their waists. I started to worry. Jim Smoke continued, "Now, I expected you to bring something to trade."

I said, "Well, how do I know you'd keep your word? Don't worry, it's somewhere safe. I'll tell you the location when my friends are set free."

Jim Smoke said, "I thought that would be the case." He

signaled at the two armed men behind us, and suddenly I felt my hands being yanked behind my back.

"Hey!" I screamed, "What the fuck?" One man held me, and the other had Josh. He forced my wrists together and slipped plastic riot cuffs over them before I could understand what was happening. Josh was putting up a fight, so one guy let me go to help the other with Josh.

I looked at Jim Smoke and growled, "I thought we were *friends*, asshole."

"Yes, but I grew tired of your shit. Now you're gonna cooperate with me so we can get this over with quickly." He said to the men, "Bring them to the front."

They pushed us forward, toward the altar where an emaciated white Jesus hung from the cross. We were forced down into the front pews, and Jim Smoke told them, "Go guard the outside and don't let in anyone who doesn't belong here."

I looked at the men walking and heard one say, "She had nice tits for an Asian." I cursed them under my breath, turned to Jim Smoke. "I thought we had a deal? What the fuck is all this for?"

He sat down on the lip of the altar stage and crossed his arms. He said, "You see, I may not have been clear. Not only were your colleagues violating the law for trespassing, so were *you*."

I scoffed. "What are you talking about?"

He wagged his head. "You're going to play dumb? Those woods around the Stovall Plantation have cameras."

My stomach dropped. I didn't think the woods would be under surveillance. Jim Smoke continued, "We have you and this gentleman on camera, trespassing. Thank you for bringing him by the way; it helps expedite justice."

"Fine, we trespassed. We didn't damage anything, so this is hardly deserved treatment for our crime."

"I'm not the one deciding the punishment for your crime. I'm merely here to prosecute in your hearing."

I asked, "Well then, where is the judge?"

"He's coming," said Jim Smoke. "Be patient."

I said, "Do you actually have my colleagues? Or did you lie about that, too?"

He stood up, "I almost forgot about them." He procured a small walkie-talkie from his pocket and said, "Bring them up." A crackly voice replied, "Yes, sir." He looked at me and said, "That loud one was giving me a headache, so we put them in the basement."

We heard a door swing open. The familiar shrill voice of Yale Law filled the church with her sermon of inconvenience. She kept screaming, "Why are you doing this? What is going on? You can't abduct us!"

I recognized the men who brought them from the cemetery. She was plopped down next to me, and Useless Idiot was put on the other side of her. He was bizarrely quiet and looked ill.

Yale Law said, "Julie, what the fuck is going on?!"

I said, "I honestly don't know. They just tied us up and put us here." I leaned to look at Useless Idiot and asked, "How is he?"

Yale Law said, "Not good, he's shaken, of course. He has PTSD from a traumatic fraternity hazing experience, and this is triggering it."

"Oh, I'm sorry to hear that," I said, grimacing. The two men who brought them up moved to stand on either side of the church.

Yale Law leaned to look at Josh. "What is your mechanic doing here?"

I said, "Uh, he dropped me off."

Her eyes narrowed in suspicion. She looked at me and said, "Do you know why they kidnapped us? What do they want from us?"

I looked at Jim Smoke and said, "That's the question I've been trying to find out."

Jim Smoke reiterated, "As I've said, you've been arrested for trespassing and theft. You'll now have to face judgment in the court of God."

I said, "I told you, I know the location of the head. If you want it, then let us go."

"What head?" asked Yale Law.

I said, "The head from the statue of General Stovall. He sent it to my room in an effort to frame me."

"Oh, I was wondering where his head went..." said Yale Law, trailing off.

I asked her, "Were you actually at the statue earlier?"

Jim Smoke interrupted, "Yes, they were. We arrested them as they were trying to take a selfie in front of the statue."

I turned to Yale Law and quietly said, "What the fuck?"

She turned a little red. "I'm sorry, we just wanted to send it to the Junior Associate group chat."

I felt stung. "There's a Junior Associate group chat?"

She said, "Yes, are you not a part of it? I'll add you." I tried to not let the pain of exclusion hurt me. After all, office me wasn't a pleasant person. I could see why they probably weren't comfortable sharing parts of their lives with that Julie.

I said, "No, it's fine. That's not important." I leaned in and whispered to her, "I have a plan. Say nothing."

Jim Smoke noticed and said, "Hey, what are you whispering to her?"

I said, "I was just asking if she had a tampon. I'm still on my period. Do you have one?"

He grimaced. "I don't want to hear about this lady stuff. Let's hear your sentence, then we'll see *if* you need one."

When I got out, I promised myself I'd hang a thousand

bloody tampons in front of his house. I leaned and whispered to Josh, "This is it. Let's get what we came for."

Jim Smoke said, "If you keep whispering, I'm putting you on the other side."

Josh said, "She was just asking me if I had a tampon."

I suddenly burst out laughing, and so did Josh. I looked at him, shaking. It was the same laughter I felt in the police station: laughter in the face of absurdity. Even Yale Law began to laugh, while Jim Smoke kept his arms crossed and scowled at us. "You think this is funny? You have no idea of the consequences you will face."

I said, "Fine, but I need answers first. What were you doing at the graveyard the night we snuck into the woods?"

Jim Smoke smirked. "Objection: relevancy."

I countered, "I think it's all relevant to why we are here. I need to establish motive."

"Motive of the criminal? We're no criminals, Ms. Chen. We're on the side of law and order."

I rolled my eyes. "I know, you keep saying that, but I want to know what you had to sacrifice the chicken for."

Yale Law interrupted, "They're sacrificing chickens down here?"

Jim Smoke sighed. "That was a ceremony we were performing, in accordance with his return."

I asked, "Did it work? Did he return?"

"Not at first," said Jim Smoke, "But by the miracle of God, he did come back."

"Who came back?" I asked.

Jim Smoke said, "You will see, very soon."

I asked, "While we're waiting, can you clarify what book you were reading from during your 'ceremony'?"

"Why do you want to know about that?" asked Jim Smoke.

"It's relevant to the case. Are you concealing evidence?" I taunted him.

"You're a curious woman, Ms. Chen, and now that's gotten you into trouble. Maybe you should learn to stay quiet once in a while."

"I'm just interested in your rituals," I said with a shrug.

Jim Smoke sighed. "Fine, I don't think it will do much harm to answer your question. It was a book, an old book discovered when the owners of the plantation house were renovating the basement."

I queried, "What were the contents of this book?"

"It seemed to be an old society that formed in the aftermath of General Stovall's assassination, created by his daughter. She was worried about the compromising of history and historical artifacts, so she established the Daughters of Pothos Historical Society. They were responsible for erecting monuments in this town, like the one of General Stovall, to make sure our great history would not be lost to time."

I was confused. "So you were reading from a history book?"

Jim Smoke looked a bit shifty. "Well, the Daughters may have dabbled in other things besides history..."

"The occult," said Josh. "Was that book written by witches?"

Jim Smoke smirked. "You're sharper than I thought, boy. But 'witch' has such a negative connotation. They prefer 'Sorceress'."

I leaned toward Josh. "How did you know it was written by witches?"

He quietly said back, "Ms. Honeypaw's mom would tell me stories about the 'White-bitch witches of Pothos' when I was young. I thought she was just doing it to scare me, but maybe she was serious."

I turned back to Jim Smoke. "How does one become a Sorceress?"

"You don't become one. You have to be born with it. It seems the women who descended from our great General Stovall were given a gift, one that allowed them to communicate between the worlds."

"Ms. Honeypaw," I said to myself. My eyes darted around. This couldn't be true or happening. She was a fraud, a fake, and ghosts didn't exist. Sally Wren was just some hyper-Christian housewife whose biggest dream was opening a gay conversion camp. I asked, "What is actually in that book then?"

He said, "It contained the procedure for bringing the General back from the dead, when the time came, and that time is now. He is needed to save our Nation."

My eyebrows furrowed. "And you happened to discover this book in the basement of the plantation house? That seems fishy. What were they doing there?"

Jim Smoke said, "They were building... a game room. The book happened to be in an alcove covered by a brick wall."

I asked, "And what happened to this society, Daughter of the Pothos Historical Society?"

"Well, now it's just the Pothos Historical Society, to allow gentlemen with similar beliefs to join."

I said, "So you made it gender-neutral? That's progressive."

"Hardly," he said haughtily. "Men were needed to help carry about the enlightenment. This is not work women can solely handle."

I rolled my eyes. "So, did you actually want the head back or was it just a way to arrest us?"

Jim Smoke pursed his lips and then stood up. He started pacing. "You're persistent, Ms. Chen. Originally I intended to leave the head in your possession to have you arrested and prosecuted. Your antics here have brought prying eyes to Pothos, and we really don't like that. I was trying to get rid of you in the kindest way, but the situation has changed. You're no longer relevant to anything, except that we want the head back."

I asked, “Is the head important for your rituals?”

Jim Smoke said, “No, but we plan to erect his statue again. It seems our conviction was strong enough that the General already returned.”

Josh asked, “Did it have something to do with the sigil in the head?”

Jim Smoke raised his eyebrows. “What sigil?”

“The one in the head?” I said guiltily. “And we might accidentally be responsible for activating it.”

He looked incredulous. “You? You think you have any responsibility in bringing back the General?”

I nodded. “Yes. We accidentally got semen on the sigil, then in an effort to destroy the evidence, I burned it.”

Jim Smoke ground his teeth together. “I hardly think that had any effect on things.”

I added, “And that semen...came from a Black man.”

Jim Smoke was taken aback. “Impossible,” he said, laughing to himself, “This is the problem with you people. Your depravity knows no bounds. You’ll say anything to get a rise out of us.”

Josh said, “She’s serious. I was there because the whole thing was a little gay too.”

Jim Smoke was speechless. Yale Law filled in the void with her shrill observation, “I’m completely riveted, but I have no idea what the fuck is going on. Is this a joke? What’s this about a book, and a head, and semen?”

I ignored her. Jim Smoke still looked at us with a hostile expression. I turned back to him and said, “I mean, someone has to tell your boss, and it’s kind of your fault since you were in charge of the head.”

Jim Smoke scoffed, “Your baseless distraction won’t work on me. This is a waste of my time.”

“Fine, fine.” I appealed. “I have another question: who owns the plantation house, and are they a part of the society?”

His eyes narrowed. "Let's just say they're an anonymous donor."

Suddenly, the lights in the courthouse flickered, and we were plunged into darkness. I heard Jim Smoke's disembodied voice. "He's here. Let's get things ready."

The two helpers began to light candles, carefully placing them at the judge's bench and along the altar. I heard the front entry doors groan open and turned to see a central figure flanked by two men holding gas lamps, purposely walking down the aisle.

By vague candlelight, I could see Jim Smoke holding a salute for the person walking toward him. We all craned our necks to see. The figure strode past us and stopped. Jim Smoke stood tall, held his salute, and said, "Good evening, General, welcome to tonight's proceedings."

The man said, "Thank you, Soldier Smoke. May God be with you." The man turned and walked up the steps on the right side of the altar. He walked to the judge's bench while two men followed. I saw one holding a silver tray. From it, he took an inkwell and a quill and placed them on the bench. The other pulled out the chair, which he sat in and shuffled forward. He grabbed a candle from the edge of the bench and brought it closer, illuminating his face. I gasped.

I had seen his face before, at the parade and at the protest. This was the face I found in a duffel bag outside my door, and brought to Josh's. The face I watched Ri'Chard clean his cum off before we threw it into the abyss. It was a face I knew well.

"General Stovall," I said quietly.

He tilted his chin upwards and asked, "These are Union traitors?"

Jim Smoke said, "Yes, they are responsible for inciting the violence in this town that led to the desecration of your statue. They are also liable for trespassing and theft of your head."

General Stovall looked down at us. "Which one has my head?"

Jim Smoke pointed at me. "It was stolen by that woman there, Julie Chen."

The General asked, "The Oriental one? Does she speak English? Can she answer our queries?"

Jim Smoke said, "Oh yes, she has quite the mouth on her."

"You," The General pointed at me. "Do you understand why you are here this evening?"

I was speechless, my mouth was agape. Ms. Honeypaw and Keli were right, and so was Mr. Lyons. His ghost had returned, although he looked very sturdy and physically present to be a ghost. Yet his eyes were milky white, and his face had a strange pallor to it.

Yale Law's voice deafened my left ear. "Excuse me, we're not 'Union traitors'. We're lawyers here to fight a voting rights case. Are we trapped in an elaborate war reenactment? Because I did not consent to participate in this."

General Stovall looked at her. "You are an enemy of my Confederacy, captured in my territory, therefore I consider you a traitor. I would reveal your intentions if you value your pathetic life."

She huffed. "What 'Union'? This is the *United* States of America. The Civil War ended like 160 years ago. Get over it."

I kicked her leg and whispered, "Shut up!"

"This war is not over," said General Stovall. "And I'm here to win it."

He turned and looked at me. "I was told an Oriental was creating trouble in this town. Your reputation precedes you, as you've been rather quiet."

"I...I...uh," I stuttered, unsure of what to say to a ghost.

"I thought you spoke English?" said the General.

Finally, I got out, "How are you here? You are dead."

"Oh, she speaks fluently enough," he said. "Yes, I remained within the ghost realm for quite some time, but I have been reincarnated to finish God's mission of preserving the freedom and liberties of this Confederacy."

I was still stunned and said, "That's impossible."

"Anything is possible when God is on your side," he said confidently.

I looked at Josh, who was just as dumbfounded as I was.

I felt Yale Law kick my leg back. "Julie, this isn't a ghost. Obviously, this is a man just pretending to be the General in order to scare us out of this town. Those are just contacts and foundation from a drug store. Get your shit together!"

I looked up at the stage and realized Yale Law was onto something. Maybe this was all fake? Everything up until this point was conjecture, but how hard could it be to dress a man up and scare people? Suddenly, I snapped back to reality. "Holy shit, you're right. This is complete bullshit. I can't believe I fell for it. They basically created a drag queen ghost of a Confederate general."

Yale Law joined, "Oh my god, I love drag shows. What would he lip sync to?"

"'Country Roads', of course," I said.

"I can see it," taunted Yale Law. "But I want something with choreo. I mean, 'Thriller' would be *hilarious*."

I said, "I can't believe I fell for this."

"I know, you should have seen your face. You were like, 'Gen-Gen-General Stovall?'" Yale Law let out an ear-piercing howl, "I can't wait to tell James about this."

I grimaced. "But everyone in the office will make fun of me." I was already imagining people constantly referencing this huge debacle for a cheap laugh. This would become my reputation. Maybe I'd have to kill Yale Law and Useless Idiot to bury this embarrassment forever, before they could message it to the group chat.

The General looked at us and remained expressionless.

Yale Law continued, "Honestly, for a second I believed it too. I was like, 'They don't teach seances at Yale Law School.'" She laughed.

Josh remained stoic. I looked at him with his furrowed brow. He was either deeply angry or skeptical of our conclusion, maybe both. I turned to Josh and whispered, "I told you this would be stupid. Let's just see what they really want from us first."

Josh whispered back, "Do you think this is all fake? I don't know, this feels weird. Also, your colleague looks really freaked out."

I looked at Useless Idiot. "He's fine. I think they're just trying to intimidate us into dropping this case, or doing this to cover up some other intention. We need to figure it out."

I turned my attention toward the General. "Excuse me, since you've come back from the dead, can I ask what your plans are?"

He said, "Do you consider me that unintelligent of a man, that I'd directly answer your query with my confidential war plans for you to report to my enemies?"

I answered, "Your enemies have bigger things to worry about. So, what's your goal with bringing back the Confederacy?"

General Stovall spoke, "With great sorrow, I have witnessed the decline of this great Nation. This is no longer a Nation of gentlemen, but a Nation of depravity and lawlessness. A woman no longer yearns to rear her young, and instead pretends that she is the equivalent of man. Man lies with man, and can even be married in holy matrimony in front of God. It's a mockery. A disgusting disgrace. And, now, they believe in the equality of races?" The

General slammed his fist on the table and stood from his chair. "I will guide this Nation to a new era. I will build an army that will lay waste to the enemies of common sense. We will create a new Nation under the will of God, who will guide us in all that is just."

If my hands weren't cuffed, I would have clapped. His commitment to the bit was impressive, even if I hated watching plays, much less ones where I was held against my will.

I said, "I have a few comments on your proposal." The General looked at me, then took his quill and dipped it into the inkwell, focusing on writing something. I continued anyway. "Firstly, building an army is a bit grandiose, don't you think? I mean, it's really expensive. Do you know what our military budget is nowadays? It's like $800 billion. That's a lot of bales of cotton. More importantly, people are really lazy now. They have phones, video games, porn, and all those that have contributed to the decline of the America you knew. You're not going to find enough restless young people to build your Christian nation; they're all stoned."

The General set down his quill and stood up. He walked out from behind the desk and started to pace the length of the stage. I continued, "A lot of women enjoy working, even if work in general sucks. Also, not everyone wants to be a mother. I know I don't want kids." I saw Josh turn to look at me, seemingly triggered by my public admittance of something I always knew.

Yale Law decided to join in. "Are you, like, a Boomer Incel? You're mad you can't get laid, and now you're dressing up as the ghost of a Confederate general to get back at all the women that won't sleep with you?"

The General said, "The two of you are surely examples of the corruption of the woman's mind. I see the grace of subservience has disappeared, replaced with greed and an unsuitable desire for power. Perhaps it would be better to get rid of you now, for the sake of our Country."

I laughed a little. "Oh, there are a lot more women like us."

The General said, "A sensible woman only needs a few examples for her to learn how to act."

"What is this really about?" I asked. "Do you want us to drop our case, or is there something else you're hiding?"

Jim Smoke said, "I don't think you get it yet. You're on the losing team, Ms. Chen. You might want to start begging for your life instead."

I rolled my eyes. "Just give it up. You won't get rid of us that easily, unless you restore the voters as I asked you to in the beginning."

"We're way beyond that," said Jim Smoke. "And I'd like to hear the General's verdict and punishment." He turned to the General. "Sir, do you have a verdict?"

The General returned to the bench and said, "Yes, I shall read the verdict as follows. For the crime of inciting a riot, I declare all parties *guilty*." He banged the gavel and continued, "For the crime of trespassing, I declare all parties *guilty*." The gavel banged. "For the crime of destruction of a cultural monument, I declare all parties *guilty*." The gavel banged again. "As a punishment fitting for the severity of these crimes, I sentence all guilty parties to *death*." His gavel banged a final time.

"Death?" said Yale Law. "That's a little dramatic. I've already been held captive for hours. Not to mention, they fed me bread with gluten, and I have bad stomach cramps. I think this has gone too far, and I demand to be released." Everyone in the office, and probably every waiter in D.C. knew about Yale Law's gluten intolerance. I sighed; at this point, I was ready for them to actually execute her.

The General stood. "Don't worry, I will soon release you from your physical bodies." He summoned one of his helpers, who brought him a wooden box. He opened the top and took out a silver, old-fashioned and ornate pistol. He inspected it and walked down the steps of the altar.

"Julie, we need help," said Josh.

I said, "Josh, that thing is a prop. Look at how old it is. This is their last test; if we don't buy this, then we win."

Josh said, "God, I hope you're right."

"Are you going to do to us what you did to the pony?" I asked Jim Smoke.

Yale Law asked, "What pony?"

I answered, "There was one hung with its guts spilling out outside the courthouse. It wasn't a Golden Retriever. I fucked up."

"Oh, Sunny is alive?" she asked.

"There's no Sunny," I told her, making her let out a sound of relief.

Jim Smoke said, "The pony disrespected the legacy of General Stovall's family. We had to make an example of it, just like we will of you all."

"What about the head?" I asked. "Don't you still want it?"

Jim Smoke smirked at me and said, "Who needs a statue when you have the real thing?"

By now, the General was standing in front of Yale Law. He looked at her, holding his pistol in his left hand, he reached out his right hand and brushed her cheek. She flinched a little, saying, "Wow, your hand is really cold. That ice pack trick is nice. I even was a theater minor at Princeton undergrad, and I'm very impressed by all this. How did you do the lighting effects?"

Jim Smoke explained, "General Stovall seems to disrupt electromagnetic fields, so the electricity goes out wherever he goes. These aren't tricks, I'm afraid. This is reality."

"Right," said Yale Law, "I actually starred in 'Chicago' at Princeton, as Roxy Hart. I know a prop gun when I see one."

The General stood in front of us, arms crossed, with a rather beautiful antique pistol now held in his right hand."Where is my head?" asked the General.

I said, "We will only give you the location once you release us. Is that what you were searching for last night? Why you went to Ms. Honeypaw's house?"

The General looked at me. "Yes, last night I went to get what belongs to me, but now I have made the decision to execute you all. I just signed the warrant for your executions on the basis that you are spies and traitors, and as demonstrated tonight, enemies of my mission to restore greatness to this Country. Now, this here is my trusted pistol," he glanced down at it, "It must be reloaded with a laborious process, so you all shall decide amongst yourselves who is the first to die and who is the last, after witnessing the deaths of all your friends."

My stomach started to become queasy. This didn't feel right, but Yale Law was still steadfast in her determination to expose the charade. She said, "Hi, I think we've done enough role-playing for tonight. We get it, you don't want us in your town. You don't have to put on a whole show and threaten us with 'execution'."

The General held out his pistol toward Useless Idiot and fired a shot. It sounded like a cannon and burst with smoke. I heard Useless Idiot let out a wild scream. As the smoke cleared, I could make out blood dribbling out a hole in his arm. He shot him, a true gunshot as the acrid smoke burned my nostrils. I said, "Lemon" softly.

Yale Law screamed, "You motherfuckers! Let us go!" She kicked out at the General who easily dodged her spindly legs. The general summoned someone to bring another box.

He answered, "Sadly, this pew is the last place you'll get to sit. Now beg for forgiveness before the altar of God." The box was presented to him, and he began to speedily reload his pistol.

The General said, "I must get this over quickly; I have a homecoming party to attend tonight."

"Julie!" I heard Josh yell.

"Lemon!" I said louder, "Ri'Chard, LEMON! LEMON!" My breaths were rapid and my eyes watering as I watched him stuff gunpowder and another lead ball into the chamber.

Yale Law looked at Useless Idiot, who was crying out in pain, and snarled, "Julie's boyfriend works for the State Department, and he's going to come in here with tanks and missiles and fighter jets to blow you motherfuckers up!"

I tensed up. Josh slowly turned to look at me and said, "Boyfriend?"

I looked at him and started to scream, "LEMON! RI'CHARD! FUCKING LEMON!"

The General held the gun to Yale Law's forehead. "Ladies first?" he asked, "This one?" Yale Law started to cry, "Please, please don't do this."

He lifted the gun from her temple and placed it on mine, the metal burning my skin. "Or this one? Perhaps I will let one of you go if you tell me where my head is."

I let out, "It's at the old quarry, we threw it in the water. You'll find it there."

The General said, "That's too bad. I shall have to consider it a casualty of war. For your confession, I shall reward you with being the first to die."

I started to cry. I heard the gun cock and felt the vibration of it clicking through the barrel against my skull. I turned to look at Josh and saw tears in his eyes, either for watching me about to die or that I lied to him, maybe both. I started sobbing and began to say, "I'm sorr—" before a gunshot rang out.

19

I was on the ground, half of me under Josh. He pushed me off the pew with his body when the gunshots rang out. I felt the church disintegrating and falling on us as the bullets pulverized its walls. The booms of each shot sounded like a cannon; it was deafening.

I heard Ri'Chard's familiar voice cry out, "Julie! Josh!"

"We're here, in the front!" screamed Josh. I felt him move off me, and I slowly lifted myself up. Our arms were still awkwardly tied behind our backs, but I managed to crawl to the edge of the pew. I could see Ri'Chard holding a flare, the panic in his face illuminated by red light. He was with Dante and another person in the middle. It took me a moment to recognize them. I could see long pink hair peeking out from under her sequined black balaclava. I gasped and whispered, "The Throat Goat."

Throat Goat was holding a giant rifle and was outfitted in tactical gear. Her camo vest was bulging with pockets filled with mysterious accessories. She yelled, "I need all you mothafuckers to stay where you are. You move, I shoot." I froze where I was.

Ri'Chard called out, "Can you guys see anyone near you? Do you feel safe to move this way?"

I scanned around and didn't see anyone near us. I called out, "I think it's clear, but where is the General?"

Throat Goat called back, "I saw some guys escape through a door on the side. I didn't shoot them because I wasn't sure whose side they were on, but next time I won't miss. How many people are with you?"

Josh yelled, "Four of us here, and someone is injured."

Throat Goat said, "Did I shoot someone? Aw shit. My bad."

I called out, "No, it happened before you came."

Throat Goat yelled, "Oh, good. Describe yourselves."

Josh stuttered, "Uh, there are two men and two women. Three of us are White, and there's one Asian woman."

Throat Goat said, "Good, now listen up, everyone. Only those four people are going to stand up. If anyone else tries to move or do some funny shit, I'm going to shoot you, and just to let you know, I have three guns on me, and I can hit moving targets. Only the people I gave permission to are allowed to stand up now."

We all rolled to our knees and righted ourselves. Josh went to help encourage Useless Idiot with Yale Law.

Throat Goat instructed us, "Good, now walk down this side aisle. Move your ass, let's go." She held the gun up and proceeded to scan the church as we hurried forward. When we got to the door, Ri'Chard held out a knife. He cut the plastic cuffs and grabbed my hand. He squeezed it before letting it go and helping the others with their cuffs. Dante put an arm on my shoulder and guided me outside. Throat Goat backed outside with the gun, and I looked to see the two "personal security" guards unconscious on either side of the door. I looked to Ri'Chard, and he said, "It wasn't me."

I looked back at Throat Goat, moving backwards with her gun trained on the entrance to the church. I needed to know who this person was, but there was no time. We were moving toward Ri'Chard's truck, which wouldn't fit all of us. Josh said to me, "I'll take the Corolla. You go with Ri'Chard."

I protested. "No, I should go with you."

Josh said, "Please, just go with them."

Ri'Chard told Dante, "Go with Josh."

Throat Goat pulled a pistol from a strap on her hip and handed it to Dante, "Don't go too crazy, cuz I know where you like to aim." She winked before getting into the truck and standing up through the moonroof, aiming the gun at the church.

I got in and watched through the back window as Josh ran to the Corolla. Useless Idiot was whimpering in the front seat, while Yale Law and I were in the back with the Throat Goat's combat boots between us.

Ri'Chard slammed the driver's door and said, "We need to get him to a hospital."

"I know," I said, "But I'm also worried about Ms. Honeypaw. They might try to get her, too." I was panicking, imagining that salt barriers wouldn't stop bullets. I instructed him to drive to the Forbidden Palace Chinese Restaurant.

We drove in silence to the restaurant. Yale Law doted on Useless Idiot from the back seat, and I looked through the moonroof up at the Throat Goat, the butt of her rifle buried in her shoulder and her pink hair blowing in the breeze. Her long, crystal-studded acrylics confidently rested on the trigger. She looked like a goddess of unknown power.

Throat Goat nudged my leg with her combat boot. She looked down and said, "I'm sorry Asian Woman. My bad."

I smiled and said, "It didn't hurt me. Don't worry."

There weren't any cars in the restaurant's lot, but it seemed to be open. We all got out, and thankfully, Throat Goat, decked out in her camo attire with multiple weapons, stayed in the truck. Ri'Chard helped out Useless Idiot, and I watched as Josh pulled in next to us. He didn't look me in my eyes. Instead, he turned to Dante and said something. They got out, and he briefly made eye contact with me before looking away. He hated me, I could feel it. Josh went and held the front door open as we all went inside. I thanked him before going in. When the owner saw us as we walked in, he screamed. "What? What is going on? Is this a gang shooting?"

I said, "Listen, I need my friends to stay here while they wait for an ambulance."

"No," he said.

I spoke softly in Mandarin. "Please, sir, there won't be any problem."

He glared at me. "You are trying to get me in trouble."

I said, "Of course not, my only intention is peace."

"That is rare for a Taiwanese," he shot back.

I said tersely, "Well, it's hard when we're constantly being provoked by our enemy."

Even though the conversation was in Mandarin, Josh could sense my anger and interjected, "Hey, sorry, but if you help us, I'll give you free oil changes for a year on your cars, does that sound alright?"

The owner smiled. "Okay! Deal." He escorted Yale Law and Useless Idiot to a booth. Yale Law looked back and said, "What are you going to do?"

I looked at her and said, "I have to go check on a friend, then we'll decide. Will you guys be alright?"

She nodded. I walked over to her and gave her a hug. She was taken aback and returned it. I said, "I'm so sorry. This shouldn't have happened. We're going to figure out how to get them."

She looked at me and said, "Go fuck them up for us, okay?"

I nodded. We all walked out front, and Ri'Chard said to Dante, "I think you should stay with them. You can take Josh's car and wait at the hospital in case they need something, alright?" Dante agreed and nodded at Throat Goat, who had moved to the front of Ri'Chard's truck, which left Josh and me to sit in the back.

As we started driving, Josh looked out the window. I tried to lighten the mood by saying, "This is crazy, but it looks like your male fantasy came true."

Josh scoffed and continued to stare out the window. "It turns out I've been living in a lot of fantasies."

I met Ri'Chard's gaze as he looked out the rearview mirror. He said, "What's the plan when we get to Ms. Honeypaw's?"

I said, "I don't know, I just want to make sure she's safe."

WHEN WE GOT to her house, I didn't see any of the lights on. We parked the truck out front, and I hopped out and ran up the porch to the front door, where I frantically banged on it.

I hollered, "Ms. Honeypaw! Are you here? Please come, this is Julie, and it's important. The boys are with me, too!" I kept knocking until I heard, "I'm fucking coming!" from inside. I smiled as she walked toward the glass.

She opened the door and said, "Bitch, why are you so pressed?"

I gave her a big hug as she struggled to rid herself of me. I let go and asked, "Are you safe?"

She looked skeptical. "Yes, but this isn't a DV shelter. I don't need you bringing this weird energy in here. You're like a bitch on the run from her pimp."

I waved for the others to come in. I told her, "We need to talk. You need to hear this."

She moved forward into the kitchen, which I had never been

in. It was dated with pink walls and light brown linoleum, but seemingly organized in its disorganization. The lighting was warm, and there was a wooden dining table on one side filled with rings from coaster-less cups.

She leaned on the counter as we moved into the kitchen. We all filed in, some of us taking chairs, when Ms. Honeypaw exclaimed, "Nah ah. What the fuck is that?" She pointed at Throat Goat.

I said, "That's Throat Goat. She saved us tonight."

Ms. Honeypaw said, "No, I don't want this big-dick-he-bitch in my house."

Josh said, "Hey, that's not cool."

I said, "Ms. Honeypaw, you can't say that."

Ms. Honeypaw looked incredulous. "I can't say that? Bitch, this is *my* house you made yourself so goddamn comfortable in, and the house rules are that you can't put on a wig and pretend you ain't got a big-ass python slithering between those legs."

Throat Goat said, "Whatever. I'm going to use the bathroom."

"Nah ah," said Ms. Honeypaw with a hand on her hip, "That bathroom is for bitches. Go pee outside in the bushes like a real man."

Throat Goat turned to me and said, "Asian Woman, this is your friend?"

Ms. Honeypaw exclaimed, "No, she ain't 'Asian Woman' you racist. Her name is Julie and she's from The Wan."

Throat Goat said, "I'm surprised you're this obsessed with dicks, but it makes sense since you're doing it for show."

"Now what the fuck does that mean?" Ms. Honeypaw asked.

"It takes a homo to know a homo," said the Throat Goat coolly.

Ms. Honeypaw's mouth dropped. "You shut your mouth. I

know my way around a dick better than you. These lips could suck the sissy out of you and set you straight."

Throat Goat said, "Impossible. My head game is mythical. This is legendary shit." She stuck her tongue out and wiggled it while I saw her eyebrows move under her balaclava.

Ri'Chard loudly exclaimed, "Enough! Enough. We have other matters at hand. Josh and Julie were almost killed tonight, and we think you might be in danger."

Ms. Honeypaw looked at Ri'Chard and pointed at Throat Goat, saying, "And you think *that* is going to save me?"

Ri'Chard said, "She is former Special-Ops. She's the most valuable resource we have at the moment."

I looked at Throat Goat and asked, "You were in the military?"

"I can't really talk about it, it was *that* deep, Asian Woman," she said.

I mumbled "Damn" under my breath. Josh chimed in, "Maybe you worked for Julie's boyfriend. Doesn't he do something important in the government?" Josh finally made eye contact with me as I flushed red with shame. I looked away and winced in anticipation.

"Bitch, you got a boyfriend?" I heard Ms. Honeypaw say. "I fucking knew it. You came in here and lied to my face. I saw it in the cards about another man, and you told me it was just some feelings for Ri'Chard, but this whole time you had a man, and you were fucking Josh on the side? Oh my fucking god, I'm done with you." She asked Josh, "Babyboy, did she break your heart?"

Josh said, "No, no, it wasn't anything meaningful... I was just surprised she kept something like that from us."

I looked at Josh. His eyes betrayed his cavalier attitude; they showed the pain I caused him, even as his jaw tensed in an effort to not show emotion. I looked at Ri'Chard, who was staring at the floor uncomfortably. I was being publicly shamed, and deservedly so.

Throat Goat chimed in, "So this seems messy...are we not going to deal with the whole kidnapper situation or just continue with your heterosexual mind games?"

Ri'Chard said, "You're right, we have bigger things to deal with." He spoke to me, "Julie, can you share what you learned tonight?"

I took a breath. My body was vibrating with adrenaline and the sick feeling of guilt. I said, "A lot of things happened in there. I learned from Jim Smoke that they were using spells from a book discovered on the plantation. He said there was a society of witches formed from the descendants of General Stovall because they had supernatural abilities, like you." I looked at Ms. Honeypaw, who raised her eyebrows in suspicion at me. I continued, "This society has been working on resurrecting the General, according to the book. However, we might have accidentally activated the sigil when we burned it, completing the rituals. He told us we were arrested for our crime and General Stovall would decide our fate.

"Then the General came. My colleague was convinced it was just a guy in makeup, but now I'm not certain. He talked with us and said we were traitors who needed to be executed. He had a gun and shot my colleague, then was about to execute me before they saved us."

"Too fucking bad. Next time, I hope he doesn't miss," said Ms. Honeypaw.

I looked at her angrily. "I think he's coming for you, too."

She said haughtily, "He can come. I'm all set. I got my own procedure to deal with these things. I don't need Miss Chernobyl Tina Turner and her guns to save me."

"Can you shut the fuck up?" I said. I lost my cool and continued angrily, "I am so tired of your shit. This is serious: we are all in danger, and you're acting like you have any fucking clue what to do. Let me tell you: you are just as vulnerable and clueless as we are. People like Throat Goat are trying to help us, so be grateful and stop being such a cunt."

The room was quiet. Ri'Chard said to Josh and Throat Goat, "Let's go in the other room for a moment. They need to communicate for a bit." Ms. Honeypaw's eyes focused on their backs as they departed before turning to me, "Well, Miss Prada and her big mouth have returned. Why don't you continue talking your shit."

I sat back. "I don't have anything else to say."

"No?" asked Ms. Honeypaw, "I cede the floor to you. Speak what's on your mind."

I remained passive. "I've already said it. It's up to you whether or not you want to accept my advice."

"Why would I take any advice from you?" She asked. "Has anything you've done worked out? First, you lost your big case against the racists in this town, then your antics incited a riot. You might have brought back the ghost of a Confederate General, so whose side are you on? It doesn't feel like you're mine. Then you went and got your coworker shot, lied to Josh, and broke his heart, and now you're telling me to be grateful for the help *you're* giving me? Bitch, are you that dumb? Do you not see the incompetency of your actions?"

The veracity of what she said burned deeply into me. She wasn't wrong about any of this, no matter how hostile her presentation of the events.

Ms. Honeypaw continued, "Not only do you have the audacity to insult me in my own home, but you tried playing mind games with my cousin and I'm fighting every instinct in me and not listening to requests from the ghost of my momma to beat your ass, because you just seem pathetic, like it's not worth even trying to break you because you're already broken. You're a fake-ass bitch, Julie Chen, just like your Prada bag."

My eyes were watering. All I could do was look at her and say through gritted teeth, "My bag wasn't fake."

Ms. Honeypaw scoffed. "As if that's the biggest issue? I took it to a pawn shop to sell, and they said it wasn't genuine."

I snarled, "Well, that's because you're a fraud and no one in this town trusts you. The bag is real, but the fact *you're* carrying it makes it fake."

I could see Ms. Honeypaw's eyes begin to water as she ground her teeth, making her jaw tense, "At least I don't lie to the people I love."

I felt my jaw start to chatter and tears fall from my eyes. I looked at her and said, "Because there's no one in your life who loves you back."

Ms. Honeypaw started to sob, and so did I. We both stared at each other as tears streamed down our faces and sobs made our chests heave. I could feel snot running from my nose as I inhaled to try and hide it, but ended up wiping it on the side of my hand. These were ugly, full-body cries that felt like a release. I cried for the old me, the one at work who felt ambition overruled human decency, for the woman who thought love came from texts and invites to prestigious political events. I cried for my mother, who remained faithful in the face of dishonesty, for the person that Josh imagined I was, and for the person I became because of him. I cried for the fear of dying, for the hatred these people felt for someone like Ri'Chard, a gentle man forged from integrity and devotion. I cried for all of this being undone by something I didn't understand, by the possibly supernatural or natural bigots whose version of America excluded those who built it. Lastly, I cried for Ms. Honeypaw, a woman just as broken as me.

Ms. Honeypaw slid on the cabinets and sank to the floor. She looked at me as she sobbed, her face red and puffy. I stood up and walked over to her and sank to the floor as well. We looked into each other's soggy eyes, and I put my arms around her shoulders as our foreheads met. We were in a union of grief, and we held each other until it passed.

Ms. Honeypaw gulped and softly said, "I can't believe he's back."

I held her a little tighter and said, "We're going to defeat him."

She cried a little bit and looked at me. "Bitch, I'm scared."

My voice wavered. "I'm scared too."

I grabbed her hand. We put our foreheads together and watched as our tears dripped onto their embrace, like the first drops of rain hinting of the storm to come.

WE BOTH LEANED against the cabinet, staring ahead. We collected enough of ourselves to stop crying. I said, "I'm sorry about what I said. That was wrong, and I didn't mean to hurt you."

Ms. Honeypaw took a breath, "I'm sorry too. I said some unkind shit, but I'm still upset about what you did to Josh."

"I know, I'm upset with myself too. I don't know why I kept the truth from him. I think it was because I didn't expect to outgrow the old me, but suddenly I felt like two different people."

"For now, I'm going to forgive you. Honestly, that's for you and Josh to deal with, and I don't need to be involved. Even if you still act like horny teenagers, you're adults and will figure this out." She took a breath. "We got bigger issues. How are we going to fight the General?"

"I think it's time to join the others. Let's figure this out together," I said. I stood up and put out a hand. Ms. Honeypaw grabbed it and I helped her to stand. We walked into the sitting room where everyone was waiting. Throat Goat was sitting on the couch using her phone while Ri'Chard and Josh were standing close together, talking. They turned to look at us.

Ms. Honeypaw said, "That's what happens when you get two bitches on their periods in the same room." She looked at Throat Goat and said, "Because real women bleed from their pussies."

I looked at Ms. Honeypaw and exclaimed, "Come on, I thought we were making progress?"

Throat Goat clacked her acrylics and said, "And I trust that you're an expert on pussy."

Ms. Honeypaw glared at her and said, "Fine. He/she/it can stay. Let's get on with this."

Ri'Chard took the lead. "Okay, Josh told me the General spoke of a 'homecoming' event tonight. We can assume it will be at the Stovall Plantation. We don't know for certain if...he's a ghost. There are two possibilities: this was an elaborate show, and that's a real person in makeup, or he's a ghost."

I said, "If he's the latter, is there anything we can do?"

"I talked with someone who knows about witchcraft, and we can try and reverse the sigil," Josh spoke to the group without making eye contact with me. He continued, "I explained to her that the sigil got semen on it, then we burned it."

"Wait," interrupted Ms. Honeypaw. "How the fuck did you get cum on the sigil?"

I looked at Ri'Chard while Josh looked down. Ri'Chard said, "Uh, I don't think that's important right now."

"It's important to me," said the Throat Goat. "Sounds like something freakier than a ghost was happening."

Ms. Honeypaw nodded towards Throat Goat. "This one can smell cum from a mile away. Finally, we have something we agree on. We both need to know how y'all got semen on the sigil?"

Throat Goat seconded. "Listen, don't you want me and her to get along? We have to know."

Ri'Chard looked mortified. Josh shifted and looked around the room. I rolled my eyes and said, "Josh and I had sex. Ri'Chard watched and ejaculated on the head of General Stovall's statue and the sigil inside of it."

Ms. Honeypaw's eyes flicked back and forth between Josh and Ri'Chard, whose eyes were equally wide in horror. I heard soft snaps of fingers from Throat Goat, who said, "Go Asian Woman."

Ms. Honeypaw turned to me with her mouth agape. "Is that why the General is trying to shoot your ass? Because Josh shot your club up while Ri'Chard watched and came on his face?"

I said, "No, he was mad because we threw the head into a quarry, and for other things unrelated to this particular incident."

Ms. Honeypaw was still in shock. She turned to Josh and heatedly said, "I blame you. This bitch used to be on the straight and narrow before you showed her your freakish ways." She turned to Ri'Chard, "And you: you should know better than to cum on the faces of Confederate Generals. Those White motherfuckers don't deserve your princely juices."

Throat Goat said, "Oh my, 'princely juices'. Maybe she does suck dick."

Ms. Honeypaw looked at Throat Goat. "Listen, there is more than one goat in this barn."

Throat Goat let out a sound of excitement while Ri'Chard said, "Okay, let's never talk about that ever again. I trust this will never leave this group."

Throat Goat said, "My lips are wet and sealed."

Ri'Chard said, "Josh, please continue."

"No," said Ms. Honeypaw, "I'm not done. What about your girlfriend? That's cheating."

Ri'Chard looked like he was on the verge of breaking out in sweat. Josh said, "Whoa, it's not cheating unless you're physically with the other person, right?"

Ms. Honeypaw said, "No, if you're with someone, you're not allowed to think of other bitches, period. That means no jerking off to porn or fantasies, you can only think about that one person."

"That's not true," I said. "You can at least fantasize about other people."

"Shut up, you are a moralless smut," said Ms. Honeypaw. She said to Ri'Chard, "You have a fine-ass woman. Why would Mulan-ica Lewinsky ever turn you on?"

Ri'Chard forcefully said, "Come on, this is really not the place to be discussing it. I know how to handle my relationship, and trust that we will be discussing this as a couple. Your outside input is not needed. Can we get back to focusing on how to defeat the General?" Ms. Honeypaw looked surprised at him cutting off the conversation, and she respectfully shut up.

Josh said, "Okay, so for reversing the sigil, we have to step backwards."

"Like the opposite?" asked Throat Goat. "That's easy, water kills fire. We just have to douse his ass in holy water and run."

"No," said Josh. "We have to go to what *creates* fire, back to the beginning. That would be wood."

"Then what creates cum?" Ms. Honeypaw asked.

"Seven minutes with me," said Throat Goat confidently.

"ThroatBitch, shut up," said Ms. Honeypaw in the friendliest way she had spoken to her yet.

Josh said, "For that, we need menstrual blood. It's the feminine and opposite of semen."

Ms. Honeypaw said, "Well, we got two regular and one GMO fish in here. Let's get to wringing out our tampons."

I looked at Ms. Honeypaw and stated, "I'm not on my period."

She let out an exasperated sigh, "I am."

"Good," said Ri'Chard, "Maybe because it's your blood, that will make it more powerful."

I looked to Josh. "What do we do with the blood and wood?"

He looked in my eyes for a moment, the way he used to, before he broke it and looked at the rest of the group. "She said we need to redraw the sigil in blood, wrap it around a wooden stake and stab the ghost."

"Fuck, you gotta shank that ghost?" Asked Throat Goat. "Who here has been to prison?"

We all looked at each other. I asked, "But what if it's not a ghost? What if it's a real person pretending to be one? We're just supposed to stab them?"

Josh finally looked at me. "We won't know until he's stabbed in the heart."

"And who is going to do that?" asked Ms. Honeypaw. "I am not going to prison for stabbing a living White man pretending to be a dead one."

Ri'Chard shook his head in disbelief. Josh said, "That's our only option, if this is a ghost."

I declared, "I'll do it." They all turned to look at me. "You all have lives here. You have responsibilities and are a part of this community. You don't need to jeopardize it for this. I don't have that. I have a job I actually hate, a failed relationship, and no close friends I could call and talk about any of this with. You all have way more to lose than I do."

"Julie, you can't," said Ri'Chard.

I said, "I want to do this. You all have shown me so much since I've been here. I've laughed, cried, and felt more alive than

I ever have in possibly my whole life. I know this is the only way I could thank you for all you have given me. I'm going to stab the motherfucker that almost shot me."

"That's the spirit, Asian Woman," said Throat Goat.

I looked at everyone in the group, even Josh.

"I hurt my wrist lifting salt bags, so I couldn't anyway..." said Ms. Honeypaw.

Josh said, "I can do it. I should do it. I can fight them off better than you."

I stared at him and smiled, as tears pooled in my eyes. "No, this is for me to do."

He looked at me with his tense jaw. I shook off my emotions and said, "We need to get to work. We need to come up with a plan to get me into the plantation house tonight."

"How will we sneak to the house?" Ri'Chard asked.

Josh said, "They said they have cameras in the woods."

"That's my forte," said Throat Goat. "I'll get you through the woods. Chances are, if they are having an event, you can pretend to be staff. No one pays attention to the people serving them. They're invisible."

"Like a caterer," said Ri'Chard.

"I can do that," I said confidently.

Throat Goat asked Ri'Chard for his keys. She said she needed to go home and grab some things. That left the four of us to figure out how to make the weapon.

Josh and Ri'Chard volunteered to look for wood while Ms. Honeypaw and I figured out how to harvest her menstrual blood.

I said, "I think you just have to stick a finger in and draw it with that."

She looked at me in disgust.

I said, "Maybe we can make some sort of stamp? Then rub it on your vagina and stamp it."

Her face remained frozen in aversion. She said, "I don't know what kind of art classes you had growing up, but I'm not about to stamp my pussy on some piece of paper."

I clarified, "You don't stamp your pussy. We make one, like from a potato. We cut and carve in it." I thought back to earlier, and the inkwell General Stovall used for writing our execution notices. I said, "You know what? I bet we mix some blood with ink and draw it."

"Will that work?" She asked.

I nodded, "I'm certain it will do. Do you have an old fountain pen around here?"

"Yeah, I have my grandfather's somewhere in here." She got up and started rummaging around an old drop-top desk against a wall. I stood near her. She opened the top, and a picture fell on the ground. I picked it up to see a young girl in pink overalls standing outside the house, when the house was in a different incarnation of its colors. I asked, "Who is this?"

"If you can believe it, that's me," said Ms. Honeypaw, glancing at the picture.

"You were cute," I said. "It's hard to imagine you were once a child who didn't curse with every other word."

"My first word was 'bitch'. I came out of the womb with this mouth."

"What does the ghost of your mother think of all this?" I asked.

"I haven't talked to her tonight. I've been busy crying on the floor with you, or planning how to assassinate a ghost, and now I'm about to go dig in my pussy for some period blood. I don't really need her seeing me like this." She found the pen and held it up. "This is it?"

"Yes!" I took it and asked her for a regular pen. We broke the inkwell of the plastic pen and put it in a dish. I waited for Ms. Honeypaw outside the bathroom until she came out, holding a used tampon by a string like a dead mouse by the tail.

"Good job, that wasn't too bad, right?" I asked her.

"Shut your freak ass up. I'm ready to finish your little art project."

I sat at the table and put the tampon in the ink. It soaked up all the ink and turned black. I dipped the fountain pen in it and began to copy the sigil from the picture on my phone.

"I'm going to talk to my mother tonight," said Ms. Honeypaw. "I'm going to call on all the ancestors to help protect your ass while you're in there."

I looked at her and said, "Thank you, I appreciate it." I dipped my pen back in the tampon.

"Yeah, so don't get your ass killed because then I can't verify the authenticity of the Prada. I need you to get that receipt," she said.

"I have it in D.C. and I'll send it to you."

"Good, so you better come out safe or all your boyfriends will be sad."

I laughed a bit. "I think after all of this I will have zero boyfriends."

I finished drawing the sigil on a small piece of paper. I asked, "Do you have your pad?"

"It's in the trash in the bathroom. I'll grab it." She came back with it folded and asked, "What do you need this for?"

"We should dip the stake tip in poison. It's time to show them that women have bled for America too."

As we let the sigil dry, Ri'Chard and Josh presented us with a short wooden stake, crudely sharpened at the end. I thanked them and wrapped the sigil around the handle, securing it with a rubber band, and used the pad as a sheath for it. I gripped it in my hand and understood what I had to do.

"Don't miss," said Ms. Honeypaw. "I feel like Ri'Chard should do it since he has the best aim."

He groaned, "Can we please forget about this?"

Throat Goat walked through the door dressed top to bottom in a camouflage ghillie suit. "Y'all bitches ready?" She changed her balaclava to a demure plain black, with newly-selected auburn hair peaking out from underneath it.

I looked at her and asked, "Do I get an outfit?"

Throat Goat handed me a bag. "Hopefully the staff dress code is black pants with a white top."

I saw brown hair at the bottom of the bag. "What's at the bottom?"

"That's a wig for your disguise. Something tells me you might otherwise stand out in this crowd," explained Throat Goat.

I went to the bathroom and took off my old clothes. I hadn't realized they were covered in dust from the church. I washed my hands and arms in the sink before putting on the clothes. The top was a bit big but I tucked it into my pants. I looked plain enough for the role. I grabbed the wig and placed it on my head. It was a shaggy brunette style with bangs that went just below my eyes. I looked in the mirror and barely recognized the vision I had become.

I stepped out and everyone looked at me. Ms. Honeypaw laughed and said, "Now you look like a basic-ass Julie." I smiled a little. Throat Goat walked over and adjusted my wig, tilting it a bit and arranging some of the hair. I said to her, "Do you wear this wig in your videos?"

She nodded, "Yes, and these wigs have mystical powers. They're like my superhero costume." She turned to everyone and said, "I present Asian Woman, our hero who will save America."

I put my hands together and bowed. Ms. Honeypaw said, "I like GeishaBitch better."

I looked at Josh. His face seemed burdened with worry and conflict. Ri'Chard said, "I think one of us should stay, though, to protect Ms. Honeypaw."

Josh nodded with understanding. "I'll stay," he said. He looked at me and said, "Please be safe."

I said, "I think this wig is actually bulletproof, I'll be fine." My attempt at humor didn't lighten the heaviness between us. I added, "You stay safe too." I asked Ri'Chard, "Are you comfortable going into the woods tonight?"

He confidently said, "Absolutely. There's no way I'm backing down tonight."

I turned to the group and said, "Let's go win this war."

20

Ri'Chard pulled in the familiar parking spot at the edge of the woods of the old Stovall Plantation. We got out of the truck, and I looked at Ri'Chard. "Are you ready?" he asked.

"As ready as I'll ever be," I said. I hoped the adrenaline rush from almost being shot and hysterically crying wasn't the reason I felt so confident about this mission.

Throat Goat organized her supplies on the back of the tailgate. She handed a rifle to Ri'Chard and said, "Big Boy, here's your big toy," adding a wink.

She handed me an elastic strap, which I examined with confusion. "It's a holster for a knife that goes on your leg. You can put your wooden stake in it."

I nodded and hiked my pant leg. Ri'Chard knelt and said, "Let me help." He rolled up my pants and slid the band halfway up my shin. He adjusted it and asked, "Is this comfortable?" I nodded. His hand firmly gripped my calf as he slid the wooden stake into the sheath. He rolled down my pant leg and stood. He stood close to me. He cleared his throat and said, "Are you sure you want to do this? You don't have to be a hero."

I felt his breath as he spoke. I saw the concern in his eyes as he spoke it from his lips. I looked at his lips and back at his eyes. I leaned in and put my lips on his.

He didn't move backward. Instead, he stayed firmly planted, as if his tightly-tied boots were cemented to the ground. It was brief, only a second. I pulled back and said, "I don't know what's going to happen tonight, so I just needed to do it once."

His brows furrowed in frustration, but he gave me a small, heavy smile. He nodded and said, "I understand."

"This shit is messier than most of the war zones I've been in," said Throat Goat. I turned my head to see her staring at us. I laughed a little.

I turned back to Ri'Chard. "I just wanted to kiss you goodbye in case things go bad in there."

"About that," said Throat Goat. "What's the protocol if you're captured? Do you want me to take you out, or can you keep your information under duress and torture?"

Ri'Chard firmly said, "That's not going to happen. We're not taking Julie out." Throat Goat rolled her eyes, though somehow, I felt that Throat Goat wasn't joking.

Ri'Chard looked at me. "If at any point you feel unsafe, just leave. If you feel like something bad is going to happen, run."

"And if you stab him and he's not a ghost, then fucking run-run," added Throat Goat. She slung a long bag over her shoulder and opened a hard shell case on the tailgate. It had various buttons and a small control screen. I asked what it was. She said, "This is a signal jammer. You said there were cameras in the woods, so this will jam up to a certain radius."

"Won't that look suspicious?" Ri'Chard asked.

I said, "The General disrupts electric fields when he's around. I'm sure they're aware everything is going to be weird tonight."

"Good," said Throat Goat. She handed me a camo jacket, lowered goggles over her head, and turned them on. "I have my night vision on, so I'm going in front. Asian Woman, follow behind me, and Big Boy can take it from the back like the nasty motherfucker you are." She purred at Ri'Chard before leading us into the woods.

THE HOUSE WAS in sight when I saw Throat Goat hold up her right arm and motion for us to get low. She took off her night vision and said, "We'll stop here." She put her bag on the ground and unzipped it, revealing a very large and intricate sniper rifle.

"Holy shit," I exclaimed. "What is that for?"

"You see those Hello Kitty stickers on the side? That's one for every life I've taken with this gun. I'm not afraid to add some more kitties to this bitch tonight." I studied it and saw a smattering of stickers on the side. I looked at her, then to Ri'Chard, and said, "I think I'll be fine."

He nodded his head, "Yep, Throat Goat has you covered."

"Don't worry," said Throat Goat, "I do my best work with big guns, and I never leave a mess." She winked at Ri'Chard.

I looked at him and said, "Maybe you will be getting laid in these woods."

He stuttered, "Uhhh, uhhh."

Throat Goat looked through her rifle scope and said, "I can see cars out front and people arriving, most of the security is out there, but I only see one guy in the rear. You see the back door over there?" She pointed at a door on the lower level.

"Yes, I see it."

"It looks like it's probably a staff back door. You're going to slip in there and then start doing something—anything. Grab a bundle of napkins and walk around with them. I don't care. Just blend in."

"What about the security guy standing back there?" Ri'Chard asked.

Throat Goat pulled out a pack of cigarettes and took one, inhaling as she held the lighter up to it. Once it was lit, she handed it to me. "You were just on a smoke break."

"And if he asks her questions?" Ri'Chad queried.

Throat Goat said, "You're a nasty girl. Flirt with him, be a bitch. I don't care, just be *believable.* Also, don't worry. If he tries anything with you," Throat Goat leaned down and put her eye to the rifle scope, "I'll put a bullet right below his receding hairline."

I slipped out of my jacket. I took the cigarette from her and looked at Ri'Chard. He grabbed my hand and gave it a squeeze before I stood up and began to walk through the undergrowth, breaking from where the woods met grass.

I tried taking a drag from the cigarette and almost choked. I had only smoked once in college, but I had to play the part. I didn't inhale, just a small puff and slow exhale. I strolled the lawn toward the brick lower section of the house. It was more daunting in person, and as I got closer I could see how well maintained it was. The owners certainly had money. When I was near the back door, I emerged into the illumination of a floodlight. The security guard turned to me. He was holding a large rifle, similar to the one Throat Goat used earlier.

"What are you doing?" he asked with hostility.

"I'm just on a smoke break," I said casually.

"Why are you coming from over there?" he asked in an interrogating tone.

"I like to walk and smoke. It's good exercise."

"You like to smoke while exercising?" he asked incredulously.

"Jesus, you're like my ex-boyfriend. Is your name Johnny?" I leaned down and stubbed the cigarette just as the door opened. A woman looked at me and said, "Oh, hey. You gotta light?"

I said, "Uh, no. I borrowed it from someone."

She said, "No problem, I'll get one of the cooks to give me one," and held the door open for me. I looked at the security guard and said, "By the way, you're way hotter than Johnny." I winked at him, and he smiled before we both went inside.

The woman asked, "Are you into meatheads?"

"Maybe just for tonight."

The staircase went down a story. It was all concrete and well-lit with fluorescent lights, seemingly new construction. I followed her down to a back room filled with boxes. I stood there for a moment trying to understand where I was. I saw the lady walk past with me with her lit cigarette. She smiled and said, "See you in there." I smiled politely at her. I took a breath and adjusted my shirt, and made sure it was tucked in neatly. I walked through a doorway in a bustling commercial kitchen. I tried to dodge the busy cooks as they made exclamations in Spanish. Everyone in the kitchen seemed to be Black or Latino, and I tried maneuvering around their bodies, busily in motion as they quickly worked the cooktops. This kitchen was an organism I had no place in. I wandered through another doorway into a small room, painted red with china cabinets along the wall. In the center were tables with platters of hors d'oeuvres on them. A woman in a blazer looked at me and said, "Are you serving?" I nodded. "Where is your uniform?"

I said, "Uh, I didn't know. I'm filling in for someone at the last minute." My mouth was dry from nervousness and cigarette smoke.

She rolled her eyes. "The pants and shirt are fine. Next time, they prefer *tight* black pants. There are extra vests hanging in the corner. Go grab one."

She had a headphone in one ear and began talking into it. I walked over to a rack and selected a gold satin vest, and put it on. I showed her, and she gave me a nod of approval. She talked into her headphones, "I'm sending out a server. Where do you need her?" She handed me a platter and a stack of napkins and said, "These are pigs in a blanket. Go to the main room and work the floor. Don't forget the slot machines by the back wall." I carefully held the platter in my right hand, napkins in my left, and stepped out.

"HOLY SHIT." I looked around, taking in a massive room that looked straight out of Las Vegas. I found myself standing in the central alley of a casino. Directly in front of me was a garish, three-tiered fountain that looked like it was stolen from Versailles. The water spilled into a small pool below, and obscured by the movement of the water, I could see poker chips covering the bottom.

To my right and left were tables where dealers in red vests stood, maneuvering cards or stacks of poker chips. The tables were filled with gamblers, well-dressed, mostly middle-aged, and all white. I noticed stacks of cash transiting between people buying and selling chips from gilded carts. Piles of cash were proudly displayed by these carts because, seemingly, people had enough money that it was safe to be left out. I stood in a motionless stupor as people walking took pigs in a blanket from my tray.

"Hey!" I heard the lady bark from the doorway behind me. "Work the floor!" She gestured firmly with her arms.

I started to walk forward. I looked at the bustling tables, people celebrating as the craps dice were rolled. I moved closer to a group standing by the table, "Pigs in a blanket?" I asked, and they selected a napkin and a greasy little sausage.

I moved along toward a crowded table where people were screaming with excitement. A man grabbed a stack of cash and held it above him. He screamed, "Yes!" His face was red with bulging veins and sweaty, making him look as if the cash weighed one hundred pounds." I peered over the shoulder of a woman's Chanel suit and saw they were playing Uno. I overheard the woman say to someone next to her, "The buy-in is $10k."

I said to them, "Pigs in a blanket?" They took them, and I progressed. I noticed the slot machines along the back way. A few men were sitting there, smoking cigars. A waitress delivered some cocktails to them, which they took without removing their focus from the flashing machines.

I slowly walked down the alley of tables toward the sliding glass doors. The sign above it read "Poker Room." I stepped in front of the glass door, which automatically opened. The room was deep burgundy in color. The doors closed behind me, and I was cut off from the noise of the main floor. This room was silent by comparison, with two tables arranged within it. The players were intensely focused. I saw a woman milling around the room. She had strawberry blonde hair with large curls that looked petrified with hairspray. The color of her skin was the same white as a full moon, blinding and almost painful to look at, punctuated by fake lashes, blue-purple eyeshadow, and intensely red lips. She was well dressed in a modest black dress and moved between the tables, checking on the gamblers.

Dealers handed out cards as the players' eyes darted back and forth between each other, searching for any tell. My only experience with gambling was watching "God of Gamblers" dozens of times as a kid. However, Hong Kong cinema did little to prepare me for the seriousness of tonight's game, as the room was dead quiet, except for the tapping heels of the mysterious lady supervising the room.

She looked at me and nodded her head toward the right side of the room. I saw a small bar along the way, tended by the woman I saw going for a smoke break earlier. I walked over and whispered, "Hi, it's my first day, and I don't know what to do."

She whispered back, "Don't worry. You don't serve poker players directly. Deborah will only interface with them." She nodded her head toward the woman working the room. She pronounced her name as "de-bore-ah", which I made a mental note of.

"Who is she?" I asked.

The bartender leaned closer. "She works for the family that owns this place, that's all I know. Apparently, they're billionaires, and they built this private casino. I guess they're really into gambling, but she takes poker *very* seriously."

"Who are all these people?" I asked.

"Friends of theirs, I think?"

I looked around at all the well-dressed patrons. Now that I was focusing on them, some looked familiar. One was a senator I'd seen disparaging gay marriage on TV, but I couldn't remember the state that he represented. Another was a host on the same network that the senator appeared on.

Deborah walked toward us and said to the bartender, "Two whiskies on the rocks." She gave me a once-over, and the bartender said, "I'm just giving her instructions. Would you like her to get any food for you?"

Deborah looked at me again. She took two fingers and delicately plucked a pig in a blanket from my tray. She took a nibble before wrapping the rest in a napkin. She said to the bartender, "A gentleman at table three would like a hamburger. Plain, only mayo on the bun, cooked medium."

My ethnic instincts made me almost vomit in my mouth. The bartender said, "Of course," then wrote it on a piece of paper. She gave it to me and said, "Bring this to the kitchen and bring the food order back, ASAP, okay?"

I nodded and left through the glass door, walking straight down the alley with the focus of someone who was being paid minimum wage to do this job. I walked back to the room where my supervisor was barking orders into her headphones. She looked at me, and I said, "Hi, this food order is from the Poker Room. What should I do?"

She groaned. "You're only supposed to be working the Main Floor. I hate when they do this shit. I'll take care of it; take the tray of shrimp cocktail and get back out there."

I refreshed my napkins and grabbed a tray of soggy shrimp arranged around a red dip in the center, similar to the menstrual blood on the wooden stake attached to my leg. I walked back out and began to circulate with the shrimp. I offered it to a man who put the whole shrimp in his mouth and extracted the tail, then put it in a bowl on my tray with a wink. I studied this crowd and recognized a few more politicians, including one who made a failed bid for president in the last election.

A man sitting at the slot machines waved me over for a shrimp, then dismissed me with the same hand. Throat Goat was right, I truly was invisible. I looked around the room and couldn't figure out what I should be watching for; it was almost too unbelievable to process. Just then, Deborah stepped through the sliding glass doors and said, "Excuse me, ladies and gentlemen." The room started to fall quiet. Everyone turned to this woman whose lunar glow commanded their attention.

Deborah continued, "We request that you join us upstairs in the Main Ballroom for a special presentation. Feel free to cash out and rejoin, or keep your chips with you. The casino is open all night." The patrons clapped and cheered while they began to stand. The man who waved for shrimp also stood. He was portly with short hair and looked to be in his fifties. He placed his glass on my tray, smiled at me, then held out his hand toward my chest and put something in my vest pocket. He turned and walked upstairs. I walked toward the back room as other patrons put glasses and dirty napkins on my tray. I entered to see my boss yelling at someone. I continued to the kitchen and put the tray down near the dishwasher.

"¿Qué haces? Quítate las servilletas antes de que se mojen," said one of the dishwashers. I bowed and said, "Lo siento." I walked back into the staging room. My boss was reading something from a clipboard. I grabbed a clean tray and said, "I'm going to collect glasses." She made a small noise of approval without looking at me.

By now, the casino was mostly empty except for the staff. I reached into my vest pocket to see what the man put in it and pulled out a black poker chip that had "$1,000" written on it. I flipped it over to see the logo of a torch. I tucked it in my pants pocket and went toward the large staircase, like something from a hotel, where the last patrons were struggling up, besides the ones in line for the elevator. I hurried up the steps and entered the old house. It was grand in its restored elegance. I saw carefully milled woodwork above the doorframes and along the angles where walls met the ceiling and floors. I followed people through a large black and white tiled foyer into the Main Ballroom.

It was cavernous; dark green walls were punctuated by white columns as crystal chandeliers hung to give this room a statement of immense wealth. This room seemed old, but well-maintained. There was a stage at the front, in front of a brick fireplace so large, I could easily stand in it. Candles were being carefully lit and placed in sconces on the wall, and I saw people carrying oil lamps and placing them on the stage.

I stood along the back wall, holding up my tray. Some people put their dirty glasses on it. My plan was working. Suddenly, the electric lights began to flicker. The crowd started to remark about it as the lights dimmed dramatically before resuming their brightness. I overheard someone say, "They're late because General Stovall only rides a horse. We could be waiting here awhile."

I tried to calculate how long it would take someone trotting on a horse to get here from the Baptist courthouse, but while I was estimating the lights cut out completely. The crowd was suddenly bathed in the warm, anonymous glow of candlelight.

Deborah took the podium and began to speak. "Ladies and gentlemen, thank you for gathering here tonight. We welcome you to the historic Stovall Plantation, recently purchased by the Everlight Foundation in an effort to preserve American culture." Some members in the audience clapped. "We never thought the owner would come home, though." She smirked as people in the audience laughed. She continued, "This country is going through a time of immense change. We've lost the essence of what makes us Americans. There are dangerous forces who want us to erase our history and shame us for having pride in our heritage. I'm here to tell you that we will never be ashamed, for we carry the blood of our forefathers with pride. We are here tonight to usher in the rebirth of America, an awakening of its people, and on the horizon, I see a golden future for our country. By the miracle of God, a long-lost leader has returned. He has conquered death to give our country new life, guiding us with a torch of light and liberty. I am utterly honored to welcome General Stovall to this stage."

The crowd erupted in applause. I got on my tiptoes to catch a glimpse of the front. I saw General Stovall walk to the stage from a side door, followed by Jim Smoke, Sally Wren, and Miss Pothos. They all walked up the stage as he took the podium, and the others stood behind him. He absorbed their applause with a stoic gaze, slowly turning to take in the crowd. Even though his face was unemotive and his chin turned upwards, I could tell he adored the attention. The General looked sinister at the podium, underlit by candles that gave his face a demonic appearance. He opened his remarks with, "Ladies and Gentlemen, with great sorrow, I have witnessed the decline of this great Nation. This is no longer a Nation of gentlemen, but of depravity and lawlessness. A woman no longer yearns to rear her young..."

As he trailed on, I realized he was just reciting exactly what he had said to me a few hours before. Perhaps this was just an actor in a costume, reciting their lines, which made me more fearful of what I was supposed to do. When he finished his statement, the crowd applauded. He continued, "We gather here tonight to assemble an Army of God. We will witness the return to true American values, and I humbly thank all the Patriots in this room who have chosen to defend our true rights. Brothers and Sisters, we will make the arduous march toward victory. Though it will be rampant with adversity and toil, the strength of our cause will propel us forward until I take my deserved position in the White House."

The crowd started chanting, "President Stovall! President Stovall!"

I muttered, "What the fuck?" under my breath. Were they supporting the ghost of a Confederate general as their nominee for the next election? Was this their actual plan? Install an immortal leader to bring this country back one hundred sixty years? This couldn't be true. There had to be some semblance of rational thinking in this room, but as I stared at the excited crowd, clapping, cheering, smiling with joy for a ghoul standing in front of them, making the emptiest of promises.

This seemed impossible, though what I witnessed tonight was already impossible. If this were going to happen, then I had to stop it. The General continued, "Tonight, I must bestow recognition to our best soldier, Jim Smoke. His bravery and leadership are why I am standing before you this evening." The crowd clapped. "I also would like to acknowledge my great-great-great-granddaughter, Sally Wren. She has maintained the integrity and mission of the Pothos Historical Society and is passing that knowledge on to her daughter. Come here, dear darling." The General held out his hand for Miss Pothos to take. She slowly walked forward and grabbed it. She stood next to him in front of the crowd as he said, "We must not let evil prey upon their innocence."

I scoffed. Miss Pothos, future witch in training and wrangler of roadkill, hardly counted as innocent in my mind.

The General sent away Miss Pothos and said, "And finally, I must acknowledge all of you tonight. You bravely stand before me to witness this moment. You are all here to reclaim the greatness of this country before it is stolen by all that is evil. Let us take a moment to pray to God and thank him for this miracle."

A man walked by me and put a glass on my tray. He joined me against the back wall and put his head down, as the rest of the room became silent. I stood uncomfortably and looked at the man next to me. By the murky glow of flames, I saw it was Mr. Lyons.

"Thank you," said the General, breaking the prayer, "And God bless you all!" He stood at the podium as the crowd cheered, basking in its admiration.

He stepped down into the crowd to mingle, followed by the rest on the stage. Perhaps he was recruiting funds for his militia so he could buy cannons and muskets. If he only rode a horse, it was going to take a while to make it to D.C. I considered all the faults in his plan before I realized it wasn't really a plan. This had to be a ploy to defraud people of money, but then why was I in trouble? Why was the "ghost" of General Stovall mad at me, and how was I ruining their plans? Whatever I did, it did not seem to justify my murder.

None of this made sense, unless the General truly was a ghost, and this was all part of an elaborate plan to bring him back from the dead to save America from the rest of us.

I saw Mr. Lyons look toward me. He said, “It was an inspiring speech, right?”

I said, “Uh-huh.”

He said, “It’s not often you get to witness history. We’re truly honored to be here, in his presence.”

I said nothing. He continued, “A beautiful young woman like yourself should be enjoying this party, rather than working at it.”

My eyes widened. He was trying to flirt with me; I guess the wig was working. I said, “Uh-hm.”

“Are you from around here?” He asked me.

I kept looking straight ahead. I knew the wig was abundant enough to hide my face from the side. I did my best fake Southern accent and asked, “Is it real? Is this really a ghost?”

Mr. Lyons paused for a moment and said, “‘Ghost’ has such negative connotations. I much prefer ‘miracle’.”

“Are you sure?” I asked Mr. Lyons. “They ain’t doing this to get some money from these people?”

He shook his head. “This is a miracle, and miracles are hard to believe until you see them for yourself. Soon, the country will understand why he was sent back to save it.”

I sighed. He really believed in this. I wanted to ask him, since I was part of the resistance, who we should bring back. Lincoln? Hariett Tubman? Instead, I asked him, “Do you think you’ll win? With this General as your leader?”

He gave a little laugh. “Let me put it to you this way: the other side is fucked. This war is just beginning, and you’re lucky to be on our side.”

I wondered if my wig bangs obfuscated my face enough that I could pass for a white woman. I asked him, "Is this about race? Do they want to keep White people on top?"

"It's not about keeping us on top, it's just accepting there is a natural order to things. There are places for men and women in society, and those of other races. Once everyone learns to respect this, they'll feel liberated knowing where they belong."

"Where is that?" I asked, knowing this answer would infuriate me regardless.

"Where? Well, I hate this idea of people on 'top' and 'below'. It makes it seem like a competition when there ain't one. White men are the natural leaders. They created the modern world as we know it. Without us, most of the world would be weaving baskets and living in mud huts. White men are responsible for all that is great in this country. Industry, modernization, the constitution. If we don't honor that fact, then how can we even call ourselves *American?*"

I felt myself grinding my teeth in frustration. I said nothing while he continued, "General Stovall understands what is needed to cure this country of its illusions." He paused for a moment and asked, "A woman like yourself must have a fine White man as your husband?"

I said, "Nope."

Mr. Lyons' voice perked up a little, "Oh, are you single?"

I said, "Not really."

"That's a very nonchalant answer."

I rolled my eyes and said with a fading accent, "Well, if you want to know, I just cheated on my boyfriend with two men, at the same time."

"Jesus," said Mr. Lyons. "You certainly are an example of a wayward woman. I see this as a result of a lack of structure in society. You're doing it because you're confused about where you belong, but I'm here to tell you, you will feel liberated when you experience your true place. All I see are women struggling under this idea of 'liberation' or 'equality'. Liberation from what? You're fighting your natural instincts to tend to the needs of your husband and your children."

"What if I don't want kids?" I asked tersely.

"Again, that's what this corrupted society has told you. All women want kids, and all women want to create a partnership with a worthy man."

"What about women who don't like men?" I asked.

"Oh, dear. Well, homosexuality is just a response to this lack of structure in society. It doesn't exist in the natural world. Do you ever see two stags raising a fawn?"

I scoffed. "Well, call me a stag-hag because I support the right for two men to raise a child, or two women. Listen, straight people aren't doing that great of a job at it, so why not let the gays do it? At least gay couples truly *want* their children in the first place."

Mr. Lyons sighed in frustration. "You're completely missing my point. What's *natural* has been corrupted by the media and by the homosexuals who control it. They're trying to see the destruction of the natural order because they are lost. There are too many lost people in this country for it to function properly, and General Stovall is going to save us." He paused, then said, "It breaks my heart to see a woman like you so confused. Perhaps tonight is an opportunity for you to find yourself."

"How should I do that?" I asked.

"You should humble yourself in front of General Stovall and see if you are worthy of being one of his chosen women," he said. Out of the corner or my vision, see him eyeing me with curiosity. Perhaps he was so focused on our debate that he wasn't paying attention to my voice. He said, "What's your name?"

Yet, I already had enough. I couldn't listen to this anymore.

If, in fact, I were about to stab a living man, prison couldn't be worse than being trapped listening to Mr. Lyons go on about a new world order. "You know what, you're right," I told Mr. Lyons. "I'm going to beg the General for forgiveness." I bent my leg and put it on the wall. With my right hand, I extracted the stake and tucked it in my sleeve. I handed Mr. Lyons the tray with dirty glasses and said, "Hold onto this."

I turned away from him. I'd grown tired of uninspired men like him long ago, with the arrogance to think they know how I should live, repeating things they've heard from other insecure men. Not all men want to be in charge, and not all women want to be subservient. To live in such a narrow mindset, their response to anything outside of their "normal" was fear. I felt that fear within myself, too, fear of so many things that melted away from my time in Pothos. Now, my only fear was about stabbing the General, and for that I had to become fearless.

I took off my vest and tossed it on the floor. I weaved my way through the crowd toward the other side of the room. I passed groups of people in conversation, laughing, or strategically planning. They would momentarily stare at me as I clumsily moved through them, brushing up against their expensive cashmere and wool suits.

Suddenly, I broke through and was in front of the General. He was in conversation with the conservative news host, who was soliciting him to come on the show. "If I could get an exclusive interview with you, your message could reach millions. We'll even come to you and shoot the segment here if you can't get to New York City on a horse." He laughed at the absurdity of his own statement.

Sally Wren and Miss Pothos were standing close to him, along with Jim Smoke. The General said, "Soldier Smoke, could you please acquire my gun from my horse? I promised this gentleman I would show him it."

The General turned to the newsman. “That certainly would be an effective means of disseminating our message. Pardon me if I’m a bit skeptical, I’m from the era of the newspaper empire.”

I watched Jim Smoke disappear into the crowd. This was my moment; he was more vulnerable now. The newsman continued, “This is the era of television, or more importantly, the Internet. You have no idea how easy it will be to get people to see your message. It’s going to resonate with many young men in this country.”

The General considered. “Yes, we need them to build our battalions. Any means of encouragement to get young men to join our cause is just.”

“Excuse me,” I interrupted in my best Southern accent, “Will you allow women to join your army?”

The General turned to me with a sour face. “Absolutely not, but perhaps you can volunteer in the nursing unit. That’s more fitting for a woman like yourself.”

I replied, “Oh, but I’m scared of blood.”

“Unfortunately, blood is a common sacrifice in war.”

“Are you afraid of blood?” I asked. He hadn’t yet recognized me.

His face was sullen. “That’s a strange question. I’ve seen a lot of blood spilled in my time, but I’ve never feared it.”

He remained quiet. I saw him focus on me. “Who are you?” he asked. I moved the stake a bit lower into my hand.

“I’m a friend of Deborah’s.” I saw her hair from the back, out of earshot, so I was safe.

“Oh, good,” said the General, “Deborah has been an incredible supporter of our cause.”

“What is she looking for out of this? Did she tell you what her plans are?” I asked.

The General looked me up and down with suspicion. I saw

Sally Wren scowl at me as well. I said, "Actually, I'm sorry for interrupting. Please continue."

I turned away and took a few breaths. How the fuck was I going to do this? I put myself in this impossible position, trying to sacrifice myself for what reason? I felt myself on the verge of crying from panic. I tried to calm my breathing and think about Ms. Honeypaw and Josh. I was doing this to keep them safe. I thought of Keli and the video she randomly sent me earlier of her drunk singing to let me know that she was alright. I thought about Ri'Chard and Throat Goat just outside, yet a world away from all this. I was doing this for them, but what was I doing for me? Was I about to sacrifice myself for an unknown outcome? I felt like a coward filled with empty promises and falsehoods. If I wasn't brave enough to tell the truth to Josh, how could I be brave enough to potentially stab a man? I bit my lip in frustration. I should have told him. I shouldn't have let it come from Yale Law. He deserved the brave me, not the cowardly one who kept making excuses.

Maybe it was the fear of not having an experience that kept me from telling him. I thought if I told Josh and he grew distant, I wouldn't have this memory of us together, no matter how painful the outcome. Yet, there I was, alone after all, about to do the riskiest thing of my life, and all I wanted were a few more simple moments with him. Moments where the hair on my neck didn't stand erect from uncertainty, or the sick feeling in my throat of self-doubt. Josh made me feel safe, and I betrayed that by succumbing to my own fear.

I looked up, and with bleary eyes, took in the crowd. They were all strangers who were beginning a war to maintain their privilege. I'd had to do the same to protect mine. The room was bustling, but through the homogeneous herd of the political elite I saw a Black woman. It was only for a second, and she was gone, but I knew I wasn't the only one coming for revenge tonight.

I felt something on my back, like a hand, but I looked over my shoulder and saw no one was touching me. The warmth of this hand relaxed my body; I breathed in confidence and exhaled uncertainty. This hand was comfort, and protection, and I didn't feel alone in the room anymore. I felt the force guide me in a slow turn. I straightened my back and stood strong. I looked at the General and took a deep breath. Whatever was coursing through my veins was no longer fear, but purpose. With clarity and intention, I would end this. I walked forward and lowered the stake into my right palm. I unsheathed it from the menstruation pad and tossed it aside. I gripped the stake as courage carried me forward.

I raised it. I stared at the General who was turning to look at me and focused on his chest. I drove the stake in with one strike.

THE GENERAL STEPPED BACKWARDS. Sally Wren grabbed his back. The newsman looked at him, then back at me, and said, "Holy shit." The General put his hand on the stake, but it made a sizzling sound as smoke lifted from his palm.

Through haggard breaths, he asked, "What is this?"

I said nothing. I looked at the smoke coming from the hole where I stabbed him. The General started to cough, then vomited black sludge on the breasts of the newsman's wife. She screamed, and the General continued to vomit black sludge onto the floor.

Everyone moved backwards. I was frozen to my spot. I saw a man muscling his way through the crowd, Jim Smoke arriving too late. He dropped the wooden box he was carrying and joined Sally Wren, who had collapsed to her knees next to the General, now writhing on the floor. "General Stovall!" he exclaimed, as he reached down to put his useless hands on the General's withering form. Deborah also pushed her way forward and she looked on in abject panic.

The veins in the General's face started to run with blackness. He looked like a true monster. General Stovall looked up at me one more time before his body started to fall apart. Skin stretched and tore as pitch black goo oozed out. Soon, he melted into a puddle on the floor, with only his uniform to define the man that was once there.

The electricity suddenly turned back on, and everyone put their hands to their eyes.

Jim and Sally let out sobs. Deborah put her hand to her mouth. Her eyes were wide, and she almost turned whiter, if that were possible. She sank to the floor in shock. The rest of the crowd was silent. The newsman tried to console his wife and slipped a bit. He lifted his shoe to reveal the pad stuck to it. "Is this a period pad? What the fuck!" He screamed.

I moved back and the crowd began parting for me. Deborah screamed, "Get her!" But no one dared touch me. I heard someone in the crowd say, "Is she a witch? She could be dangerous."

When I made it out into the foyer, I hurried toward the front door. I heard something behind me, half expecting it to be someone ready to shoot me, but I was perhaps even more unsettled to see Miss Pothos. She stood in the foyer in her pink polyester dress, watching me without expression. I hurried to the front door and grabbed the patinated brass handle.

I opened the front door and walked outside, welcoming the air. Two security guards nodded at me, unaware of what was happening inside. I said, "Smoke break," to them and quickly walked down the steps. I saw the General's horse tied to a tree out front, nibbling on some grass.

The crunch of stones under my feet was all I focused on as I crossed the drive toward the side of the house. I heard the same sound and turned to see a deep blue Rolls-Royce driving by me slowly. The back window was rolled down, and I could only see darkness inside. But I could feel whatever was within this car staring at me. I stared back. After a few moments, the window rolled up, and the car drove away. I glanced at it as the red taillights cast a hellfire glow along the drive.

I had to keep moving, and as I made my way around the side of the house, across the perfectly cut lawn, I ran toward the woods. I heard my name quietly called: "Julie! Julie!" It was Ri'Chard.

My legs hit the undergrowth, and I felt like I was transported from a dream back into reality. I grabbed Ri'Chard and gave him a hug, my fists holding a bunching of his shirt. I didn't want to let go of him.

I heard Throat Goat say, "Asian Woman, give me some information."

I pulled back and looked in Ri'Chard's eyes. I smiled while tears formed in mine. "We did it."

"Well then, we got to get the fuck out," exclaimed Throat Goat. She started to quickly dismantle her rifle and pack up.

Ri'Chard asked, "Are you alright? What happened?"

I blinked a few times. "I don't know, but it worked. He's gone."

Ri'Chard grabbed my hand and held it as Throat Goat guided us back in silence through the dark woods. We went as fast as we could, leaving us all panting by the time we made it to the truck.

Throat Goat told me to sit in the front. I got in and took a deep breath. Ri'Chard peeled out of the parking spot, and soon we were back on the main road.

Ri'Chard said, "We'll go to Ms. Honeypaw and let her know."

"I think she already knows," I said.

I felt a hand brush my left arm and saw it was Throat Goat. She held out her pointer finger, and on the edge of her long acrylic nail was a little Hello Kitty sticker. "For your first kill, Asian Woman."

I took it from her finger and wondered where to put it. I felt it in my pocket and pulled out the poker chip. I turned it in my fingers, examining the only artifact from this evening, and put the sticker next to the lit torch.

21

We pulled in front of Ms. Honeypaw's house. The night was still deep, the sky the same puddle of blackness that General Stovall dissolved into, yet filled with the light of stars. I was happy to see the familiar glow of lights from within her house.

I got out of the truck and walked toward the porch. I was surprised to see Ms. Honeypaw sitting outside. She looked at me and smiled. She said, "GeishaBitch, you can take off your nasty-ass wig now. The fight is over." I laughed and slowly walked up the steps. I took a seat next to Ms. Honeypaw, close enough that our arms touched. I pulled off my wig and asked, "Where's Josh?"

"He's inside, on the phone with CrystalBitch. When I knew it was over, I told him to relax." I took a breath and felt the sadness within. I think I wanted him next to me.

Throat Goat and Ri'Chard stayed by the truck. Throat Goat showed him some of the equipment she brought, but I think Ri'Chard sensed Ms. Honeypaw and I needed a moment. I asked her, "How did you know it worked?"

"I told you I'm psychic."

I smiled. "I'll never doubt you again."

"Good," she said with force, "Because I've been trying to help your ass this whole time not to create this mess you're in."

I looked at my hands. "How is Josh doing?"

"I think he's sad, and definitely worried about you, but I know this is good for him. That boy hasn't opened his heart in a long time."

I said, "I don't think I've opened my heart, ever."

"I could tell the moment you walked through my door. I thought, *Who is this uptight bitch with a fancy bag?* You were so... eh." She made a sound of disgust. "Then I got to know you more, and I can't say I like you, but I kinda fuck with you now."

I laughed. "I kind of fuck with you, too." She looked at me as the corner of her mouth turned into a smile. I asked, "How did you know that it worked?"

"I told you I was going to call upon my ancestors." She looked out ahead and took a deep breath. "I saw Betsey." Ms. Honeypaw's eyes began to water. I reached out and grabbed her hand as she continued, "I finally got to talk to her. I thought I'd say all these things to her and curse her out for leaving her child in the fucking town, but I just cried like a bitch." Ms. Honeypaw put up a hand to wipe her tears. "She told me how much it hurt to leave her child, but she thought he might have a chance at living. She said..." Ms. Honeypaw's voice cracked, "She was so proud that he survived and had a family. She was so proud to see me." By now, Ms. Honeypaw was using both hands to wipe tears from her eyes, "She told me never to be ashamed of where I came from. She left her baby out of love, not hate, and prayed every day that he would be alright." Ms. Honeypaw looked at me with her wet cheeks that formed a smile, "And I was the result of those prayers. My momma was the result; all of us were her dreams come true." I hugged Ms. Honeypaw as she sobbed into my chest.

After some time, I said, "I feel like Betsey helped me too. She saved me, I think. I was so scared, and felt I couldn't do it, but I saw a woman through the crowd and suddenly felt a hand on my back that reassured me in a way I'd never felt before. She gave me the courage to do it."

Ms. Honeypaw sucked the snot up her nose, "That was Betsey. She told me you did it, GeishaBitch. I'm proud of you." Ms. Honeypaw raised her head and gathered herself. "Damn, I don't think I cried that much since Prince died."

"You liked Prince?" I asked.

"Yeah, there was just something girly about him that I thought was fresh."

I asked her, "Why is it okay for Prince to be girly but not Throat Goat?"

She looked at me and said, "Because I could still fuck Prince up. Throat Goat is a different breed, but I'm starting a basketball team, then that bitch is my first pick."

I agreed. "Throat Goat is indeed a different breed. We're lucky she's on our side." I looked at Ri'Chard and Throat Goat challenging each other to see who could assemble a rifle the fastest. Deep inside, I felt a bit unsettled, like we were still on the battlefield.

Ri'Chard picked up his cell and looked at me. He walked toward the porch and up the steps. "My nephew just texted from the hospital and said your colleague is alright. They had to do a minor surgery to remove the bullet, but he should make a full recovery."

I let out a sigh. "That's good news. I'm glad."

He looked at me and asked, "Where's Josh?"

"He's inside." I stood up. "I'll go check on him."

They both nodded in understanding as I went inside. I stood in the foyer. I could hear his voice talking to someone, "Yeah, it was good to catch up too. Hopefully we can talk again soon, and thanks for helping. Seriously, you have no idea what's been happening here." He paused and laughed a bit before saying, "Okay. Talk to you soon. Bye." He walked out of the room while looking at his phone and was startled to see me when he looked up. "Hey! You're back!" He reached out and gave me an enveloping hug. "Ms. Honeypaw told me it worked. Is that true? Did you really kill the ghost?"

"Yes, but not after becoming a waitress in an illegal casino. That was the weirdest night of my life."

"Casino? What?" Josh asked with confusion in his voice.

"Let's talk about it later." I grabbed his hand and said, "I think we need to clear the air." I led him into the living room, and we sat on a couch. He held my hand and met my eyes. I took a breath. "I'm so sorry for not telling you I was in a relationship earlier. I think I was scared that I wouldn't have the chance to get to know you if I told you, and there was just a feeling in me that made me want to have this experience with you.

"I'm so glad I trusted that feeling because you showed me so much. You showed me tenderness and respect; you showed me desire and made me feel so beautiful." I started to choke up. "When I think back to myself before I knew all of this, I don't like that person. That old me was so judgmental, and after tonight, listening to all these people express judgment for how others live, I realized that, like me, they don't know anything." Josh's face was processing my words, a bit confused as he took in all I was revealing to him.

"I can't believe I used to think I knew everything. I thought I was doing so well in life, with my fancy job in that stupid city. It took coming to this small town and becoming friends with you all for me to realize, I have no idea what I'm doing." I smiled at Josh and squeezed his hand. "I only know that I'm thankful for getting to know you. I don't know what will happen after this, but I'll always care about you."

"Julie, I care about you too." He leaned in and put our foreheads together. He pulled back and said, "I also will never forget this time we had. You made me realize a lot of things myself, and I didn't realize how much fear has been holding me back. After all this...I don't know. I just feel different, like I'm starting life over again. Who knows where I'll end up."

I bit my lip and tried to not cry, "I feel different too." I wanted to tell him that I hoped he would end up with me, but I couldn't trust myself to know if that was a decision out of certainty or just chasing this feeling of falling for someone. I told him, "I just want you to be happy."

Josh nodded. Our cheeks lifted as we smiled at each other.

After more tears, more deep breaths, and the comfort of Josh close to me, he went and got the others to join us. We all gathered in the sitting room so I could explain what happened tonight, starting from the moment I descended the staircase into the basement. When I finished, everyone looked just as confused as I was.

Ms. Honeypaw exclaimed, "There's a fucking casino in their basement? Damn, all I have are spiders and old paint."

Throat Goat said, "I got my bunker in my basement."

"A bunker, for what?" Ms. Honeypaw asked.

"Did you not listen to this story? This government is filled with people doing funny shit. You should always be prepared for The Takeover," said Throat Goat.

"You got a guest bed in your little bunker?" Ms. Honeypaw asked.

Throat Goat looked at Ms. Honeypaw and said, "It's not little, bitch."

Ri'Chard tried to get everyone back on track. "What Julie

saw seems to indicate this is a coordinated effort, with deep pockets."

I nodded. "Yes, whoever the people who own this property are, they have an agenda, and this agenda is spread out across politics and media."

Josh asked, "What can we do about it, though? We're just normal people from Pothos."

"Normal is a word that only applies to some of us here," said Ms. Honeypaw, who looked at Throat Goat.

I said, "This is way beyond all of us, except maybe her." I gestured to Throat Goat.

She looked surprised. "Honestly, I'm pretty retired from all this bullshit. It never ends. If I were you guys, I'd just start stocking your bunkers and getting ready. That's why I'm making all my tapes, because I know nights down there are going to be lonely."

Throat Goat was right. I thought of a future where we were all trapped in our concrete holes, waiting for the world to return to normal...but was it ever normal?

"So what do we do?" Josh asked.

Ri'Chard said, "I also don't have any ideas. This is too big for any of us to deal with. We just have to hope they move on, leave this town alone, and forget about us."

Ms. Honeypaw said, "I agree. Let's just pretend this didn't happen and act normal. I'm done with these witchy bitches. I haven't slept right since all this shit started happening."

I said, "So that's it? Do we just forget about this? We can't do that. I think we should report what happened in the courthouse tonight. There's definitely evidence to corroborate our story."

"Listen," said Throat Goat, "You'll have to leave me out of your little story you're going to tell. I don't need my name coming up *anywhere*."

"Who will you report to?" Ri'Chard asked. "The police here are corrupt, hell, probably across the state."

I reassured everyone. "I'll talk to my boss about it. I'm sure we have contacts at the FBI. This might be a case for them since it definitely involves illegal gambling."

"FBI? Shit. I mean, I have questions too, but something is telling me to mind my business on this one." Ms. Honeypaw said. I also felt powerless. I didn't know where to start, and my hope of escalating the case to the FBI seemed as far-fetched as a ghost when I first got to Pothos. I thought back to looking into the void of the Rolls-Royce, and it made my spine tingle. I knew there was so much more to this.

"You can try talking to your boss," said Ri'Chard, "But I don't know if it's safe for you here. They might try to get you again, and it could be worse if they figure out you're the one who stabbed the General. I think it's best if you leave tomorrow."

Everyone nodded. "What about Josh?" I asked. "Won't he be in danger?" All eyes turned toward Josh.

He answered, "Maybe, but in all honesty, I'm a White guy. It will be harder to get me than anyone else. I also know some of the officers. They weren't there tonight, so maybe they're still the good guys?"

"They tried to kill you, Josh" I reminded him.

He looked uncertain. "I know!" announced Ms. Honeypaw. "Why don't you go and shack up with CrystalBitch? Lay low for a minute until we know what's going on."

The thought of that immediately made me a little jealous, but it felt ridiculous. I tried to fake a smile and said, "I'd tell you to come to D.C., but that might be difficult with—"

"Your man there?" Ms. Honeypaw interrupted. "You want to bring the man you cheated with to crash on the couch of the man you're dealing with? That's some progressive shit."

I stuttered for a second and said, "I was thinking of cost-of-living, housing, what his social life would be, that kind of stuff."

Josh said. "I'll reach out to Alana, that's a good idea." I smiled at him. Maybe it was for the best. I wanted him to be happy, and that probably wasn't with me in D.C. He said, "I'll go call her again and see." Josh went into the other room and I heard his muffled, "Hey again" after she answered on the first ring.

"Are you really going to report this? Do you think they'll actually arrest these people?" Ri'Chard asked.

I reasoned, "We have the temporary courthouse as evidence. Ri'Chard should have some recordings from tonight, and the hospital should report the shooting injury of my colleague to the police."

"You can't hear what they were saying on the recording, and it places us all in the church too," said Ri'Chard. "What if they use that to pin the church shooting on us?"

Throat Goat forcefully chimed in, "And I wasn't actually there, either."

I reasoned, "I still think there's a strong case, especially with our witness testimonies."

"I am not setting one goddamn foot in that courthouse," said Ms. Honeypaw. "As of this moment, I don't know shit. I'm with Throat Goat; leave my name out of this." Throat Goat let out a sound of agreement. Ms. Honeypaw continued, "And if you ever try to drag us into your case, we'll support each other as sisters. We were getting our nails done, and her set of nasty acrylics took the whole goddamn night, isn't that right, Sir Suck-A-Lot." She gestured to Throat Goat.

Throat Goat casually said, "These 'nasty' acrylics cost $300 a set. You couldn't even afford a French-tip on your pinkie."

Ms. Honeypaw was taken aback, but I saw her give a curiosity-tinged smile. I think Throat Goat was growing on her. Josh returned to the room and said, "It's all good. I'll leave for Asheville tomorrow."

Ri'Chard nodded and looked down; Josh looked at me and feigned a smile. I looked at everyone and said, "Ri'Chard is right; it's best if I also leave town tomorrow. It will draw too much attention to you guys if I'm still around. I'll have to see what actions I can take from afar."

Josh and Ri'Chard looked at me. I could see the sadness and understanding in their faces. Ms. Honeypaw also looked pained. Perhaps she was a bit sad, too.

Throat Goat broke the silence and said, "Bye, Asian Woman."

Ri'Chard said, heavily, "I agree with Julie. It's best if we try to keep a low profile from now on."

Ms. Honeypaw looked at me and shook her head. "As someone familiar with having to hide from people you might have wronged, I also agree. Skip town, don't look back, and try to change your Social Security number if you can."

I furrowed my eyebrows. "I can't change my Social Security number."

"I'm only suggesting what I've learned. Take it or leave it," said Ms. Honeypaw.

I nodded and said, "Maybe next time, we'll all be meeting under better circumstances." As I said this, I felt the strain of reality against my optimism.

"I GUESS THIS IS GOODBYE," I said to Ms. Honeypaw. The group of us stood outside on her porch in the darkness of early morning. I had changed back into my regular clothes, baptized in church dust.

She looked me up and down and said, "I guess this is

goodbye too. I can't say you'll be taking a vacation to Pothos anytime soon."

"I don't think so, but I'd still like to visit someday."

Ms. Honeypaw said, "I'm not good at goodbyes, so I hope everything goes well for you in D.C. and you get yourself a new Prada bag or whatever."

"I don't think you'll be seeing 'Miss Prada' again."

"I'll miss her, but I guess this Born-Again-ho version of you is alright," said Ms. Honeypaw.

I reached out and gave her a hug. I held her tightly until I was ready to let go. We smiled at each other, and I turned to walk down the porch steps. Josh and Throat Goat got into the back while I took the front. I offered to take the back, but Throat Goat said, "You're a killer now. I can't have my back to you."

I chuckled and said, "I don't know if ghosts count."

"They count," everyone said in unison.

We drove back to my hotel. Dante came with Yale Law so she could rest and pack. We dropped Josh at his garage so he could grab my Volvo and drive it to the hotel. When we arrived, Dante was waiting outside the Corolla, smoking a vape.

Throat Goat said, "That's my man, looking suspicious and fine as hell."

When Ri'Chard parked, she got out and went over to her man. It was just Ri'Chard and me in the truck. I looked at him and said, "Hey, I'm sorry about kissing you earlier. I don't know what came over me."

He said, "It's fine. It was...it happened."

I said nervously, "I don't want to cause trouble in your relationship, though. I know how much you love Aisha."

Ri'Chard took a deep breath, "Yeah, we're going to have to talk through these things. I already let her know something happened."

"You did?"

"Yes, I told her immediately after it went down. I figured it was better to not let time build it up into something bigger. We scheduled a call to talk about it tomorrow."

"How do you think she'll take it?"

Ri'Chard wondered and said, "It's not going to be easy. I'm sure she has an automatic fear of 'the other woman', but she doesn't know you're not a bad person."

"A homewrecking whore?" I offered.

"Yeah," he said, "That might be her instinct, so I'll just have to explain to her who you are."

I nodded. "I'm really impressed by how you're dealing with this. I'm taking notes for next time." I looked down, then met his gaze. "I think you're a really good man. You're going to be a great husband and father." His face softened. I continued, "I'm so grateful to have spent this time with you and Josh, and I hope someday our paths cross again. I'd also like to meet Aisha as long as she doesn't hate me."

"Thank you, that really means a lot. I think you're one of the bravest people I've ever known. To go into that place alone and kill a ghost...I'm in awe. I hope you know that."

"I didn't feel alone, though. It felt like all you guys were with me."

Ri'Chard smiled. "I can't wait to tell Aisha about it. She's going to think I'm crazy, but I have to tell her."

"Do you think she'll believe it?"

Ri'Chard looked out the front windshield and thought for a moment. "I don't know. But I don't want to spend the rest of my life trying to convince people about what happened. I believe you, though. I do."

I looked out the front window too. I watched Dante grab Throat Goat by the hips as she playfully pushed him off. He turned her around and grabbed her from behind, swaying their bodies together.

"It's nice to see it work out for them," I said, gesturing to Throat Goat and Dante.

Ri'Chard chuckled a little and said, "You know, it's good to see him be comfortable. That's all I want for him, to not feel like he has to keep secrets." Before, that would have stung, but I had grown past it. It wasn't shame, but understanding, and the hope to never do it again.

Ri'Chard said, "I hope your return home goes well, too." Those words stung. It didn't feel like I was going home; Pothos, in a twisted way, felt like home. He reached out over the center console and gave me a hug. He rubbed my back while we embraced and I took in his presence for possibly the last time.

We pulled back, and I said, "You should get going, you've had a long night."

"So have you. I hope you can rest before you head back tomorrow."

"I'm pretty wired. There's so much racing through my mind right now to keep me occupied on the ride back."

Ri'Chard said, "Don't think about it too much. Sometimes ignorance is bliss."

I agreed, but I couldn't unsee what happened tonight. There was so much more to this story, so much that I could go crazy trying to figure it out. I asked him, "Will you see Josh before he leaves?"

"Of course," nodded Ri'Chard. "He's going to see me on the way out of town tomorrow."

"Good." I got out of the truck while Ri'Chard called for Dante and Throat Goat to get in.

Throat Goat walked up to me and said, "Asian Woman, I'm proud of you." She held out her fist as I bumped mine against hers.

I said, "I'm proud of you, too. I learned a few things from that video, you know."

She gave me a knowing look. "I'll tell you, that officer who came to verify his alibi marched straight onto my couch. I thank you for that."

I said, "Oh, that sounds like an abuse of his power."

"I know," said Throat Goat, "But as much as I say 'Fuck the police', sometimes I suck the police."

"Suck the police...maybe that would make them not be such huge assholes," I said.

"Listen, you're onto something. I wanted to start an intelligence gathering program where instead of torturing terrorists, we sucked their dicks. Men are so stupid and easily controlled by their dicks. They share anything when hypnotized by The Suck. I know all my regulars' ATM pins."

I said, "Wow...that is a thought. I will think about that heavily on my ride back to D.C."

Thankfully, Josh arrived with my car, which seemed like a natural moment to end our conversation.

"Yeah, you think about it. We'll talk more next time I see you," she said. She got into the truck.

Dante came up and shook my hand. "Thanks, Julie. I hope we can meet again, under better circumstances."

"I'm always happy to help out," I said to him. The doors closed, and Ri'Chard started to drive slowly away. I felt Josh put his arm on my shoulder. Ri'Chard rolled down the window and held out his hand in a static wave as he headed back to his home.

Josh asked, "Did you get to say your goodbyes?"

"I did, but now it's time just to say goodbye to you."

He said, "I also suck at goodbyes." I leaned in and kissed him, and after a moment, he pulled away. He focused on me and pulled me in again. We shared a long kiss before we put our foreheads together.

"Do you want to come to my room for a bit?"

He looked at me and said, "I'm happy to. It felt rude to ask."

We walked holding hands back to my room. Once we were through the door, I leaned against a wall while Josh kissed me. He pulled my shirt over my head and began to kiss down my chest and neck. I said, "I should shower, I feel pretty gross after tonight."

He picked me up and carried me to the bathroom. He started the shower and still kissed me while the water warmed. We moved inside and began to lather our bodies with cheap hotel soap. Our hands explored each other's slippery skin as the soap gathered between the gaps in our fingers. We took turns washing and making out, cleansing ourselves of all that happened tonight. We both grabbed towels and dried off, then fell onto my bed.

I was on top of him, but slightly to his left side. He pulled my thigh up and lightly caressed it. I held his face and kissed him, then stopped to look in his eyes. I couldn't believe I'd be leaving those eyes; I tried to memorize the feeling of him looking at me. I moved my fingers along his stubble, up to his lips. I traced his lips, their softness. I ran my fingers down his neck and back up to his ears. I pinched his earlobes. I took in the vision of him and accepted that I was in love with a man. We were meant to come together, and that union healed something in both of us, but this wasn't meant to be forever. We both had to leave in the morning.

I had already let go of my old self, but it felt tragic that I'd only have a moment with him as my true self, with no pretensions or lies, and at my most exhausted and vulnerable. I kissed him, then pulled away, and turned to look at the wall.

"What's wrong?" Josh asked with tender concern.

I tried to hide the tears that pooled at the corner of my eyes. I felt his thumb wipe away one as it tried to escape down my cheek. I was caught.

I looked into his eyes and said, "I'm just sad that now I feel like I can be myself around you, and we barely have time left."

Josh rubbed my cheek. "Do you feel like you weren't yourself around me before?"

"I plead the fifth," I told him, cheekily.

"So that first time we kissed, or made love? That wasn't you?" Josh began kissing down my neck, my chest. "Or when you made me put on your underwear to show off for you? That wasn't you either?" His kisses moved lower, circling my navel. He moved even lower and looked up at me. "You forget that I know what you taste like, so let's see if this is the real you."

He pushed my legs up as his kisses landed on my pussy. He began to devour me with an insatiable hunger. In between tantalizing licks, he slowly got out his statement, "I...will never... forget...the way you...taste."

I watched him consume me. He was in ecstasy as he whet his appetite with my wetness. His head writhed back and forth and his grip on the back of my thighs remained firm. He wasn't letting me go until he confirmed he had already tasted the real me. I looked into his eyes. "Devilish" wasn't a term I could use to describe them. I had already seen the eyes of the Devil, but Josh's eyes were different. Perhaps I was seeing the real him, his raw sexual desire. He let go of one of my thighs and reached up toward me with a cupped hand.

"Spit it in my hand," he ordered me. I did as I was told. He brought his hand down and tipped it so the spit slowly fell onto me. I felt it hit my already sensitive folds. Some of the spit lingered between his hand and my pussy, like a nearly invisible thread. He lowered his hand and started to put his fingers inside me. He looked at me and said, "Will you show me the real you?"

I nodded. He said, "Then make me lick you."

I bit the bottom of my lip as I smiled. I wiped a little spit from the corner of his mouth and put my hands in his hair. I knew what he was telling me to do. He was telling me to accept my power, my need for pleasure. I hesitated; the Julie that came to Pothos would never even let a man get in this position. She'd never fought for her pleasure. Yet, that was a different Julie. I now had this man between my legs, waiting for me to grant him permission. I felt his hands grip my legs tighter. His breaths cooled the slickness on me. I looked him in the eyes and pushed his head down into me.

He was voracious. I leaned back as I held his head down. I slowly gyrated my hips against him, feeling the discomfort of his stubble against my sensitive skin, but I didn't care. I moaned and gripped his hair tighter. I screamed as he moved faster and deeper, "Ooooh, Josh, I'm coming!"

I released my breaths and felt my eyelids grow heavy. I felt Josh move up until he was face to face with me. He paused, laughing a little as he looked at my smiling face. "Can I kiss you?" he asked.

I was scared for a second, then said, "Yes, I want to taste me too."

He leaned down and gave me a taste of my other lips on his. It was a little salty with a subtle tang. I kissed him intensely, signalling that this was not over. I rolled him over and got on top of him. I put both his arms above his head and held them down with my left hand. With my right, I felt for his cock. I held it behind me as I teased him, moved my hips to rub him along my ass, until the moment I was ready to have him in me. I gave him permission, once again, as he let out a deep moan of satisfaction. I grabbed one of his hands and put it on my breast. He lightly squeezed as I slowly moved up and down. I liked the power of commanding him, driving him like a manual car, until it didn't feel right. Our relationship wasn't a power struggle, and I wasn't gaining anything by trying to dominate him.

"What is it?" He asked.

I looked at him and said, "Make love to me. I just want to be with you."

I moved himself upwards while I continued to straddle him. Our foreheads lightly touched and he reached around and put his hands on my back.

We slowly moved in a rhythm and I kissed him slowly.

So much of sex I knew up to this point was like a commute to work with a partner. It was the same routine with the same destination, though I usually had to find a parking spot after they had already arrived. With Josh, sex was like driving on back-country roads, my GPS signal going in and out, without a hurry to get to any destination. I tried to remember the way he'd kiss the inside of my arms, or the feeling of his fingertips barely touching as he dragged them across the top of my thighs. I took in his moans and shared mine with him. We didn't speak; the lust was replaced with deep intention. We gazed, kissed, and felt.

He whispered into me, "Julie, I'm close."

"Me too," I told him, my hand resting on the back of his neck. The pace quickened; he said, "Julie, I'm coming!" His hands gripped my ass tightly, and he kissed me as he whimpered. I moved my hips deeper, as the tingle that built from deep inside me became an electric jolt that spread throughout me.

We lay on our sides facing each other. Our bodies were slick with sweat again, but I didn't want to it wash off. I just wanted to stay close to him. I felt him rub the inside of my palm with his finger. He was a man that liked to keep his hands busy. Our stares didn't break. As I looked at him, I saw a tear form in the corner of his eye and run down his cheek. I shed a tear too. We didn't have to say anything, but it was enough for both of us to know we were together in this feeling.

. . .

Toward dawn, I felt Josh shift. We had been holding each other, waiting for this moment. We roused ourselves and got dressed. I walked him out to the parking lot and stood in front of the Corolla, holding hands.

"This is it," he said.

"This is it," I echoed. "That was a pretty good goodbye in there." He smiled. "What time are you leaving tomorrow?" I asked him with reservation.

"I'll pack up and try to leave tomorrow morning. I'll stop at Ri'Chard's house, just to say goodbye."

"Good. I'm sorry I got you into this mess, and your boss Steve might get mad at you."

"He'll understand. I'll tell him it's a family emergency. I think I'll only be gone for a week, but just to give us some time for you to start your investigation."

"Yes," I reassured him. "Once that starts, they won't mess with you."

He laughed and leaned in to kiss me. "Bye, Julie. I hope our paths cross again."

I didn't want to lose the feeling of his breath on me. I felt myself choking up. I managed to say, "I hope so too." My vision started obscured with tears, and I was unable to hold my sobs back. "Josh, I hope it works out for you in Asheville."

He brushed his thumb across the top of my hand. His voice was shaky, but strong as he said, "I hope it works out for you in D.C., too."

We embraced and held each other tightly until I could see dawn breaking over his shoulder. We didn't let go of each other until I said, "Okay."

He looked at me and asked, "Okay?" I nodded.

He got in the car. He rolled the window down and looked at me. He asked, "Will you miss her?"

I looked at my Volvo and back at him, “She might get jealous if I say ‘yes’.”

He gestured to my Volvo. “I wouldn’t want her getting jealous because of me. Besides, I’m taking this lady to Asheville.”

“You’re taking this thing all the way there?”

“Of course, it’s great on gas and surprisingly comfortable. Maybe not as fancy as your car, but it gets the job done.”

I looked at the car then Josh, and said, “It does get the job done.”

He turned and grabbed something, holding out his hand to me. I put mine out and felt him put a small rock in my palm. It was the citrine he put in my cup holder when he first gave me the Corolla. “It’s for good luck,” he said, then winked at me. I thanked him as he put the car into gear and started off. I held the rock to my heart as I watched his taillights as he turned onto the main road and drove toward the rising sun.

A FEW HOURS LATER, I sat in my Volvo and looked around. It felt foreign to me, and I immediately wanted to be back in the Corolla. I waited for Yale Law to put her suitcase in the back and get in the front.

She took an exaggerated breath. “I slept like shit. Surprisingly, this hotel has cable, and I watched a ton of reality shows to help get my mind off things. What did you do?” She asked.

“I didn’t sleep,” I said confidently.

Yale Law looked shocked. “Julie, how can you drive?”

“Don’t worry, Volvos are supposed to be the safest cars.” I put the car in gear and began to move out of the hotel parking lot.

“Do you want me to put in directions to the hospital?” She asked.

“Sure, thanks.” As we were leaving the hotel lot, the GPS told me to turn right, but I went left.

"Uh, Julie, you made the wrong turn."

"I know, I just want to go see something."

"Are you sure you can drive?"

I rolled my eyes. I had ten-plus hours of this ahead of me.

We drove toward downtown, where the ruins of the old courthouse loomed over the town. I slowed down to take in the blackened piles of ash that were starting to be shuffled around by parked machinery, and the flimsy brick walls that climbed towards the morning sky. I turned at the island where the statue of General Stovall once stood and lorded over the town before it was toppled. I drove down a few blocks before I saw flashing lights ahead.

There were police cars and firetrucks parked on the road. Steam rose from something obscured by the trucks. I pulled over. We both got out and hurriedly walked down the street.

A familiar crowd had gathered on the sidewalk behind the emergency response crews. My heart was pounding as we jogged closer, until the charred remains of the Baptist courthouse came into view.

"Holy Shit," said Yale Law. "Was that the place we—" I shushed her.

We merged into the group of people standing behind the caution tape. The tree where the pony once hung was singed as fire engulfed its thinnest branches, encouraged by the breeze. I could feel the heat emanating from the remains of the building. It was easier to burn it than explain why it was riddled with bullet holes, also erasing any evidence we might have for our case. A pit in my stomach formed, weighted by anger and frustration.

I heard, "Well, we keep meeting at these scenes. Is that a coincidence?"

I turned to see Mr. Lyons close to me. I said, "A 'coincidence' is a series of events that seem related but happen organically. This wasn't an accident."

"Miss Julie, are you inferring this was a crime? It was an old building, and, well, you know how these things go."

"So the ghost of General Stovall isn't responsible for burning it?" Mr. Lyons looked at me and said nothing. I continued, "I'm leaving now. I'll be heading back to D.C. with my colleagues. You don't have to worry, the ghost finally scared me off."

Mr. Lyons tried not to smile and said, "I'm sorry, this is the last thing you'll see in Pothos."

"If you keep burning the town down, there won't be much of Pothos left." I took in the scene as firefighters tried to douse water on a hopeless cause. There was nothing left of the Baptist courthouse, its secrets burned with it.

"Tell me one thing Mr. Lyons: the first warning you gave me, did the woman actually see the ghost?"

Mr. Lyons had to think for a moment. "Oh, Ms. Lee? Of course. I would never lie about warnings from the beyond realm." It was bullshit. I knew he made it up just to try and scare me. My investigative instincts threatened them, even if I had the whole story wrong from the beginning.

I said, "Whatever that's happening in this town that you don't want me to find out about, just know these secrets don't often stay in the grave." I looked back at the courthouse, then to Mr. Lyons. "And when they do come out of the grave, I'm not afraid to deal with them."

I looked beyond him and saw Sally Wren holding Miss Pothos against her. They were both wearing the same outfits they had on last night, though they looked like they were stained with dirt. I caught Miss Pothos' gaze. Her face held a slight grin. She lifted her arm and showed her hand balled around a lighter. She held it in front of her, and struck it with a dirt-stained thumb that had chipped, red glitter polish. She let the fire burn for a moment, smiled at me, then blew out the flame.

THE SECOND COMING

The darkness drops again; but now I know
That twenty centuries of stony sleep
Were vexed to nightmare by a rocking cradle,
And what rough beast, its hour come round at last,
Slouches towards Bethlehem to be born?

William Butler Yeats

ABOUT THE AUTHOR

B.Z. Pierce is a deeply flawed human being whose core is grounded in fundamental decency and a passion for connecting with others, no matter where they come from. He delights in creating characters shaped by the same contradictions and complexities.

www.bzpierce.com

www.ingramcontent.com/pod-product-compliance
Lightning Source LLC
LaVergne TN
LVHW090549110826
845146LV00001B/83

* 9 7 9 8 9 9 4 8 3 1 0 1 4 *